Piers leaned over her, so near that Aisley could feel his breath,

yet she knew no fear, only thrilling anticipation.

"I am glad you are loyal," he said, "but I think 'tis time that I made you my wife in truth. 'Tis time we both know that you belong to me—and to no one else." Then he paused, his body still as his large palm lay against her throat. "'Tis no fault of mine that you chose me, Aisley," he said, his voice low and serious, "but you did. So heed this well—I hold what is mine."

The threat was implicit, and Aisley had no doubt that he would kill any man who would presume to take his place—and perhaps her, too. He had the power, she knew, and should he decide to choke the life from her right now, there was naught she could do....

Dear Reader,

Our featured big book this month, *The Honor Price*, by Erin Yorke, is a stirring tale of adventure and forbidden passion. One of Harlequin Historical's most popular authors, Yorke brings readers the story of Alanna O'Donnell, a young Irishwoman whose flight from her uncle's treachery brings her into an uneasy alliance with Spanish nobleman Lucas del Fuentes— a man she should by all rights hate.

Cheryl St.John's first book, *Rain Shadow*, was part of our March Madness 1993 promotion. Don't miss *Heaven Can Wait*, the gripping prequel to *Rain Shadow*. Heartland Critiques gave both books a GOLD ★★★★★ rating!

Aisley de Laci is wed to a knight rumored to be in league with the devil in *The Devil's Lady*, a remarkable medieval by Deborah Simmons. And finally, Laurel Pace's *Winds of Destiny* is the long-awaited sequel to *Destiny's Promise*.

We hope you enjoy all of these titles. And next month, be sure to look for the new Theresa Michaels, *Fire and Sword*.

Sincerely,

Tracy Farrell
Senior Editor
Harlequin Historicals

Please address questions and book requests to:
Harlequin Reader Service
U.S.: 3010 Walden Ave., P.O. Box 1325, Buffalo, NY 14269
Canadian: P.O. Box 609, Fort Erie, Ont. L2A 5X3

DEBORAH SIMMONS

The Devil's Lady

Harlequin Books

TORONTO • NEW YORK • LONDON
AMSTERDAM • PARIS • SYDNEY • HAMBURG
STOCKHOLM • ATHENS • TOKYO • MILAN
MADRID • WARSAW • BUDAPEST • AUCKLAND

ISBN 0-373-28841-7

THE DEVIL'S LADY

Copyright © 1994 by Deborah Siegenthal.

Books by Deborah Simmons

Harlequin Historicals

Fortune Hunter #132
Silent Heart #185
The Squire's Daughter #208
The Devil's Lady #241

DEBORAH SIMMONS

Always drawn to writing, Deborah Simmons began her professional career as a newspaper reporter. She turned to fiction after the birth of her first child, when a long-time love of historical romances prompted her to pen her first book, published in 1989. She lives with her husband, two children and two cats on seven acres in rural Ohio, where she divides her time between her family, reading, researching and writing.

Special thanks to Lynn Moser for her help
with this story and so much else

Chapter One

Aisley felt like a Christmas gift.

Or maybe a goose, all trussed up and waiting to be devoured by the hungry knights who milled about below like a pack of surly dogs. They were all full of wine and ale and food and eager for a prize. One would think the holy day was already upon them, the way the men feasted here at Edward's court.

Frowning in disgust, Aisley saw the approach of her servant and turned away, unwilling to have Edith see her as she usually was not: powerless. But the woman had been with Aisley since birth and could tell her mood. "What is it, my lady?" she asked softly.

Aisley laughed bitterly. "What is it?" she echoed, her normally lyrical voice harsh with anger. "I feel like a tournament prize, all wrapped up—" she whirled a hand downward to take in her fine new gown and ermine-lined cape "—and ready to be bestowed."

"My lady—" Edith whispered, her tone urging caution.

Aisley cut off her words. "Edith," she said, "in the months since my father's death, his holdings have continued to prosper under my hand. Yet instead of receiving a reward for my efforts, it seems I am *to be* the reward given to some foul-smelling, money-grubbing wretch, simply because of our good king's greed."

"My lady!" Edith protested.

"'Tis not fair," Aisley whispered, as she had so often in the past weeks. No matter how cleverly she had managed her father's estates, how many suits she had successfully defended, how many crops she had brought to fruition—not to mention the household that ran so smoothly and tightly that it fairly sang like the string of a vielle—it was all for naught. In but a year the king's summons had come, ordering her to wed.

"Hush," Edith said. "It could be worse. At least you may select your own husband, and from the finest knights of the land, I might add."

"Ha!" Aisley scoffed. "That *honor* comes to me only because I had enough money to pay for the privilege. Think you the king gave me a choice because of his love for me?"

"Hush," Edith warned again. "Stop this dangerous, foolish chatter and be still. For once in your life, behave yourself and pick wisely, using your head instead of your spleen!"

Aisley smiled grimly, unoffended by her servant's words. Edith had been more a mother to her than anyone else, and Aisley could not curb the good woman's tongue even if she tried. Instead, she sought to comfort the angry servant. "Don't worry. I will pick wisely, dear Edith. I have a plan," she said.

Edith's mouth dropped open and she stepped back a pace in horror. "Oh, heaven help us," she whispered. She was long familiar with Aisley's schemes—schemes that never failed to get the young woman into trouble. Feeling the press of panic, she moved forward again, her hands clasped together in supplication. "My lady, please, cast aside whatever poor design you have devised."

Aisley smiled, this time more sweetly. "I am only taking your advice to cull sagely, Edith," she said. "The king told me that I must select one of his knights, did he not?" Without waiting for a reply, she continued, "He said any of his knights. That includes all in his realm, does it not?'' Aisley paused, ignoring Edith's confused and wary expression.

''My lady—'' she interjected.

''So I have made up my mind,'' Aisley said. The self-satisfied smile that tilted the corners of her dainty mouth told Edith that Aisley was up to no good, and she shivered for the fate of her charge. Since the cradle, Aisley de Laci had been a handful, growing up with three brothers in a rough-and-tumble fashion, with no mother to teach her mild ways. Now, the two eldest boys having succumbed to a fever, the third having been killed in the latest Holy Crusade and her father only recently gone, Aisley was the only survivor. She had proved hardier than all of them—strong and clever—but she was also stubborn and sometimes foolhardy.

Privately, Edith thought that marriage to a decent man would do her charge good. To be ruled by a firm but warm hand and have babies of her own to raise might bring out the girl's gentler nature. Edith had even held out hopes that this decree of King Edward's would turn out well, for Aisley was already seventeen and showed no interest in pursuing a husband herself. Yes, Edith had hoped, but she had not taken into account her mistress's willful nature, which was making itself quite apparent in the lady's tone of voice.

''And if he does not approve my choice, then I am, I assume, free to return home,'' Aisley concluded smugly.

Edith's mind raced as she sought to fathom Aisley's plan. For some reason her mistress thought the king would not allow her to marry the knight she would name. Edith blanched as one solution presented itself. ''My lady, you would not ask for a man already married!'' she asked in startled accents.

Aisley's eyes widened in surprise. ''No, I had not thought of that, truly,'' she said. She tilted her head to the side as if considering such a course. ''No, I do not think Edward

would accept that. But he will hold to my choice. He must,"
she said more firmly.

Edith took a breath, afraid to learn the worst, but compelled to ask. "And who will it be, my lady?" she queried.
Aisley's slow smile reminded her of a cat that had strayed
into a dairy, and her trepidation grew.

Feeling the first pleasure of the day, Aisley let her gaze
sweep disdainfully over the knights assembled below before turning to Edith. "I shall choose Baron Montmorency," she said. She paused, expecting her old servant
to be awed by her cleverness, but instead, Edith's eyes
flickered and closed as she sank to the floor in a swoon.

Aisley squared her shoulders as she stepped into the hall,
empty now but for Edward, his queen and a few of his servants and retainers. The king had had the grace to give her
a private audience, but Aisley was not sure if that was a
blessing or a curse. Should Edward attempt to overturn her
decision, he would find it more difficult in front of a room
full of followers. Here, with only this small group... But
Aisley would not let herself think of defeat. A warrior did
not.

Edward was still handsome, tall and long legged, with
golden hair and bright blue eyes, but Aisley had never been
swayed by a man's figure. She eyed him dispassionately as
she knelt before him. "Good evening, Aisley," he said. "I
hope you have found your stay at court enjoyable."

Aisley nodded, forcing a smile. "Yes, of course, my
lord."

"I hope you have spent your time judiciously, so that you
might find the best husband among my knights assembled
here?" he went on slyly, and the others grinned and chuckled at his teasing.

Aisley did not, but licked her lips nervously at the impli-
cation of his words. "My lord did not limit my selection to

those at court," she said as calmly as she could. "I may take to husband any of your knights, may I not?"

Edward's eyes narrowed in surprise, but he only nodded curtly in answer.

Aisley lifted her chin, prepared to speak, yet she found the name harder to utter than she had thought. She took a breath, slow and even, and loosed it. "Then I choose for my husband Baron Montmorency of Dunmurrow," she answered.

Her announcement was greeted by the response she had expected. Gasps and the hushed murmurs of shock surrounded her. She did not have to strain to catch the phrases so often associated with Montmorency. "The Red Knight...the devil's own...a sorcerer...a follower of the black arts..." Although Aisley had heard it all before, somehow the words sent a shiver up her spine now that they were being directed at her.

She shook off the dread that seemed to threaten and glanced at those present. Everyone was looking at her with varying degrees of horror. Everyone, that is, except the king and his wife. Anger showed on Edward's face, though he masked it quickly, and Aisley tried not to smile in triumph. Naturally, he was piqued because she had won. Now, would he be gracious enough to hold to his word?

Edward appeared about to speak, but was halted by his wife, who leaned toward him and whispered something in his ear. Perhaps the queen would temper his rage, Aisley thought, for it was well known that Eleanor was a softening influence on her husband.

Although listening to his wife, Edward glanced sharply back at Aisley, and she tensed under his regard. His blue eyes seemed to search into her very soul, assessing her strengths, her weaknesses—the very tenor of her heart. She held his gaze, though, and as she did, Edward smiled. She felt herself relax when she heard him laugh softly. He thought it all amusing, she realized with relief. He would be gracious enough to concede her victory, and she could soon be on her way, a free woman! He leaned toward her and grinned. "Montmorency it is then," he said.

Aisley's eyes widened in surprise. She had expected the king to deny her decision, perhaps to force her to choose another, but never to let her marry the Red Knight, a virtual recluse who shunned those outside his dark demesne. She felt herself sway on her feet, then stood firm, gathering her wits about her.

The king was smiling at her shock. Obviously, displeased with her attempts at trickery, he would punish her for her outrageous behavior. Oh, dear Lord, Edith was right. She would now be in worse trouble than before unless... unless... Aisley's thoughts, already rushing to form a new plan, were interrupted by Edward's speech.

"Quite naturally, I expected you to choose one of the barons you have met here during your stay, but, as you pointed out so succinctly, I did give you leave of all my knights," he said. "You have made an unusual choice, one that I would not have made for you, but I see no reason to deny you your heart's desire." His words were so softly laced with sarcasm that Aisley felt a shiver run up her spine.

"I think you will be good for Montmorency—a bright angel for our Red Knight. Mayhap you will tame him, eh?" he asked, directing his question to the others, and his audience laughed nervously.

Eleanor smiled serenely beside him, and Aisley knew she would have no help from that quarter.

"Very well then," the king said, looking satisfied. "I give you good journey. You may leave on the morrow, and you will be at Dunmurrow before Christmas." He nodded in curt dismissal, and Aisley stared, aghast. So soon? She recovered herself enough to curtsy and mutter her thanks—empty, hollow, phrases—and then left the hall, quite unable to believe that she was to marry a man she knew only by black and menacing rumor.

* * *

Aisley was in the midst of packing when Edith appeared, trembling, at her elbow. "Well, my lady?" the servant asked breathlessly.

Aisley did not even bother to turn around, but folded a gown into her chest. "We leave in the morning ... for Dunmurrow."

Edith let out a wail that resembled a funeral chant, and Aisley finally turned around to eye her servant. "Don't fall into another faint, please," she snapped. "I have other things to do than pick you up off the floor."

"But, my lady, why? Why would you choose such a monster when you had your pick of the handsomest knights in the land?" Edith protested. "Lackland or de Fiennes would have been happy to wed you, and they would have been kind masters."

But they still would have been masters, Aisley thought. And that was a notion she could just not accept. Never in her life had she suffered a master. Her father and brothers had left her to her own devices. She never had been forced to do another's bidding or follow anything but her own inclinations, and she was not about to start now, she thought as she shoved a pair of slippers in with her clothing.

"But Montmorency!" Edith gasped, crossing herself. "He is evil! 'Tis said he is an alchemist, a practitioner of the black arts, a worshiper of the ... devil himself! That is why they call him the Red Knight, because he is league with the devil! And now he has holed up in the keep of Dunmurrow, never venturing out, calling wizards and sorcerers to him there to learn their secrets, and then casting them out as he conjures for his own dark purposes. 'Tis said that no one who enters his lair ... ever returns." The words that had tumbled out so rapidly seemed to die on her lips as Edith bent her head and shivered with fright.

Aisley finally turned from her task and took the servant in her arms. "Rumors! What nonsense!" she scoffed. "All the great warriors have nurtured legends about themselves so as to strike fear into the hearts of their foes," she said. "This Red Knight is but mortal man. You will see." She patted Edith awkwardly and bid her sit down upon a stool, while she turned back to her packing.

"But why, my lady, why?" Edith moaned. "Was this your wretched scheme—to send us into evil?"

Aisley's hands halted their task but for a moment before she reached for her Psalter. "I admit I had hopes that the king would not favor my choice, but he cared not to admit that I had tricked him. He seeks to teach me a lesson, that is all," she said as she placed the holy book in with her other belongings.

Edith wailed again, a soft keening sound that set Aisley's teeth on edge. "Stop this foolishness at once, Edith," she ordered, straightening. "Have no worries about this fearsome knight. I promise you we will not be at Dunmurrow long enough to be frightened of him."

Edith's head shot up, a look of bemused inquiry on her face, while Aisley smiled grimly. "Think you that Montmorency wants a wife prying into his dark businesses?" Aisley asked. "I think not. He has no interest in court intrigues and does not quest for money. He will refuse me, and I shall be free to return home, unwed," she said, with more certainty than she felt.

"But that would be folly!" Edith sputtered. "Even the Red Knight could not defy an order of the king."

Aisley shrugged. "I have heard that Montmorency lives under his own rules."

"Yes, but surely he will not gainsay Edward?"

Aisley smoothed out the garments that she'd hastily stacked in the chest and reached for the heavy wooden top. "And if he does not, than I shall be wed. One brute is the same as another to my way of thinking," she said. She slammed down the lid, so forcefully it nearly broke in two.

* * *

The air was frosty when they set out, the mounts steaming in the cold morning air, and Aisley pulled her fur-lined cloak more tightly around her. One of the king's own men, Delamere by name, led the small band, with a guard of six and servants to attend them. Aisley scanned the group with practiced eyes, her gaze halting on a small man in ecclesiastic robes hurrying to catch up with the procession. "Who is that?" she asked.

"'Tis the priest, of course," said Delamere. "He is to make sure that you are well and truly wed. Perhaps the king suspects that no chaplain lives at Dunmurrow...." He shot her an amused glance, and Aisley frowned at his insolence. She turned her mount away, trying to still the uneasiness that crept over her.

Although she had used Montmorency's black reputation to try to outwit Edward, Aisley told herself she did not believe a word of it. She knew how fast gossip traveled and how exaggerated it soon became, and she suspected that all the talk about Montmorency was just that—talk. If no chaplain served at Dunmurrow, it did not mean that the Red Knight had driven the man away with his foul practices.

Aisley almost laughed aloud at the notion. She suddenly found the presence of the holy man in her train vastly amusing. Perhaps Montmorency would even want to keep the fellow on, but certainly not to perform any marriage ceremonies. You may lead a horse to water, Aisley thought, lifting her chin, but you cannot make him drink. She may have chosen the Red Knight, but he had not chosen her, and, priest or no priest, she could not imagine anyone forcing him to wed. And when he refused, she thought, allowing herself a small smile of triumph, she would be free....

The king's man had no liking for her, that was plain, and each day he drove the wedding party harder—as if they were off to battle and not traveling to the groom's holding. Edith whined and fussed over the pace, but Aisley did not complain. The sooner they reached Montmorency's demesne, the sooner she would be on her way home.

Upon their arrival, however, Aisley felt no relief. Even the countryside was forbidding, for around them stretched seemingly endless, flat land, while a great, grim forest marched like a menacing presence beside them. It was nearly nightfall when she first set eyes upon the Red Knight's castle, and despite all her brave resolutions, she shivered at the sight.

The sun was setting, casting deep shadows across the walls, but Aisley could see the rectangular keep, old and gloomy, rising from behind the rough stone, its arrow slits black as narrow eyes. Hugging the ground, a gray mist seemed to grow out of nowhere, wreathing all of Dunmurrow like a ghostly shroud.

The effect was so eerie that Aisley drew in a sharp breath, and for one chilling moment she wondered if Montmorency did have powers at his command, powers that could summon a fog to hide his home from prying eyes and unwelcome visitors.

Edith's soft wail of fright brought Aisley out of her somber thoughts. When she saw a few of the servants cross themselves, Aisley shook off her hesitation and rode forward toward the reluctant priest, who was mumbling under his breath—whether prayers or curses, she could not tell.

Aisley waited while the king's garrison went to the gate house. At least she would have a fire and a bed for the night, and, hopefully, no snow on the morrow when they left. No matter how haughtily Delamere had behaved so far, he could hardly refuse to escort her home. But if he did object, she would beg some men from the knight who would soon spurn her as his wife. The thought made her lips curve into a smile of mischief.

It was wiped from her face by the approach of Delamere, who reined in beside her with a furious look on his features. "We have been denied permission to pass through the walls," he informed her tersely.

"Why?" Aisley asked calmly. Although she was anxious for a warm bed, this treatment was cause for celebration, not dismay, if it meant she would never have to face the Red Knight. Should Montmorency refuse even to see her, then she could be on her way home to Belvry even sooner than she had anticipated.

"Because the castle is closed for the night, and all visitors are forbidden entrance until morning," Delamere answered.

Aisley drew in her breath in surprise, just as she heard Edith gasp beside her. A quick glance at her servant confirmed that she threatened to swoon upon her mount, and Aisley nudged her horse closer to prevent the woman from falling. "What nonsense is this?" she asked the king's man. "I demand to speak with Baron Montmorency," she said.

"As did I," Delamere answered with an angry grimace. "But my request was rejected until morning." Aisley watched, speechless, while he ordered the servants and guards to make camp in the very shadow of Dunmurrow.

A groan from Edith again claimed Aisley's attention, and she looked to her servant, who was sagging on her palfrey. "Stop this at once or I shall drop you onto the ground," Aisley warned, unable to curb her annoyance with the woman.

"Oh, my lady, it is as we feared," Edith whispered. "He is a creature of darkness."

"If he were a creature of darkness, he would be out here enjoying it," Aisley snapped. "He is more a creature of rudeness! It is unheard of to deny visitors entrance. And to think we are here on the king's business! This Red Knight dares much." Although she had no wish to sleep in a cold cart again when hearth and table were within reach, she was impressed by Montmorency's open defiance. It boded well for her plans.

"He's a devil, mark my words," Edith warned.

"And you mark my words," Aisley said, with a smile playing about her lips. "He is an ill-mannered, reckless man who will defy the king's edict tomorrow! And then... then we shall go home," Aisley said, her blood tingling in anticipation.

In the morn, the drawbridge was finally lowered over the massive ditch that surrounded the castle, and the wedding party rode into Dunmurrow. Accustomed to the busy workings of her home, Aisley was surprised to find the bailey nearly deserted, the buildings seemingly empty. She refused to look at Edith, knowing full well what the servant would make of the inactivity.

Although she scorned the Red Knight's dark legend as so much nonsense, when the drawbridge groaned back into place behind them, Aisley felt a prick of dread, for they were well and truly locked inside his lair and at his mercy....

Aisley tried to throw off her unease as a guard led them into the keep, but the great hall of Dunmurrow was no comfort. Huge and dark, it smelled musty and smoky, and she could see the dirt that caked the once-painted walls. She sniffed. What manner of man was this, who kept his home in such a condition? The narrow windows were shuttered, letting in but the feeblest bit of sunlight from so high above that it could barely pierce the gloom below.

Lack of light was not unusual, especially in such an old keep, but normally candles, rushes dipped in grease, and flares were lit, at least during the day. Yet this hall boasted only a few, which did little to drive away the shadows.

Aisley shivered as most of her retinue found seats on benches along the trestle tables. The fire seemed too far away and too low for her taste, and she walked closer to its bright warmth. From her position, the other end of the vast room seemed impenetrably dark, and she felt cold despite the nearby heat. She refused to look at Edith, who was cowering near the priest.

The group was silent, the oppressive atmosphere settling over them like a pall, with the only sounds coming from Delamere as he strode back and forth impatiently. The king's man obviously was accustomed to being treated with more deference, and he did not care to be left cooling his heels, especially after an ignominious night spent outside the walls.

Just when Aisley thought Delamere would burst with the force of his own fury, a servant announced that Montmorency wished them to dine. Although it was early for the midmorning meal, the men fell to, as if hungry for something with which to occupy themselves as much as for food.

"Come. Eat, my lady," Edith said, beckoning Aisley to her side. Aisley sat, though she knew she would hardly take a bite—not with the magnitude of the task ahead of her. Suddenly her clever plan seemed too bold, too uncertain, to be successful, and Montmorency's home appeared strange and unsettling. So far, she noted ruefully, the man was living up to his reputation.

Aisley watched the one servant move back and forth from the tables to the kitchens, putting out ale and trenchers of stew, and was dumbfounded. "Where is everyone?" she asked. Her hall at Belvry rang with the sounds of ladies, knights, squires, pages, servants and visiting villagers dining together, not this eerie silence. The castle was too quiet, its hollows echoing with the slightest noise.

Edith gave Aisley a look of eloquent horror in answer. "He is inhuman, I tell you," she whispered.

Aisley snorted. "'Tis not inhuman to live poorly," she said. "But I am just realizing, dear Edith, how much I have taken for granted," she noted pensively. "The castle father built when he was young is still new today and full of light, lovely murals, fine tapestries. Many servants, all doing their duties...."

"Much of it owing to you, my lady," Edith said proudly. "Men left to their own devices naturally run awry of good food and cleanliness," she said with a frown of distaste.

"I can tell that," Aisley answered. From what little she could see of it, Castle Dunmurrow was filthy. The rushes on the floor were old and did nothing to dispel the smells of rotting food and close garderobes. The walls were black with smoke, the tables rough and unclean. Aisley looked down at the trencher she shared with Edith. It was swimming with grease, and she wondered if it had been as sorely neglected as the rest of the household.

Whether clean or foul itself, the wooden vessel was filled with unsavory food. After one taste Aisley leaned back from the table, pulling distractedly on a hunk of bread while the others ate. And ate. The meal seemed to last forever, and Aisley found herself on edge by the time it was ended, the trenchers cleared away and the cups refilled with sour ale.

As sad as was the fare, it seemed to have set the group more at ease, but for Delamere, who still appeared irritated, and Aisley, who was fast working herself into a fury, too.

"Here, my lady, have a drink," Edith urged in a placating tone.

"I want nothing, Edith, but to be finished with our errand," Aisley said with annoyance. "Let Montmorency come and be done with us, so that we might be on our way!"

"Hush," Edith warned with a glance toward Delamere.

Aisley ignored her. "Why the delay? Why are we made to wait here like beggar children after spending the night outside the walls?" she said, her voice rising.

Edith only shook her head helplessly. "My lady, please watch your tongue! It would not be wise to cross swords with the Red Knight."

"I don't care if he is the devil incarnate. If we are not admitted into his unholy presence without further delay, I am leaving. And hang the king's edict!'' Aisley said. She moved to stand, while Edith raised her hands to her cheeks in breathless worry, and Delamere shot Aisley an angry glance. As though on cue, a servant named Cecil stepped forward.

"If my lady and her escort would follow me, my lord is ready to receive you now," he said.

Aisley would have taken Edith, too, but thought perhaps it was best to leave her servant behind. If the Red Knight were even half as bad as his reputation, Edith would probably swoon again.

Cecil led them toward a hole in the wall, where a stair spiraled up into such blackness that Aisley climbed it with difficulty, grateful for the servant's directing touch upon her elbow. She did not realize that they had stopped at a door until he flung it open and bade them enter.

Aisley assumed they were in the great chamber, the Red Knight's own den, but she could not see much. Warmth met her after the chill of the steps, and she walked toward the fire. If there were any windows in the room, they must have been shuttered, for the only light was thrown by the blaze behind her. The setting was a fitting one for Montmorency, Aisley thought, for what she could see of the room glowed eerily, as though the walls were crimson.

Delamere moved next to her, and it seemed as if the space around them was a small, red cocoon carved out of the night of the surrounding chamber. With no torches or candles to brighten it, the rest of the room lay deep in darkness.

Far across from them, in the heaviest of the shadows, sat a huge figure flanked by a pair of enormous dogs.

Was it Montmorency? Aisley strained her eyes, trying to see him better, but her gaze could not pierce the gloom. He was big, bigger by far than Delamere—that much was apparent even though he was seated. But that was all Aisley could determine. His clothing, his features, his hair and his coloring were all indiscernible. Although she knew instinctively that she faced the Red Knight, she could not even see his face.

The unusual setting gave her pause, and she drew in a breath warily. What kind of man was this? Did he seek to frighten them intentionally? Aisley had never feared the night, had never believed the stories whispered about the man before her, and yet she felt a shiver travel up the back of her neck just the same.

Edith would have fainted dead away.

Chapter Two

"I have read this edict you bring me from the king," the figure said softly. His voice was deep and strong and laced with mockery. Or was it annoyance? Aisley was not sure which, but it irked her, coupled with the fact that he had spoken without even greeting them properly. She thought of the long, cold night spent outside Dunmurrow's walls, of her stay in the filthy hall below, of the darkness that hid her host from her eyes, and she grew even angrier.

"I am glad, my lord," she said, "for we waited so long that I began to think none in your castle were able to read it."

His head snapped up at her thinly veiled insult, and Aisley sensed rather than saw his eyes burning into her. She was beyond caring. "If you do not wish to comply, then tell us so, that we may depart. I have a long journey ahead of me, and many *more* nights to spend out in the cold before reaching my home."

Silence met her speech, and Aisley felt like stalking across the room to slap him to attention, to make him rise and pay her the homage that was her right instead of skulking in the shadows, red devil that he was.

"My lady..." Montmorency paused as if he could not remember her name, and Aisley gritted her teeth at the slight. "Lady de Laci," he said. "This missive states that you were bidden to select any knight in the land to wed and you chose *me*.'' He spoke in a dry tone that intimated he could see right through her ruse. ''Why?'' he asked.

Aisley licked her lips, unnerved by the direct question. She had expected Montmorency to refuse her and send them on their way—perhaps with a polite demur, perhaps with a rude scold—but she was not prepared for this bold query.

When she hesitated, he barked at Delamere, ''You, sir— is she such a shrew that none at court would have her?''

Aisley drew in her breath, her cheeks flaming, while Delamere choked back a laugh beside her.

''She is known to be willful, my lord, but many would gladly marry her,'' Delamere answered.

''Yes, for she has great wealth, does she not?'' Montmorency said softly.

The insinuation was not lost on Aisley. How dare he suggest that only her holdings made her attractive as a wife? She bit her tongue to keep from shouting at the beast across the room.

''Think you that she is comely?'' the baron asked suddenly.

Aisley blushed again as Delamere turned to her, his eyes sweeping over her in the first appreciative sign she had ever seen from him. ''Yes, my lord. Her figure is spare, but fine, her hair so pale it is nearly white and so rich that it rivals the finest silver. And her eyes . . . her eyes are silver, too, with depths that sparkle like a gemstone.'' The king's man seemed to catch himself, and turned away. ''My lady's beauty is renowned,'' he concluded.

''Along with her temper?'' Montmorency asked wryly.

Delamere had the grace not to answer, but smiled grimly, while Aisley clenched her fists as they discussed her like a prized ox about to be roasted for their Christmas feast.

''And so you chose me, my lady,'' Montmorency said slowly, in a threatening way that made Aisley shiver despite her anger. ''Perhaps the fine gentlemen at court were too weak for your taste and you thought the Red Knight equal to the task of taming you?''

Delamere chuckled beside her, and Aisley stiffened. "I can see that it was a mistake, my lord," she said as coolly as she could.

"Yes. It was a mistake—your mistake, wasn't it?" Montmorency asked, his voice as menacing as his castle. When Aisley refused to answer, the silence stretched between them, making her heart pound so fiercely that she dug her nails into her palms.

"But what's done is done," Montmorency finally said, his tone even again. "So be it. Cecil, have the chapel prepared and see that the priest is taken there as soon as it is ready. I am afraid we are not used to having many visitors here," he said, addressing them once more, "and the hospitality of my hall is limited. But we shall do our best." He waved a hand in dismissal, and Aisley felt her blood run cold.

"Wait!" The single word rang out in the stillness, the panic edging it evident even to Aisley's ears. She eased in a breath, and when she turned to Delamere, she spoke more calmly. "You may return to the hall." Glancing back she went on, "My lord, I would speak to you alone, if I may."

"You may," Montmorency said. Delamere, obviously relieved that his duties were nearly completed, left hastily, ushered out by Cecil, and Aisley was left alone with the huge form hidden in the shadows. What kind of man would shroud himself in total darkness during the daylight hours? Aisley felt her will waver as she stood before him, but with a great effort she gathered her courage and took a step toward the menacing figure.

One of the dogs growled low. "Stay, my lady," Montmorency said. Aisley halted, confused, then took another step forward. The dogs growled again, frightening sounds from deep in their throats.

"Stay, I said," Montmorency repeated angrily. "Sit," he added more gently, his arm pointing to the settle near the fire. Aisley sat down quickly and hard, as obedient as any pup. She ran her tongue over her lips nervously.

"My lord, I assure you this is all a mistake," she began, her hands bunched tightly into fists beneath the flowing fabric of her gown.

"Yes, it is," Montmorency said, his irritation evident. "And you made it. Think you I would defy the king's order?"

Aisley did not answer. Montmorency laughed, a bitter bark in the quiet chamber. "So you did."

"Your reputation is great, my lord," Aisley said softly.

"I see," he said. "Perhaps you thought I would simply wave a hand and make the edict disappear with a sorcerer's trick?"

Aisley stifled a gasp at his phrase, and she could swear she saw the flash of white teeth, smiling tauntingly in the shadows.

"Well, my willful Lady de Laci, your machinations have gone awry, for no matter what you might have heard about me, I do not defy my king. I owe Edward much, and if this be his wish, then I will obey. Now," he said, rising, "you made your bed. I suggest you lie in it." A tap on the door signalled the servant's return, and Montmorency bade him enter.

"Cecil, please show my bride to her room. We will be married as soon as possible," the Red Knight said, his words echoing in Aisley's head like a death knoll.

Although Aisley sat motionless in her chamber, her mind raced. She could run yet. She had only to open the door and find her way out of the keep. It would be easy enough in the darkness that blanketed the interior, she told herself. But what awaited her outside? Could she talk her way past the guards? And what of the drawbridge? It had been raised behind them, locking them into the bailey. Aisley swore softly, one of her father's curses rolling from her tongue in unladylike fashion at her predicament.

Despite all her hard work, all her planning and scheming, she was to be wed, and not to some biddable fop, but to a man who wouldn't even show his face in daylight—who would not even let her approach him! Aisley felt a quiver of dread and quelled it promptly. The brute was not going to frighten her. And she was not going to run. She was a de Laci, and she would be strong.

A knock upon the door halted Aisley's thoughts, and she turned, annoyed at the prospect of facing Edith. She could not bear to hear the servant wail at their plight. All her concentration was expended trying to remain composed herself; she doubted whether she could soothe her servant, as well.

It was not Edith, however, but the ever-present Cecil who answered her summons to enter. "My lord bids you come to the chapel, my lady," the man said, his expression unreadable.

Aisley blanched, unable to believe that the time had arrived so swiftly. She had none of her chests and was still dressed in the gown she had hastily donned this morning. She did not even have a brush with which to smooth her hair. Clenching her fists, she bit back a protest. What did it matter? She certainly did not care what that oaf, the Red Knight, thought of her. With a brief nod, she loosed a calming breath and followed Cecil with as much enthusiasm as if he were leading her to her own execution.

They traveled through narrow passages cut into the stone until they stood in a chapel as shrouded in gloom as the rest of the castle. Having lost all track of time, Aisley wondered if it had indeed grown late, but then she realized they had not even partaken of supper. No, the night within these walls was not natural; it was of man's making.

Lifting her chin, Aisley kept on walking beside Cecil, past the pitifully few figures assembled to witness this union. Was that Edith crossing herself and whispering fearfully? Aisley thought she heard the word *blasphemy* and something about devil worship as she went by.

She struggled to retain her serene demeanor, for despite her outward show of courage, she was not immune to the forbidding atmosphere of Dunmurrow, and the perpetual shadows, the musty smell and the brooding silence did little to make its chapel seem like a house of God. Even less did the solemn assembly resemble any wedding party that she had ever seen.

With great effort, Aisley tamped down her uneasiness, unwilling to let Edith's words frighten her. Just because the Red Knight appeared inclined toward darkness did not mean he was a necromancer or some sort of evil creature, she told herself; besides, she had faced worse than a bit of shadow in her life.

Her head held high, she approached the altar. Montmorency was already there, a tall, mysterious figure standing before the priest. Aisley stepped beside him, nearly tripping in the gloom, and was surprised when his hand moved to her elbow to steady her. She glanced up at him, but she could not discern his features, and she had to suppress a shiver at the sight of the great, faceless form. There was something wholly pagan in marrying a man whose face she could not even see.

Refusing to be intimidated by him, Aisley turned to the priest, who, flanked by candles, was the only person in the entire chapel who could be viewed clearly. The little man gazed at her anxiously and then down at his book, as though he wanted no part of this ceremony. Aisley could not blame him. The blackness was like a living thing, pulsing around her, and she took a deep breath to still her panic.

When Montmorency touched her, Aisley nearly jumped out of her skin. Although she knew the contact would be brief, knew she must let him take her hand for the duration of their vows, she was not prepared for it. With great effort of will, she relaxed her hand in his grip and was pleasantly surprised, for, despite Edith's predictions, Montmorency presented no hoof or talon. His hand was normal enough. It was large and warm and strong, his fingers callused and dry. Still, Aisley shivered in reaction.

'Twas not a tingle of fear, though, but a surge of excitement that ran through her. Startled, she felt her breath catch and her heart beat a little faster, for she was extremely aware of every bit of her skin that met Montmorency's. It was a sensation such as she had never before experienced, and with sudden horror she wondered if her behavior was the result of some sorcery. Had the Red Knight cast one of his wicked spells upon her?

The thought made Aisley nearly wrench herself free from his grasp, but she tried, instead, to concentrate on the priest's words. When they didn't calm her, she counted to ten. She told herself that she was far too educated to believe in the black arts, but the argument seemed woefully unconvincing when she was swathed in shadows, holding on to a man she could not even see.

That was it, Aisley decided. The unusual act of clasping someone's hand was making her feel strange. She was unaccustomed to that sort of closeness. Never one to seek or show affection, Aisley was used to the rough company of her brothers and her to father's cool respect. Touching was foreign—and usually repugnant to her.

Aisley vividly recalled an encounter at court when Baron Rothschilde had cornered her behind a tapestry. In a revolting attempt to woo her, the knight had pushed her up against the cold stone and put his fat, wet lips on her mouth. Aisley had kicked him in the groin and made her escape, more determined than ever never to submit to a husband.

And yet she was marrying a man infinitely more repulsive than Rothschilde. Or was she? Aisley did not feel revulsion now, but rather a sort of thrilling pleasure that she could not explain. There was something both frightening and compelling about the Red Knight, she realized. And it was the compelling part of him that made her the most uneasy.

She shot a glance up at the knight who towered over her, making her seem tiny and defenseless. Whether by might or by magic, he was powerful, Aisley sensed. The hand holding hers undoubtedly could crush her like a walnut shell. And tonight? Aisley balked at the thought she had not dared let into her mind.

You have made your bed, now lie in it. Montmorency's words returned, mocking her, and Aisley shifted uneasily. The fingers that held hers now in supplication before the priest might lose their gentleness in the privacy of the great chamber. Big and featureless to her, the Red Knight might well be some kind of demon, just as they said, yet Aisley knew that she must lie with him tonight. She shuddered with dread.

As if in answer, Montmorency squeezed her hand tightly, and, raising her chin, Aisley turned her attention to the ceremony. She could not say whether she drew strength from the man beside her or whether he simply forced her own innate courage to the fore, but somehow, some way, she pledged him her troth.

Although she had the odd notion that the baron had given her reassurance when she needed it, Aisley was glad when he released his hold upon her. Her relief was short-lived, however, for before she could turn away from him, the man grasped her arms and pulled her up against the unyielding expanse of his chest.

Aisley gasped in surprise at the strange feel of a man's body pressed to her breasts. Perhaps if she could see or be seen, the sensation would not be so alien, but the chapel was so dark that it seemed as if they were alone—just as though a great chasm had opened around her and her only anchor was the Red Knight.

Disoriented, Aisley raised her hands, her fingers finding purchase in the fine material of his surcoat. Montmorency immediately loosened his grip on her arms and slid his hands up her shoulders to the back of her neck. Aisley felt the gentle pressure of his fingers and palms, giving warmth and life to every bit of skin they touched as he turned her face upward. Then his lips met hers, for a brief, hard kiss.

It was over before she even realized what he was doing. Stunned, Aisley blinked up at his face, but she could see nothing. As if they moved in a dream, she waited breathlessly—for what, she was not sure. Montmorency's hands glided back down her arms slowly, and Aisley marveled at the heat he generated even through her sleeves. His grip tightened, and she leaned into him, lifting her head . . . .

He put her from him forcibly. "You may retire to your room, but I will expect you for supper," he said roughly, leaving her to stand staring stupidly after him into the blackness.

Dazed by all that had occurred, she might have stayed there indefinitely, but for a sound from the altar that caught her attention. Turning, Aisley gazed up at the priest, surprised by his presence.

Had only a moment passed? It had seemed to her as if she and Montmorency were alone in the silent blackness for an eternity, and yet . . . the chapel did not look quite as dim now, and she could hear the movements of the guests. Everyone was still here, making noises, oblivious to what had happened to her.

What *had* happened to her?

Aisley wasn't sure. For a moment, it had seemed that there was no chapel, no priest, no wedding party—only her and Montmorency together in the shadows . . . touching. She shivered. She could still feel the imprint of his hands on her, the pressure of his chest, his mouth. . . . Aisley lifted a finger to her lips and had the odd impression that her new husband had marked her as his own.

She dropped her hand abruptly as she realized that Edith's tales were making her fanciful. It was a marriage kiss, nothing more, she told herself, and, being unaccustomed to the handling of men, she had been a bit overwhelmed. The unusual circumstances of their union had played tricks on her senses. She must have imagined that Montmorency squeezed her hand to comfort her, too, for he was obviously still angry with her. His curt dismissal had made that clear enough.

Aisley licked her lips nervously. Things were happening too fast—and too strangely—for even her quick wits to grasp. She felt out of her depth, and she did not like it. By nature and by vocation, Aisley liked to run things. She needed to be in command at all times, yet she was beginning to feel powerless here in Dunmurrow. She was naught but a prisoner of the gloom, an unhappy bride for an unwilling husband.

She drew in a shaky breath. It seemed impossible that the clever scheme she had set in motion so many weeks ago had led her to this, but it was true. She was wife to the Red Knight—a dark, forbidding figure who threatened to shatter her control not only with his eccentricities, but with his very touch.

Back in her bedchamber, Aisley was greeted by her chests, which had been placed inside the door like a final reminder that she could not go home. Restlessly she fingered the heavy ring that Montmorency had set upon her finger as she realized that she would have to live in this cold and forbidding keep. She felt like throwing herself upon the bed and weeping.

Instead she sharply ordered a whimpering Edith to unpack her belongings. She stepped out the door and called back a retreating Cecil. "Are there more candles that I

might have?'' she asked. He eyed her nervously and nodded. ''Then bring them to me, please. I cannot abide this
darkness. Have you any serving women or men who clean?''

He shook his head. ''There is a laundress.''

''Have her brought to me at once,'' Aisley said. He paled,
but nodded swiftly, then was gone.

''I want someone to clean this chamber,'' Aisley said to
Edith. The servant, who had not moved from her spot, was
still moaning softly at their plight, so Aisley ignored her and
flung open the shutters. The air that met her was frosty, but
fresh, and she welcomed the light as she put her hands on
her hips and surveyed the room.

It was small and bare, except for her chests, the bed and
the settle that stood in front of the hearth. The walls were
gray, the floor nearly black and the bed hangings dusty.
Aisley wrinkled her nose in disgust.

'''Tis an insult to give you such a shabby place!'' Edith
said, her grief over the wedding overshadowed by her outrage at their lodgings. '''Tis a disgrace to any lady, and especially to you, for you are used to such fine things. Why,
there is not even a chair here.''

''Judging from the lack of furnishings in the castle, I
would say I am lucky to have the settle,'' Aisley replied.
''And we can make cushions for it easily enough.''

Edith sniffed in reply, drawing a smile from Aisley for the
first time since she had entered Dunmurrow.

''From the age of the keep, I would say I am fortunate to
even have a hearth,'' she noted. She shivered, imagining a
cold, windowless cell, and was truly thankful for what she
had. Then she pictured the great chamber, where the baron's wife would normally be housed, and shivered again, a
different sort of shudder that encompassed both her uneasiness and a strange sensation she could not explain.

Shaking off the peculiar feeling that thoughts of her new
husband engendered, Aisley opened her mouth to say she
was glad not to be in the hot, glowing darkness of Mont-

morency's lair, but she thought better of her words. The room did bear a faint resemblance to descriptions of the devil's residence, and Aisley did not care to hear Edith make comparisons. She had heard enough silliness about her husband from her servant.

"This chamber will suit me well enough once it is cleaned," she insisted, more sharply than she intended. The room was in sorry condition, but, as elsewhere, seemed to be afflicted mainly with dirt, something Aisley knew could be remedied. "If the laundress cannot help, then you and I must do the work ourselves until more women can be brought from the village," she said. "And they will be! I care not what expense . . ."

Aisley broke off her words with a start of surprise. "Money," she said softly. "Edith! Perhaps this ferocious Red Knight is poor. He might have few servants because his demesne is not productive. . . few candles because he can not afford them or does not have skilled help in sufficient numbers to supply them."

Although Edith looked dubious, Aisley continued almost eagerly, grasping at this possible explanation for the state of the castle. "If the problem is funds, it can easily be remedied with income from Belvry. Or better yet . . . a move to Belvry!" She sat down hard on the bed, stunned by the idea and the hope that it brought her.

Perhaps, just perhaps, Montmorency would be happy with a thriving estate and would be willing to live there at least part of the year. Aisley's eyes, bright with expectation, flew to Edith, but the servant shook her head woefully. "Maybe, my lady," she said. "Yet there must be enough wood nearby to provide torches to light the hall, and still it lies in blackness."

Aisley stared at her servant while her burgeoning hope dimmed. Edith was right, of course. There would be no move to Belvry. The Red Knight, she suspected, was right at home here, in the darkness.

Chapter Three

Her head held high, Aisley followed the everpresent Cecil to supper. Her bedchamber and the tiny storage room attached to it were now neat and clean, and everything was tucked away. She tried not to think of her spacious quarters at Belvry, or of the solar, with its oriel windows, where she had spent so much of her time. Perhaps she could send for some of her tapestries to cover the cold, damp walls of Dunmurrow, and to cheer her....

Aisley turned her mind away from its painful path and concentrated on her steps. After the meal, she would order a bath, she decided, trying to focus on details. Perhaps if she gave her attention to such small matters, she wouldn't be forced to ponder the larger issues, such as the enormity of her mistake.

She had erred, Aisley admitted now to herself, though not to Edith. Her plan had relied too much on the reactions of others, and when the king and Montmorency had behaved unexpectedly, her scheme had been ruined. Far from gaining her her freedom, her actions had bound her to this dismal place forever.

Aisley knew she should have chosen someone else, yet when she considered the other knights, there were none she wanted. Faces swam before her, all of them objectionable, for in truth, she did not want to be married to anyone. Of course, if Edith was to be believed, Aisley *still* wasn't married to anyone, for the servant insisted that Montmorency was not mortal, but a ghost or a demon. While cleaning, she had seen fit to repeat every rumor she had ever heard about the Red Knight, making him everything from the devil incarnate to a formless specter.

Aisley smiled to herself at her servant's foolishness, for she put no stock in the tales. Reflecting upon them, she decided that perhaps she had not picked so poorly after all. The faceless Montmorency might be more suited to her than a real, live man, and a shadow ought to be much more malleable than an arrogant noble. With a sigh, she discarded her fancies. No matter what he was, the Red Knight would not be easily ruled, she suspected.

Following Cecil along a cold, narrow hall cut through stone, Aisley nearly tripped in the gloom. Choking back an oath, she was suddenly infuriated by the senseless darkness and wished she had taken anyone but Montmorency to husband. If she had picked one of the knights from court, she would be facing other problems now, but at least she would be able to see! Dunmurrow's infernal night was beginning to weigh heavily on her, frustrating her efforts to pretend that all would be well.

Aisley was not surprised when Cecil led her to the great chamber. It was not unusual for a lord and his favored vassals to dine there, where he also slept, but she was not pleased to be back in the Red Knight's lair. The room was even blacker than she remembered, its eerie red glow limited to the area in front of the hearth, the fire being the only source of light.

A table had been set up in the shadows, and Aisley could see the huge figure of Montmorency seated there, waiting for her. Although she had scoffed at Edith's stories about him, she couldn't help feeling a twinge of uneasiness. She was reminded of a huntsman and its prey, and when a low growl emanated from his direction, she nearly jumped.

"Quiet, Pollux," Montmorency said, and Aisley realized with giddy relief that the sound had come from one of the dogs and not from her husband. Still, the unholy darkness and the presence of the animals made it hard for her to dismiss Edith's whisperings. Perhaps the Red Knight was some beast, a hideous thing whose face was distorted by a snout, sharp fangs and unnatural red eyes....

"Sit, my lady. I will not bite you," Montmorency said in that dry, almost insulting way of his, and Aisley's uneasiness fled, replaced by annoyance. She lifted her chin, swallowed a sharp retort and sat down.

"My lord," she said with a nod. Then she deliberately glanced away from the forbidding figure he made, looking for any sign of her entourage. As far as she could tell, no other places were set at the table. "Where is the priest? And the king's man, Delamere?" she asked.

Montmorency's head came up, and his voice sounded wryly surprised. "They are gone," he said. "They left after the wedding, anxious to start the long journey ahead of them."

Aisley felt cold and hot at once. She could not believe that the small band had not been invited to stay. Even if winter stores were limited, some ale and bread could have been provided. It was unheard of to send off wedding guests without a meal.

She was appalled, outraged and more than a little disquieted, for with the knowledge of their absence came the realization that she was alone now, locked in with the Red Knight—all contact with the outside world severed. "You bade them leave without—without a word from me?" Aisley asked, trying to keep her voice steady.

"I did not know you wished to speak with them," Montmorency answered, his massive shoulders shrugging. "They were eager to be on their way."

Aisley frowned. No doubt they were eager to fly from the Red Knight's den, cowardly curs that they were, she thought with contempt. "No wedding feast? No celebration?" she asked as evenly as she could.

"Celebration? I saw no cause for it," Montmorency said, his tone bitter.

Aisley felt as if he had slapped her. "I see," she said sharply. "Very well. Perhaps you will have greater cause for rejoicing when you receive an accounting from Belvry. I know not how much you need, but I have just made you wealthy!"

"I desire not your wealth!" Montmorency answered angrily, slamming down his fist on the table.

Aisley decided to ignore the outburst. "You do not?" she asked, more calmly. "From the look of the keep, I would say money is just what you need." She casually reached for some bread and broke off a piece for herself.

"Perhaps I should remind you that it was you who came here uninvited, Lady de Laci," Montmorency hissed. "It was you who forced me into a marriage I did not seek or want. Did you give any thought at all to your...victim?" he asked in a deceptively pleasant voice. "What if I was pledged to another? Did you even consider that? What if I care for someone else?"

Aisley was momentarily taken aback—and appalled. Marriages among noble families were usually business arrangements, but there were many tales of courtly romance. Although the Red Knight was the last person she would have suspected of such devotion, she knew it was possible that he might want another woman for his wife—a woman with whom he was in love. "Do you?" she asked abruptly.

Montmorency leaned back as if regarding her, although Aisley knew that he could not really see her in the gloom. Or could he? An ordinary man could not, but the Red Knight was anything but ordinary. He did not reply immediately, dragging out the silence between them until she felt like screaming. Although she had no idea why, the answer suddenly was very important to her, and she wanted—needed—to hear him deny that he cared for another.

"No," he finally said.

"Oh!" She slammed down her knife, angry at him for taunting her.

"But what if I were?" Montmorency asked, cutting off any further protests. "You certainly did not give a thought to me, or to anyone else when concocting this wild scheme to escape the altar," he said, a hint of disgust in his voice.

Aisley frowned. He was twisting things around to make her appear the villain when it was Edward who had forced her to wed and Montmorency who had been foolish enough to agree. "Of course I gave no thought to you, my lord," Aisley snapped. "I never dreamed that you would actually marry me."

Montmorency grunted in answer, as if her words confirmed his thoughts.

"What does that mean?" Aisley asked, her annoyance growing. It was bad enough that she couldn't see the man. Now, apparently, he was not even going to talk to her coherently.

"It means, my dear wife," Montmorency said, "that you are just what I suspected—a spoiled brat."

Aisley was stunned. "How dare you?" she asked, incensed.

"I dare because I am your husband," he answered smoothly. "Perhaps you ought to try to remember that."

"As if I could forget," Aisley muttered. She thought she heard the low rumble of a chuckle, but discounted it as only a sound from one of the dogs. She attacked her food, too irritated to speak to him further.

Montmorency was no fool, she realized, and she would need all her cleverness to outwit him. Her mind raced, searching for a way to bring him to his knees—or at least remove that mocking tone from his voice. And it came to her, so clearly that Aisley nearly choked, stunned as she was by the revelation.

Their union could be voided.

Marriages could be dissolved on the grounds that they had been contracted against the will of one of the parties. Although Aisley certainly had not wanted to wed anyone, she had chosen Montmorency in front of the king and his witnesses, so she could hardly claim coercion. No, she could not, Aisley thought, a slow smile spreading across her face. But Montmorency could.

The Red Knight had made it clear that he wanted no part of her. During her audience yesterday, the rude figure had intimated that she was desirable only because of her dowry. At the time, Montmorency had plainly stated that he accepted her to wife only to obey Edward—and hadn't he just complained that she had forced him into a marriage he did not seek or want? He had been contracted to her, against his will, by the king's decree!

Aisley was grinning now, certain that they had a clear case for dissolution. She had but to convince Montmorency, and they could end this farce. She would be free to return to Belvry, having chosen a knight as Edward had ordered. And Montmorency could not be faulted; he, too, had done his king's bidding by wedding her. No one, after all, had declared just how long this marriage was to last.

Assuming her most cajoling attitude, one she used to bargain with peddlers of fine cloth and spices, Aisley presented her case. "There is a way, my lord," she said.

"A way what?" Montmorency asked with a grunt.

"A way to be rid of me," she answered sweetly.

He snorted. "If there is, I should like to hear it."

"Marriages contracted against the will of one of the parties can be voided," Aisley explained. "Therefore, we have only to wait a sufficient time and then petition for the marriage to be dissolved."

"Dissolved?" Montmorency asked loudly. "On what grounds?"

"On the grounds that one of the parties was forced, against his will," she repeated, exasperated. Did he not understand?

In the gloomy darkness Aisley heard strange noises, as if the baron were choking or sputtering, but she could not recognize what he was saying. And perhaps it was only the dogs again. "Well? Are you agreeable?" she prodded.

"You're serious!" Montmorency shouted in a stunned tone.

"Of course I am serious, my lord," Aisley said pleasantly. "'Tis the perfect solution to our dilemma. When our union is declared null and void, we will both be free to return to our former lives."

More sounds emanated from the Red Knight's direction, but Aisley wasn't sure if it was Montmorency or the pets growling at his feet. "Well, what think you of my plan?" she asked.

"I think you are mad!" the Red Knight roared. Aisley heard him rise and then sit back down, his great bulk making the bench creak under his weight. He appeared to be breathing heavily, and she felt a prick of uneasiness. What was he getting so angry about? Had he not just complained that he did not want her for his wife?

When Montmorency spoke again, he seemed to be calmer. "Now, let me make sure that I understand this new scheme of yours," he said evenly. "You were ordered by Edward to choose a husband, and you picked me. Now you want to turn around and petition the Church and Edward to dissolve our marriage on the grounds that you were forced into it?"

"No, no," Aisley said. "You misunderstand me, my lord." She thought she caught a relieved sigh from across the table, and continued more easily, "*You* are the one who was contracted against your will, therefore you must make the petition. I shall support you, of course, and attest to the fact that you married me only because of the king's decree.''

"Me!'' This time Montmorency's bellow shook the room, and he leapt to his feet, knocking the bench aside. "You want *me* to claim I was forced to wed you?''

"Of course,'' Aisley said slowly, uneasy with his show of temper. "'Tis true, is it not? 'Tis what you told me.''

Montmorency growled like a beast, and for a moment she thought he might lunge across the table at her. Unaccustomed to such displays, she sat very still, trying to fight off the feeling of fear that threatened her. It was not so much the way he loomed over her, a great dark shadow, unseen and unknown, but the strength of his ire that made her uneasy.

Aisley had always found strong emotions of any kind disquieting and had dreaded funerals, for the outpouring of grief disturbed her. Even at her own father's burial, she hadn't been able to summon the wails that came so easily to Edith and others. She licked her lips nervously as she wondered whether to remain where she was or flee the Red Knight's wrath.

When he made no further move toward her, she ventured a comment. "I take it you are not in full agreement with my plan?''

Montmorency groaned. Aisley thought it an improvement over the growling, and she relaxed slightly. She heard him right the bench and sit down. "No, I am not in agreement with your plan,'' he said quietly. "In the first place, 'twould be a lie, for no one has ever forced me to do anything against my will.''

"But you said—''

Montmorency cut her off. "I said I did not seek or want this marriage, but neither was I coerced into it. 'Twas done to please Edward, though I am thinking 'twas even more of a sacrifice than I first suspected.''

Aisley was stung by the comment. Must his tongue always be so sharp? "You act as though you are the only one suffering, but I am not pleased by our union, either," she pointed out. "Think you that I wish to live here?"

Montmorency was not stupid. He caught the contempt in her words. "But live here you will," he said, so deliberately that Aisley's heart skipped a beat. She was suddenly reminded just who sat across from her and how dangerous he might be.

When the baron talked easily to her, annoying her with his dry comments, Aisley could forget his bizarre reputation and the odd surroundings and could speak freely. If she closed her eyes, she could almost imagine herself seated in a sunny solar or dining in a spacious hall next to a great, if rather surly, knight. But she was not. She was trapped here in the blackness with a man she had never seen, about whom tales that could make one's blood run cold abounded.

Aisley drew in a deep breath. It would be wise to remember just who Montmorency was and tread carefully, especially until she knew more about him. Thinking frantically, she decided that it would be better to reason with him than to argue. Although he obviously did not want her as his wife, he was unwilling to dissolve the marriage. Perhaps he would agree to a separation of sorts.....

"My lord," Aisley said softly, "if you are so unhappy with me, why not let me go back home? We could remain wed, but could live apart. You could come and go at Belvry as you wished," she offered magnanimously. Warming to her topic, she would have said more, but Montmorency interrupted her.

"You are my wife, and you will stay here, whether it pleases you or no," he said. His tone brooked no resistance, but Aisley could not surrender her freedom so easily.

"But I am needed at Belvry," she said, trying another tactic. "'Tis a very prosperous holding, my lord, and if we are to continue to receive a good income from it, I must be there to—''

Montmorency didn't even let her finish the sentence. ''I told you that I want none of your precious money! I need it not!'' he growled.

''Then why are guests not offered proper repast? Why is the castle in such poor repair? Why are there not more servants to keep it clean? Why are there not more fires to warm us and more candles to drive away this wretched darkness?'' Aisley's voice had risen along with her frustration. How could Montmorency deny his need for money? Why was he rejecting the very thing that every other man craved? And if he did not want her, then why not let her go to Belvry? She could make no sense of him and wanted some answers.

She did not get any. The baron remained ominously quiet until the silence seemed a presence in the room. Aisley would have thought the man himself gone, but for the shape of his huge form, a menacing figure in the shadows. When he spoke again, his voice evidenced no anger, only that dry tone that had become too familiar.

''If you are afraid of the dark, my lady,'' he said, ''you should not have chosen me.''

Aisley had swallowed enough humiliation. Perversely, she deemed Montmorency at fault for not defying the king. He could have refused her, could have fought back. She had only her wits to save her, and this time, her wits had failed her.

''You will excuse me, my lord,'' she said. It was not a question, but a statement. She stood, her hands curled into fists at her side. ''I have had enough . . . supper.'' Without waiting for an answer, she turned and stalked to the door, groping her way into the blackness of the winding staircase.

''Cecil!'' Montmorency's voice rang out, and as if by magic, Aisley heard the soft sound of the servant's slippers, rising up from below to greet her. He held a candle, and Aisley thought herself never more happy to see one.

"I am taking my meal in the hall tonight, Cecil," she said, and the normally expressionless servant shot her a startled look. Aisley suspected that the man feared his master's wrath, but she told herself that she was not frightened by the Red Knight. Just let that rude oaf try to drag me back to his chamber, Aisley thought. She was prepared to fight him every bit of the way.

With effort, she slowed her steps and attempted to calm her racing heart, for she knew that she must appear her best for the throng in the great hall. As the new chatelaine, she must act her part, however loathsome it might be. With a lift of her chin, Aisley assumed her most gracious demeanor, determined to meet and eat with those who lived and worked in Castle Dunmurrow just as though she were a happy bride and not the most miserable of women.

Moving from the blackness of the steps into the hall, Aisley was in her element. Lady of the castle was a role familiar to her, and she stepped forward confidently, only to find her feet faltering when they met the old rushes. For a moment, she stood and gazed around her, unbelieving. Then she sucked in a breath that was nearly a sob at the sight of the vast chamber that lay before her.

No knights or ladies or servants crowded the long tables. No servers rushed to and fro from the kitchens, and none sought to place their pallets upon the floor for the night. Dunmurrow's great hall was deserted, its dark silence more ominous than anything Aisley had yet witnessed in the castle that was now her home. She trembled as her last threads of hope unraveled.

Edith was waiting for her, half asleep, her short, squat figure curled up in the settle by the fire and an empty cup and trencher at her side. "Oh, my lady," she said, starting as Aisley shut the door. "Have I nodded off? Is it late?"

Disregarding her previous plans to call for a bath, Aisley decided to try for sleep herself. "It is early yet, Edith, but you are tired. You may go to your chamber now."

Edith looked stricken, her normally rosy, plump cheeks pale as she twisted her hands in her lap. "Perhaps I—I could sleep in the wardrobe," she suggested, referring to the small storage space separated from Aisley's room by a curtain.

"If you are afraid to go to your own chamber, yes, you may lay your pallet in there," Aisley said.

"I'm afraid, by all that's holy, I am," Edith whimpered. "I'm afraid of what evil might befall me alone in this wicked place and I'm afraid for you, my lady." She paused as if she could not go on, and when she spoke again, her voice was hushed. "Do you know what to expect this night—your wedding night?"

Halted in the act of unfastening her belt, Aisley drew in a sharp breath. God's truth, she had forgotten all about what awaited her this evening. She had been far too busy scheming and arguing with Montmorency to worry about bedding him. She shot her servant a piercing glance and found that Edith's round face showed a blush to the roots of her brown hair, now laced liberally with gray.

"It should be your mother's place to tell you, but since, God rest her soul, she is not here..." the woman's quiet words trailed off. "Do you want to know?"

Aisley nodded slowly, her eyes never leaving Edith, who now took a deep breath. "When a man takes a wife, he acquires the rights to her body, to use as he will," she said, shuddering as though the thought of the Red Knight using anyone's body filled her with horror.

"You saw enough of your brothers to know that men are made differently. 'Tis so they may fit themselves between your legs and thus take their pleasure. It is...painful, my lady," Edith whispered. "But you are strong, and you must think that you might be getting a wee babe inside you by it."

The servant looked down at her clasped hands. "That's what I used to hope, but God saw not to bless me so." She lifted her head and gave Aisley a watery smile. "Yet I was charged with you, my lady, and watched you grow beautiful and clever. Lord help us, I never thought to see you wed to such a one as this!" Edith broke off her speech to wail softly over her mistress's fate.

Taking pity on the older woman, Aisley held out her arms awkwardly and let Edith weep against her shoulder. Her own eyes remained open, staring into the bright fire as she pictured her strapping brothers and their accoutrements and then envisioned the far larger figure of the Red Knight. The thought of him forcing a part of his anatomy into her body made her blood run cold. She was strong, yes, but...

When Edith's sobs had finally faded, Aisley released her and smiled reassuringly. "Do not fret. I am not worried," she said, lying boldly.

Edith seemed to take some small comfort from the words as she sniffed and wiped her nose. "At least it doesn't last more than a few minutes, my lady," she added, dabbing at her eyes. Then she lifted her head. "At least, it shouldn't. That—that devil might have some other evil planned. Oh, my lady, I am afraid for you!" She shook her head. "Who knows what the beast will do? Did you get a good look at him? Perhaps he is made like the horned one, with a goat's body—"

"He is just a man, Edith," Aisley said, cutting off what promised to be another diatribe about Montmorency's strange reputation. She thought privately that the phrase *just a man* hardly described the Red Knight, but she was not going to mention that.

"But, my lady, the stories they tell about him and his love for blood and his black ways," Edith protested. "What if he casts some spell upon you to make you do his bidding?"

"Stop it now," Aisley said. "Your constant nonsense grows tiresome." Edith was sweet, but foolish. Although the woman loved her as a daughter, Aisley had never been able to return that affection as strongly, and she always felt a little guilty about it. "Get some rest," she said more gently.

Edith nodded, but remained wide-eyed with apprehension. "Well, my lady, I shall be close by, and if you should scream, I will come running," she promised.

Aisley's lips curved into a bitter smile. "And what will you do?" she asked, knowing that the combined strength of two women was no match for a knight—especially this one.

Edith appeared flustered for a moment, then gave Aisley a determined look. "I shall hit him over the head with something," she said.

"And then what?"

"We shall flee, my lady!" she answered eagerly. "We shall flee this dreaded castle and be rid of the devil forever!"

Aisley's smile grew more grim. "And as two women, alone in the winter countryside, where shall we go?"

"We shall seek sanctuary at the nearest nunnery!"

Aisley patted her servant, unwilling to destroy whatever dreams were a comfort to her. But somehow she thought the king would frown upon her murdering her new husband in his bed. "Take your pallet into the wardrobe, Edith, and get some sleep. Things will look brighter in the morning," she said softly.

After Edith had gone, Aisley built up the fire. Despite her brave words, she felt a need to drive away the darkness, and she lit several of the candles Cecil had given her, placing them on a chest near the bed. Then, finally, she removed her clothing and slipped under the covers. Leaving the bed curtains hanging open, she sat up against her pillows to wait for Montmorency.

Time seemed to drag by more slowly than possible, and she wished she had not been so quick to quit the Red Knight's presence. At the very least, she could have lingered over her meal, putting off the inevitable as she attempted conversation with the man . . . or beast.

Aisley breathed in and out very slowly while she struggled to put aside Edith's fearful rantings. Her husband was no demon, but a man, she told herself. Yet that was little comfort, for he was a man whose manner she did not know and whose face she had never seen.

And he did not want her as his wife. That fact chilled Aisley to the core. She knew Montmorency was angry with her for choosing him. What if he decided to take out his displeasure upon her tonight? Now that the time of reckoning was near, she decided that perhaps she ought not to have argued with him at supper . . . or to have stalked away from his table.

As the night wore on, Aisley wished that Montmorency would come and be done with it, for she little relished this waiting and wondering. Yet he did not arrive, and she had many an hour to envision the worst, her disquiet growing. She wished then that she had not let Edith sleep in the adjoining room, for the presence of her servant meant Aisley must remember one thing above all else.

Whatever happened, she must not scream.

Chapter Four

Aisley wasn't sure how long she kept her vigil, fighting her uneasiness as she waited for the appearance of her husband, but eventually she dozed. Although she was briefly disoriented when she awoke, she had the habit of becoming instantly alert, so it did not take her long to remember Dunmurrow and its dark lord. Her eyes flew open and her heart began to pound. Was he here?

Fighting her panic, Aisley dared to look beside her, but no mysterious form lurked in her bed. She was alone. Breathing easier at the knowledge, she glanced around. The chamber was as she had left it, except that the candles had guttered out and the fire was burning low. Had Montmorency come and gone without touching her? She tried to ignore the eerie feeling such thoughts engendered. Then, with a shaky laugh, she realized no inhuman visit had wakened her. She had been roused by the dawn, which was now trying to find a way into her room through the heavy shutters.

Aisley sat up straight and gasped in surprise. Montmorency had not come to her! Relief surged through her so rapidly that she felt giddy. What did this mean?

It meant that he truly did not want her.

Aisley threw off the brief sting of that barb, for she certainly did not care for him, either. Who would? The Red

Knight was naught but a faceless, formless being who skulked in the shadows and frightened everyone with his dreadful reputation and terrible temper.

Aisley thought herself well rid of his attentions, and since he had not sought her out on their wedding night, it was more than likely that he never would, she reasoned. She could hardly believe her good fortune. She would not have to lie with the Red Knight, face his fearsome passions or try to be strong through some painful ordeal that could only be humiliating in the extreme.

This was truly the first good thing that had happened to her since she had set foot in Dunmurrow, Aisley decided. Now, if only she did not have to stay here. Obviously, Montmorency did not desire her. Would that she could convince him to let her go home.... Aisley recalled her arguments at supper and frowned in frustration.

For a man who practically professed to despise her, the Red Knight was awfully possessive. Men! Their way was to rule and direct others, for no other reason than habit. Perhaps he held her here only as punishment for choosing him, Aisley thought suddenly. The notion gave her pause, but for all his growling, she did not really think Montmorency that cruel.

Drawing her knees up to her chest, she hugged them to her and sighed. Too bad he would not agree to dissolve the marriage, she mused, for she certainly could not do so without him. Nay, she could not claim to have been forced into the union, but... Aisley gasped as a new idea came to her.

There was another way to get the Church to declare the union null and void, and it would not require Montmorency's consent. Relationship within the fourth degree made a union spiritually unlawful. Of course, Aisley was not related in any way to Montmorency, but she need only claim that she was....

She smiled. She knew that men sometimes fabricated false ancestries so as to rid themselves of their wives. Such a scheme for herself was unlikely, perhaps, but not impossible! Slipping on her chemise, Aisley jumped from the bed, chuckling with joy at the thought of regaining her freedom. It would be quite a pleasure to thwart the Red Knight!

The sound must have roused Edith because Aisley heard her servant call from the wardrobe. "Come," she answered gaily, and Edith rushed in, looking around her with a startled expression.

"Good morning, Edith," Aisley said. "Now that we have finished with my chamber, I think we shall begin on the rest of the castle." Unwilling to share her secret hopes as yet, she turned her thoughts to her new, albeit temporary, home, and the tasks that would keep her busy until such time as she might return to Belvry.

"What?" Edith looked at her blankly.

"I'll send you to the village for some women, and before nightfall we shall have help who can cook and clean properly. We'll need men to repair the walls and paint," Aisley said, ticking off the tasks on her fingers while Edith stared. "And we'll need tapestries, and a cupboard for the hall, perhaps. I shall know more when I've had a good look around," she concluded, smiling at her servant.

"He's going to let you improve the castle?" Edith asked in amazement.

"Well…" Aisley hesitated. She refused to admit that she had not exactly discussed the matter with her husband. "I'm sure Montmorency will approve of the changes," she said. "Admittedly, Dunmurrow is not as new or spacious as Belvry, but it has a certain stark beauty. We can only try, and see what we have when we are finished! We shall start with the kitchens. I must have a look through the pantries and cellars and find out who has been cooking the slop Cecil serves."

Edith, who had been noting her charge's improved mood with approval, suddenly moaned and clutched her throat. "My lady, no! You cannot mean to go into the cellars!"

"Why not?" Aisley asked.

"Because that's where he probably does his conjuring!"

"Who? Montmorency?" Aisley asked, puzzled.

"Yes," Edith answered seriously. "'Tis no doubt where he works his alchemy and sorcery. The place is probably hot as the devil's own home with smoking furnaces and tables lined with star charts, flasks and retorts filled with ghastly substances!"

Aisley laughed aloud, finding it hard to picture the dry-witted Red Knight bending his great bulk over a hot furnace or a dainty flask. "Oh, be still, Edith!" she said lightly, smiling to herself. After last night, Montmorency seemed a little less menacing and a lot more manageable. Let him growl all he wanted, she thought with a smile. In the end, she would get her way.

"My lady is up and about this morn," Cecil said as he helped his master into his surcoat. "She appears to be in fine spirits, my lord."

Montmorency grunted by way of comment. He felt no need to explain that his bride's happiness could probably be traced to the absence of himself from her chamber last night. He had suspected Aisley would be thrilled by her lack of marital duties. In fact, he would hardly be surprised if she broke out the best wine to celebrate.

"She has requested an audience with you," Cecil said.

"Meaning she demands to see me," Montmorency said dryly.

"Yes, my lord," the servant answered without looking up.

Montmorency shrugged his great shoulders, smoothed the cloth into place and grunted. "Tell her to join me for dinner," he said.

Cecil paused in his ministrations. "Think you that wise, my lord?"

Of course, it was not wise, Montmorency noted with a grimace. But today, for the first time in months, he had awakened thinking of something other than that which consumed him. This morning he had thought about pale hair and gray eyes....

He could still hear the husky tenor of her voice, still smell the musk scent she wore. Earthy and inviting, it had aroused his senses when he had kissed her in the chapel. Montmorency felt a surge in his loins at the memory of her soft breasts pressed against his chest and sought to control himself. It had been a long time, he noted ruefully, but he had no desire to remind Cecil of that small matter. "I wish to eat with my wife. Have you any objection?" he asked mildly.

Cecil was silent for a long moment before he spoke again. "Do you trust her?" he finally asked.

"No, I do not trust her," Montmorency answered grimly, "but I find her intriguing." That statement was true enough. Although he thought Aisley's scheme to defy Edward had been foolhardy, he admired her courage in devising it. He was even more impressed by the grace she showed in defeat, for when her plan had failed her, Montmorency had expected her to run. The fact that she had not both complicated and enlivened his existence in a way that he did not deign to examine.

"'Tis dangerous, my lord," Cecil warned before backing away.

God's teeth! Of course, it was dangerous, Montmorency agreed silently.

"Perhaps you might be best served by voiding the marriage," Cecil suggested.

Montmorency turned swiftly toward his servant, not certain he wished to hear more. But he mustn't be stupid, he told himself. He must consider all his choices carefully when it came to the dispensation of his new wife. "How?" he asked sharply.

"You may not have considered it, my lord, but the ban against consanguineous unions provides general grounds for dissolution," Cecil explained. "Even relationship by marriage can be invoked. 'Twould not be difficult to produce a few witnesses to claim that you and Lady de Laci are related in some way."

Montmorency sat down on the edge of the bed and rubbed his chin. "Of course," he said softly. "Why did I not think of that?" He was reminded of the night before, when Aisley had spouted that nonsense about his being forced to marry her. Why had he not thought of it then?

He knew why, though he cared not to admit as much to his servant. He had been too enthralled with her voice, her entertaining chatter, her absurdities, her backbone, her fragrance...everything about her. Aisley could scatter a man's wits as easily as wind could scatter chaff.

He had best be rid of her. Montmorency recognized that, but something held him back: the memory of her presence across from him, filling the dark room with life. He clung to it, to her unplanned disruption of his lonely world, and he hesitated.

"Edward will not let a maiden retain such prosperous holdings," Montmorency noted, the stubble of his beard rough against his fingers. "Even if the Church agrees to void our marriage, the king will simply bid her take another husband."

Cecil moved away as he continued his usual morning routine of straightening the chamber. "Yes," he answered over a shoulder, "you are probably right, my lord. But she would no longer be a threat to you."

The baron grunted. He pictured Aisley leaving Dunmurrow and tried to ignore the sense of loss that struck him at the thought. Whom would she choose next? Montmorency held many of Edward's knights in contempt. Those he did not might have wives by now, for circumstances had forced him to sever contact with all but a few trusted friends. He imagined Aisley wed to another, her silver hair spread out upon a pillow, her pale thighs open as someone else pumped into her. It was a vision he could not ignore.

He stood up abruptly. "I do not wish the maid to suffer under some other's hand," Montmorency said. In truth, he did not want another man bedding his wife, and who could blame him? "Edward would not be pleased by such trickery, either. He is a firm believer in marriage. 'Tis best to leave it be for now," he said gruffly.

"You are right, as always, my lord," Cecil wisely agreed. "But surely you do not intend to let her remain here? If she has such a prosperous holding, will you send her there?"

"No!" Montmorency turned and bellowed his answer. He felt a surge of possessiveness for his dainty wife and a rush of anger at Cecil's interference. Although he knew the man spoke reason, he did not care to hear it. "She is mine," he hissed. "And just like any other wife, she will live with her husband. Do not overstep your bounds, my friend."

"Yes, my lord," Cecil said meekly, but his loud sigh told Montmorency he was not in accord. "You will tell her then?"

"No, I will not tell her!" the Red Knight barked. "And you will not, either. You will keep your mouth shut, even should she try to trick you into revealing something! Aisley is clever, make no mistake, even though some of her schemes are ridiculous."

"But, my lord, how will we manage? What will you do?" Cecil asked.

Although the man sounded truly concerned, Montmorency cut him off with a wave of his hand. "We will continue as we have since she arrived," he said. "Begone now. I will think upon your advice, but I must make my own judgments in the matter of this wife I acquired so suddenly."

After Cecil left, Montmorency leaned an arm against the wall and grunted in annoyance. The dogs, sensing his mood, roused themselves and came nosing at his free hand, begging for attention. He absently scratched their ears.

"What say you, Castor? And you, Pollux? What think you of your new lady?" he asked. The animals whined happily at the sound of their names, and Montmorency snorted. "Fickle hounds. Yes, she is very tempting," he mused, smiling to himself.

"I know what I would like to do with our little Aisley," he mused aloud. "When she uses that haughty tone with me at dinner, I would like to knock aside the trenchers and take her right there on the table." But that was out of the question... wasn't it?

Montmorency scowled. "What I should do is send her back to Edward, who is probably laughing himself hoarse over the whole business," he concluded harshly. The dogs thumped their tails against the floor in agreement.

Aisley tried to keep the note of triumph out of her voice when she greeted her husband, but she could not help the happiness that sang in her. She had been right. Things did look better in the morning.

"My lord," she said, approaching the table. Even the sight of the eerily glowing great chamber and Montmorency's mysterious form hidden in shadow did not disturb her. Somehow, after last night, he appeared less threatening, and Aisley was full of optimism. Perhaps they could make some arrangement to live in peace together just as she and her father had done.

"My lady," Montmorency acknowledged as she took her seat opposite him.

Aisley felt like humming as she nibbled at the meal. She had overseen preparations of it and it was probably the first decent food Montmorency had been served in a long while. "I hope you like the venison pie," she said.

"Why? Is it your doing?" he asked.

"Yes," she answered. "I looked over the kitchens today and would clean and arrange them better, but I need more help. I would like to go into the village this afternoon and bring back some free women or villeins to work here at the castle," she continued.

Aisley modulated her voice carefully, making the words not a request but a simple statement of her intent. Then she paused, holding her breath, until she noticed that her hand was suspended over her cup, giving away her apprehension.

She dropped her arm and waited tensely for the Red Knight's arguments, for she had already decided that she would not back down. Today she would not let him intimidate her with his dark form or his wicked temper. If he was going to insist that she live at Dunmurrow, then he had better let her make it livable. Ready to do battle over the improvements, Aisley was surprised by his answer.

"By all means," Montmorency said, very smoothly.

Aisley felt herself relax and drew in a deep, calming breath. "Thank you, my lord," she answered. "I'm sure you realize that as your seneschal, Cecil should be overseeing the duties of others instead of constantly waiting on all of us. We need servants, and some men to help with repairs, whitewashing, painting and the like. Of course, we need a better supply of candles, a weaver and a wardrober. I could see to the dairy and the farming, too, if you wish it."

"You are full of energy, my lady," Montmorency said softly in that dry tone of his, and Aisley felt a blush stain her cheeks. She looked down at her trencher and made no comment. Did she detect a note of sarcasm in his words? Was the Red Knight pleased or angered by her enthusiasm? Aisley could not tell. His voice told as little as his shadowed countenance, and she was sharply reminded that the brooding master of Dunmurrow was not as other men.

Having no desire for him to bait her into some new dispute, Aisley kept quiet. She ate quickly, eager to be about new duties, but Montmorency was not finished with her yet. After a long silence, he spoke more genially. "Your father is dead?" he asked.

"Yes," Aisley answered. "A year now."

"And you have no one else?" Montmorency asked.

"I had three brothers," Aisley said, picking apart a piece of bread. "Two died of the fever when I was younger, and the third was killed in battle."

"It must have been hard for you, alone," Montmorency said, his voice softening.

"No," Aisley answered curtly. "I have managed very well. In fact, I have run Belvry for many years, the last solely on my own, and the holding has prospered. I could have continued but for our good king, who felt the need to cast me from my birthright."

Montmorency grunted. "Had you never a longing to wed?"

"No," Aisley answered truthfully. "I ran Belvry myself. What need I for a man to make war and bring ruin upon my lands?"

A disquieting silence followed her words. "To give you sons?" Montmorency finally asked.

"So that they might die?" Aisley replied bitterly. "No, thank you." She reached for her cup, thinking the conversation had turned entirely too personal, and took a long swallow of wine.

"Then we are in agreement," Montmorency said dryly.

"Oh?" Aisley's own voice was heavy with sarcasm.

"Yes," he answered. "You have no wish for a husband and I have no wish for a wife. 'Tis too bad that we find ourselves married to each other."

Aisley nearly choked. When she regained her composure, she snapped, "I can always count on you, my lord, to both ruin my meal and remind me of my folly in choosing you." She thought she heard a low chuckle, but told herself she must be mistaken. Montmorency was far too inhuman to ever laugh.

"Was there no one else you might have picked?" he asked slowly, as if mulling over the question. "A friend of the family? A distant relation? A neighbor?"

Aisley laughed bitterly. "My neighbor is a pompous ass who has always coveted my lands," she said. She did not add that Hexham had turned a lustful eye on herself, too, for she had no desire to hear Montmorency scoff. The Red Knight's opinion of her was so low that she was sure he could not imagine anyone wanting her. But Hexham did, and Aisley knew it. The idea was not comforting. "Do you know Baron Hexham?" she asked.

"No," Montmorency answered.

"How lucky you are," Aisley said. "For I can tell you, 'tis a friendship better left unmade. Hexham is a conniving liar and thief, always coming to Belvry with oily smiles and sweet words, while he tried to encroach on our demesne behind our backs."

"He never attacked the holding?" Montmorency asked, his voice suddenly hard.

"No," Aisley answered. "In truth, I think he has not the courage to fight, but does his business by scheming and intrigue. He has Edward's ear, and I'm sure he is blistering it now with his outrage."

"He wanted to marry you himself?" Montmorency asked.

The fierceness in the Red Knight's words made her pause, but Aisley nodded, forgetting for a moment that they were in darkness. "Yes," she said when she remembered. "He has always wanted Belvry, and with my father dead, he saw his chance. He became such a pest that I finally had the gate barred against him. I—I did not trust him." She remembered the look in his eye when last they'd parted. One of her attendants had informed her that Hexham might dishonor her in order to force her to wed him. From then on, she had refused to see the baron, though he still sent a barrage of messages, begging her audience.

Aisley drew in a breath. "I truly think the man too dense to realize that the de Lacis have always seen right through him," she said lightly. "He is so full of himself, too, that he probably couldn't imagine a maiden telling him nay. He gained his demesne through marriage, fooling his poor wife with his looks and his feigned charm, no doubt."

"He was married?" Montmorency asked harshly.

"Yes. Hexham's wife died several years ago, probably from being locked up in his tower for most of her days," she answered. She lifted her head, suddenly wishing that she could see Montmorency to judge his reaction. "He will be angry when he hears that I have chosen you," she said.

"He actually thought you would pick him?"

Aisley laughed at the skeptical tone in Montmorency's voice. "Yes," she said. "I am sure that he did, for he sees himself as quite the courtier, and since I have known him for so long, he probably presumed that I would take the familiar."

Montmorency grunted at that. "You did not choose the familiar," he said.

"No, I did not, did I?" Aisley agreed, and suddenly the shared jest made Montmorency seem almost . . . likable.

It did not take long for Aisley's gay mood to be overset, and by the time she was shown into the great chamber for supper, she was fuming. The darkness that had seemed of little import in the morning now appeared as a black barrier erected by the devil himself, and she took her seat without even speaking to the form that loomed across from her.

"My lady," Montmorency said softly in greeting.

"My lord," Aisley answered stiffly. She said no more, but toyed with her fish, hating this cat-and-mouse game that Montmorency apparently so enjoyed. By faith, she was used to plain dealing. Her brothers and her father had been cold, but reasonable, and they would never have played her falsely as had the man hiding in the shadows. She ate quickly, wishing all the while that she could stand up and fight him face-to-face rather than mince about in the gloom.

The silence stretched into infinity as they took their meal, with only the low rustling of their movements and the snuffling of the dogs giving any relief. Aisley felt oppressed. Even when dining in her chamber at Belvry, she had rarely been alone. If no guests joined her, still the serving women were present, but here the solitary Cecil presented the food and departed, leaving the two of them in blackness. Aisley felt like she was entombed, with an evil shade her only companion.

The sense of eeriness grew, and she wondered how she possibly could have enjoyed even one moment in the Red Knight's company. He was probably every bit as bad as Edith's stories claimed him to be, and appeared remotely civil only when he wanted information from her.

Aisley gritted her teeth as she thought of their long conversation at dinner, of how he had drawn her out and led her to talk about her family and Hexham. What had been the purpose of that? she wondered. What did he want from her? Was it all some form of punishment for forcing him to wed her, or did Montmorency have more fiendish plans in mind?

How he must have laughed at her enthusiasm and all her plans for his bleak castle! She bunched her fingers into fists when she thought about his amusement. He had told her blithely to go ahead and do what she wanted, knowing full well that she could not . . . .

The dreaded voice broke into her thoughts. "'Tis a good meal tonight," Montmorency said. "And the bread is better, too, I have noticed."

Aisley refused to acknowledge the compliment.

"You have done well with the kitchens," he said.

He obviously wanted a response, but Aisley would have braved the fires of hell before thanking him for his paltry praise. "Yes," she said instead, signaling her agreement. She decided not to utter another word. If Montmorency knew nothing about her or her wishes, then he could not hurt her as he had today. Other hurts and the means to inflict them, she did not deign to consider.

She hoped to finish her meal and be gone. Once back in her chamber, she would begin fabricating her new ancestry—one that would result in a familial relationship with the Red Knight. This morning she had thought to set Dunmurrow to rights before leaving, but now she wanted only to have her marriage dissolved as soon as possible.

"How went your afternoon?" Montmorency asked.

His question destroyed her resolutions to remain silent. "You know very well how it went," she answered through clenched teeth. "Edith could get no women from the village to come here, let alone live in the castle." She paused, trying to calm herself, but failing. "If you did not approve of my plans, why did you not tell me so? Why make us go to all that trouble? Was it simply to taunt me? Do you despise me that much?" Realizing that her voice gave away more emotion than she would have liked, Aisley shut her mouth to contain her despair.

"I don't despise you," Montmorency said softly.

"You don't? I would not know it from what you put me through today!" She felt her temper getting away from her and took a slow breath. "And my servant, too. Edith came back even more terrified than before, for the villagers simply fed her fears. They all think you are a demon!"

"And you do not?" Montmorency asked.

"I am not an ignorant peasant who has never been two steps beyond my doorway," Aisley answered. "I am well aware that knights cultivate their own legends to better strike terror into the hearts of their foes."

"And I take it you are not terror stricken?" Montmorency asked wryly.

"I am not your foe! Think you I am?" Aisley asked sharply. When the Red Knight gave her no answer, her ire grew. "I grow weary of your scorn, my lord," she said. "You should be thankful for my choice! From the look of Dunmurrow, you need nothing more than a skilled chatelaine, and now you have one staring you in the face. I handled my father's holdings, before and after his death, directing the steward in all his tasks."

"I have supervised building repairs, the farming, the cooking, the dairy, the wardrobe and the larder," she continued, her voice rising. "I have collected rents, defended lawsuits and handled budgets for the entire demesne. I can fly a falcon, read and write, play chess and tables, and am thought to possess a fine singing voice. All this in addition to the large marriage portion I brought. And I'll swear to you that any other man would be happy to have me!"

Montmorency's fist crashed down onto the table, shaking the cups with the force of the blow. "But I am not any other man," he shouted. Aisley heard the scrape of his bench as he leapt to his feet. "And you knew that when you forced yourself upon me! God's teeth, I have no use for a wife meddling in my affairs!"

Aisley rose, too, fearful of him for the first time this day, and she stepped back, away from his wrath.

"You know nothing about me! Nothing, you foolish woman!" Montmorency growled. Aisley heard him coming around the table, and she felt the urge to run, to race for the door rather than face the enormous black shape that moved toward her in anger. But she was a de Laci, and she would not flee. Although her heart thudded wildly at his approach, she stood her ground, her chin held high.

Montmorency's hands closed on her arms, and Aisley thought surely he would either break them, or shake her like the branch of a tree. She knew that violence between a man and his wife was not unusual, yet she had never dreamed it would be part of her life. She opened her mouth to protest, for she was not about to cower before her husband, no matter who—or what—he was. But instead of striking her, Montmorency pulled her against him.

His mouth was hot and rough on hers, taking, not giving, and Aisley felt her fear spiral into a different direction. And yet... slowly the kiss changed. His lips were softer, gentler, as they played on her own. Although one of his big hands slipped up behind her neck and held her captive, Aisley knew the time for fleeing was past. She had no intention of going now, for she felt no fright, only a strange, breathless excitement that kept her where she was—pressed up against the Red Knight. Montmorency's kiss was nothing at all like Rothchilde's; it was not like anything she had ever known.

Floating in darkness, Aisley existed solely for the exquisite touch of his lips. When she felt his thumb at the corner of her mouth, urging it open, she complied, and his tongue swept inside in a white-hot burst of sensation.

The glow of the eerie room swam before her as she closed her eyes, a crimson vision flooding her being. The ensuing blackness was an enveloping cocoon, as was his chest, strong and alive against her breasts. Aisley lifted her trembling arms to encircle his neck and bind the two of them together, closed to the outside world.

Montmorency's tongue was like a brand, firing her senses as it stroked her. His fingers were dry and callused on her neck, while his other hand slid down her back and under her behind, lifting her from the floor and up against him, hard. Her short gasp of surprise was lost in his grunt of pleasure, a sound that inflamed her even more, and she sent out her own tongue to taste his.

Montmorency growled low in response, a deep, primitive noise that found an echoing note in Aisley's blood, and she felt herself slipping away into a void inhabited only by the Red Knight. *Lead me husband,* her blood pounded. *Take me with you....*

"Aisley, Aisley...sweet wife." Montmorency's voice, bereft of its usual wryness, seemed to be breaking, and she lifted her head at the urgency in it. His hands again moved to her arms as he gently put her away from him, and although she could see nothing of his features, Aisley sensed that he was searching for words.

"I must keep to this life for my own reasons, but I will grant you this," Montmorency whispered. "You may do your cleaning and your repairing and your furnishing. If the women will not come, get men to do the work. And if they will not come, tell them I shall personally drag them by the scruffs of their scrawny necks to do their lord's service. Now go." The softness in his voice robbed the order of its rudeness, but when his hands dropped from her, Aisley felt a physical loss.

She walked away, too bewildered by her still-trembling limbs to realize that she had just won major concessions from the Red Knight. At the door, she turned, gazing back into a darkness as impenetrable to her as the mind of her husband and tried to still her thudding heart. She was not sure which bothered her more—Montmorency's dismissal or the knowledge that she truly did not want to leave him.

Chapter Five

Aisley awoke the next morning feeling oddly restless. The night before she had lain awake for hours, alone in her bed, yet she felt no relief at Montmorency's absence. The memory of his kisses returned to make her blood throb in her ears, and she wondered if instead of rejoicing at his neglect of her, she should be insulted. Perhaps he found her wanting, Aisley reflected, a notion that was oddly dissatisfying.

Aisley knew that she was thought comely, although she had spent most of her lifetime trying to ignore the fact. Keeping up with her brothers, helping her father and being recognized for her accomplishments had been more important to a lone girl in a household filled with males. They cared not how she looked, but how well she served as chatelaine.

Yet other men valued such superficial things as beauty, Aisley realized, lifting a hand to her pale cheek, and some were even known for their preferences. Suddenly, she wondered if Montmorency's tastes ran toward tall, dark, voluptuous women. Then she drew in a sharp breath, surprised and disgusted at her own musings. What cared she for the Red Knight or his desires!

Aisley told herself she was interested only in the concessions he had made to her last night, and already her head was spinning with plans for the castle. In truth, Dunmur-

row would not be so bad if he allowed her full reign, and
Aisley suspected that he would. A change had come over
him at supper. And what a change! One moment he was
growling like the evil beast he was supposed to be, and the
next . . .

Aisley raised a finger to touch her lips, amazed by his
kisses and her own passionate response. For the first time
since her wedding, she wondered what she was missing in
her marriage. Then she sighed at her own foolishness. A kiss
was one thing; sharing a bed was quite another. Aisley reminded herself that the Red Knight was no ordinary man,
but an enigma whose face or form she had yet to see.

She shivered, finding it hard to believe that she had put
her arms around him willingly when he was such a
stranger—and so very strange. All the things she had heard
about him, but had never really believed, returned to her
mind and made her uneasy. Edith was wrong about one
thing, though, Aisley thought with a smile. Montmorency
was definitely no shadow, but hard, solid flesh. She could
attest to that. She shivered again, this time as a rather delicious warmth spread through her at the thought of his embrace.

With a sigh of annoyance, she shook off her odd mood.
Although the Red Knight's kisses were not . . . objectionable,
and although he had deigned to allow her improvements to
his home, Aisley was not ready to put aside her latest
scheme. She still planned to concoct her false ancestry and
to have her marriage declared null and void—and with all
speed.

Meanwhile, she would put Castle Dunmurrow to rights.
Now there was a job she knew she could handle well, she
thought, bounding out of bed. If her appearance did not
satisfy Montmorency, there was little she could do to alter
it, but she could change Dunmurrow. And eventually, even
the Red Knight might be pleased by her efforts. Aisley

smiled at the notion, then dismissed it scornfully as she called for Edith.

Truly, it did not matter what Montmorency thought of her. And it was certainly not with him in mind that she donned one of her favorite costumes, a pale blue gown with a brilliant turquoise surcoat that she knew flattered her unique coloring. Her father, never given to flowery speech, had once said it made her look like a bright blue jewel set in silver, so Aisley took heart, though she had no glass in which to view herself.

She had Edith braid her hair and arrange it over her ears. Now that she was married, she knew she should no longer let her pale tresses fall loosely. And since she was going to the village, she let the servant coax her into a wearing a jeweled net upon her head, although normally she would reject it as being too gaudy.

"You look lovely," Edith said, her eyes growing moist. "If only we were back at court, and you still had your choice of knights, every man in the realm would be asking Edward for you."

"But we're not, and they're not, and fie on them all anyway," Aisley said. "I have never dressed to please a man, nor do I intend to now," she claimed.

For a moment, she wondered if Edith were teasing her, but the servant would hardly accuse her of trying to impress her husband. Edith would think she had gone witless for trying to beguile the Red Knight—which she was *not*. "I am going to the village myself this morn, Edith, and I intend to look my part as chatelaine of Dunmurrow Castle," Aisley said, defending her raiment.

Edith shook her head sadly. "You may look like a queen, my lady, and you do, but you'll not change the minds of the villagers. They say that the Red Knight was awarded Dunmurrow but two years past and was too busy fighting with Edward in Wales to even look at the place. Then, when he did come, he locked himself in and has not been out since.

While the place falls to ruin, he works his dark spells. They say—"

"Hush!" Aisley cut her servant off impatiently. "I am well aware what everyone says and thinks of Montmorency, but we need help here, Edith, and I intend to get it. Do you doubt me?" she asked, gazing directly at her servant. Edith shook her head again, as if poised between despair at their situation and loyalty to her mistress.

"Think what you will, then," Aisley said. "You may stay here...." Her words trailed off as she noticed that Edith was wringing her hands nervously. "What is it?" she asked.

"Consider this, my lady," the servant said, her eyes suddenly bright with excitement. "I could go with you, and we might make our escape from this evil place!"

"Edith! I beg you to cease bothering me with this nonsense," Aisley said briskly. "We are here, and here we shall stay unless something occurs to alter our situation. I am shocked that you would think a de Laci ready to run from a challenge," she scolded.

Edith stared at her with wide eyes. "You think Montmorency a—a challenge?" she squeaked.

Aisley frowned. "Of course not. I am referring to the castle and carving out a life here," she said. "There is nothing wrong with Dunmurrow that cannot be fixed with a little cleaning and painting and furbishing."

"And Montmorency?" Edith asked.

Aisley dismissed him with a wave of her hand. "He will be content to leave us to our own devices," she said. Then she swept out of the room, leaving her servant standing slack jawed behind her.

Eager though she was to get to the hall, Aisley had to slow her pace to make her way through the dimness. She told herself that her enthusiasm had everything to do with the improvements she had planned, and nothing to do with the Red Knight. Still, she felt a tiny tremor of anticipation, for she expected to find Montmorency waiting for her in the gloom. She hoped that he would take her to ~~~~ himself, both to make good his promise that she wou~~ servants, and to spend some time with her.

When she found the vast room empty except for the ever-present Cecil, Aisley felt a sharp stab of disappointment. "Will my husband not be joining me this morn?" she asked the servant.

"He is busy elsewhere, my lady," Cecil answered, "but he left instructions for me to accompany you to the village."

Aisley sought to hide her frustration, for she was chagrined to think she might be chasing after her own husband. "Let us go then," she said curtly, irritated that Cecil was to be her companion again. The fellow was polite, if taciturn, and not unpleasant company. It was just that he seemed to be there every time she turned around.

Instead of being impressed by Cecil's many skills, Aisley thought perhaps he might be the reason the castle had fallen into such a poor state. One man could not do everything, she knew, and for all her own talents, she had often been forced to delegate responsibilities to others. 'Twould be best, to her mind, if Cecil did the same.

The village of Dunney was not far away, and Aisley was pleased to see that it was not as gloomy nor as destitute looking as the castle. When word traveled about that the Red Knight's bride was passing through, people gradually drifted to their doorways to gawk. At first Aisley felt awkward at the cold glances of dread sent her way, but gradually the tenor of the townsfolk seemed to alter.

She smiled slightly to hear them whisper of her beauty, for, in truth, she normally did not attend to it. However, if her face could win her a place with these people, then Aisley was determined to press her advantage. She smiled wider when a group of children broke away from their parents to surround her palfrey.

"Are you truly the Red Knight's lady?" asked a young boy, bolder than the rest.

"I am indeed," Aisley answered. "What is your name?"

"I am Kendrick," the boy answered proudly. "And this is my sister Moira."

A little girl with dark curls who had been hiding behind her brother peeked around him. "Are you a witch?" the child asked breathlessly.

"Certainly not!" Aisley answered.

Although Kendrick gave his sister a black look, it did little to quiet her. "But you are married to him—the Red Knight," Moira protested.

"Hear me, Moira, and all of you," Aisley said, lifting her head and raising her voice. "Baron Montmorency is no devil or demon, but mortal man, like any of you. These stories about him are but foolishness designed to frighten his foes. You are his people and are under his protection. You have no cause to fear him!"

"Aren't you scared of him?" Moira asked, her black eyes wide.

Aisley laughed gently. "I fear no man," she answered, "and most assuredly not the Red Knight." She heard the excited whispers of the villagers as they argued among themselves over her words. Good, she thought, for the brisk exchange of ideas suggested that at least some of the people believed her. Although she knew she could not expect to change all their minds in one day, she had planted the seeds.

Regretting that she had no sweets to give to the children, Aisley passed out coins instead and watched them scurry off, cheering their new lady. If only the adults would be so easily won over, she thought wistfully as she looked over the crowd in search of any who might come with her.

To Aisley's surprise, Glenna, the widowed mother of Moira and Kendrick, spoke up almost immediately. She agreed to come cook at Dunmurrow, for she had been faring poorly in the village without her mate. Then Glenna's sister and her husband and an orphaned boy decided to come, too. Although disappointed in the slim number, Aisley was pleased to have anyone at all, for she heard some dire comments that those who rode with her would not be seen again.

"Nonsense!" Aisley shouted. "I intend that these people do my business with the village—to help it thrive. You will see some of them tomorrow, when they come to do the marketing." Then Aisley drew herself up in her most regal stance, looking down at those who surrounded her in a manner designed to remind them she was a noblewoman.

"And hear this," she added. "All who wish to prosper by your association with Dunmurrow be warned: do not slander the good name of my husband!"

As she rode away, Aisley heard the murmurs of the villagers behind her, and thought she had made a good beginning. They would have much to talk about, and tomorrow, when she sent one of her new servants back to the market, they would be reassured that their lord was no demon.

Pleased with herself, Aisley slanted a glance under her lashes at Cecil and was startled to find him watching her warily. Realizing that he disapproved of her words, she felt a momentary misgiving over her brave speech. Perhaps she had said too much. Perhaps she should have said nothing at all.

For, in truth, who was she to defend the Red Knight? She had never even seen his face.

All in all, Aisley counted the day well spent. The new cook immediately lent her hand in the kitchen, providing a proper meal for Aisley, Edith, the old servants and the new. And as soon as it was cleared away, she set everyone to work cleaning out the hall.

By the time Cecil called her to supper, her gown was dusty, her jeweled headdress had been put aside and her braids had fallen down her back. She realized belatedly that all her efforts to appear beguiling were for naught, but she was too tired to care.

Montmorency was in a sullen mood, anyway, and only a cat with its special night sight would be able to discern her fine clothes in the gloom that hung over his chamber, Aisley decided. Was it a wonder that she held no appeal for her husband, when he had yet to see her in the light? She felt a brief surge of irritation at the thought, but was too pleased with this day's work to be annoyed for long, and even the Red Knight's silence could not deter her.

Although not by any means talkative, Aisley found that she enjoyed relating her success. She told him of the villagers' initial resistance, of the welcome she'd received from the children and of those she had brought back with her. "It is a beginning, my lord!" she concluded.

Ignoring Montmorency's unenthusiastic grunts, she laid out her plans for increasing the tie between Dunney and the castle. "Once the villagers see that you don't eat people for supper, we shall surely have our pick of able-bodied workers," she added as she broke off a large hunk of bread.

"And how can you be sure that I don't?" the baron asked, his voice low and menacing.

Aisley was sharply reminded of his strangeness, of the aura of danger that existed in the room, dispelled but briefly by her chatter. Her spirits were still high, however, so she resisted an urge to shiver at his daunting words and answered him lightly. "For one thing, you have yet to eat me."

The noises that ensued then were truly frightening, until Aisley realized that the knight was coughing violently. "Are you choking?" she asked, half rising in concern.

"Stay," Montmorency muttered. "'Tis nothing."

Assured that he was in no danger, she immediately turned her attention back to the conversation. "I have been thinking about preparations for Christmas," she said. "A proper celebration might well and truly win over the villagers, and there is time to ready a small feast. We would need more spices for gingerbread and seed cakes, and the larder is so low! But still, we could do something. 'Twould go a long way toward gaining their trust, my lord,'' she said.

"Aisley." Montmorency's tone held none of its usual dryness and immediately gained her attention. It was such a little thing, his calling her by name, but it sent a tiny thrill through her.

"Yes, my lord?" she answered, a bit breathlessly.

"Piers. My name is Piers," he said.

"Piers," Aisley repeated. She decided that she liked his name and the way it rolled around on her tongue. Then she remembered his tongue mating with her own yesterday and blushed, glad for the concealing darkness. Would he kiss her again? Aisley's heart beat fiercely at the idea she had held at bay during the meal, and then her thoughts ran wild as images of his embrace flooded her being.

She realized, with a twinge of shock, that she wanted him to kiss her. She actually *wanted* him. He was a great, hulking, shadow—a mystery, and a wicked one, perhaps—but still Aisley could not help herself. She wished for just one kiss....

Drawing in a sharp breath, she clenched her hands in her lap and listened for the sound of movement across from her.

The dogs snorted and settled more comfortably somewhere about Montmorency's feet. Piers's feet, she amended. Piers. Although she repeated his name silently, like a plea, the object of her desire apparently was oblivious to her bold thoughts.

"You boasted of your singing talent," he said suddenly. "Care you to exhibit your skill?"

Aisley silently released the breath she had been holding. "Certainly," she answered in a shaky whisper. What was the matter with her? Surely she was not longing for the Red Knight's attentions? She'd had too much wine, she decided. The day had been long, she was tired and she had drunk too much wine with her food. That explained the bizarre turn of her thoughts... didn't it?

She realized that Montmorency was speaking and tried to heed him. "I've a mind to have Cecil fetch the village boy to accompany you. I heard him plucking at a vielle this evening," he said.

"Think you that wise?" Aisley asked, shaking off her odd mood. She was anxious that the youngster not be drawn into the Red Knight's lair. After her relative success this morning, she hardly needed embellished tales of Montmorency's frightening figure to make their way back to the village.

"No, I imagine it is not, but I thought you meant to defend my name against all who would slander it," Montmorency answered. Aisley blushed again, embarrassed that Cecil had repeated her words to the Red Knight. She said nothing.

"Did it ever occur to you, Wife, that I *like* the stories told about me and that I am pleased that they keep people from my door?" Montmorency asked smoothly.

"But why, my lord?" Aisley asked, truly curious.

"Piers."

"Piers," Aisley repeated, unnerved by the heated demand in his voice. "Why?"

"'Tis no matter why," the Red Knight answered gruffly. "However misguided your loyalty, I want you to know that it is duly noted. Now, since you have seen fit to bring all these people to the castle, let us make use of them. Cecil!" he bellowed.

The servant entered immediately, as though he had nothing more pressing to do than wait outside his master's door for a summons, and soon the young man was brought into the great chamber. Cecil sat him by the fire. Perhaps the youth thought only that his newly married lord wished to share the darkness with his bride, for he did not falter, but played with ease.

Aisley sang an old love ballad and then another. She ran through her entire repertoire and still Piers entreated her for more. She was forced, finally, to refuse, but she felt warm when she finished, flushed with her success. Although her husband often baffled her, one thing was certain: he liked her singing.

He didn't say much, really—just a few whispered words, but they were spoken with a reverence that seemed to strike to her very core. Aisley knew she had received more effusive praise before, but none more sincere.

Piers loved her voice. Long after she had left, he heard her clear tones ringing in his ears, more piercingly beautiful than anything he had ever experienced. He was still seated on his bench, unwilling to move from the spot where he had taken so much pleasure, when Cecil came in to attend him for the night.

"She has lighted torches in the great hall," the servant said, and Piers felt an unreasonable anger at the man for interrupting his reverie. "The shadows are banished, and there are people there, from the village, putting their pallets down for the night."

"So?" Piers asked, an edge of irritation in his voice.

"So you have one less place to walk in your own home, and more bodies underfoot, roaming the castle," Cecil said.

"So?" Piers asked again, with uncharacteristic recklessness. "It has begun, as we always knew it would."

"Yes, my lord, it has begun," Cecil answered gravely. "But what shall become of your lady?"

His lady. Piers was silent at the words. Strange though it was, Aisley was his wife. What would happen to her when the world he had struggled so hard to maintain came tumbling down about his ears? He did not care to speculate.

He swore softly and waved Cecil away, sitting alone at the table. Why should he care what happened to the woman who brought about his downfall—the willful, outrageous maid who plunged headlong into the darkness without blinking?

Piers sighed. He knew she was all of these things and he knew her responsible for his impending doom, and yet all he could think of was her singing, clear and lovely as that of an angel dropped down from the heavens to him at this yuletide.

Aisley let Edith help her into the small tub. She had been tramping about the grounds, inspecting the dairy and the fields, and was eager to wash away the dirt. She sighed audibly as Edith handed her the soap. There was nothing like a good, hot bath.

Watching her servant smile at her pleasure, she felt even better. No longer predicting their eminent demise, Edith had finally removed to her own chamber, but she was still wary and scowling most of the time. "It is good to see you cheerful again, Edith," Aisley commented as she sank into the water.

"Humph!" Edith snorted. "I cannot say I'm happy here, and I still wouldn't trust the red devil as far as I can spit. But seeing that he is treating you fairly and letting you take charge of everything, as is your wont . . . well, I suppose I shall be staying for now," she said.

Aisley chuckled, for she knew Edith never had any intention of deserting her. She relaxed for a long moment, enjoying the warmth that seemed to melt her very bones, and realized that she was actually quite content. The thought made her smile in surprise, for she had never dreamed it possible that she could count herself happy as the lady of Dunmurrow. And yet . . . here she was, practically purring like a cat after a long, busy day.

Despite his initial hostility, Piers had let her take her rightful place as chatelaine—and had even let her begin improvements on the castle. Edith, who knew her well, was right. Aisley's life had always revolved around running a large household, and she reveled in the duties, the responsibilities and the details.

Dunmurrow was not as big as Belvry, perhaps, but the changes it needed presented other challenges. Belvry, meanwhile, was in the hands of a trusted steward, who she knew could manage without her for some time. And perhaps in the spring she might visit....

"I'll say this much for the wretch, at least he knows how to please you. Though with his powers, that should be no surprise to me," Edith said. She paused as she laid out a fresh gown on the bed. "I'm glad you are settling in so nicely, my lady, but..." The servant's words trailed off, and Aisley lifted her gaze to Edith's stiff back. What now? she thought tiredly.

"Sometimes I fear that you are not truly content, my lady—that your mood is simply a trick of his sorcery," Edith said grimly.

"What are you babbling about?" Aisley asked.

The servant turned and wrung her hands together. "He hasn't put one of his spells on you, has he? I've been afraid that he's...bewitched you!" Aisley could have laughed, but for Edith's pitiful look of concern.

"Cease your worrying, Edith. Montmorency has not bewitched me," she said. She sank further down into the water, unwilling to hear more conjecture about the Red Knight and his evil doings. So what if he cloaked himself in shadows? Aisley didn't care if he stuck feathers upon his head and danced about like a chicken, as long as he let her do what she willed. She knew her life could be much worse, although she did not say as much to Edith. Truly, Aisley suspected she could have ended up with a husband far less to her liking than Piers Montmorency.

Baron Hexham, her widowed neighbor, immediately came to mind. Aisley remembered well how the overbearing, pompous knight had treated his first wife. The poor lady had been shut away as though feeble of wit while he cavorted with one mistress after another.

Or she could be struggling with Baron Humphries, whose cold stare had seemed more evil by far than Piers's darkness. And then there was Rothchilde, with his fat, wet lips... Aisley shuddered in repulsion.

"At least he does not expect you to bathe him," Edith said, drawing Aisley out of her thoughts. She shot her servant a startled glance and then waved her away. The intimacy—or lack of it—between herself and her husband was one topic she refused to discuss.

Let Edith believe what she might on that score, Aisley thought as she began to wash herself, her pleasure cooling with the water. She had no intention of letting Edith know how right she was—that Piers did not bid her do any of the more personal tasks normally associated with a wife. Aisley frowned, for although she knew she should be grateful for such a reprieve, for some reason, it galled her.

Glancing down at herself, naked in the water, Aisley admitted that she was not well endowed. She possessed a slender, more boyish frame than perhaps she might, and she disliked the notion that her husband might find her wanting. She had never in her life tried to appeal to a man. On the contrary, she—or rather, her brothers—had nearly had to beat men off with sticks. And during her recent court visit, she had been besieged, presumably by greedy wretches anxious for her land, though they seemed quite eager for her body, too.

How did one attract a knight? Aisley recalled some of the court ladies in their fancy finery. They were always batting their lashes and whispering and thrusting out their bosoms. Aisley snorted at the thought of such tactics, for she knew that in the darkness of the great chamber, Piers would not be able to see any messages her eyes might send him. Nor could he view her breasts, which would be difficult to thrust out, considering their small size. And he'd never gotten close enough to hear her whisper...except once.

Aisley blushed as the memory of the other night returned and she reviewed his kisses again in minute detail. She savored the episode like a fine wine, shivering at a sudden heat not brought on by the water. But, like any other memory, it was beginning to fade, and Aisley sometimes wondered if it had all been a dream. Had it been just days ago? It seemed like forever.... Aisley lifted a finger to her lips, then, scoffing at her own foolishness, she doused herself with water and determinedly scrubbed her hair.

When she had finished and Edith was handing her the fine clothes she had brought with her from Belvry, Aisley still could not put her earlier thoughts entirely aside. Perhaps it was her contentment or only her curiosity, but she decided to look her best for supper with her lord.

She wore a deep red surcoat that hugged her small breasts tightly and a pendant that dangled heavily between them, drawing attention to her bodice. She even donned the jeweled net for her hair. And in the gloom of the Red Knight's lair, she batted her lashes and leaned provocatively over the table. But as far as she could tell, Piers was indifferent.

Aisley did not even know if he was looking at her. She did not know why she was making the effort, and she suspected that Edith would consider her witless for pursuing a man who hid in the darkness like a leper—or worse. She should probably be down on her knees thanking the good Lord that he chose to leave her be! Pushing aside her trencher, Aisley tried to convince herself that her odd stirrings and frustrations were the products of some ill wind or changes in the moon.

And yet when he spoke, the low, dry tones of her husband's voice made her skin tingle. "Will you sing for me tonight?" Piers asked.

"If you wish," Aisley answered. "Shall I call for the boy to play?"

"No," he said. "Your voice is so beautiful that it needs no accompaniment." Flushing at the compliment, Aisley sang, one song after another. His favorite was a melancholy love ballad, and she ran through it again before stopping for the evening. "No more?" he asked, his voice coaxing in that wry manner of his.

"No more," Aisley said with a laugh, "or I shall be hoarse as a frog come the morn."

"Very well," Piers said. "I shall excuse you then, for it grows late."

Aisley was suddenly conscious of how alone they were, together in the darkness, without the boy musician or even Cecil. She stood up and walked to the table, but instead of moving toward the door, she hesitated. She turned to her husband's form, trying to discern him in the shadows, and then, without planning it, took a step toward him. One of the dogs, whose presence she had forgotten, growled, halting her progress.

"What is it, Aisley?" Piers asked warily.

"I would bid you good-night, my lord," Aisley answered. Her blood was thundering in her veins, and she licked her lips nervously, for she was aware that her words could be interpreted in more than one way. But she did not care. Bold by nature, tonight she felt even more reckless and daring, pushed by her strange longings, her curiosity to know the great dark figure that waited only a few steps away.

"Goodnight, Aisley," Piers said. His words were a dismissal, and for a moment she stood still, confounded, unaccustomed to being spurned. Then she turned on her heel to go, thinking herself foolish for seeking a kiss from such a one as the Red Knight.

As she followed Cecil to her bedchamber, Aisley brooded upon the folly of her actions. Was she really interested in further encounters with the Red Knight when but a few nights ago she had been in abject terror at the prospect of his embrace? No. Yes. Aisley shook her head in uncharacteristic indecision. Usually, everything was so clear to her, but the gloom of the castle seemed to have cloaked her thoughts in confusion.

She had enjoyed his kiss. And he was no cloven-hoofed devil. His hands were not talons, his teeth not fangs and no glowing embers shone where his eyes should have been. And she liked his voice, deep and dry, yet oddly comforting.

Aisley sighed, for she wasn't sure of anything except that after but a few days of marriage, the Red Knight was more compelling than forbidding.

Chapter Six

After Aisley left, Piers sat in the darkness, pondering his wife's behavior. He was increasingly aware that she was all that he thought about. He existed for dinner and supper, even though he knew that Cecil did not approve of courting danger so recklessly. He could not help it. He could no more avoid her than he could avoid breathing. She had become a symbol to him of life itself, and although he had once entertained thoughts of eagerly riding to his death, he found that he wanted to live. Despite all, he wanted to live.

Piers was drawn to her lilting voice and the sweet smell of her. He loved listening to her quiet, efficient recitation of her day, and at those times, he could almost fool himself that they were truly husband and wife and that he was like any other man. He knew that they could not continue on indefinitely as they were, and yet they did, for he could not do otherwise.

A knock on the door roused him from contemplation, and he shouted casually for entrance. "Come!" he said, expecting Cecil. Then his somber mood lifted, for it was not his servant, but his vassal who was crossing the chamber with great strides.

Piers stood, glad to greet the young man who had fought at his side for many years, a man who even now oversaw his soldiers and his lands, a man he counted as his greatest friend. "You have been long in coming!" he said, slapping Alan heartily on the back.

"Too long, apparently," his vassal answered. "The moment I approached the village, I was assailed with the news that you had wed! What is this?"

"I have married," Piers said, his voice even. "'Twas arranged by Edward."

"You jest!" Alan protested.

"Would that I did," Piers said softly.

"But what did she say? Does she know?"

"No!" the baron answered roughly. "And she will not find out."

"But how can you keep such a secret?" Alan asked, seemingly stunned.

"Just as I always have," he answered bitterly. "Concern yourself not with it." He suddenly wished his vassal anywhere but here, now, at Dunmurrow, while at the same time he felt a surge of possessiveness for his wife. By God, let no man question his joining, not even Alan!

Piers frowned, trying to put aside this anger and turn his mind toward more productive matters. "What news have you of my lands and my men?" he asked.

Aisley put on one of her oldest gowns. She had work to do today, and in truth, if she did not look her best, who would care? Certainly not her husband. The darkness he embraced kept her hidden whenever they were together. In fact, Aisley decided that if she did not have to pass Cecil to get to her seat, she could probably dine stark naked, and Piers would never even notice!

The ridiculous notion made Aisley smile, until she realized that her husband could do the same. What if he were sitting across from her without any clothes on at their meals? Aisley put both hands to her flaming cheeks and sat down hard as she tried to imagine that great body, to which she had once been pressed, without covering.

Really! She scolded herself with a nervous giggle. She was spending an inordinate amount of time thinking about the Red Knight, and improperly, too. It was a waste of energy that could be well spent elsewhere, she told herself firmly, and she stood up, determined to put him from her mind. He had made it quite plain last night that he had no interest in her, Aisley reminded herself, still piqued by his rejection.

She was piqued by his rejection? Aisley drew in a sharp breath, shocked at the very idea. Surely she was not upset that Piers had denied her a kiss? Surely she was not pining away for the touch of the Red Knight? She frowned and stared down at her slippers, an eerie feeling intruding on her shocked surprise. Perhaps Edith was right, and he had bewitched her in some way....

Aisley admitted that the man had been too much in her thoughts, and she well remembered how she had practically begged him for a good-night kiss. Perhaps it was not her own fault, but Piers's doing.

A love potion? Aisley laughed at the image of the huge, shadowy figure of her husband stirring strange herbs into her cup or sprinkling powder onto her food. In truth, she hardly thought the man interested enough in her to make the feeblest effort to secure her attentions!

Aisley scoffed at her own fancies. She must be growing addle witted to believe Edith's ranting. Each day the servant seemed to lay some new tale of horror at the Red Knight's door, and yet, in the time that Aisley had known him, Piers had never shown any evidence of these alleged powers. He had never mentioned sorcery, except in oblique jest, and if he had some dark dungeon where he conjured, she certainly had not found it.

With a sigh, Aisley gathered strands of her hair to braid it, then dropped her hands. Why bother when there were none here at Dunmurrow to frown upon her for wearing maidenly tresses? And, if the truth be told, she was still a maiden anyway, Aisley reasoned. Lifting her chin, she let her hair fall free and went to join Edith in the great hall.

Aisley found her servant standing near the entrance to the kitchens with a sour look on her face. "I sent both of them to Dunney, as you requested, my lady," Edith said, "though I think one person could have done the marketing as well as two."

"'Twill reassure the villagers to see them both," Aisley said, dismissing Edith's complaint with a smile. She looked about the great hall, with its newly painted walls, its scrubbed floors and its hearth burning brightly, and was proud of her accomplishments. She wanted to display them.

"What would you say to a Christmas feast?" Aisley asked. "Although the larder is low, we could send for some supplies from Belvry later to supplement the winter stores. 'Twould certainly do much to bring the villagers around, would it not?" She ran a practiced gaze over the vast space, mentally filling it with more trestle tables to accommodate the guests. When she glanced at Edith for affirmation of her plans, however, the servant only shook her head sadly. "What is it?" Aisley asked.

"'Twill not ease the fears of the villagers to fill them with food and drink," Edith said.

"Nonsense," she answered. "Many a body has been brought round with a full belly and some Christmas bounty."

"But 'tis Montmorency that frightens them, my lady," Edith said, lowering her voice. "And no celebration will change that, unless he shows himself, and he will not."

"He might attend," Aisley said stiffly, even though she, too, felt certain he would not. As far as she knew, Piers never left his room. *He never left his room.* The realization made Aisley's head spin. Was it true?

When she'd arrived at Dunmurrow, the entire keep had seemed a fitting domain for its dark lord, yet now she had cleaned and lit fires and opened shutters. Although the place would never be as bright as Belvry because of the narrow windows, there were more candles and torches, and old hangings had been stripped away. The shadows that had haunted Dunmurrow had been banished—except in the great chamber. And that's where Piers stayed.

Why did the man not show himself? Why did he keep to the darkness? Aisley could think of no explanation other than Edith's bizarre claims that he was a demon, but he wasn't... was he?

The servant's snort drew her from her disturbing thoughts. "He will not come, and you know it!"

"Hush!" Aisley scolded, trying to think.

"No! Don't hush me," Edith said, her agitation growing. "I'm glad that you are keeping busy by running things as you like, but that doesn't change the fact that you are married to the Red Knight. And as if the devil himself were not bad enough, we must deal with that servant of his, who is everywhere at once!" she added, glancing about warily. "He is more than likely a familiar, a beast that takes both animal and man shape to do his master's bidding!"

"Oh, for the love of heaven, Edith," Aisley snapped. "I have heard enough of your babble!"

"I'm sorry, my lady," the servant said. "But just because you seem to have accepted him doesn't change the opinion of the rest of us. How can people trust a lord whom they have never seen? And what am I to say when they ask me about him? How can I explain to anyone that I have lived in the castle for days and the only time I caught a glimpse of the baron was during that black ceremony you called a wedding?"

Edith crossed her arms belligerently across her chest and gave her mistress a challenging stare. "You tell me," she urged. "What does he look like, and why does he hide himself?"

Aisley gazed at her servant, at a loss for an answer to the blunt query. In truth, her days had become so full that she hardly had time to muse on the Red Knight's eccentricities. She hated the darkness of the great chamber, yes, but she was becoming accustomed to it, and she did not think that Piers was truly evil. Yet she felt an eerie prickling sensation when she realized that no one at Dunmurrow, with the possible exception of Cecil, had ever laid eyes upon their lord.

It was so strange it nearly took her breath away, but Aisley was not about to admit as much to Edith. Truly, the woman was a trial! Why must she always stir up trouble? The servant did more harm than good for Aisley's cause here at Dunmurrow, and, for the first time in her life, she thought about sending Edith away, back to Belvry without her.

Such an action would probably both thrill Edith and break the woman's heart. It would also leave Aisley alone with the Red Knight. She lifted her chin. Unaccustomed to lying, she simply tried to state the facts to the best of her knowledge. Turning a glare upon her servant, she said firmly, "My husband is tall and dark."

Unfortunately, Edith had known her too long to be taken in by that curt reply. "Oh, my lady," the servant gasped. "My lady, it is as I feared. You have not seen him, either. That wicked creature has put a spell upon you!"

"Nonsense!" Aisley said again. "Fie on your foolishness!" she added in an effort to rout her own doubts, as well as Edith's.

"*Aaeeiii!*" The sound of a child's high-pitched wail brought their argument to a swift halt, and both women rushed toward the kitchens.

There they found little Moira crying loudly, while her mother, murmuring soothingly, held her close. Glenna looked up when Aisley entered. "A burn, my lady, but not a bad one. I have told her time and time again to stay away from the fire...."

"Poor Moira," Aisley said, stepping closer. She dropped to her knees and held out a hand to the girl. "May I have a look?" The child shook her dark hair dolefully. "I won't hurt you," Aisley promised.

"No, I don't want you to see it. 'Tis ugly," Moira said.

'Tis ugly. Aisley rocked back on her feet, nearly falling from the force of the revelation that shot through her at the two words. "'Tis horrid looking!" Moira added, warming to her topic. "'Tis frightful! You might faint."

Aisley heard the girl's innocent prattle, but she did not see the tiny white hand clutching Glenna's sleeve. She saw instead the tall figure of her husband, lurking in the darkness. *'Tis ugly...* A burn or a disfigurement might prompt a man to hide himself away, Aisley thought, drawing in her breath, and she felt a deep, keen relief at her discovery. Here was a reasonable explanation for her husband's behavior—one that did not involve the black arts. Piers might be marked, but he was no beast.

Turning her attention back to the child, Aisley smiled gently. "I have a very strong stomach," she said. Moira shrugged, obviously tiring of her game, and held out her arm. The skin was red and mottled, but not terribly. "'Twill probably heal without even a scar to show for it," Aisley assured her. "Let me prepare a poultice."

She rose to her feet, still giddy at the possibility that Piers's isolation had a practical cause. Even as she smoothed medication on the child's arm, her mind was racing ahead to the possibilities. She had seen burns before, and some were, indeed, frightful. But surely nothing could be as bad as the constant shadows.

It might not be a burn that plagued him, Aisley realized, as she walked back to the hall. The Red Knight was a fearsome warrior. He might have lost a limb or been maimed beyond recognition during some battle. Oddly enough, the thought was comforting—far more comforting than the eerie tales of sorcery that clung to him. If vanity kept him in darkness, then, perhaps in time, she could draw him out.

"Good morning!" Startled by the sound of an unfamiliar voice, she glanced up to see a stranger approaching from across the room. Instead of answering, she stood stock-still, shocked at the sight of someone new and different in the closed world of Dunmurrow.

The man was average in height, but strongly built, with an unruly mop of brown curls, and he smiled at her pleasantly as if it were the most normal thing in the world. With a shock, Aisley recognized just how far from civilization she had come when a man's greeting set her back. "Good morning," she returned, belatedly remembering her manners.

Alan was glad that he had spoken before he got a good look at Dunmurrow's new lady. When he had called out to her, all he had seen was a dull brown gown and a flash of light hair, but now that he stood before her, it was all he could do to keep his jaw from dropping.

Piers's wife was the most beautiful woman he had ever seen.

Alan noticed the hair first. She wore it loose, letting it fall straight down her back past her waist in a shimmering curtain so blond that it was nearly white. She was not tall, but she was well-proportioned nonetheless. Dainty was the word that came to Alan's mind. She was slender as a reed, but it was apparent even from her flowing surcoat that she was gently curved in all the appropriate places.

Her face was a pale oval, her nose straight and narrow, her lips pale pink and lush, and her brows arched intelligently over eyes that were the color of newly wrought silver. Alan tried not to stare. He could not believe that the vision before him was wed to his lord.

Piers had said little about his marriage—only that Edward had arranged it. Although Alan could not understand why the king would give Piers a wife, he suspected the woman to be some dowdy, landless maiden who needed a husband but could not easily find one. Never in his wildest dreams had he imagined Edward gifting Piers with the loveliest creature in his realm. What madness was this? Had the girl earned the king's disfavor? Was she a shrew?

Alan sensed there was far more involved here than Piers's terse explanation, and he decided he would enjoy getting to the bottom of it. He had dallied this morn, in no particular hurry to greet the baron's bride, but now he grinned broadly, realizing that he would relish a nice, long stay at the castle.

"My lady," he said. "I am Alan Clinton, the baron's vassal. I have just returned from a survey of his lands, and I am most delighted to be at your service." He bowed gracefully, and Aisley couldn't help smiling at his friendly manner.

"I am Aisley de ... Aisley Montmorency." Aisley corrected herself with a blush. "It is a pleasure to meet you. We will welcome your company." That, Aisley decided soon enough, was an understatement.

The presence of a new person, especially a man of a talkative bent with tales of the outside world to share, was like a ray of sunshine in their recently dismal lives, making Aisley realize just how strange her days had become. The emptiness of Dunmurrow and the darkness that shadowed her existence were momentarily banished by her guest.

Time seemed to fly by while they sat and talked by the hearth, Alan with a cup of ale at hand and Aisley listening to him tell of the demesne, the villages and the people who lived there. The vassal seemed truly interested in Dunmurrow and complimented her effusively on the changes she had made. His warmth made it easy for her to talk of her plans for a Christmas feast and for expanding the castle population.

"I can help you there, my lady," Alan said. "When I pass through the countryside and the other villages on the baron's lands, I will simply spread the word that he is looking for people to work here."

Aisley drew in a breath in pleased surprise. "Do you really think anyone will come?" she asked eagerly. Then she cast her eyes down to the floor, unable to discuss the possibility that they might not and, more importantly, *why* they might not.

Piers's vassal seemed undisturbed. "There are always those who need work, my lady, and they will be glad to join you here," he reassured her. Aisley was suddenly swamped with a surge of affection for this man, the first to show her any help or encouragement since her arrival. She smiled at him gratefully.

Alan had to keep a grip on his jaw again to prevent his mouth from falling open. If Piers's lady was lovely in repose, when she smiled, the sun itself rose to illuminate her beauty. Alan practically had to shake himself or risk lapsing into a stupor. And so much for one of his theories: the woman was not a shrew.

"Where is your home, my lady?" he asked, searching for a clue to this strange alliance between her and the lord of Dunmurrow. "Did you live near here?"

"No," Aisley said with a wistful look. "I come from Belvry. Perhaps you've heard of it?"

Belvry? Who hadn't heard of it? It was only one of the richest holdings in the west. "Yes, I know Belvry, though I have never been there," he answered. "'Tis rumored to be very grand."

"Oh, 'tis not so grand." Aisley deflected his praise with a wave of her hand. "But it is spacious and very comfortable. Of course, 'tis of more recent construction than Dunmurrow," she hastened to add. "My father built it himself before I was born."

"You're a de Laci?" Alan couldn't help the surprise that crept into his voice. At her nod, he mentally discarded another theory: this lady was no dowerless maid, but a very wealthy woman. How had she ended up here...with Piers?

"You were a ward of Edward's then?" he asked, no longer subtle in his quest for information.

"Not exactly," Aisley said, her lips tightening, and Alan suspected that there was no love lost between the lady and her king. "Although he did... take an interest in me after my father's death."

What? Had Edward coveted the lands? Alan knew that the dictates of politeness called for him to end his personal queries, but he couldn't stop now. He was dying of curiosity. "And you met Piers...?" He deliberately let his words trail off, waiting for her to finish the sentence.

She did not. "I had never met Piers," she answered, a bit coolly. Then she regarded him with those silver eyes, now glittering dangerously, and Alan wanted to apologize for even asking. He cleared his throat.

"I'm afraid all this talk has made me hungry, my lady, and I must tell you that I eagerly await the changes you have made in the kitchens since my last visit. 'Tis a fact that I have never boasted over the fare to be had at Dunmurrow." When he made a wry face, she laughed, and he nearly wanted to weep with relief. She had forgiven him.

And suddenly, Alan realized just why Piers was acting as surly as a baited bear. Lady Montmorency could scatter a man's wits in a thrice with her beauty, her soft voice, her gentle ways and that musky fragrance that, in itself, was enough to drive a man wild. He, for one, would gladly eat from her hand. What of the fearsome Red Knight?

Aisley called for dinner to be served in the hall, without even waiting for Cecil to attend her, for she did not want the man to summon her to her husband's table. She felt light-headed at the prospect of escaping a meal in the great chamber. The pleasant atmosphere of the room around her and the sounds of her household enjoying their food was like a bracing draught that lifted spirits sagging under the weight of Dunmurrow. Aisley reveled in it.

She felt guilty.

Despite her best efforts not to compare Alan with her husband, Aisley knew the difference between them was as night is to day. For one thing, there was the small matter that she could see Alan. She could actually watch him move, meet his eyes, catch his gestures and frowns and grins. Like everything else in her life, it was something she had taken for granted before coming to Dunmurrow, but which now seemed fresh and new for the lack of it.

And Alan was easy to look upon. He did not stare at her with the greedy eyes of the men at court nor with the disapproval of the king's emissary. He treated her not with the veiled hostility she had so often marked in her husband's behavior, but with the pleasant manner of a friend, and his compliments, which she might once have shunned, were treasured after her doubts about herself. For one usually so distant toward others, Aisley drank in the attention like a thirsty seed.

"My lady!" Alan said, pushing aside his empty trencher. "I suspected the fare here might have been improved. It could hardly have gotten worse," he added with a grin. "But I never expected such a delicious meal. Truly, I must keep the men quartered away, so that they do not become fat as hogs and roll about, unable to do their duties!"

Aisley laughed softly, but Edith did not share in their jest. "Why are the men kept quartered away?" the servant asked, slanting a glance toward Aisley that reeked with suspicion.

"The baron's lands are wide, encompassing several manor houses and villages," Alan explained without hesitation. "But do not fret, Edith. We are never far away, and there are always soldiers left at the castle, though we have no cause to expect attack."

Aisley nearly laughed at that, for who would dare to beard the Red Knight in his own den? She had felt many things since coming to Dunmurrow, but never had she felt unprotected. She could not imagine a man brave enough to ignore the black rumor that surrounded Piers Montmorency or strong enough to match his fearsome reputation in battle.

"If you are concerned, I will send a guard to attach himself to your chamber," Alan suggested.

Edith's gray brows lifted in surprise, and she nodded soberly. "Very well, thank you," she agreed, looking mollified for the first time in many days.

Aisley sent Alan a grateful look. For a moment he stared at her, then he seemed to collect his thoughts. "Well, my lady, now that I am stuffed full of your wonderful food, I feel the need to ride off my fat belly. Have you seen the lands around Dunmurrow? Would you care to come with me?" he asked.

Aisley stilled, the prospect sending waves of pure, unadulterated pleasure through her. It was such a simple thing to go riding, something she had always done until she came to Dunmurrow, and something that she sorely missed. She swallowed hard, unwilling to show Piers's vassal the depth of her gratitude for his casual invitation. "Yes," she managed to reply. She resisted an urge to run to the stables.

Donning her fur-lined cloak, Aisley looked down at her dowdy gown and smiled. How wrong she had been this morning to think that no one would notice! How different the day had turned from what she had planned. Eagerly mounting her palfrey, she followed Alan from the bailey.

Once out in the brisk air, Aisley decided she would never deny herself this pleasure again. Whether she had to drag Alan with her every day or beg Piers for companions, she would ride. She felt as though she had been brought back to life after being entombed.

She felt guilty.

As they left the walls behind, Aisley glanced up at the grim keep, wondering which arrow slit marked the window of the great chamber, and for one eerie moment it seemed as though the Red Knight were looking down upon her, unkindly. With a shiver, she dropped her gaze and urged her horse forward.

The lands that had looked so bleak on her arrival seemed touched now with a stark beauty, and Aisley was delighted with the nearby forest. Alan appeared to know the area well and led her through the trees to a large pool fed by a waterfall. "'Tis lovely," she said softly.

"Yes," he answered, and for a time they were quiet, listening to the birds calling and the sounds of the animal life around them, busy even in the chill of winter.

Aisley gazed at the pond with longing and decided that it would make a fine place for bathing come summer. Then she drew in a breath and mentally shook herself. She should not be thinking that far ahead. By the time warmer weather arrived, she might be gone, back to Belvry, her marriage dissolved and Dunmurrow nothing but a dark memory. That was what she wanted, wasn't it?

Aisley glanced up to find Alan's gaze upon her, his brow furrowed in question at her strange mood. She smiled. "Thank you for showing me this place. I vow 'tis the loveliest spot I have seen on the baron's demesne."

Alan nodded. "'Tis beautiful, to be sure, but 'tis growing cold. Perhaps we should be getting back."

"'Tis mild for this time of year," Aisley protested, loath to give up her day in the sunshine for a return to the castle.

Alan took note of her hesitation and grinned. "Well, then, shall we go round to the village and back?" he suggested.

Aisley agreed happily. "Do they know you there?" she asked as Alan set a leisurely pace out of the forest.

"Yes," the vassal answered. "I have often gone there, taking care of business for the baron."

Because he will not go himself. Aisley looked away as she thought of Piers, bound by some design to his castle and sending his man in his stead. "You have served my husband for many years?" she asked.

"Yes, my lady," Alan answered.

What does he look like? Aisley could not give voice to the question, though it sorely plagued her. *Why does he hide himself in darkness?* There was so much that Alan might tell her, but Aisley knew it was not right for her to ask, nor was it his place to answer. She forced her thoughts to the village, and changed the conversation accordingly. Still, all during the ride, she found her mind returning to the mystery of her husband, a mystery upon which Alan might be able to shed some light.

The residents of Dunney were welcoming, but still wary of the lady of Dunmurrow and her husband's vassal. Aisley again found her staunchest allies in the children, to whom she handed out coins. Talking with one of the little ones, she laughed and looked up to catch Alan watching her intently. Pausing for just one moment, she was struck with the fervent wish that he was Piers, that the Red Knight would show himself, come to the village and attend to his wife.

Aisley sighed, shaking off the odd notion, and sent the boys and girls running off to play. She stopped to speak with some of the villeins and promised to send some ointment back to an old man with stiff joints. Before she knew it, her precious sun was lowering in the sky, and Alan was urging her to his side. It was time to return to Dunmurrow.

On the way back, Aisley decided to speak about that which troubled her. She had spent most of her day with Alan and had found him to be forthright, honest and good-hearted. Although she knew it might be unfair and even unwise to jeopardize their new friendship with queries about Piers, she longed so desperately for information that she took the risk.

"The villagers say that the baron has never been to Dunney," Aisley noted, sliding a glance toward the man who rode beside her.

"I do not know," Alan answered, and she noticed a veiled look come over his previously open features. Although he spoke of his lord with affection, Aisley sensed that he did not care to discuss the baron's behavior. "I have not spent much time at Dunmurrow, having been busy looking over the lands and keeping his men in readiness, should we be called to battle."

"Piers does not train the men himself then?" Aisley asked.

"No," Alan replied cautiously. "He used to, but since he was awarded the castle, he has had other concerns to occupy him."

What concerns? Alchemy? Sorcery? Aisley almost asked about the Red Knight's foul reputation, but held her tongue. She told herself she did not believe any of that nonsense, yet she must know why Piers lurked in the great chamber, never venturing out among his people, never greeting the day....

Why does he cloak himself in darkness? Aisley almost blurted out the query, but something held her back. With an abruptness that was nearly painful, she realized that Piers might not skulk in the shadows with his vassal. He might greet Alan in the light, hiding not his features and form from his trusted man-at-arms—a man more trusted than his bride. Aisley swallowed hard.

Too ashamed to let Alan know that she had never seen her husband, Aisley desperately sought for a way to rephrase her question. She clenched her fists in frustration. Here was a man who could tell her all, but how could she ask without revealing her own bizarre position as a wife who was not a wife? She drew in a deep breath, unwilling to let this moment pass.

"Alan, you have known my husband for many years and you seem to hold him in great regard. I must ask you, why... why does he stay so much to his room?"

"My lady..." Looking pained, Alan refused to meet her eye. Instead, he sent his gaze to where the sun would soon set behind Dunmurrow's walls. "My lady, 'tis not for me to say," he answered finally. "Come, we must return to the castle 'ere suppertime or Piers will have my head for keeping his lovely bride from his side!"

Disappointed, Aisley let out the breath she had been holding and nearly snorted aloud at Alan's words. As if the Red Knight cared a whit where she was or with whom she kept company! More than likely, he was probably rejoicing right now that she was out of his way for a day. He was probably glad to be rid of her.

Chapter Seven

Piers was furious. He stalked back and forth within the confines of the great chamber, trying to concentrate on what Cecil was saying, but it was difficult. The servant was telling him things he didn't want to hear, and each word flayed upon his temper like a lash. "And where are they now?" Piers growled.

"I was informed that they went to the village, my lord," Cecil answered softly.

"After a cozy chat, a nice meal and a tryst in the woods," Piers said through gritted teeth.

"Apparently so, my lord. Though I would be remiss if I did not note that I hardly expect either one to behave in a manner inappropriate to their stations," the servant added.

"Inappropriate!" The Red Knight's bellow rang out, booming off the walls as he slammed his fist down upon the table so hard that the slab of wood jumped. *Inappropriate* was a feeble word to describe what could be happening, and Piers's agile mind replaced it with more graphic phrases: unfaithfulness, adultery, cuckoldry....

"My lord, perhaps you should be more concerned with what Alan is revealing to your wife than their actions," the servant said, "for if she learns the truth about you, she would have a dangerous weapon to wield."

On some level, Piers knew Cecil was right, but it was concern over what his vassal and his wife were doing that prompted his anger, that made him walk the room, jealousy tightening his chest, rage engulfing him. He struggled against the helpless fury that had become so much a part of his life, for what good did it do to rant and rave and strike out like a child?

With an effort, he gained control of his temper, and when he spoke again, his voice was soft and even, though still deadly. "Please inform my wife and my vassal that I wish them to dine here with me this evening," he said. When Cecil lingered as though he would comment, Piers snapped at him. "Now! Go, and make sure that you find them before they run off somewhere else together!

"God's death, whether I would have her or no, she is mine now—in the eyes of Edward, in the eyes of the Church and in the eyes of man!" Piers said. "I want them both here with me where I can judge for myself just how...inappropriately they are behaving."

Piers stood, leaning his arm against the wall until he heard Cecil close the door. Then he turned again to his pacing, striding back and forth in the space in front of the chamber's enormous, elaborate bed. The irony was not lost on him.

Aware of the late hour, Aisley hurried through a bath and let Edith help her into a fresh gown. For once, the servant was not prattling on about the dark lord of Dunmurrow and the latest doings she put at his door, but talk she did—about the guard Alan had sent to her.

"His name is William, though he told me to call him Willie. As if I would be so familiar!" Edith said scornfully. "I told him to call me Mistress Edith, and you should have seen the way he grinned at me! I tell you, my lady, I would feel safer in a viper's bed than with that one at my door."

"If you truly fear the fellow, then ask Alan to replace him," Aisley said.

Ignoring that advice, Edith sniffed loudly. "I doubt even that he is a soldier, for he is short and skinnier than a shaft of wheat—hardly the kind to afford protection! Perhaps your handsome vassal gave me this fool apurpose, to spite me," Edith said.

Aisley sighed. "He is *not* my vassal, but my husband's," she reminded Edith firmly. "And I'm sure he gave little enough thought to which of his men you would find most pleasing."

Edith scowled at her and put her hands on her hips. "Well, if this William is an example, 'tis a poor lot your Alan has in his ranks—if he has any men at all," Edith said, shaking her head. "Since we have yet to see this great army that guards us, I think that these soldiers are naught but shades, like their master."

Aisley waved her servant away, eager to be rid of her ceaseless chatter. "Just make sure the man gets something to eat," she said.

"That I will!" Edith answered quickly. "I shall fatten him up, my lady. Then perhaps he will look more substantial than a blade of grass, ready to blow away in the first stiff breeze."

When the door closed behind her servant, Aisley sighed with relief. She lifted her long hair, but it wasn't totally dry, so she let it fall loose again as she mulled over Edith's words. At least the woman had something new to complain about, she thought, and the irreverent Willie might well keep her mind off the Red Knight and his doings. With a slow smile, Aisley realized she was grateful to Alan for providing the guard. She would have to thank him.

Her grin faded, however, when she remembered how Edith had referred to the vassal as "hers." It would be easy for the villagers and Dunmurrow's people to look to Alan in the absence of their lord, but it would not be right. Aisley knew, with a sense stronger than logic, that Piers would not like it. The very idea made her nervous, and she licked her lips, anxious to have the evening done.

Truth be told, Aisley was not eager to share a meal with Alan and her husband. A lingering guilt over enjoying her day out-of-doors plagued her, though she knew it was foolish. She had done nothing wrong—had only escaped the castle for a little while. Why then did she feel as if she had betrayed her husband? Because she preferred light to darkness?

A knock drew Aisley from her thoughts, and she hurried to the door. The minute she opened it, she knew something was amiss by the look on Cecil's face. Aisley had often wondered if the man ever changed his expression. She could not imagine him laughing or grieving, for he always seemed stern, rarely giving away his own opinion or making conversation. But tonight... something was different. The servant appeared positively concerned. Aisley gazed at him in surprise.

"My lord bids you join him for supper," Cecil said, and something in the way he said it made Aisley eye him again, sharply.

"Yes, of course, I always take supper with the baron," Aisley said. Was it her imagination or had a flicker of trepidation passed across the servant's features? "Cecil? What is it?" she asked, suddenly wary. Was Piers up to some devilment?

"My lady, naturally it is not my place to say, but..." Cecil hesitated.

"Please feel free to speak," Aisley urged. Silently, she wished that Piers's servant might reveal something of his master. *Tell me, Cecil. Tell me.* But when the man spoke, he did not divulge any of the Red Knight's secrets.

"My lady, the baron seemed ill pleased by your preference for his vassal's company. Perhaps he fears there will be talk...." Cecil's words trailed off, revealing his discomfort.

Aisley drew in a breath of astonishment. "Talk? Talk? Who is there in this godforsaken castle to talk?" she asked. All her fears about her husband fled on the heels of her anger. How could Piers begrudge her a visit with someone from the outside world? The guilt she had secretly harbored over her enjoyable day disappeared in an instant.

"How could anything said about me ever compare to the tales about him, the Red Knight? It seems that daily I am treated to some new tidbit from my servant! If he is not purported to be burning sacrifices in the cellar, then he is eating children's hearts for dinner!" Aisley snapped.

At her outburst, Cecil's demeanor returned to its usual fixed state. "Yes, my lady," he said. And then he stepped back for her to precede him as he did every night, without the slightest indication that their conversation had occurred. Refusing to lose her decorum further, Aisley fumed quietly as she walked to the great chamber.

Talk! Aisley was outraged that her husband, who never took her outside, never ate in the great hall and never gave her the slightest encouragement, had the gall to take offense at her entertaining his vassal—his very own vassal, a trusted man who presumably had sworn fealty to his lord.

Aisley's cheeks blushed red at the thought that right now Piers might be berating Alan for his attentions—or worse, accusing him of some perfidy! And to imagine that she would betray him so easily! As much as she enjoyed being with Alan, the thought of anything further between them had never crossed her mind.

Alan was handsome, yes, but not wildly so. He was nice looking and well mannered, like many knights she had met before but had not given a second glance. In truth, the only thing that set Alan apart from the others was his presence here, cheering her in the gloom of her prison.

At Belvry, Aisley had been surrounded by people and had had her choice of conversation, but here at Dunmurrow, her options were few. Piers never spoke to her except at meals, if then, which left her to Edith's increasingly bizarre dialogue or the limited topics of the servants. Alan had been a welcome respite from the sometimes lonely atmosphere of the castle—until the Red Knight had ruined it for her. And that was what annoyed her the most—that her simple joy in her fine day spent in the bright outdoors with a companion was now gone forever.

Aisley entered the great chamber sullenly, her eyes searching the shadows for the huge form of her husband. She intended to give him a piece of her mind, but the sight of another figure at the table stopped her. "My lady," the man said softly, and Aisley recognized Alan's voice. Perhaps Cecil had exaggerated Piers's displeasure, and she had agitated her spleen for naught, Aisley thought in confusion.

"My lady," Piers said, his familiar tone as dry as usual, and Aisley felt a small measure of relief as she took her place across from him. She was a little startled to find that Alan sat beside her, but at least she was not expected to share his trencher. What was the Red Knight's game to seat them so?

"Piers, you neglected to mention that your wife's beauty rivals that of the finest gem," Alan said, and Aisley nearly choked on her wine. Was he trying to rile the Red Knight purposely, or had he no notion of the devil's displeasure?

"In the village they spoke of an angel for our Red Knight, but I had no idea that they spoke so literally," the man continued. Aisley tensed, waiting for her husband's explosion from across the table, but it did not come.

"Yes, I am told that she is thought comely by all who are privileged to gaze upon her loveliness," Piers said. A mocking tone had entered his voice, and Aisley fought with the dread that he sometimes could induce in her. Her anger, which had burned so fiercely only moments before, fled before the sinister form looming across from her. The danger that emanated from him seemed to pulse in the darkness. Did Alan not feel it?

Apparently not, for his next words showed no caution. "Piers tells me that your marriage was arranged by Edward, my lady," he said. "Were you not surprised to find yourself betrothed to the Red Knight? There are those who would be daunted by such a prospect, considering his reputation."

Was the man insane? Aisley gulped down in one quick swallow the bite of food she had taken. "No, I was not surprised," she answered. "'Twas my own doing. I chose him," she said sourly. And what a mistake that appears to have been, she did not add.

"You chose him?" Alan asked, as if taken unaware by her answer. "I do not understand."

Aisley sunk lower on the bench. Would that she could crawl under it! This morn she had thought Alan's curiosity deterred by her cool responses and by the dictates of courtesy, but here he was, posing his questions even more boldly than earlier—and in front of the Red Knight himself!

"Edward gave me leave to pick my husband from all of his knights, and I took Baron Montmorency," Aisley mumbled. Since Piers showed no objection to the conversation, she fully expected him to note that the decision was not to his liking, but he made no comment. What was he thinking there in the darkness? If only she could see him....

"Really?" Alan said. "But you told me that you had never met Piers before. What prompted your selection?"

Would the man never stop? Aisley shuddered, fully expecting the Red Knight's fist to slam down upon the table in rage at any moment, but all was quiet from the shadows. Obviously, he would neither hinder nor help her with her replies. "The baron's reputation is great," she said simply.

"Ah! You had heard of his prowess in battle?" Alan asked.

"Yes," Aisley murmured. Feeling sorely tried by the vassal's questions, she decided that if he asked her one more thing, she would spill the entire story, whether Piers liked it or no. What would the good Alan say when she told him she had hoped to be denied the Red Knight, that she had never dreamed she would really become his wife?

Alan smiled into his food. There was obviously more to this story than what the two were telling, and he would love to hear it all. Having known Piers for years, he was well aware of the rumors surrounding the Red Knight, rumors that would surely discourage the most stouthearted of maids. And yet the beautiful heiress to Belvry had picked the lord of Dunmurrow. Why?

Only a woman with a taste for sorcery or other unusual inclinations would seek out such a man, and yet Alan could swear that the new lady was an innocent who preferred the light to the darkness. "So you wanted a great warrior to protect your holdings?" Alan asked.

Aisley gritted her teeth in frustration, and then suddenly decided there was no reason why she should be trembling on the edge of her seat. Alan must be aware of the rumors that clung to Dunmurrow's lord. If he had served as Piers's vassal for many years, the man probably knew far better than she just who—and what—the Red Knight was.

"I chose him on the basis of his reputation," she answered. "Surely you have heard all that is said about Baron Montmorency, or shall I enlighten you? He is called the Red Knight because he is in league with the devil."

"He is a great sorcerer, drawing wizards to him from afar to learn their secrets, then casting them aside to conjure alone. He is an alchemist, an astrologer, and is responsible for all manner of black deeds. In fact, he is blamed for everything bad that has happened in the area for the past few years, from sour ale to disease and death. With such powers at his command, he must be the mightiest in the land, greater even than Edward. Wouldn't you say so, Alan?"

Aisley asked slyly, pleased to turn the tables on her tormentor.

The baron's vassal appeared, for once, to be at a loss. When he finally spoke, his words were formed cautiously. "Perhaps the tales of Dunmurrow's master have been a bit exaggerated by the common folk," he said.

Aisley smiled, glad that no one could see her mirth. "Perhaps, but you would be ill-advised to irritate him, Alan, or he may turn you into a toad right there where you sit," she warned. Or keep you locked up here with him in the shadows, she thought recklessly. Which would be the worse punishment? She reached for her cup, determined to answer nothing more, and thought she caught the rumble of a chuckle from the darkness.

"Fret not, my lady," Alan assured her. "I'm much more useful to Piers as I am. A toad would have a difficult time commanding the respect of his men. 'Twould be hard to understand his croaking, and to find him a mount, too, I would imagine."

At the idea of a froglike creature riding a horse, Aisley choked back a giggle, but she heard no answering sound from the blackness this time, and her amusement faded. Piers did not appear to share their humor, and Aisley thought Alan would be wise to pay more heed to his lord's mood. Although she didn't really believe Piers could transform his vassal, she knew there were many ways the baron could vent his displeasure.

And he was obviously displeased. The master of Dunmurrow was a dark, brooding presence throughout the meal. For a while Aisley managed to coax the two men into talking about their experiences fighting against the Welsh, but then, as if by tacit agreement, the subject was dropped, leaving a long period of quiet. Even Alan's natural enthusiasm seemed to diminish in the gloom.

Finally, Aisley spoke of the afternoon they'd shared, but Piers seemed little interested in the villagers or the condition of his land. He grunted a surly response to any query directed toward him, and Aisley felt his black mood like a funeral pall spreading over the room. How soon could she leave without offending him? she wondered.

"I must admit I was astounded at the changes your lady has made to Dunmurrow," Alan noted. "I never thought the old hall could look so welcoming, and I'll not be complaining about the food this time."

"My wife is well suited for her position, is she not, Alan?" Piers asked in an odd tone.

"She is, my lord. You have been truly blessed," Alan answered.

Aisley colored and pushed her trencher aside. Somehow she did not think the Red Knight shared his vassal's view concerning her descent upon his household. His reply, however, belied her thoughts.

"Yes," Piers agreed, his voice low. "She is my Christmas gift, a prize unlooked for, but treasured nonetheless."

Aisley frowned at his words, unable to believe for one moment that he meant them. For the sake of courtesy, her husband was agreeing with Alan, pretending to be pleased by his marriage, when she knew how much he hated Edward's edict. Aisley felt an odd stinging in her chest at his game and wanted nothing more than to retreat from his company.

Yet how could she truly blame Piers for his bitterness? It was not his doing that had made her his wife. This was a fate she had brought upon herself. Suddenly, Aisley felt truly miserable, her pleasure in her bright day destroyed, the busy life she had created here revealed as a sham. The stinging in her breast turned into an ache, and she realized with surprise that she was hurt by the Red Knight's rejection.

She told herself it was just a bit of bad beef giving her indigestion. To care what Piers thought or did was truly foolish. And hadn't she, long ago, erected enough walls around herself that the careless words of family members would not pain her? Clenching her fists tightly at her side, she opened her mouth to excuse herself from the table, but she was not quick enough.

"I have heard that you sing more beautifully than any bird, my lady. Shall we be treated to a sampling of your talent tonight?" Alan asked.

Aisley drew in a breath. The last thing she felt like doing was performing for these two like a trained pet. Truth to tell, she was heartily disgusted with both of them—and with the entire male gender. But before she could formulate a not-too-scathing reply, her husband spoke for her.

"Not tonight," Piers answered. "I would retire early. Alan, you must be weary after your long day," he said pointedly.

"Yes, I am," the vassal agreed mildly. Taking the hint, he rose immediately from the bench. Aisley nearly stood herself, until she realized that it would not be wise for her to leave with her husband's man. Alan bowed in her direction. "It has been a pleasure, my lady," he said. Then he turned to Piers. "Again, may I congratulate you, my lord."

Piers grunted in response, making Aisley's cheeks burn in embarrassment. Some undercurrent existed between the two men, but exactly what its source or what her own role might be, Aisley did not know. She only knew that she longed to escape from this room as soon as possible. Saying nothing, she sat straight with her hands folded in her lap until the door had closed behind Alan. Then she, too, rose. She was halted by Piers's voice, deep and soft, speaking her name as if it had been torn from his throat. "Aisley."

"Yes?" she asked. Surely he was not going to lecture her about her relationship with his vassal! Although she faced her husband's figure in the shadows bravely, knowing that she had done no wrong, Aisley felt too weary to fight with him. She just wanted to end this long day with the forgetfulness of sleep.

"Leave no candle burning tonight in your chamber and draw your bed hangings tightly closed," Piers said. She heard the gentle click as he set his cup down upon the table. "I will come to you tonight, my wife."

Aisley nearly swayed on her feet, suddenly swamped as she was by surprise and no little fear. She looked at his form, trying without success to pierce the blackness that surrounded him. Then she licked her lips, knowing that she could give no answer but one. "Yes, my lord," she said softly.

She stepped blindly out the door that Cecil held open for her, but waved aside his assistance and walked alone. She needed the time to think, to master the emotions that surged in her breast.

The fear Aisley understood and sought to put behind her, for she truly did not think her husband a beast. She was fairly certain now that Piers suffered some disfigurement that kept him in the shadows. Although the thought of bedding such a one was frightening in itself, she found her dread overshadowed by a swift, sharp leap of excitement, making her even more unsure about her reaction to joining with him. He was not rejecting her, that was certain, and that thought was enough to send a shaft of elation through her, which confused her further.

Cecil was in her room, turning down the bed when she arrived, and Aisley dismissed him dazedly. She sat down on the bed, glad that Edith would not be returning this night, for they had developed a routine that allowed Aisley her privacy after supper. Until now, it had been a time for her to read or plan the following day's activities. She had not thought—not since that first night, really—that this time would ever be used for its intended purpose, and yet... tonight it would.

Suddenly, she felt panicked, as if the lord of Dunmurrow would arrive at any moment. "Leave no candle burning," he had said, and Aisley glanced around the room quickly, searching for the stubs of wax until she realized, with a start, that all the candles had been removed. For a moment, she wondered if Piers had spirited them away magically. Then her thoughts flew to Cecil, who would normally not be in her chamber at this hour. He must have taken the candles with him when he left.

Aisley sighed with relief, but it lasted only briefly. All too soon she remembered that she had left Cecil at the door to the great chamber. Yet she had found him here, by her own bed, when she entered! She gasped aloud and shivered, a long, chilling shiver that pierced her very soul, for even the swift-moving Cecil could hardly accomplish such a feat unless...

Unless he truly was a demon. All Edith's warnings returned to play havoc with her senses, and Aisley gripped the edge of the bed. Tonight, of all nights, why must she be faced with such a monstrous revelation? Tonight, of all nights, when she awaited the imminent arrival of Cecil's master, the Red Knight himself, *her husband,* who would this evening claim his rights...

With a soft moan of alarm, she reached out to grasp the bedpost and leaned her head against it, seeking some respite from the turmoil that raged within her. She found none, for when she looked down, she saw with dismay that her hands were trembling.

A noise outside her chamber made her gasp, and for the first time since her wedding day, Aisley feared what she might see of her husband in the light more than she disdained the darkness. With swift efficiency, she undressed, climbed into bed and pulled the hangings tight, shutting the bed off from even the dim glow of the fire and plunging herself into pitch blackness.

Chapter Eight

~~~~~~~~~~~

Aisley waited, clutching the covers as if they would somehow ward off the Red Knight and his magic. She thought herself a sensible woman, a woman of logic and facts. She had never been to a soothsayer, had never begged potions from any of the old village women and had never truly believed any of the tales about the Red Knight. And yet…there was no denying that Cecil had been in two places at once. Aisley could think of no reasonable explanation, and all others that popped to mind were too dreadful to contemplate.

The sound of her own breathing, coming fast and shallow, was so loud in the enclosed space that Aisley did not even hear him. When the bed hangings suddenly parted, then shut again, she gasped in surprise, and when she felt a figure slip in beside her, bare skin sliding against her own, she shivered in mortal dread.

"Are you frightened of me, my wife?" Aisley recognized the dry tones of her husband and knew some relief. It was only Piers, after all, not some fire-breathing demon. She had always liked his voice, had enjoyed the hard press of him when he kissed her, and he had never really frightened her. If only… She wanted to tell him about Cecil, to ask him about his servant's mysterious appearances, but her tongue seemed to cleave to the roof of her mouth. In truth, she feared the answer he might give her.

"Aisley, Aisley, my wife," Piers said, so tenderly that the words touched her very soul. "Tell me now, do you fear me?"

Aisley lifted her chin. "No," she answered, for in her heart she did not. It was just that...

"I thought not, or I would not have come to you," Piers said.

Aisley wetted her lips nervously, unable to see even the outline of his form in the darkness. "Why—why did you come?"

In answer, he grunted, a sound that somehow indicated both need and anger. "I find that I am very jealous, wife, to know that you are so eager to spend time with my vassal," he said, with a kind of mocking desperation.

Aisley's trepidation dissolved, and she felt a lump in her throat. Earlier, she had been furious at the suggestion that she had spent too much of the day with Alan, and she should have been outraged by any insinuation that she had played her husband false. Yet instead of anger, she felt some other emotion, warm and alien, flood her chest. The Red Knight jealous? Aisley could hardly believe it, but if he was, she longed to soothe him. "My lord, I am an honorable woman. I would never—"

"Good," Piers said, one of his fingers poised upon her cheek. He leaned over her, so near that Aisley could feel his breath, yet she knew no terror, only thrilling anticipation. "I am glad to hear it, but I think 'tis time that I made you my wife in truth. 'Tis time we both know that you belong to me—and to no one else," he said. Then he paused, his body still as his large palm lay against her throat. "'Tis no fault of mine that you chose me, Aisley," he said, his voice low and serious, "but you did. So heed this well—I hold what is mine."

The threat was implicit, and Aisley had no doubt that he would kill any man who would presume to take his place—and perhaps her, too. He had the power, she knew, and should he decide to choke the life from her right now, there was naught she could do.

Aisley was not frightened, however, for she had never wanted any man but her husband. And at this moment, her longing for him was surging through her so swiftly that she was weak with it. What was it about him that affected her in a way no other ever had? Was it his voice, his strength, his mystery—the very darkness surrounding him that drew her?

Aisley knew not, but again she had the odd sensation that the world had dropped away, leaving only herself and Piers, together in a great, black void. There was naught but his warmth over her, and his palm, although just resting upon her, seemed to spread heat to all her extremities.

Her plans to dissolve the marriage fled under the pressure of his touch, but she felt no loss, for they seemed foolish schemes. The potent force of the man over her drove away all other desires, banishing her concerns in a shadowy promise of things she had never yearned for, yet which now seemed seductively appealing—and within reach.

She reached out.

Drawing in a deep breath, Aisley turned her face toward Piers's arm, her cheek grazing it like a subtle caress. She felt him tense in surprise, then heard his low exhalation of approval. She wanted to say something, although she had no idea what, but his thumb brushed her lips, effectively halting her speech as he lightly traced them. His fingers moved across her features—her eyes, her nose, her brows—in gentle exploration. The sensation was heady and sweet, and Aisley's heart pounded to the rhythm of his as his roughened touch moved over her, outlining her ear, sliding down her neck....

With one swift movement, Piers threw off the blankets that covered them, and the suddenness of the action made

Aisley wonder if the pain Edith had warned her about was imminent. She stiffened, but her husband only took up strands of her hair and arranged it over her, smoothing it along her flesh.

"Such hair, like fine silk," he whispered. He lifted more, and Aisley felt a tug as though he was rubbing it against his cheek before letting it fall back against her bare breasts—a seemingly innocuous movement that sent a ripple of exhilaration through her.

He kissed her then—tender, drugging exchanges that made Aisley crave more. Hesitantly, she put a hand to his cheek. It was smooth, with just a trace of stubble along the strong jaw. He must have shaved, she thought, just before his tongue grazed her lips. Then she couldn't think. She made a soft sound, and he grunted in response, forcing her mouth open wider and sweeping his tongue inside. This time she moaned louder, amazed at the strange delight flowing through her, and Piers responded, tasting her and thrusting his tongue into her until Aisley felt dizzy and hot.

She slipped her hands to his wide shoulders, enjoying the interplay of muscle beneath his sleek skin. He was warm and pleasing to the touch, and Aisley ran her fingers along his side and over his back again and again as he kissed her, undaunted by the barely restrained power in his massive warrior's body or the scars that marked it.

Brushing aside her hair, Piers put his hand upon her breast as if it were the most natural thing in the world, and Aisley wondered if he could possibly be aware of the feelings he engendered in her. She made a noise that gave her away.

"Lovely wife. Aisley, you are so lovely," he whispered. "Small, but beautifully formed." His rough fingers caressed her softly, his thumb flicking against her nipple, and she gasped, clutching his shoulders.

He kissed her again, a deep, lush communion, before breaking it off. Aisley was bereft for a moment—until she felt his tongue upon her breast. "Piers!" she whispered, startled by the excitement that leapt in her. He answered by making sweeping circles around her nipple and then taking it into his mouth.

Aisley arched against him, and her hands, as if by their own will, went to his head. Her fingers threaded through hair that was smooth and cropped, and without thought or shame, she pulled him closer. In response, he sucked harder, his hands moving along her back, cupping her bottom and sliding along her thighs while his lips lavished attention on her breasts.

Then his mouth traveled lower, trailing across her stomach. "Open your legs for me, beautiful wife," he whispered. Without hesitation, Aisley spread her limbs, unable to deny him. Through the haze of desire, she suddenly felt fearful again, wondering wildly if Piers was indeed a sorcerer who had placed a spell on her, so willingly did she do his bidding.

"Piers," she whispered, her voice thick as she struggled for words. His hands closed around her calves, easing her knees upward. She felt them move, yet she was incapable of stopping him. "Have you...bewitched me?" she managed to ask.

He tensed, and Aisley sensed his attention on her face though she could not see him. "I have put no spell on you, my wife, other than that which is as old as time itself—the attraction between a man and a maid," her husband answered in his familiar, dry tone. "I have no need of spells, Aisley, for you and I..." His voice was deeper now and strained as his words trailed off. "We shall make our own magic this night."

With that, Aisley felt his mouth on the inside of her thigh. She started, blinking in the blackness, and then he was kissing her...there between her legs. She gasped as his tongue traced her. She gasped again, and then her gasps turned into moans, deep moans of pleasure that would not be held in check.

Aisley could not believe what was happening. For once, she was grateful for the darkness, so that she could not see herself, see her knees up in the air and her legs spread wide—while the Red Knight knelt between them. His big hands cupped her buttocks tightly as he pressed his hot mouth to the innermost part of her. And she felt no shame, only a wanton desire for more as she lifted her hips to him. More...

Aisley didn't realize she had spoken until she heard Piers grunt in response. "More? Yes, Aisley, you shall have more," he whispered hoarsely, moving over her. "I have thought of little else since the moment I wed you. I have dreamed of riding you, my wife." He spoke breathlessly, as if it cost him great effort.

"Know you how I suffer at our meals? Yes, I must eat, but it is not food I crave," Piers said as he guided the broad head of his shaft to her entrance, dipping it in the warm wetness there. "Know you that every time I sit across from you at the table, I want to kick it aside and take you down with me onto the rushes or to toss you upon my bed?" he whispered.

He spoke with such fervent heat that Aisley's body grew taut, her senses stimulated beyond endurance. She felt him run his moist tip along the most responsive spot of her body, stroking her again and again. "I want to bury myself in your pale softness...." he whispered with a hoarse growl. The rest of his words were lost on her as Aisley lost herself. She dug her fingers into the thick muscles of his upper arms and cried out, release thundering through her.

Mindless with the ultimate fulfillment, she was only vaguely aware of him entering her, her attention drawn more by his voice than his movements. "I can feel your pleasure," Piers muttered as though he was on the brink of death. Then he was still and quiet for a moment, his breathing loud in the blackness, his huge knight's body heavy upon her own delicate frame, before he spoke again.

"I feel, too, your barrier, and know that you are truly untouched, my wife," he whispered. "Know you now that you are mine, and mine alone," he said, with a ring of triumph. Then he surged into her, and Aisley cried out again, biting back what would have been a scream as he buried himself to the hilt. She tried to squirm away from him, but Piers held her hips fast, withdrawing only to slide into her again and again, the length of him filling her until, shouting his pleasure, he spilled himself deep inside her, shuddering in her arms.

For a moment, Aisley could only shiver against the ache, then she became aware of other details: Piers's weight, oddly comforting, atop her; the sweat that made his massive arms and shoulders sleek as she stroked them; the locks of his hair that rested against her temple; his breathing, low and rough and strangely vulnerable. Lying entwined with her husband as if one with him, Aisley felt something more than pain or pleasure—something that moved her to the core.

Taking his head in her hands and lifting it above her, Aisley traced his brow, the hollows of his eyes, the strong cheekbones and the curve of his ear. Then she kissed him, pressing tiny, feathered kisses to his lashes and cheeks and chin until their mouths met, gentle at first, then eager and hungry. With her husband's face grasped tightly between her slender fingers and his form heavy upon her, Aisley noticed a swelling pressure inside her and realized that he grew hard once more.

This time there were no words as they moved together in the darkness, hands and mouths exploring hard muscles and soft curves, slick with sweat and musky scents. Piers lifted her legs, and Aisley wrapped herself around him, so that there was nothing between them but this intangible something that went beyond the intermingling of their breaths— that went beyond the slow, sure rhythm of their bodies. It enveloped them, surrounding them like a living thing that thrived on their sounds of pleasure, the communion of their touch and the hot, heaving ecstasy of their release.

If Aisley hadn't known better, she would have called it love.

When Aisley awoke, she thought for a moment that a strange dream had plagued her. She shivered, suddenly cold in the black cocoon of her bed, then scents assailed her, along with an ache between her legs, and she sat up, putting a trembling hand to her swollen lips. "Piers?" she whispered into the darkness.

Cautiously, she moved the hangings, only to gaze out into the deep shadows of her chamber. Though she could see little by the light of the dying fire, the bleak quiet told her he was gone, and she rubbed her arms as if chilled. Slipping out of bed, she threw on a robe and walked to the hearth. She built up the blaze, then sat down in the settle nearby, amazed by what had taken place this night.

She stared into the flames, her heart thudding wildly as she recognized that she could never now dissolve her marriage, for she had no wish to part from her husband. Piers had been mysteriously compelling before, but now he was far more than that.

Clasping her arms around herself, Aisley recalled their joining. She was astounded at her own wantonness even as she knew that should he bid her to, she would do it all over again—and again. She smiled to herself, unable to lay all the blame upon her husband because whether he bade her or not, she wanted him. She wished he were still here in her bed, for if he were, she would go to him now, kiss his lips and caress his firm muscles, his massive, hard warrior's body until...

His body! Aisley drew in a sharp breath of dismay at the memory, for she knew that Piers was well formed beyond her imaginings, with no hideous disfigurement to make him lurk in the shadows. She had traced his face with her fingers and found no signs of sores or burns or warts or even unruly hair. A scar did run from one eye, but it was minor, not something that would make even a vain man seek the darkness.

Gripping her arms tightly, Aisley shuddered, unsure whether her newfound knowledge brought relief or a disappointment. For if her husband was, in truth, whole, why then did he live as he did? She struggled against the answers—Edith's answers—that assailed her. There must have been something she missed, something that in the dizzying depths of desire she did not notice, Aisley thought frantically.

And what of Cecil, his servant, who seemed to move through walls like smoke? In the hot pleasure of consummation, Aisley had forgotten that the man had been in two places at once. She licked her lips nervously as she pondered questions for which she could provide no easy solutions. Foremost among them was the one she most dreaded: was her husband truly a sorcerer? If so, Aisley knew not if her new feelings for him were given of her own accord or urged from her by some wizardry.

The memory of Piers's visit to her chambers haunted Aisley all day, making her blush and squirm at odd moments. She was thankful that she did not see Alan, for she was not quite certain she could meet his eyes. She was not surprised when Cecil told her that the knight had left early in the morning on another errand; Piers had made his jealousy clear. Still, she hardly thought it right for him to punish his vassal, and she planned to tell him so.

The sight of Cecil turned her thoughts to other matters, however, and she called back the retreating servant, anxious to learn the truth about him. "Cecil," Aisley said, piercing him with a cool, steady gaze, "did you remove the candles from my room last night?"

The man did not hesitate. "Yes, my lady," he answered. "'Twas by my lord's order."

"But..." Aisley struggled to say more. She wet her dry lips and opened her mouth, yet nothing came out, only a rapidness of breath that gave away her distress. "You may go," she finally said, dismissing him while she could still hold up her head. He nodded, eyeing her dispassionately, and turned away.

Aisley's shoulders slumped as she was assailed again by vague suspicions about her husband, and then memories of the past night returned to drive away her concerns, making her heart race and her body ache for his touch, despite his strangeness—despite everything.

With an impatient gasp, she threw on her cloak and walked out into the bailey, into the bracing air, with the hope that it would clear her head. But her confusion stayed with her, and her gaze was drawn upward, irresistibly, to the keep where her husband waited in his dark lair. And she knew that whether by sorcery or her own desire, she wanted him desperately.

Piers did not call her to dinner, however, and Aisley ate in the hall with Edith and the others, trying to avoid her servant's eye. She did not know if she could hide either her new suspicions or the blossoming of her woman's body from Edith's gaze. She was also a bit piqued that, after what had passed between them, Piers did not seek her company.

Then Aisley remembered his words from the night before, describing their meals together as torturous for him, and she realized that it was probably best that she not join him. Still, the thought of Piers kicking aside the table and taking her down among the rushes or tossing her upon his bed did not fill her with fear and loathing—only a rather disconcerting thrill, which she firmly quelled. Her cheeks scarlet, she glanced around and was grateful to see that Edith was occupied.

"And who gave you leave to eat with me?" the servant was asking a short man who sat down across from her.

Despite Edith's unfriendly tone, the man took no offense, but grinned at her, displaying a wide mouth full of healthy teeth. From the deep creases in his brown cheeks and around his eyes, it was apparent that he had spent much of his life in pleasant humor. Good, Aisley thought, wishing that his cheerful disposition would pass on to Edith.

"Alan Clinton gave me leave, mistress," the fellow replied. "Told me to stick by your side day and night, he did. And I do, too," he added, sending a broad wink toward one of the servants near them.

So, Aisley thought, this was the infamous Willie, whom Alan had set to guard Edith. It appeared to be a lively pairing, for the two seemed as oil and water together. "Oh!" Edith shrieked. "You'll keep a civil tongue in your head, my man, or you'll be out on your ear, make no mistake about that."

"Now, don't be telling me such tales, Edith, when you know you would miss me, especially during the long, cold nights," Willie said with a leer.

Aisley drew in a surprised breath, certain the man was in for a good walloping—or a ferocious scolding, at least—but Edith only snorted. "As if you could do aught to protect me when you haven't a bit of meat on your bones," she said scornfully.

Willie sat back, grinning even more widely, if that was possible. "Aye, but I've enough meat where it counts, now don't I, Edie girl?"

"I'll not listen to such foul talk, you rascal!" Edith said, puffing up like a toad with her outrage. She darted a glance toward Aisley. "Especially in front of my lady."

Willie's gaze followed Edith's, and Aisley smiled in greeting. The man's once-black hair was dappled with bristly gray, leading her to suspect he was old enough to be past worrying about his speech. She was proved right quickly enough when Willie set down his ale with a dramatic thump.

"My lady has the look of a woman well loved," he replied, "which is no surprise, given the size of her husband. I don't think she'll take offense at a few words between you and me." While Aisley tried not to blush at the guard's astute observation, Edith rose from the bench in a huff. "Here now, I haven't finished my meal," Willie protested.

"You can go or stay, for all that I care," Edith called over her shoulder. Willie grumbled briefly, filled his mouth with food, grabbed the last of the bread in his hands and took off, following after Edith like a loping dog.

Watching in fascination, Aisley noted an unfamiliar twitch in Edith's skirts as she walked away. Since the death of her husband, the servant had never flirted with any man that Aisley could remember. Could it be that she was less ruffled by her new guard than she pretended to be? Aisley sighed with relief. At last Edith had something—or someone—to claim her attention. Perhaps now she would finally accept her new life at Dunmurrow.

The thought made Aisley acutely aware of her own change in circumstances. After last night, she could hardly consider the castle as her temporary residence. She was here, firmly wedded and bedded, her plan to dissolve her marriage abandoned in the heat of her husband's embrace.

Truth to tell, she longed to take her place as Piers's wife in all ways, but she knew the easy byplay that existed between Edith and Willie could not be theirs. She suspected that Piers would never sit with her in the great hall or accompany her on her errands, and the thought made her a little heartsick.

The Red Knight was still steeped in mystery, perhaps now more than ever, and despite the passion they shared, Aisley remained uneasy about her husband. In many ways, he continued to be very much a stranger to her.

* * *

Although Aisley spent the afternoon engaged in wearisome tasks, her thoughts kept returning to Piers and the supper she would share with him. Despite her best efforts, she could not seem to banish the vision of her husband making love to her in his own eerie chamber, and her new fears about his dark powers did little to diminish her longing. Like something forbidden, it seemed all the more enticing, and Aisley could imagine him bearing her down onto the great bed where he slept, a shadowy form made substance by her touch...his body, hard and smooth, over hers; his mouth, hot and moist against her skin....

To her dismay, she found the image lingering in her mind when she greeted her husband at the appointed hour. "Good evening, Piers," she said, keeping her voice steady only by strength of will.

"Wife," he answered shortly, with a nod of his head in the darkness. His surly tone brought Aisley up short, unexpected as it was after the night of intimacies they had shared. Was this to be the way of it—meals as usual, with no soft words between them to denote the change in their relationship? Or perhaps there was no change, Aisley thought dismally. Last night might have been nothing more to Piers than a duty performed only to make her his wife.

The thought was sobering, and Aisley ate in silence. Yet as her teeth sank into a piece of fowl, she was reminded of her husband's gentle bites against her flesh. Once again she was glad for the darkness that cloaked her blush and her sudden trembling as she reached for her wine.

"You are quiet this evening," Piers barked at her. "Is there something amiss?"

Aisley put down her cup slowly, considering her reply. Although it had been bothering her all day, she could not bear to ask about Cecil, for she was loath to further darken Pier's already ill mood, and in truth, she dreaded the answer he might give her. Neither could she broach the question of the shadows that cloaked him, and she certainly did not feel inclined to mention the longing for her husband that even now gnawed at her. "No. 'Tis nothing, my lord," she said.

Piers snorted at her brief answer, and they continued in silence, Aisley waiting for some sign that the figure across from her was the lover who had come to her in the night.

"I hope you are not waiting for Alan," Piers said abruptly.

"No," Aisley answered cautiously. "Cecil told me that he left early this morning." She paused. "Think you it fair to send him away so soon—and at Christmas?" she asked.

"So you miss him already?" Piers voice was low and menacing, and she felt a shiver run up her spine. This man was dangerous, she reminded herself. Piers Montmorency was famous for his savagery in battle, and she knew very well how huge and strong he was. The same hands that had caressed her tenderly might just as easily stop her breath....

"I miss the company," she said slowly. "Not the man."

Piers snorted, obviously still jealous of his vassal, and Aisley smiled down into her trencher. Perhaps last night had not been such an obnoxious duty for him, after all. Perhaps even now he wanted her just as she wanted him.... The thought made Aisley draw in a quick breath, and her heart began beating wildly. *Take me. Take me down among the rushes.* She tried to form the words, but courage failed her, and she picked up her cup, taking a long gulp.

"Have you not plenty of...company?" Piers asked scornfully. "Have you not your Edith and Cecil and the new servants you insisted we must have, and the villagers you cultivate, filling my hall?"

Aisley swallowed hard. "Yes," she said softly, but even as she answered, she knew that it was his company she sought, his attention she yearned for. It was absurd, she thought bitterly. Always fiercely independent, she had gone her own way, never *needing* anyone. "'Tis not the same," she answered with a frown. "For they cannot discuss varied topics, nor read, nor play chess, nor go hunting...."

Though she had not intended the slur, it was there in her words, Aisley realized. Many of those things required light, and Piers could not do them, either. She had just put the Red Knight in the same class as a unschooled freeman or villein, and she knew that he would not like it. She hurried to correct herself before he exploded in rage. "Perhaps you could venture out with me sometime," she began.

"No!" he answered roughly.

Aisley sighed in exasperation. "Why?" she asked. "Why must we always be shrouded in darkness? I know you are not the devil you would have others believe you are."

"Do you?" Piers's voice was dry, as usual, but edged with hardness, and Aisley was chilled by his taunt. She rose from her seat. "Where do you go?" he growled.

"When you seek to bait or frighten me, I find I do not care to remain with you," Aisley answered, lifting her chin.

"Perhaps you desire another?" he asked.

"Perhaps if I saw more of you, I would not be lonely, my husband!" Aisley hissed between clenched teeth.

"Long you so for me?" Piers asked in mocking tones.

"Yes," she admitted softly. "And if you would but attend me, you would know that is true. 'Twas a joy yesterday to view your lands. Why can we not ride out together? I would show you the plans I have for the dairy. The wood is beautiful, and there is a waterfall—"

"Enough," Piers said. "Do not speak to me of what cannot be."

"But why? Why, Piers?" Aisley asked, exasperated. "I am your wife! Can you not explain to me what this thing is that keeps you in shadow?"

"My wife!" Piers scoffed. "An uppity wench I have never seen before storms into my keep demanding that I wed her!" he said bitterly. "And you would have me trust her?" He laughed, but the sound held no humor.

Aisley stared at his black form, appalled at his jibes. And she had thought to love him? She trembled at her own folly. Lifting her chin, she swept from the room, slamming the door behind her.

Chapter Nine

In her own chamber, the candles were back in place, and Cecil did not come to take them away. Although Aisley concluded that Piers would not be visiting this night, still she waited, sitting up in her bed in the darkness, wanting him and feeling angry with herself for her own foolish desires. So this was to be the way of it, she thought bitterly. Her husband had done his duty, taking her maidenhead only to prove his ownership, and he would not come to her again.

Aisley told herself she should be relieved to be done with the Red Knight's attentions, but her rebellious mind returned to the night before when he had held her, moving inside her, making her feel things she had never dreamed possible. Damn his black soul! She longed for him . . . like a woman bewitched.

Despite her angry ruminations, she finally dozed off, and when she awoke it was not to the presence of her husband, but to Edith's panicked voice. "My lady! My lady!" the servant whispered.

"What is it, Edith?" Aisley asked, alert in an instant. Fire, brigands, an assault on Dunmurrow—all were possibilities she considered as her eyes flew open. The bed hangings had been pulled aside and Edith stood over her, grasping a candle in one hand and tugging anxiously at Aisley with the other.

"Just listen, my lady!" Edith said. "'Tis the red one—outside in the bailey—doing his devil's work! Conjuring, I thought he was, and loud enough to wake the dead, but when I stuck my head out the window..." Edith paused long enough to cross herself. "I saw someone down there with him. A human sacrifice, that's what it is, my lady. I'll swear to it! And that useless guard of mine will do naught!"

"Hush! Hush!" Aisley said. "I can hear nothing over your ranting." Rising to slip on a robe, she went to the window and peeked through the narrow slit. A pale moon cast a dim glow upon the ground below and upon her husband's unmistakable form. Aisley gasped when she realized that he appeared to be attacking someone with his sword. Her eyes searched the bailey for marauders, and, finding no one, returned to Piers.

Although he seemed to strike repeatedly, his foe neither moved nor fell, but remained still and upright. "'Tis nothing but some sort of quintain," Aisley said, annoyed at the relief that swept through her. She turned in exasperation to her servant. "My husband merely practices his swordplay upon a piece of wood and straw, and you think him a demon!"

"Edith! Are you in there?" Both women turned at the sound of a voice calling from outside the chamber door, and Aisley immediately recognized the unmistakable drawl of Willie, Edith's personal guard. "You come out here right now and stop meddling in the baron's business!" he warned.

"I'll thank you to leave me be, you worthless excuse for a soldier! I might as well have one of the village boys protecting me, for all the good you do me," Edith snapped. With a sniff of disdain, she turned back to Aisley. "But, my lady, your lord has been shouting and cursing something terrible," she said. And as if to mark her words, a bellow, obviously Piers's, erupted from below.

"Damn you t'hell, Cecil, you gutless coward!" The words were loud enough, but so badly slurred they were barely understandable. "Where's my vassal? Send for Alan, for I would strike swords with him!"

Aisley frowned at the speech, recognizing the reason for its garbled accents. "'Tis too much drink, that is all, Edith," she said. "Have you not heard men in their cups before, my own brothers included?"

Her servant eyed her with no little skepticism. "Are you sure that's all it is, my lady?" she asked, her brows knitted in worry. Aisley nodded.

"Edith, if you don't come out this minute, I'm coming in. Beg pardon, my lady," Willie called.

Edith had the grace to look ashamed and mumbled an apology. "'Tis all right," Aisley said softly. "I am glad you woke me. They're disgraceful, his drunken shouts." She had every intention of taking her husband in hand, but did not care to tell Edith so, lest the woman fear for her safety. Blood and sacrifice—what rot!

"Good night, Edith," she said as evenly as she could. "Please go back to bed before Willie breaks into my room."

A hearty snort met her words, and Edith mumbled something about the uselessness of her guard, soldiers and men of short stature in general. When she opened the door, Aisley caught a glimpse of the object of her derision, glowering unhappily. "Now what did you have to go and bother his lady for?" Willie whispered heatedly.

Edith's undoubtedly bruising retort was lost in the closing of the door, and Aisley stood for a moment, smiling after the mismatched pair. An angry shout from the window drew her attention back to her husband, however, and she slipped a cloak over her robe and made her way down to the bailey. To her surprise, no guards stood by the entrance, and she walked freely into the night. Although Aisley had every intention of continuing on until she reached her husband, the sight of him stopped her dead.

Dressed in full mail and helm, Piers was something to behold, even in the darkness. Tall and broad as a giant oak, he smote a target set into the ground. His moves were graceful, despite his drunken state, but the wine was obviously affecting him, for he seemed to have difficulty striking his goal.

Still, he was magnificent, and Aisley drew in a breath in admiration. The Red Knight, her husband, was beyond the measure of most men, and the power emanating from him made her heart trip apace. She had watched her brothers practice their skills innumerable times, and she had been witness to other tourneys at court, but never before had a man affected her so.

With a shock, Aisley discovered that she wanted him, right here, right now, on the ground in the starlight, his lips hot on her own, his heavy body still garbed for war. She swallowed hard, dismissing the wanton thoughts as wholly unlike her and a product of the moon's dark spell.

Her husband appeared to be too drunk for such play anyway, Aisley noted, and he would, more than likely, not welcome her attentions. She frowned at the thought, but pushed it aside. Whatever Piers's feelings on the subject, she was his wife, and it was her duty to see to him. In this case that meant putting him to bed, so the rest of the residents of the keep would not lie awake in fright at the sound of his sport. She'd opened her mouth to call to him when he shouted a curse.

"She thinks me half a man!" Piers growled, swinging viciously at the post.

Did her husband speak of her? Aisley wondered with surprise. She did not know who else he could be talking about, but why would he attribute such thoughts to her, when she knew full well that he was more man than most? The ferocity of the blows he was raining upon the quintain alarmed her, and she realized then that he was angry, more angry than she had ever seen him. Sucking in a sharp breath, she felt like shrinking back into the keep, but Piers must have heard her, for he drew up short, his body rigid as if he were listening.

"'Tis not true! She cares for you, my lord," said a voice, and Aisley noticed Cecil standing in the shadows a safe distance away from his master. "If you could but—"

Cecil's speech was drowned out by Pier's roar. "Be still, you fool!"

The outburst directed toward Cecil gave Aisley new courage to face Piers's rage, for if the servant could not sway him, who could? The task, she knew, fell to her. Wetting her lips anxiously, she walked forward. "Come to bed, husband," she said quietly.

Although she had witnessed his fury, Aisley was unprepared for his response. Piers whirled around, an enormous dark figure, a black knight in the shadows, and like an avenging angel, his sword arced through the air with enough force to take off a man's head. Aisley knew that had she not been standing well away from him, she might have been cut down. She drew in a sharp breath of fear.

"Aisley?" he asked hoarsely.

"Come to bed, Piers," she repeated, as evenly as she could. "'Tis too late for such practice."

His unexpected bellow of pain and wrath shook her to her very soul, and Aisley stepped back, shocked by the anguished sound. Before she had time to gather her wits, Cecil was at her side, dragging her into the building again. "'Tis best you return to your room, my lady," he said.

Although at that moment she wanted nothing more than to run and hide from her husband, Aisley knew she could not. She clenched her fists at her sides, drawing from reserves deep within her the strength to face him. "No! He sounds as if he is hurt," she said. She tried to shake off the servant's hold as she sought her husband's shape in the night. "I must tend him."

"Nay, my lady," Cecil said. "He had too much wine is all."

Aisley felt the cold of the stone wall pressing against her back and refused to budge. "Cecil, I demand that you step aside and let me see to my husband," she said as coolly as possible.

"Nay, my lady. I cannot," the servant said, taking her arm. "My lord would kill me if I did."

He moved to pull her with him, and Aisley caught a glimpse of Piers's form. As she watched, his great blade swung out and took off the entire top of the quintain. Though she knew not its source, Aisley recognized his fury as a pulsing, living thing. Greater than anything she had ever known, it seemed to fill the bailey, and her heart thumped in terror. Giving up all her efforts to aid him, she turned and fled up the stairs, so quickly that she barely heard Cecil's last words.

"'Twould kill *him*," the servant said.

Aisley avoided him. She busied herself with a trip to the village so that she would not have to share her early meal with him, and she would have refused to sup with him, too, were she not fearful of his rage. She had seen it last night— rage that had turned him into a rampaging beast—and she cared not to view it again.

Of all the frightening things about the Red Knight—and there were many, if she listened to Edith—none could compare to the excess of emotion she had witnessed. It was so profound as to be unsettling, so out of control as to disturb Aisley in ways she could not determine.

She had discounted the rumors that surrounded him, had even managed to pay no heed to Cecil's mysterious ability to be everywhere at once, yet she could not deny the Red Knight's terrifying temper.

When she entered his lair to sup, Aisley half expected him to be gnashing his teeth and beating his breast. But he only sat cloaked in shadow at the table, as usual. She took her place, finding it hard to reconcile the still figure, sparse of movement, with the wild man she had glimpsed the night before. Piers Montmorency was a man of many sides, and Aisley hesitated to consider just how little she knew of him.

"My lady," he said in his customary dry tones.

"Piers," Aisley acknowledged. "How are you faring this evening?"

"I am fine," he answered roughly.

"I thought you might have been hurt last night," Aisley said slowly. "You are well?"

"Other than an aching head that kept me abed for most of the morning, I am thriving," Piers said.

Though she was certain he spoke the truth, Aisley caught the sarcasm in his voice. She decided to ignore it. "I am glad."

"Are you?" he asked wryly, as though he believed her not.

"Yes, I am glad you are well. I was concerned about you," Aisley said. She looked down at her food. Although she knew he could not see her, sometimes she had the eerie feeling that his gaze pierced her being, baring all to him.

And suddenly, of all the memories that had plagued her from the night before, the one that returned was the vision of him as she had first seen him, great and powerful and graceful, and filling her with longing. She again imagined herself lying underneath him on the moonlit ground while he moved inside her, and she drew in a breath and reached for her wine. Was he bewitching her still?

"I am sorry you were witness to my...display," Piers said. "I am old enough not to frolic in my cups like an un-weaned lad, but I seemed to have lost my wits for an evening." He paused as if he found it difficult to continue, then spoke curtly. "Cecil said you were most determined to come to my aid, despite my foul temper. I apologize if I offended you."

"No, not at all," Aisley said, hastening to smooth over any ill will between them. An apology from the Red Knight?

The man would ever surprise her. "I hope..." she began. Then she licked her lips anxiously. "I hope I was not the cause of your anger." She hurried on, unable to stop herself now that she had gone this far. "I know that we quarreled, but I would hate to think that I... that you would be so... incensed with me," she said softly.

It was true. His wrath had frightened Aisley more than she cared to admit. She could not bear to have it directed toward her, especially after the night they had shared. The passionate interlude may have meant nothing to Piers, but Aisley held it close to her heart as her one untarnished memory of the Red Knight.

Piers was silent for a moment, and Aisley felt tension emanating from him, though he made no movement. "No," he answered shortly. "'Twas not your doing. Now let us forget the incident. Tell me of your day," he urged.

Aisley did, and as she spoke, she relaxed. A man was not himself when he drank and should be forgiven for much of what he did when in his cups. She had seen her brothers behave poorly, too, and yet she had never witnessed anything like the Red Knight's ire. 'Twould be well for her to remember that her husband was capable of emotions greater than any she had ever known.

Reaching for her wine, Aisley suddenly stopped, her hand halting as she was struck with an odd notion. If this man could rage so fiercely, what of his other feelings? Love, for instance? Could the Red Knight cherish a woman as strongly as he felt his rage? Giddily, Aisley wondered what it would be like to be loved by her husband—not just to be held and caressed, but to be truly loved from the depths of his being. With the force of his passion, 'twould surely be beyond anything imaginable....

She set down her vessel sharply, annoyed at her own foolishness. Her mind was tripping along useless paths. She had never sought affection from anyone, not even her father, and if she thought to win it from this giant, mysterious knight, she was surely mad...or bewitched. Besides, displays of any kind made her uncomfortable. Why, then, would she long for them from this dangerous man?

"I like your scent," Piers said abruptly. "A musk, is it?"

"Yes," Aisley answered, flustered. "I like the way you smell, too." She clutched her cup in a white fist, realizing how silly she sounded and longing to call back the remark. But her husband did not laugh.

"Thank you," he said huskily, and Aisley felt her body respond to the warmth in his voice. Perhaps he could be a wild beast; perhaps he was a creature of the dark. But she remembered when he had come to her bed and held her and kissed her, and she flushed with the strength of her desire.

"Will you sing for me tonight?" Piers asked.

"Yes, of course," Aisley said. Pushing aside her trencher, she stood and began a folk song. "I stood in Maytime meadows by roses circled round, where many a fragile blossom was bright upon the ground...." One after another, she sang ballads that she knew Piers enjoyed, while he sat still as stone, listening.

Although he neither moved nor spoke, and though she could not even see his face, somehow Aisley sensed that she'd never had a more appreciative audience. When she finished, she felt full of contentment...and yearning, for the words of the love songs seemed potent and real here in the eerie glow of the great chamber.

"Beautiful," Piers said softly. "You sing like an angel, Aisley, my treasure."

Aisley blinked in surprise at the fulsome praise. Silence stretched between them as she sought a response, but no clever quips leapt from her tongue. Floundering as she was in a great stew of confusion, she could find no words to describe her feelings for the man who sat across from her.

"Thank you," she said finally.

"'Tis late," Piers added gruffly. "You may go."

After his tender remarks, the curt dismissal stung, and Aisley was even more dismayed. Would she ever understand the Red Knight? She rose shakily, feeling as though her limbs would not hold her, and knew suddenly that she did not want to leave him.

"Wait," she said, before she could help herself. She reached across the table for his hand, unprepared when she touched him for the jolt of lightning that shot up her arm, making her breasts ache. She nervously wet her lips, glad he could not see her discomfiture, even though she knew he sensed it.

"Yes?" Piers asked, his voice low.

"I would know...will you come to me this night, my lord?" she asked, her cheeks flaming at the question. If he should refuse her or mock her or shout at her...

Stillness and silence met her query. Then finally Piers spoke. "Do you want my company?" he asked.

"I do," Aisley whispered.

With a grunt, he pushed back his bench, the sound loud and grating, and before she knew what he was about, he was around the table moving toward her. "You shall have it," he growled. He reached for her, his hand grasping her out of the shadows, and picked her up as if she were light as a rag doll.

Flinging her arms around his neck, Aisley felt his mouth upon hers, and she whimpered, a low, joyful noise as his tongue sought hers. She was held tight against his chest while he strode to the bed. Then he laid her down and moved over her, impatiently pulling at the bed hangings with one hand while the other worked at her clothes.

With a final tug at the curtains, Piers immersed them in utter blackness, and Aisley could see nothing. She could only feel Piers's weight driving her down into the bed, his lips hot and stirring against her ear as he removed her gown. 'Twas bliss....

Piers closed his eyes. He felt the pain recede, desire surpassing it, and soon there was nothing but the woman in his arms and the hot need in his groin. It was so great that it daunted him, and he forced his body to stillness. Aisley was so small, so dainty that he knew he ought to hold back, to keep himself in check. He had the other night, difficult though it had been, because it was the first time, but tonight...

Tonight, Piers wanted her more than he had ever desired anything in his life. He wanted to bury himself in her until nothing existed but Aisley, all tight and smooth limbed around him. He lay unmoving over her, his hands poised at her waist, his mouth at her throat. "Do you still want my attentions?" he asked.

"Yes," Aisley breathed. "Yes. I wanted you last night— and the night before when I found you gone," she admitted, her hand stealing up to his hair. "And I wanted you tonight, here among the rushes...."

Piers's only reply was a growl of pleasure, and he fell upon her with a wildness that echoed the fierceness of his drunken rage. Ah, yes, Aisley thought dimly. Everything about Piers Montmorency was larger than life when loosed, his passion as well as his anger.

For a moment, as he tore her shift, the raw power of his need frightened her. But then, as if her husband had tapped some inner lode of which she was unaware, Aisley found herself responding in kind. Never had she dreamed that she would pull at his tunic, bite his flesh and grasp him so boldly in her hand while he grunted and jerked! Never had she imagined that she would writhe and gasp and scream out her pleasure... like a woman bewitched.

"Why are you called the Red Knight?" Aisley asked softly. She was curled up beside her husband in his enormous bed, her mind and body fully sated by the fury of his lovemaking.

Piers sighed, and Aisley thought for a moment that he would not answer. But then he spoke, his voice low, his breath warm against her hair. "'Twas a long time ago, when I first fought with Edward in the Holy Land. Because of a particularly gory incident, I was covered in blood from head to toe, more so than is usual even in battle," Piers explained.

"Although very little of it was my own, our foes dubbed me the Bloody One, or the Red Knight, and were awed that I fought on. So began the rumors of sorcery, too," Piers noted dryly. "'Twas said that only a master of the black arts could survive such terrible wounds. Of course, Edward thought it all vastly amusing. He dubbed me the Red Knight himself, and it stuck."

"And you fought on," Aisley said, "your reputation growing."

"Yes," he whispered. He rubbed his cheek against her tresses, so softly that she tightened her arm against his massive chest as if to hold him closer. "'Twas not healthy, as I see now," he reflected. "A reputation for immortality only invites challenges from others."

Aisley drew in her breath. "Many sought to kill you?"

"Many sought to kill me," he repeated, lifting a long blond lock and letting it fall against his skin.

"But you fought on until..."

His hand stilled in her hair. "Until Edward gave me Dunmurrow," he said.

Aisley waited for him to continue, but Piers only combed his fingers through her tresses again, spreading the strands across them both. "Then you came here and locked yourself away from the world," she prompted.

Piers made a low sound and turned onto his side, facing her. "Apparently, the locks weren't stout enough," he said dryly as his hand traveled down her leg, "for one tiny beauty, who feared not the Red Knight, stormed my keep and claimed me to husband."

He stroked her ankle and then took her foot in his palm and lifted it gently. "Your feet are so small and fine, my dainty Aisley, my brave little wife," he said softly. Then he kissed her slender arch.

Aisley giggled. Piers grunted in approval and started teasing her sole, stroking it lightly with his thumb. She laughed and tried to pull away, but he held her until she was breathless. "Stop! Stop! What are you doing?" she finally managed to gasp.

"I'm tickling you, Wife," Piers answered, his voice revealing his surprise. "Have you never been tickled before?"

"No," Aisley said soberly. She could feel his big body slide against hers as he moved back to her side.

"Did your brothers not tickle you?" he asked.

"No," Aisley answered. "We were never close," she said, searching for words to explain the relationship she had shared with her older siblings. "I loved them, of course, but..." *But they never tickled me or made me laugh or hugged me....* Aisley turned her face away, although the dark hid her features. "They were older and too busy with manly tasks for such nonsense."

Piers grunted in disapproval. "Had I a sister such as you, as beautiful and as piercingly bright as the sun, I would have spoiled her terribly."

Aisley felt an odd lump in her throat. She remembered her plans to dissolve their marriage by claiming to be related to her husband, and she swallowed hard. "'Tis glad I am that you are not my brother, Piers," she said hoarsely.

He laughed, a gentle roar that made her smile. "I am in agreement," he said. "'Twould be unnatural to feel such desire for a sibling." His voice became a low growl that communicated his eagerness for her body, and he pressed a kiss upon her shoulder before sending his tongue sensuously up her neck. His hand covered her breast, making languid warmth spread through her entire being. Then his teeth nipped at her ear. "'Tis desire such as I have never known, Aisley, this wanting you again and again and again," he whispered, turning her on her side to face him. "Surely you have bewitched me, Wife."

The words brought Aisley up short. "Piers," she said. "Do not jest about such things!" She thought of her own wild suspicions, of her husband's penchant for the dark and of his mysterious servant, and she opened her mouth to question him. But his lips were moving across her face, spreading sweet, hot kisses on her cheeks and her eyelids. Then, before she could speak, he claimed her lips, and at the heart-tripping sweep of his tongue, Aisley forgot her fears.

Piers pulled her up against his hard chest, and she moaned at the sensation as her breasts pushed into the smooth planes of his body. Cupping her bottom in a big hand, he drew one of her slim legs over his own, and before she even knew what he was about, he was sending his hot member deep inside her again.

Aisley caught her breath in surprised pleasure, and then his mouth closed over hers again, his tongue seeking hers in a slow, sure rhythm that matched the thrusts of his body. It was far different from their earlier mating, yet Aisley enjoyed it no less, and soon she was pressing herself to him, begging him to go faster, to ease the ache between her thighs.

Just as she thought she would weep from longing, Piers took his hand from her buttocks and slipped it between them. He pressed his thumb to her pleasure point, and Aisley cried out, her head thrown back, her fingers digging into his muscular arms as spasms swept through her.

In an instant, she was on her back, gasping from the heavy weight of him as he thrust into her fast and hard and so very deep that she came again before he shouted his pleasure into the darkness, his great body shuddering with the strength of his release.

"Ah, Aisley, what a fierce little lover you are," Piers whispered when he finally rolled from her. "Who would have suspected that my dainty, dedicated chatelaine would be so passionate?" His massive arms enfolded her in their warmth, promising so much and making her feel things she had never felt before, never known. If it were not for the confusion, the strangeness that would not leave her except when his hands were hot upon her...

"Piers," Aisley said, her head slowly clearing after the force of their union. "All the rumors of your sorcery are unfounded?" she asked.

He tensed as if he sensed something unsaid in her words. "Why? Do you wish me to cast a spell for you?" he asked wryly.

"No, I..." Aisley licked her lips. "I just...I feel as if I am bewitched!" she blurted out.

Piers laughed, throwing back his head in loud mirth. "God's wounds, Wife," he said, as he hugged her to him, "I thought you refused to believe all that!"

"Of course I don't believe it!" Aisley protested, her cheeks burning crimson. "I simply wondered..." She halted again, unsure of what to say. "What of Cecil, then?" she asked boldly. "Or know you not that the man can be two places at once?"

Her husband laughed even louder, until Aisley was annoyed with his amusement. "I fail to see what is so funny," she said. In her irritation, she tried to wiggle away from him, but his strong arms held her fast.

"Cecil!" he bellowed, and to her dismay, Aisley heard the door swing open. She scrambled under the covers, pulling them up to her chin, while Piers swung back the bed hangings. Although she doubted that anyone could see her in the shadowed room, she wouldn't be surprised if Cecil's odd powers included spying in the night like a cat.

"Yes, my lord," the servant answered. Had he been waiting just outside the door?

"Bring your brother to me," Piers ordered.

"Yes, my lord," he said. Then Aisley heard the door shut.

"Put on your gown, my wife, so you are ready to receive my servants," Piers said, chuckling. Aisley, still fuming over his laughter, left the bed immediately, and sought her fallen clothing in the darkness. She was so annoyed that she forgot the presence of the dogs, but Piers did not. "Castor! Pollux! Away!" he commanded when the beasts sniffed and growled at her approach, and she heard the thumps of their big bodies as they lay down out of her way.

The torn shift Aisley tossed aside with a blush, but she found everything else and was seated demurely at the table when Cecil returned. "Stand by the fire," Piers ordered his servant from the bed, and Aisley peered at the two men who moved to do their lord's bidding. Both were short, middle-aged, brown of hair and serious of countenance. They looked very much alike. Aisley drew in a breath. They were identical.

"Tell my lady your names," Piers directed.

"Cecil," the two answered in unison.

"You are twins," Aisley finally said, awestruck.

"Yes, my lady," one answered. The other nodded.

"But your names?" she asked, puzzled.

"Our mother said she had but one name picked out and that we must both take it," one of the servants said. Aisley released a breath in surprise and relief.

"You may go, both of you," Piers said, and Aisley grinned, no longer begrudging her husband his laughter. How utterly foolish she had been, succumbing to Edith's suspicions!

"Come back to my bed, Wife," Piers said. His husky tone beckoned, and Aisley turned toward where he lay. But her smile faded as she realized he was but a voice in the utter blackness beyond the firelight, a shadowed form, an enigma, her knight of the night.

"I—I just donned my clothes," she said. Her breasts rose and fell rapidly as her yearning to flee the gloom warred with her longing to fly into his arms. Truly, who was this man, and how did he gain such power over her?

"Come to bed and fear not," Piers said warmly. "I shall not use you again, my poor wife. Are you sore, Aisley?"

Her cheeks flamed while she stood undecided, her mind seeking excuses to go to her chamber, bright with candlelight, even as her heart wanted to return to her husband, hidden in the shadows. "No," she mumbled.

"Then come," Piers urged.

Drawn irresistibly to him, Aisley walked into the deep darkness at the edge of the bed. Although she made no further move, she soon felt his hand upon her wrist, dragging her down beside him, before he pulled the hangings closed again. When Aisley discovered what he was about, she tried to stop him.

"Piers, no!" she shrieked, but her words did not sway him. He removed her slipper and stroked her foot until she drew her knees up against her chest in helpless laughter, kicking and squirming in his firm hold. "Please, please!" she whispered, until he finally heeded her. "Why do you torture me so, you fiend?" she gasped.

"Because I like to hear you laugh," Piers said. Aisley, taking in great gulps of air, was still too weak to protest when he removed her gown in the darkness. She felt his hands against her bare flesh, and she tingled, every bit of her alive and awake.

"Why?" she whispered.

"Because it eases me," Piers answered, pulling her naked body into his embrace. True to his word, he did not try to join with her again, but only held her against the warmth of his chest. His strong arms made a cocoon for her, and Aisley felt a sudden, fierce joy as she nestled there.

"You ease me, Aisley," Piers added hoarsely, and for a moment, he grasped her so tightly that she thought she might break.

Chapter Ten

Aisley wanted to sleep with him. Curled up beside the great, warm length of her husband and tucked under one of his strong arms, with the sound of his soft breathing in her ears, she was content. It was unlike anything she had ever known, this closeness. It was alien, yes, but for once in her life Aisley did not want to flee from it. She breathed in the manly scent of his skin and wanted to stay in the shelter of his body forever. Odd that she took such comfort from the Red Knight, but she did. She knew comfort and warmth, and she felt ... wanted.

In the darkness, Aisley could almost imagine that theirs was a normal marriage—perhaps even better than normal, for they seemed to care for each other, which was unusual in noble unions. Aisley knew that she felt deeply for Piers, and despite his initial hostility, she thought she had discerned in his passion and in his teasing a bit of affection toward her, too. She was certain he held her in some regard, but not enough to show himself to her.

There her pretention to normalcy ended, for what wife never looked upon her husband?

Aisley tried to picture him. She had traced his features with her fingers, but she was no artist and she was unable to conjure up an image from touch alone. Was the hair that felt crisp under her hands raven black, dusty brown or a rich red, to match his name? Try as she might, she could put no color to it, but made it a blur in her mind.

"Aisley..." His voice, low and deep, drew her from her thoughts. He pressed a kiss to her forehead, and she smiled. Would the man never let her rest? Aisley sighed and snuggled closer. Although she was nearly asleep, she knew she could be persuaded to join with him again...and again. "'Tis getting late," he said. "You had better be going to your own chamber."

Aisley's eyes flew wide open, though they met with naught but darkness. He was sending her away? She was not allowed to spend the night with him? The warm, wonderful feelings that had begun to grow in his embrace shattered like shards of ice. She sat up at once, searching impatiently for her gown, and when her hands could not find it in the blackness, she cursed softly. Or was it a sob?

"Aisley, love..." She disdained the endearment. So what if his voice was aching? There was no good reason for him to toss her from his bed like some easy wench, paid for with coin. She was rooting desperately among the bedding now, as though seeking not only her clothes, but her dignity, until his hands on her wrists halted her frantic movements. He was behind her, his chest hot against her back, drawing her to him like a flame, but she refused to melt against him. She slipped free, swept aside the bed hangings and stepped upon one of the dogs.

"Oh!" Aisley reeled back against the bed as it yelped and moved out of the way. At this point, she was ready to wrap herself in a blanket just to get to her room, but when she turned, she was met with her things. Piers held them out to her, and she took them, dressed quickly and prepared to go.

"Aisley...your slippers," he said. Was he laughing at her? She grabbed them from him and slid them on while she hopped away from the great bed, longing to put some distance between her and what had happened there. Had she only dreamed of his affection?

"Good night, my wife," Piers called softly. "Sleep well."

Angry now, Aisley would have slammed the door, but she knew it was too heavy, and, anyway, one of the Cecils awaited her outside. She let him escort her to her chamber, although she knew the night would be a long one. Suddenly, her own bed seemed vast and empty and lonely. How could she sleep well?

The next morning, while Edith helped her dress, Aisley told herself to act more sensibly. Truly, she must be losing her wits to jump so freely into the Red Knight's bed only to find herself reluctant to leave it. She had spent a lifetime protecting her heart. Why, then, did she seemed compelled to hand it on a platter to her husband?

Sitting down to have her hair dressed, Aisley was assailed by the scent of him, and of their lovemaking, lingering on her body, and she flushed at the gentle reminder. If she begged a bath this early in the day, however, Edith would surely be moved to comment, and Aisley did not care to hear another fervent lecture on how the Red Knight had cast his spell upon her.

Aisley eyed Edith guiltily, expecting the servant to accuse her of joining with Piers in his foul practices, but she realized, with some surprise, that the woman was not paying her one whit of attention. Instead of railing about her desperate lot at Dunmurrow, she was busily braiding Aisley's long locks . . . and humming.

Edith had obviously found something to be cheerful about, Aisley thought with a twinge of envy, and suddenly she felt more alone than ever. She had become accustomed to siding with her husband against her servant's slander; now who would prod her to his defense?

"I have discovered how Cecil can be in so many places at once," Aisley said.

"Have you now?" Edith asked, pausing in her humming only long enough to pose the question. She then began another tune, so horribly different from the prescribed notes that Aisley smiled.

"Yes," she answered. "He is no familiar. He is not even one man, but two—a set of twins," she said, waiting for the other's gasps of revelation. They did not come.

"Is he now?" Edith asked, chuckling softly. "No wonder he does twice his share of work. Or mayhap they are getting by without doing all that they should, if there are two of them!"

Aisley turned to look at her, astonished by the woman's bright smile and light words. She had expected amazement, argument and a tirade about the evils of the Dunmurrow household, but instead the servant seemed to accept Aisley's explanation with equanimity.

"There you go, my lady," she said, patting the braids neatly arranged on Aisley's crown. "You do look lovely this fine morning. Will you be needing aught else now?" she asked.

Staring, Aisley shook her head numbly. If she didn't know better, she would say Edith was the one bewitched....

With a frown at her own foolishness, she rose to begin her day. She threw herself into her work, attacking a stack of mending, but like a ballad that presses to be sung, the memory of her husband taunted her, making her long for him again and again.

The warmth of the hearth forced her mind to the heat of him, and she ached for his touch and the sound of his voice, growling his pleasure. But it was not only the thought of his lovemaking that disturbed her. Aisley recalled, perhaps with more discomfiture, his kindness, his tickling and the security of his embrace.

Maybe Piers had put a spell on her, and she no longer had a will of her own. No, that was untrue, Aisley decided. She had a will, just a weakened one. How then to get her old self back? She caught sight of one of the Cecils and frowned.

Piers's servant had turned out to be no evil being, and her better sense told her that all of Edith's other tales about the Red Knight were false, too.

Although Aisley doubted that Piers possessed special powers to enthrall her, there was no denying that she felt something for him, enough to throw herself at his head, tumble into bed with him and be tossed out like the veriest strumpet. That treatment still stung in the light of day. Hadn't she learned a long time ago not to yearn for closeness? After all these years, the rebuffs were no easier to bear. In truth, it was more painful now, after the intimacies she had shared with the Red Knight, to face his rejection.

Aisley told herself that she had never wanted or needed anyone in her life. Why then did she feel so drawn to her husband, a mysterious dark figure who would not even show himself? She felt like a boy's tilting doll upon a stick, thrust this way and that by her husband's moods, powerless to control her fate. It was a disturbing image. Aisley resented it, resented his constant intrusion on her thoughts, and suddenly she wished for nothing more than to be indifferent to him, as she had always been to all other men.

Abandoning her task, she went to the kitchens with the hope that some company before the midday meal would drag her from her ill mood, and Glenna greeted her warmly. "Thank you for taking such good care of Moira's burn," said the cook. "'Tis healing very nicely."

Aisley smiled sincerely, but the servant's words jarred her. Had it been only a few days ago that she had treated the child and imagined that Piers, too, had been burned, or had some physical reason for keeping to the shadows? She sighed, for she knew now that that was not the case. There was nothing wrong with her husband, yet she knew not why he stayed in darkness.

Again, Aisley felt assailed by suspicions, never quite believed, but never quite discarded, concerning the Red Knight. He'd claimed all the rumors about him were nonsense, had laughed at her unease, and yet...who would admit to practicing sorcery?

"'Tis good to have a lady who heals in Dunmurrow," Glenna said softly.

"Aye," a voice agreed. "I would trust my lady any day over the village healer." Aisley looked up, recognizing the young man who had accompanied her when she sang. Thomas, she thought, remembering his name.

"You mean Widow Nebbs?" Glenna asked.

"Yes, I would sooner tend myself than take that one's advice," Thomas said.

"Widow Nebbs is wise beyond your ken," the cook said. "She is old now and rarely practices her healing arts, but she has great knowledge of herbs."

"Humph. Love potions and the like," Thomas said with derision.

"'Tis not good to disrespect your elders," Glenna noted in her best mother's voice. The young man, taking the hint, became quiet, while Aisley thoughtfully returned to the great hall.

Widow Nebbs. Aisley had heard of the village healer before and had planned to stop sometime to share recipes with her. Like other women with her skills, the widow was viewed with awe by most of the villagers, who talked of her alternately as a saint or a witch, depending upon the outcome of her treatments. Aisley was inclined to agree with Glenna, though. These old women often knew more than they let on, for they had accumulated a lifetime of knowledge, perhaps even a bit of magic.

Magic. Aisley scoffed at her own thoughts. She had never believed in such nonsense before—but she had never been bewitched by the Red Knight before, either. She wondered if Widow Nebbs knew how to break such a spell....

Edith came in, laughing gaily at some quip from her guard, and though she sat by Aisley, she had little attention for her mistress. Aisley did not mind, for she was glad that

Edith was finally growing accustomed to Dunmurrow. Still, it was easy to envy the two older people their carefree exchanges.

"Do you need me this afternoon, my lady?" Edith asked. "For if you do not, Willie has promised to take me walking outside the walls." She blushed rosily, and Aisley was struck by the notion that the woman looked years younger—and prettier, too. Willie grinned widely, his black eyes bright.

Aisley shook her head. "No, I won't require your attendance." She thought of the mounds of sewing she had left to finish, but decided that Edith could help her another time.

"Why don't you come with us, my lady?" the woman asked suddenly. "'Twould do you good to get out."

Aisley smiled. "No, but thank you for inviting me." She enjoyed eating with them, however, for the amusing banter and suggestive looks they shared made them lively companions.

"Are you sure you won't join us, my lady?" Edith asked as they rose to leave. She shook her head again, smiling, and watched them wistfully as they went.

"Come on then, my girl," Willie said to Edith. "I've a bit of lovely country to show you."

"Hold up, you dolt!" Edith scolded. "You are supposed to wait for me, are you not? Some guard you are!"

Aisley chuckled, then fell silent. Truth be told, she coveted their light chatter, while cursing her own ties to the somber darkness. With their departure, her thoughts turned inward, toward the great chamber, for even now he called to her, and Aisley knew that she would forgo even an outing in the sunshine to spend the day in his bed. Would the time come when she would cling to him, never leaving the shadows, finally becoming a creature of the night herself—a shade like the Red Knight?

Aisley shivered at the thought. She had wanted to be his wife in all ways, but now she recognized the danger of growing closer to him. She had been better off before, in a world filled only with duties and accounts, not with dizzying longing and...emotions she would prefer not to feel. If only she could turn back time! Rising from the bench, she grabbed her cloak and headed toward the stables. It was time to pay a call on Widow Nebbs.

Two of the castle guards insisted on accompanying her, and Aisley let them, though she said little during the journey. She left them down the road and walked to Widow Nebbs's hut alone. Although Aisley told herself it was only customary for one healer to call upon another, she wet her lips nervously when she knocked upon the door.

A woman's gravelly voice bid her enter, and Aisley stepped inside, into gloom that reminded her of the Red Knight's chamber. It was difficult to see, and smoke made the small room so close that for a moment Aisley thought it was empty. Then her eyes made out the form of an old woman seated on a stool, stirring a pot that hung over the fire.

Aisley laid the basket she had brought on the table. "Widow Nebbs? 'Tis Aisley Montmorency. I have some bread and cheese for you."

"So you are the new lady of the castle," the woman said. "Come closer so that I may have a look at you."

Perhaps it was a reflection of the odd mood that had gripped her all day, or maybe too much time spent at Dunmurrow listening to black rumor about her husband, but Aisley felt a chill when normally she would have reached out to the woman. She suppressed the urge to leave and stepped closer.

Widow Nebbs was very old, with thick white hair that flowed down her back. Her face was creased with great, deep wrinkles, but her cheeks were sun browned, and though small and bent, she did not appear frail. Aisley smiled.

"So you've come to take my place, have you?" the widow asked.

"Not at all!" Aisley protested.

The old woman grinned. "'Tis time, child. I am too tired to care for these ungrateful creatures any longer." With a graceful sweep of her arm, the widow gestured to the hard-packed dirt floor, and since there were no other seats, Aisley dropped down near the old woman's feet, her slippers tucked under her gown. Over the smoke, she could smell garlic, lavender and saffron, and she looked up to see great bunches of herbs hanging from the low ceiling.

She felt the old woman's eyes upon her, like tiny, glittering stars hidden in the rough folds of skin, and she glanced away toward the fire. The only sounds were the gentle hiss of the blaze and the scrape of the spoon against the pot. The widow never stopped stirring, her arm gliding in a gentle rhythm while Aisley watched.

"So what ails you, child?" the old woman asked.

"Me?" Startled, Aisley drew her gaze, with difficulty, from the pot. "Nothing. I am fine."

The widow laughed, a low, dry chuckle. "No one comes to me for nothing. What can you be wanting? Are you ill?"

Aisley admired the smooth movements of the woman's bony wrist as she pondered her reply. I'm bewitched, she thought to herself. Then she smiled at her own foolishness.

"Ah. I see," the widow said. She stirred silently for a moment before speaking again. "As a healer yourself, you must know there are some ailments for which there is no cure."

"Yes," Aisley said, nodding slowly. The fire was making her warm and drowsy, for she had done little enough sleeping last night, and she found it difficult to pay attention to what the old woman was saying.

"And, of course, in some instances the cure is worse than the disease," the widow said with a soft chuckle. "'Tis always the way with cases of the heart...."

Aisley drew in a breath, trying to stay alert. What had the old woman said? Something about liver complaints?

"If only you didn't fight it so, child. But I can see you are a stubborn one." The widow made a clucking noise in her throat. "So many would welcome such a great love. They come to me craving spells and potions to conjure pale imitations of what you have. Do you truly not want it?"

Want it? Want what? Aisley lost all train of thought as her head drooped and nodded.

"Foolish girl. I shall give you what you desire, but I cannot swear to you that it will work. There are some things, child, that are meant to be, whether we poor humans want them or no, and meddling in them can be worse than doing naught."

Aisley yawned and glanced up at the widow only to find the stool empty. When had the old woman risen? She stood, and there the widow was at her elbow, pressing a packet upon her. "Mix this in a bit of warm ale and drink it all down. It may help you," she said. "And stop by any time, my lady. I have enjoyed our talk."

Aisley tucked the paper of herbs into her now-empty basket and nodded her goodbye, feeling a bit disoriented. Truly, she didn't recall much of her chat with the old woman, for the fire had been so warm and she so weary. Shaking her head as if to clear it, she walked outside.

It wasn't until she was back at the castle, returning the basket to the kitchens, that she was reminded of the packet. "What's this, my lady?" Glenna asked, holding it up.

"Oh, Widow Nebbs gave that to me," Aisley said, rather distractedly. She could see Cecil motioning to her out of the corner of her eye.

"'Tis one of her potions," Glenna said. "Be it for you?"

Aisley nodded and stared at the little paper, trying to remember exactly why she had brought it home. Glenna turned back to her cooking, but Aisley remained where she stood, staring at the bundle. She had the vague notion that it had something to do with Piers, but that made no sense. Lifting a hand to her face, she rubbed her eyes.

She had gone to the old woman to discuss rememdies, but the visit had been so strange. Had she fallen asleep there? Aisley recalled wishing that she could rid herself of her growing attachment to her husband, but surely she had not voiced her desire to the widow...had she? With a growing sense of horror, she realized that if she had, the herbs might be meant to counter his spell....

She dropped the paper suddenly, as if it burned her.

Nonsense. Aisley told herself that she did not believe in love potions and such. Piers was no sorcerer, Cecil was no familiar and a harmless old village woman could not break the bond that had grown between her and her husband, no matter how much Aisley wished to sever it.

Or did she?

She leaned back against the stone wall, struggling to make sense of her confusion. She had been miffed by Piers's treatment of her, that much she admitted. And caring about him made her seem...helpless, a sensation that she did not like at all. But what of all the other sensations he made her feel?

With a red-hot jolt Aisley remembered what he did to her body—the way she soared when joined with him. She remembered the warmth of his arms when he simply held her, the dry humor in his deep voice and the pleasant companionship that she had never before known. Did she really, truly, want to give it all up and return to her previous life of calm, cold emptiness?

Whether good or bad, Piers made her feel, and Aisley knew, deep down inside, that she was alive now for the very first time because of him. She would not risk it all by taking some strange old woman's concoction.

"My lady!" Aisley was drawn from her thoughts by one of the Cecils, who, failing to get her notice, had finally walked to her side. "Alan sent some workmen to help us, and I would know where to lodge them."

Aisley looked at the servant blankly for a moment before recovering herself. "Oh, yes. Good. I am sure we can find some place for them...." Her attention focused upon Cecil, she began walking with him back to the great hall, and so she did not see Glenna bend down to retrieve the fallen packet.

"'Tis for my lady," the cook said to her new helper. "Stir it into her ale."

Aisley was in a hurry to get to the great chamber. She did not wish to be late, she told herself, although she suspected the rapid pulsing of her heart was due to other reasons entirely. Would her husband greet her pleasantly? Throw her down among the rushes? Take her to his bed, where she would find wild passion and gentle rapport—until he tired of her presence? Aisley was not sure what to long for as she entered Piers's room.

"My lady," he said, and Aisley sat down quickly.

"Piers," she acknowledged, a bit breathlessly. Then she reached for her cup. The ale was warm and sweet this evening, but her throat was dry from her nervous anticipation, so she drank deeply.

"The day has been long without you, my wife," Piers said softly, his tone low and melodious.

Aisley blushed even as she felt her body respond to his voice. It was a like a caress, reaching across the table to her, robbing her of her breath and of her good sense. But she would not succumb tonight without a bit of resistance, however brief. "'Twas a long night without *you*, my husband," she said pointedly.

She heard his chuckle in the darkness and took another swallow of ale to calm herself. Finishing the cup in a gulp, she set the vessel on the table. "The drink is rather poor tonight, is it not?" she asked.

"Is it? I notice naught but you when in your company," Piers said. Aisley smiled at the words, feeling the pull of him like a lure out of the darkness. The refreshment had eased her, as had Piers's obviously good mood. Despite her annoyance with him, she found her thoughts racing ahead to the night that would follow their meal. Would he tear at her clothes or simply leave them on her, growling of his urgent need for her?

Heady with desire, Aisley leaned toward him slowly, but something pushed her back. With a start, she sat up straight on the bench, overcome by an odd, prickly sensation.

"Aisley?" She heard Piers's voice, but it sounded discordant and shrill, and when she tried to move again, it was as if she were caught between opposing forces grappling for her insides. Then her stomach cramped violently and she cried out, slipping to the floor.

"Aisley!" Piers was at her side in a moment, but his touch seemed to burn her flesh, and the darkness of the room weighed her down, smothering her.

"Don't!" Aisley managed to croak between gasps, flailing at him with her arms, and finally, his fingers left her.

"Cecil!" he bellowed, and soon the servant was lifting her with cool, capable hands and carrying her away from her husband, who was muttering curses in a harsh tone. When the chamber door opened, Piers's voice faded away, and the air that met her seemed fresher. Taking great breaths, Aisley clung to Cecil all the way back to her room.

Then she was lying on her own bed, and Edith was there, whispering words of comfort. Clucking softly, the servant put a cloth to her head, but it did nothing to cool the battle that raged within her. Closing her eyes, Aisley surrendered all thought.

"Well?" Piers could barely restrain his impatience. It seemed as though his servant had been gone for hours, while he paced his room, consumed with worry for his wife.

"She is not well, my lord, but 'tis hoped that it will pass," Cecil said.

"Of course, 'tis hoped that it will pass!" Piers snapped. "Do not try my temper with platitudes fit for an infant. What ails her?"

"The cook, Glenna, says that your wife took a potion obtained from a village healer. The cook assumed it was some sort of purge and stirred it into her ale, but now the woman is beside herself and there is some confusion over whether your wife actually intended to take the brew."

"A purge?" Piers sank down on the edge of his bed, puzzled. Why would Aisley seek out a healer? Had she been ill? Just yesterday she'd appeared hale and hearty in every way, Piers remembered, recalling fondly each bit of her sleek flesh that had slid under his fingertips, quivered beneath his mouth....

Perhaps she had some female complaint, he thought suddenly. And then it struck him. He knew of one particular reason why women sought purges, but surely not Aisley.... "No!" he shouted, rising to his feet. "'Tis not so!"

Cecil's voice was soft and reasonable, as usual, and he seemed to read Piers's mind. "She could be with child," he suggested.

"'Tis possible," Piers admitted with a fierce growl. "But she could hardly know if it were so already!" God's wounds, it had been only a few days ago that he had taken her maidenhead.

"Your wife might fear that any offspring of yours would be a demon—" Cecil began.

"No!" Piers's cry of anguish rent the room, cutting off the servant's speech. It was not true, could not be true! Aisley did not fear the Red Knight, nor did she believe the tales about him. Why then would she beg a potion from a village hag to rid herself of his baby?

"No!" With another angry bellow, Piers slammed his fist into the wall. He did not look up when Cecil left the room, nor did he notice the blood that flowed down his fingers to drip upon the floor.

"There, there, my lady," Edith said softly. "You'll be fine now, you will. Can't be anything more for you to bring up, you poor thing. Here. Drink this, and 'twill ease your pains and make you rest." Aisley felt something trickle down her parched throat, and she groaned.

"Hush, my lady," the woman crooned. "It appears that you got a bit of something bad from the village healer. You should know better than to trust some old peasant woman. Naught but crazy, most of them are! Now, you must rest, but I'll be right here, should you need me," Edith assured her.

Aisley's eyes were closed and her limbs heavy, but her head throbbed and her stomach churned, making sleep difficult. And when it came, she was plagued with dreams, strange and vivid, like a tableau in which the Red Knight figured prominently. Aisley tossed and turned and cried out, seeking escape from the nightmares, until she felt Edith's comforting hand on her brow, and then, somehow, she slipped away into blackness.

She noticed when the atmosphere in the room changed sometime later. It became charged somehow, like heavy air before a lightning storm, and Aisley struggled for breath. She felt a presence then, standing over her, but it was not Edith. It was dark and hot, and she turned away from it, back toward her dreams....

"Here, my child," the Widow Nebbs said. Her wrinkled face was brown, her eyes knowing as she held out a packet of herbs. "You have only to mix a little in his ale, and you will be rid of him forever."

"What are you saying?" Aisley asked in confusion. Had she dozed by the fire? "I don't understand."

"But you do," the widow asserted. "This is for your husband, for Montmorency. Give it to him, and he shall bewitch you no more."

Aisley stepped back, horrified. Was the old woman telling her to poison Piers?

"You would be free then, my child," the widow said with a smile. "Free to return to your old home, your old ways, to run your own household without interference . . . or distraction."

Aisley nodded. That much appealed to her. "Yes, but—"

"Then you have only to put a pinch in his cup, child," the old woman urged.

Aisley backed away, shaking her head. She saw the great dark figure of her husband looming in the shadows, remembered the sleek muscles of his body moving under her hands, recalled the sweet comfort of his arms around her. She imagined the familiar, dry tones of his voice being stilled by death, and she cringed. No matter who he was or what he was, she could never kill Piers. She could never kill anyone! "I can't," she cried.

"Silly girl. You don't have to murder him. Just put a bit in his ale, and you will be rid of him forever. That's what you want, isn't it? To be rid of him? It's what you want. . . ."

Aisley found herself huddled in a cramped corner of the hut, and still the old woman came toward her, her voice slow and rhythmic. "It is what you want, isn't it?" she asked again and again, while Aisley shook her head in denial.

"You must make up your mind now," the widow said, and Aisley felt herself rise and struggle against some unseen force. "Is it what you want?" the old woman asked.

"No!" Aisley screamed. She, who rarely raised her voice, shouted at the top of her lungs and sat straight up in bed with the force of her conviction. "I want Piers!"

"I'm here." The deep voice chased away the nightmare. And suddenly his arms were around her, cradling her in their warmth against his massive chest, making her feel safe and sound and . . . wanted.

Sometime before dawn Aisley awoke again. She drew in a deep breath of relief, feeling as well as only a person who has been ill can feel—and grateful for it. Fingering the covers, she recognized her own bed, but opened her eyes to darkness. A strong arm tightened around her, and she realized she was resting against her husband's firm chest.

"Piers?" she asked softly, surprised by the squeak that came out. Her mouth felt thick and dry as she struggled to speak—and remember. She recalled visiting Widow Nebbs, returning to Dunmurrow, sitting down to eat with Piers . . . and then only a void filled with horrible nightmares.

The widow had handed her some herbs, but Aisley could have sworn she had tossed them aside. She knew that she could not give up her husband, no matter how difficult and strange he might be. Why then did she feel as if she had taken the potion and been torn asunder by her newly forged loyalties?

Aisley turned to Piers, sliding her hand across his massive trunk to assure herself that her great, mysterious husband was still solid flesh and still breathed, despite her attempt to exorcise him. He pulled her close, his fingers gently smoothing her hair while her cheek lay against his tunic.

"Aisley?" he asked softly. "You are well now?"

She nodded into the material that clothed him, not trusting herself to speak. What an idiot she had been! How could she ever have wished to break the spell that shimmered between them, warm and beckoning? Aisley wished now that she had never even heard of the Widow Nebbs.

"Why?" Piers asked. His voice was hoarse, and Aisley ached for him. How much did he know? She felt ashamed for visiting the healer, embarrassed by her own weakness and stupidity. She should never have brought the packet home, she realized, for somehow it had gotten into her belly, damaging her health, her peace of mind and her tenuous truce with her husband.

"What was the potion for?" Piers asked. Steadier this time, his tone told her that he intended to be persistent. With a sinking heart, Aisley knew she would have to tell him something, yet she couldn't bear to admit the truth. She felt Piers stiffen at her continued silence, and she wanted to weep into his side. *Don't turn away from me now....*

"Was it a purge to rid you of our child?" he asked abruptly.

Aisley blinked in surprise and sat up straight. "Piers!" she said, horrified. "I would never do such a thing." Truly, the thought of a baby had never crossed her mind, though she supposed it would be a natural enough outcome of their joining.

A baby... what would it be like, the son of the Red Knight? Such thoughts brought new worries, but Aisley dismissed them. She had made her choice, and it was too late to go back to her old life, a life without Piers Montmorency.

"Are you saying that I'm pregnant?" Aisley asked in amazement.

"No," Piers answered softly. "'Tis too soon to tell, unless your monthly flow is overdue."

Aisley blushed at his words and mumbled a denial. "But I might be, might I not?" she asked hopefully. "Though I suppose this—" she hesitated and clutched her stomach "—might have killed it." She sucked in a sharp, painful breath at the thought and sat up straight, staring into the darkness toward her husband.

"Oh, Piers, I did not mean to take anything, I swear to you! 'Twas all so strange, like a dream.... I went to the old woman's hut to discuss remedies, and when I returned, Glenna found the packet of herbs. I—I dropped them to the floor, and then Cecil asked me about something and I forgot all about it. Glenna must have assumed . . ." Her words trailed off into a sob. "Dear Lord, if I have hurt a child . . ."

Piers's arms curved around her again, drawing her back into his embrace. "'Tis too early to tell," he said gruffly. Did he sound relieved? Surely he did not think her capable of murdering her own baby? But what was he to think? Would he be comforted to know the real task of the potion was to rid herself of him? Aisley hugged him tightly, as if to make up for the betrayal.

"Do you . . . want children?" Piers asked.

"Yes, of course," she whispered.

"Then we shall make some when you are feeling better," he said, his voice turning husky, and for the first time since waking, Aisley felt the force of his allure, an allure that she knew was more real than any wrought by magic. "I shall make love to you again and again, my wife, until my seed is firmly planted in your belly." His low promise made her tingle all over, and she closed her eyes, thankful that the herbs had failed.

"You are not to take anything more from that village healer. Fools and worse, they are," Piers said firmly.

Aisley nodded, smiling. "I am cured," she said. She snuggled closer to her husband, and for this moment, at least, she did not regret choosing the darkness.

Chapter Eleven

When Aisley awoke later, Piers was gone, and she wondered just how much of the past day and night had been dream and how much reality. She remembered visiting the Widow Nebbs with the vague hope of breaking the spell that held her in Piers's thrall, but she did not think she'd actually asked the old woman for such help. Still, the widow had obviously given her something, and somehow she had ended up drinking it, for she recalled becoming ill and purging her body of just about everything *except* her feelings for Piers.

They were obviously going to remain with her, for they were not the product of any sorcery or potion. In the aftermath of her sickness, Aisley realized that her bewitchment had natural causes. It sprang out of a previously untapped well of emotion that could not be denied, nor dismissed by any cure.

Like it or not, she cared for Piers, and she told herself she might as well get used to it, for she suspected that her attachment to her husband was more likely to grow before it diminished. If she could only ignore the shadows that surrounded him....

By afternoon, Aisley was well enough to be restless, though Edith would not let her up. "I've strict orders to see that you don't strain yourself, my lady," she admonished. Since Aisley could not imagine Edith taking orders from anyone, she assumed that the directive was of the servant's own making. Although she bristled under the enforced rest, she stayed in bed until supper, when she tried again to rise, telling Edith that she must join her husband in his chamber.

"Nay, my lady," Edith said, pushing her back against the pillows. "Cecil says you are not to leave your room this evening. Your husband wants you to take care of yourself," Edith noted, with approval in her voice. Aisley stared at her servant in amazement. Was this the same woman who had hated and feared the Red Knight more than any other? "Here, my lady," Edith said, plying her with a cup of thin soup. "Glenna hoped that this would sit well with you."

Aisley took it with a disgruntled nod. Of course Piers did not want her with him. He was probably still angry with her over her illness. The thought made her breath catch in her throat. Had he found out from Glenna, or even Widow Nebbs herself, what the potion had been intended to do?

It would be all too fitting if, now that she accepted him, he were to turn her aside, Aisley decided, and her heart raced in panic. Handing the empty vessel back to Edith, she lifted her chin. "I want my husband, I want to see him," she said firmly. Although she knew the plea resembled that of a whining child, she could not help herself. Suddenly she needed the comfort that only the Red Knight could provide.

Edith made some soothing noises and patted her hand. "And so you will, my lady. I shall have Cecil give him the message. Will you be wanting anything more then this night?"

Aisley shook her head, a bit miserably. She stopped just short of ordering Edith to make sure her husband came to her. Lord help her, she was pathetic! Although Edith appeared to suffer the Red Knight more easily than before, Aisley could not envision her servant braving his lair and dragging him by the ear to her side.

With a tremulous smile at the very idea, she sank down under the covers. Then, before Edith could leave, she sat up again. "Edith! You may...extinguish all the candles, please," she said. "And pull the bed hangings closed."

"Yes, my lady," Edith replied. "I'll do that, so you may get some sleep."

Aisley slipped down again among the blankets, sighing softly at Edith's mistake. She did not require darkness to rest, but to receive her husband.

She did not have long to wait after Edith left. A faint stirring of the air told her that the curtains were moving, and soon Aisley felt him beside her, a great solid presence in the utter blackness. She reached out a hand and was surprised when it met thick material. Piers obviously was wearing a robe of some sort. With sudden pique, Aisley realized she did not want him wearing anything.

"You summoned me, Wife?" he asked, his voice wry, as usual.

"Yes," Aisley admitted, feeling awkward. Had she only dreamed that he had held her close earlier this day, comforting her with his embrace while they spoke softly together? Silently, she cursed his strange moods, which always left her guessing. But tonight she could not be angry with him. She was too much aware of her regard for him, the discovery still fresh after her bout with illness.

Knowing that she could not change what she felt for Piers did not make the deep emotions any easier for Aisley to bear. It was painful, this aching, wanting need; no wonder she had shied from it. She had ever been brave, however, and she resolved to shy away no longer. Although she could not alter her longing, she knew how to ease it. "Did I imagine it, my husband, or did you not this morning promise me children?" she asked.

Aisley felt his body tense at her words, but she did not shrink from him. Boldly, she slipped her hand inside the cloth that draped his body. "I seem to remember a pledge that you would plant your seed within me, often," she whispered. She felt the muscles of his chest and stomach contract at her touch, and she let her hand roam downward. "Deep inside me," she added, breathlessly.

Piers was already hard, but she stroked him, enjoying the feel of him and the low, rumbling noise he made in response. He was still for a few moments, as if stunned by her actions, and then, in one swift motion, he turned and covered her, his knee separating her legs before he groaned and made good his promise.

To her relief, he spoke naught of her illness, but made love to her with a singular gentleness. He left her while she was sleeping, and although Aisley was disappointed when she awoke and found him gone, it was much better than being asked to leave his bed.

And so they established a routine. During the day, Aisley managed the castle; during the evening she dined in the great chamber; and for a few precious hours each night, she bedded her husband. She told herself it was more than enough, told herself that her experience with the Widow Nebbs's concoction had driven all thoughts of sorcery from her, but still she wondered why Piers kept to the shadows and why he would never stay with her until dawn. And, as many could attest, it's the thing forbidden that is often most desired....

For a while, Aisley was satisfied. Preparations for the Christmas feast were keeping her busy, and she had little time to ponder her husband's mysteries. After checking with Glenna about the day's meals one morning, she returned to the hall, where she sat down to write a letter to her Belvry steward. Her concentration was soon interrupted by the arrival of Edith, with Willie in tow. The servant was wreathed in smiles, while her guard did not look pleased.

"Slow down, woman!" he complained as he buckled a sword belt round his waist. "I told you I wasn't ready to come down yet. Now why would you go and run off like that without your guard?"

Edith made a depreciating noise. "I've work to be doing, William Gallway, and cannot lie abed all morn like some soldiers I know."

"Are you calling me lazy, wench?" he asked, the grin on his face removing the sting from his words.

"If the shoe fits, you may wear it," Edith said loftily, while Aisley watched in fascination. Recently, Edith had walked about like one in a funeral party, but now she was acting like herself again. *More* than herself. Edith had a cheery, girlish quality about her that Aisley could never remember seeing before. Had her relationship with her guard gone beyond flirting?

Aisley had not been concerned when the servant had not attended her this morn. Truth to tell, her mind had been elsewhere, but now she wondered just what had delayed Edith....

"Hold there, Edie!" Willie ordered, in a more serious tone than Aisley had ever heard him adopt. "I think 'tis time you learned who is your master, my girl."

"Is that so?" Edith asked.

"Yes," he said. "Now sit." Although they were some distance from her, Aisley watched Willie guide Edith down onto one of the long benches. His back was turned, but there was no mistaking the firm set of his shoulders.

"Now, my girl, let me tell you the way of it," Willie said. "'Tis many years since either one of us was married, and perhaps we need to refresh our memories a bit on how a man and a maid get on."

"Seems as there are some parts to it that you recall very well," Edith said, smiling up at him jauntily.

"Well, uh, yes," he admitted, and Aisley wished she could have seen his face as he responded to that sally. "But there are other things that you may have forgotten—namely, that a woman must obey her man. I know you've been used to doing on your own for years, but I expect now that you'll listen to me, for 'tis the natural way of things."

Aisley leaned a little to the left to catch a glimpse of Edith's face. Her maid's expression was deceptively mild, and she wondered when the storm would break. "You want me to defer to you in all things?" Edith asked.

"Yes," Willie answered, though he did not sound as positive as before.

"All right," Edith replied. Aisley nearly slipped from her seat in astonishment until she saw the servant fix her with a bright gaze and wink broadly.

Willie, who was walking back and forth in front of Edith, made low noises of approval. "Well, then, that's a good girl. I'm glad that you are able to see reason. I'll have you answer to me now," he added, with a bit of bravado. Aisley found it hard to choke back her laughter.

"If that's settled, I have a bit of mending to do for my lady," Edith said. Willie nodded his agreement, and Edith turned away from him.

Aisley tried to wipe the smile from her face, but it was difficult when the woman wore such a conspiratorial look. "I'll be getting to that mending now," she said loudly when she stopped before Aisley. Then she leaned closer, whispering for her mistress's ears only, "Always let them think they're having their way. And then do what you please."

While Aisley swallowed her mirth, Edith winked again, then trotted off to the wardrobe, Willie at her heels like a trained pup—but a happy one, Aisley reflected.

For a moment, she felt a pang of envy for her servant's friendly liaison. Edith and her guard were not bound to the evening, like secretive partners, but bantered day and night, their affection apparent. Aisley had never seen the like before, and she was surprised at the strange yearning it evoked. She promptly quelled it.

Truly, she was a lucky woman. Foisting herself upon a stranger steeped in rumor, she had found herself a man who let her run his household, pleasured her in bed and, for the most part, gave her good company. Was she so shallow that she was unhappy with these gifts?

No, Aisley told herself, and she put aside thoughts of the darkness that shrouded her life and the curiosity that plagued her. She turned her attention back to her writing, but the words were difficult to compose. She kept thinking of her husband up in the great chamber, alone in the gloom.

What did he do all day? Did he miss hunting and hawking and training his men? Aisley knew that at one time Piers must have done all those things. What had led him to this solitary life? Was it truly an interest in sorcery, or something else? She frowned, frustrated by all the questions for which she could find no answers. She had always solved any of the myriad household problems that had faced her by approaching them logically, yet the Red Knight's bizarre behavior seemed to defy reason.

She was consistently blocked in her efforts to discover more about him. Cecil would tell her nothing, Alan had been close mouthed and Piers went into a rage whenever she broached the subject of his exile. And if there was one thing that distressed her more than the shadows, it was Piers's temper. She had no wish to draw it upon herself.

From the corner of her eye, Aisley saw Cecil head toward the cellars and realized that she had been lost in her somber thoughts, the letter to her steward unwritten before her. With a sigh, she turned her attention to her task. When finished, she rose and chanced to notice the other Cecil hurrying outside. 'Twas rare, she knew, that neither brother was attending his master.... Was no one guarding the Red Knight's lair? Aisley felt a sudden impulse to see for herself.

Without stopping to consider her actions, she quickly slipped into the dark stairwell that led to the great chamber, her sense of braving the forbidden becoming stronger with each step. Of course, no one was ever allowed into

Piers's room uninvited except the Cecils, who presumably did all the cleaning and were the only ones to wait upon their lord.

Although one or the other of the twins was usually lingering outside, there was really no need for a guard. Who would dare approach the Red Knight's own den? Even those with an invitation were apt to be reluctant; Aisley could not imagine anyone entering without permission.

And yet, that's exactly what she planned to do.

She couldn't help herself. Here was an opportunity to learn more about her husband, for what could be more revealing than his own chamber by day? Would he be there? When alone, did he allow some light to pierce the gloom? Aisley tried to picture Piers's room ablaze with candles and could not, but it might be so. And if it were, perhaps she could catch a glimpse of him. Or, if he were gone, mayhap she could find some clue, an answer to her eternal questions about the Red Knight.

Her heart was thumping wildly by the time she reached his door and found no one waiting outside it. Without hesitating, she pushed open the heavy wood, then slid inside and quietly shut it behind her. She turned slowly, breath held, to take in the scene, but no revelations met her questing gaze.

As usual, the great chamber was dark, glowing an eerie red near the fire, steeped in shadows elsewhere. Was he gone? The only sound was the hiss of the burning wood. Then Aisley heard something else, a thump and the soft padding of feet. The dogs! She had forgotten them, she realized, as she saw one move around the edge of Piers's bed and lift his head to stare at her.

"Aisley?" She nearly jumped from her skin at the sound of Piers's voice, emanating from the blackness. "What is it, my wife?" he asked. Aisley tried to judge her husband's mood from his tone, but her heart was pounding too loudly. Was he angry or pleased at her entrance, uninvited?

She wet her lips and tried to speak. "Piers, if I may disturb you for a moment?" Her unsteady words threatened to give her away, and she forced herself to talk calmly. "I have written a letter to my steward—at Belvry—that I would read to you, for your approval."

"Where is Cecil?" he asked.

"I saw him going out as I came up," Aisley said, declining to explain her precipitous rush to the great chamber. "If you are too busy..."

"No. Sit down, please." His dry tone, back in evidence, told her in no uncertain terms that he saw right through her ruse. "Read me this missive," he said.

Aisley sat by the fire, held up the letter to the light and did as her husband bade her. When she'd finished, she put it down, pleased that her voice had not wavered. Now she had only to wait for his response.

Although Aisley cared for Piers more than she had ever thought possible, he still had the power to intimidate her, and like a guilty child stealing a sweet, she knew she had sought forbidden fruit by coming here. Would he scold her? She tensed, dreading his ferocious temper.

"Very well done," Piers said, and Aisley felt weak with relief. "I would send it with all speed. Did you miss me, Wife?" he asked, so suddenly and so smoothly that Aisley was slow to heed the change in topic.

"Yes," she answered, for 'twas the truth. She always missed him, although she tempered her longing as best she could.

"Then come here," he urged huskily.

Surprised and pleased, Aisley walked into the shadows, ignoring the dogs, which now nudged her legs in greeting. Somehow she met Piers in the darkness. "You are a hot wench who cannot stay away from her husband," he said hoarsely, his lips moving against her hair.

"'Tis the sad truth," she replied, slipping her arms around his waist. She rested her head against his great chest, while his fingers combed through her hair. He lifted a heavy handful and kissed it.

"Sad for you, perhaps, but a delight to me," he said softly, his voice oddly serious.

Aisley hugged him tightly, though it was like gripping the bole of a tree. "No. 'Tis a joy to me," she whispered.

"Aisley..." The word was like a groan, torn from his throat, and then his mouth was upon her own, making her blood leap in response. The mysteries that surrounded the Red Knight were momentarily forgotten as he worked his undeniable magic on her, and Aisley let her duties go unheeded to spend the morning in her husband's bed.

As the day of the feast rapidly approached, Edith become more and more willing to help. In fact, the change that had come over the servant since their arrival at Dunmurrow truly astounded Aisley. As often as not, she found Edith humming to herself merrily while she went about her duties, and this morning was no exception.

"I believe we shall have plenty of cakes, my lady, but we should bake more bread, so that the villeins may take some loaves home with them," Edith said.

Aisley smiled to herself. "So you think now that a bit of extra bread will bring them around?" she asked as they watched more benches being hauled in for the upcoming festivities.

"Yes, my lady," Edith answered readily. "'Twill do the people good to have a day of plenty and celebration."

Edith's comment was so different from her initial opinions about the feast that Aisley could not help teasing her a bit. "Even if the Red Knight does not join them?" she asked.

"Well, you understand that I still can't approve of him, but seeing as how Willie says he's a good man and must have his own reasons for doing what he does, I guess I shall reserve my judgment," Edith said.

Aisley felt a brief stab of pique that her servant would believe Willie over herself, until she realized that she might not have defended her husband adequately—or vehemently—enough. Certainly, she had always scoffed at the rumors about him, but had she actually told Edith that her husband was good and kind and gentle and... passionate? Aisley flushed. "Of course he's a good man," she said.

"Well, I suppose he must be, as Willie thinks so highly of him, though I admit I still have my doubts." Edith gave a swift shake of her head. Her musings were interrupted by Willie himself, who ambled in from the kitchens, a cup of ale in his hand.

"Edie, Glenna wants you in the kitchens," he mumbled, his mouth full of something edible.

"And just what were you doing there?" Edith asked, accusingly pointing a finger. "Filling yourself up with the seed cakes meant for the feast, I suppose!"

Willie grinned, showing telltale crumbs in his teeth but not one bit of remorse, and Edith marched off, clucking loudly.

Smiling absently, Aisley turned her attention to the additional tables, then abruptly glanced back at Willie, who had seated himself at a bench by the fire. Suddenly, as if seeing him for the first time, she realized that he knew her husband.

According to Edith, Willie thought highly of the Red Knight, so he must know the man, perhaps know him well. Presumably, Willie had been in the baron's service for some time, so he just might have answers to some of the questions that plagued her.

Aisley felt her heart quicken at the possibility, and she seated herself near him, all the while keeping an eye out for Edith. She wanted this conversation to be private. "Willie," she began, hardly daring to look at him. "You have served the Red Knight for a long time, have you not?"

"That I have," he answered gruffly before taking a deep draught of ale.

Aisley waited, but no more comments were forthcoming. Willie simply wiped his mouth with the back of his hand and stared into the hearth flames. Apparently, the soldier was voluble only when the mood struck him—or the topic was one of his own choosing.

"How long?" Aisley asked.

"Oh, years, my lady," he answered, but it was not much of an answer.

What does he look like? Aisley desperately wanted to ask, but she felt shame brighten her cheeks. How could she admit to this man—this friendly, wise swain of Edith's—that she had never set eyes upon her husband?

"Them that join with the Red Knight usually stay, for he is a fair man and a great warrior," Willie added.

But what does he look like? So close but yet so far from discovering some truth about her husband, Aisley clenched her fists tightly in her lap. "I imagine his size alone was imposing to the enemy," she said aloud.

"Yes," Willie replied with a nod. "He's a big man."

And? Aisley felt like prodding Willie with her knife in order to get the information she sought. What about his hair, his eyes, his face? "Did he . . . frighten them?" Aisley asked.

"Well, of course," Willie said. "Especially after he got his name, the Red Knight, from Edward Himself. And then all the stories rose up about him." He made a sound that denoted his disgust with the strange rumors.

So Willie did not countenance the tales of sorcery, either, Aisley mused, but the soldier did admit that Piers was frightening in appearance. She drew in a sharp breath at the revelation. Piers must have been born with some deformity or been scarred hideously in battle, yet not in a way she could detect with her fingertips. "Willie," she said seriously, "why doesn't he train the men himself any more?"

The soldier gazed down into his cup and then up at her, his dark eyes forthright. "Well, I can't say for sure. We, the lot of us under the Red Knight's command, thought that when he got the place here he deserved a rest, and I just imagine that's what he's doing.''

A rest? Aisley nearly choked on that answer, which did nothing to explain the myriad mysteries surrounding Piers Montmorency. "But he never leaves his chamber!" she protested.

"Is that so?" Willie asked. His voice was bland, giving the impression that he did not think the Red Knight's behavior odd or even interesting. "I wouldn't know, my lady," he said, rising. "Now, if you will excuse me, I am supposed to keep an eye on Edith, you see."

Aisley stayed where she was, watching him go and knowing that he would reveal nothing. Piers had chosen those around him well, she acknowledged, while the bitter taste of being left in the darkness lingered in her mouth.

With a frown, she moved to pick up Willie's forgotten cup. It still held some ale, which had been warmed by the fire, and the feel of it reminded Aisley of the Widow Nebbs's potion. If only there was some herb that would make men talk freely, then she would have all the answers she sought, Aisley decided with a wry smile.

She drew in a sharp breath as an idea struck her. Unfortunately, she knew of naught that would make a man speak truthfully, but there were many other herbs, each with its own special powers....

Aisley clutched the sleeping draught tightly in one hand while she lifted the other to knock upon the door to the great chamber. She heard Piers's brusque call to enter, and yet her feet faltered at the entrance.

It was not too late to turn from her task. Aisley knew she had only to slip what she held into her gown and be done with it. But she rarely wavered from a course once she had set it in her mind, and this night was no different. Wetting her lips nervously, she opened the door and stepped inside.

"'Tis Aisley, my lord," she said.

"You are early, my wife," Piers noted. "Are you eager for your food this evening?" She heard the wry note in his voice, which suggested she might be anxious for his love-making, and she hesitated. Although always ready for her husband's attentions, she could not afford to receive them now, for it might spoil her plans. She needed Piers in her bed later this night—not here, not now.

"Yes, I am starving!" Aisley answered, as if oblivious to his hints. Although Piers spoke no more, she could feel his disappointment. It emanated from him, and she would have smiled had she not been so wary.

She seated herself on her usual bench, and, discovering the table empty, eased out a long, slow breath. Usually, the food was in place when she appeared, but tonight, as she had hoped, she had arrived before Cecil. To fill the quiet, Aisley spoke of her day and her duties, her mind ever elsewhere, her ears listening for her husband's servant.

At last the knock came, and Aisley schooled herself to sit immobile until Cecil put out the trenchers. The man must have the eyes of a cat to pierce this gloom, Aisley thought, suppressing a shiver of apprehension. What if he should note her deed? But it was too late to change her mind. When Cecil put down her husband's cup, her hand shot out, ostensibly to settle it firmly in place, and in that moment, she opened her palm and shook out the contents of the packet she'd been clutching.

Tonight her husband would sleep with her.

Cecil was dismissed, and the meal progressed, as usual, in the darkness. Aisley told Piers of her preparations for the Christmas feast as she picked at her food, her hand stilling every time he lifted his cup. Had she given him too much sleeping draught? Not enough? He was a big man, and the timing was so crucial. When Aisley heard him yawn, she moved to her feet.

"Come to me, Piers," she said softly. "I will await you in my chamber." She heard the soft sound of his pleased chuckle, and then she was out the door, trying to slow her racing heart as she hurried back to her room.

Although they had shared both her bed and his, Aisley knew that Piers preferred to come to her so that he might leave before dawn. Always he kept to the darkness, and in the darkness, he held her, his hands and mouth knowing all of her, his man part thrusting deep within her and making them seem as one until she cried out in ecstasy, and yet...

Despite all the intimacies that had taken place between them, she knew that if she met her husband in the daylight, she would not know him.

The situation was intolerable. Aisley could not understand the shadows anymore now than when she'd been first ushered into his presence. She clung to the idea that her husband was disfigured in some way not readily apparent, that some discoloration marked his face or that he was misshapen in a manner her fingers could not detect, for the alternative was even more ominous.

Although Edith no longer offered her opinions, Aisley could easily recall the rumors that surrounded her husband. She knew that the man who bedded her was no evil sorcerer, and yet a niggling doubt crept upon her during the long daylight hours without him, a doubt she wanted to put to rest.

She had hoped that with time, Piers would come to trust her, that he would reveal himself to her as he did to Alan and the Cecils. Truth to tell, she was stung by his lack of faith in her, by the barrier that he put between them. Perhaps someday he would relent, but Aisley was not a patient woman. She would wait no longer.

Tonight she would view her husband's face and form.

Aisley lay against Piers's broad chest, listening to his even breathing and the slow, sure beating of his heart. Her own was racing as she tried to remain still and judge whether he only rested or truly slept. Piers had moved slower tonight, as if the herbs were already working, urging him to slumber, yet Aisley had enjoyed his attentions no less. At the memory of their passion, a sob formed in her throat. Was she doing the right thing? Now that the time had come, she felt more dread than relief at the prospect of viewing the Red Knight.

"Piers?" she whispered. He did not answer.

Although loath to hurry, Aisley was unsure just how long the potion would keep him sleeping, and she had no desire to be caught staring at him. The very notion sent fear tingling up her spine. This was the Red Knight, the scourge of the north, a man reputed to be in league with the devil himself....

She sat up and pulled back the bed hangings, determined to say she was tending to a call of nature, if Piers should waken. Silently, she slipped on a robe, moved to where her gown was lying and groped for the pocket in which she had hidden a thick candle. In her haste, she nearly dropped it, and she cursed softly before she stepped to the fire and lit it with trembling hands. Then she forced herself to walk to the bed.

Drawing a deep breath, Aisley bent toward her sleeping husband and raised the candle. The light fell upon a man tall and broad, a knight of enormous stature, and though shivering with dread, she pulled back the blankets that covered him to look upon the body of her husband for the very first time.

His legs were huge and muscular and covered with fair hair, lending his skin a warm cast. His maleness, big even at rest, lay in a dark blond thatch at his groin, and above, his flat stomach rose and fell gently with each breath. One of his hands reposed there, large and long fingered, and seeing no disfigurement, Aisley raised her eyes further.

She saw that his chest was smooth and broad, his skin golden, his shoulders incredibly wide, his arms bulging with strength, and she gasped. There was nothing wrong with his body, Aisley thought giddily. He looked like a golden god, sculpted to perfection.

With a tremor of trepidation, Aisley lifted the light to his face, where she would surely find the reason why he cloaked himself in shadows.... Slowly, his features became illuminated, and a sound of shock and amazement died in her throat at what she beheld.

Piers Montmorency was beautiful.

Burnished hair lay close to his head and curled along his neck. His brow was clean and straight, his eyes deep set with thick lashes. High cheekbones led down to a strong jaw and lips that were generously curved, but not too full. His narrow nose had a bump in it, as if it had been broken, but that did nothing to mar his face—the face of an archangel—nor did the scar that slashed across one eyebrow toward his hairline.

Aisley stepped closer. Holding the candle with one hand while the other clutched her throat in dismay, she looked for something—anything—to explain the darkness in which this man hid himself. Tentatively, she reached out to touch the white scar, none too old, that ran to his eye, and released an uneasy breath. She had seen worse, far worse, on other knights, and it did nothing to take away from Piers's beauty. On the contrary, it made his handsome visage more potent, more real . . . as if Gabriel had come away from a joust with the devil.

The devil. Aisley couldn't, wouldn't think it, and she backed away, whispering a prayer. As she stared, Piers stirred, and suddenly the enormity of what she had done struck her to the core. She nearly dropped the candle in her rush to pull the bed hangings closed. Then she blew out the stub and fumbled to replace it in her gown. Finally, she returned to the side of the bed, but she only stood there uncertainly as confusion swamped her.

Aisley licked her lips, afraid to return to her husband's side, yet ashamed of her own fears. She clenched her fists, angry with herself, as she struggled. Before her marriage, she had never been frightened of anything—not the dark, not the absence of her mother, not tales of ghosts or evil beings that made Edith shiver, not even the hollowness of a life she had filled with duties instead of love.

With a sob, Aisley slipped off her robe and climbed under the blankets. Tears that had not marked her cheeks for years fell unheeded as she put her arms around her husband and rested her head against his massive, perfect chest. With blinding clarity, Aisley realized that no matter who he was or what he was, the Red Knight had filled up an emptiness inside her that she had never known existed.

She loved him.

Chapter Twelve

Aisley awoke gently to warmth and comfort. She rubbed her cheek against heated skin, reveling in the scent and feel of her husband. Was she dreaming or did his great chest rise and fall beneath her head? At the thought, she came alert in an instant, for she knew instinctively that he should not be with her.

What time was it? Aisley felt a swift surge of panic as the memory of her recklessness the evening before returned. Her misdeed had been compounded tenfold, she thought wildly, for she must have given Piers too much sleeping draught. Obviously, it had kept him abed with her all night, and now there was no way to pretend that nothing had happened. There was no way they could go on as before....

For the first time, the image of her husband took shape in her mind, and Aisley shivered. She saw the golden god who lay with her, knew every aspect of him save the color of his eyes and realized that nothing could have sent him into darkness but a pact with the devil.

As if her thoughts troubled him, Piers stirred beside her, and Aisley wondered again at the hour. Then she had her answer, for she heard Edith's knock upon the door. "My lady, are you well?" the servant asked as she entered. "'Tis past your time to rise."

Aisley swallowed hard. "Yes, I am fine, Edith, but I wish to stay abed awhile longer," she said evenly. "Go about your other duties and leave me for now."

Despite her dismissal, Edith moved to the window, for Aisley heard her footsteps and the creak of the shutters. "Are you sure you are all right?" she asked, and Aisley cursed her servant's concern. What if the woman opened the hangings?

"I am fine, Edith. I am with my husband. Leave us!" she commanded.

Nothing could have sent Edith scurrying away with more haste than mention of the Red Knight, and Aisley couldn't help smiling when she heard the door shut firmly.

Her smile faded at the sound of her husband's bitter groan. "'Tis morning?" he asked groggily.

"Yes," Aisley answered. "'Tis the morning before Christmas," she said evenly. "And you are in my bed." With more calm than she felt, she pulled aside the curtains and sat back upon her heels. For a moment, she hesitated. Would she find him transformed into a hideous beast with the dawn? Whatever the consequences, she knew she must look, and with her heart thudding in her breast, she turned to see light streaming onto the bed, illuminating her husband.

Aisley drew in a breath, for despite her fears, Piers had not changed into a horned creature with the morn. He was even more handsome than she remembered. She had suspected that the candlelight might have given him a glow that had enhanced his charms, but she was wrong. Even in the harsh sunlight, Piers was glorious.

He was a huge man, but well proportioned, his broad chest tapering to a flat stomach and narrow hips that disappeared under the blankets. His muscular arms were covered with blond hair, the same hair that lay in bright waves upon her pillow, shining in the light. He lay on his back, one thick arm flung across his eyes, his brows drawn down in anguish, as if to deny her presence. But there was no mistaking the high cheekbones, the strong jaw and the generous lips that she had glimpsed last night.

"You are beautiful, my husband," Aisley said softly as her eyes traveled over him. She longed to reach out to him, as if by her touch she would make this vision real, but Piers rolled away from her and threw his legs over the other side of the bed, thrashing angrily at the curtains.

"Leave me!" he bellowed. "Call Cecil to me, and leave me, you stupid wench!"

Flinching at his words, Aisley rose and slipped on a robe. Instead of summoning Cecil, however, she walked around the bed to where her husband sat, his head in his hands. She felt something heavy in her chest as she approached him, something that made her throat thick and her eyelids sting.

It was not fear, even though Aisley knew he could easily knock her across the room with a careless swing of his arm. She knew how intense his wrath could be, how very frightening he was in a rage, and yet she could not turn from him. Swallowing hard, she knelt before him and touched his fingers, dragging them from his face. "Do not send me away," she whispered.

With a groan, Piers lifted his head, and Aisley was again shocked by his beauty. Golden hair framed a face such as she had never imagined, and then she drew in a quick breath of surprise. Eyes the color of the brightest, loveliest robin's egg returned her gaze. Overwhelmed by some emotion that threatened to choke her, she swallowed hard, unable to turn her attention from his eyes. Such a beautiful blue they were, and yet...

They saw her not.

Aisley fell back on her heels, reeling with the force of the revelation, and suddenly everything became clear: the darkness, the isolation and the ever-present servants. The Red Knight was no sorcerer, and he took not to the shadows because of any disfigurement.

The Red Knight was blind.

Piers remained still under her regard, his face closed and hard as if he was prepared for some blow. It was a chilling look, a look that would have sent the fainthearted scurrying away, but Aisley was strong and she did not move. "When?" she asked.

She was unprepared for his sudden movement and tottered on her heels when he burst from the bed. He thrust her away from him, knocking her to the floor, while he cursed viciously, his normally dry voice roaring in fury. Aisley got to her feet, her heart in her throat as she watched him, for he was truly like a rampaging beast, crashing around the room, kicking aside the settle and all else in his path. When he tripped against a chest, he hefted it high and tossed it against the wall, breaking the heavy wood to pieces while Aisley cowered against the bed.

She was frightened then, more frightened than she had ever been in her life. Her dread of sorcery, of spells and shadows and night creatures, was as nothing compared to the terror that gripped her now, for here was a stranger, a huge, ferocious, unpredictable stranger, who might be capable of anything. And there was no reasoning with him, she knew. Putting her trembling hands over her ears to shut out his bellows, Aisley closed her eyes tightly against the sight of such raw emotion raging out of control.

The ensuing silence made her open her eyes again, and she saw that Piers was still now, panting, his face turned toward her, its handsome features twisted with hatred. "I ought to kill you," he said softly.

Aisley felt the words like a blow, and truly, she would rather have been struck. Did she mean so little to him? All the gentleness, all the teasing, all the passion that existed between them ... had it all been as nothing? And just as suddenly as it had filled her, the fear drained away, replaced by an emptiness, an unnatural calm that settled over her as though she were dead inside.

Aisley lifted her chin, steeling herself against useless tears. God knew she had spent enough of them last night, and for what? This morning her precious husband wanted her dead. "Do not speak to me so, even in anger," she said evenly. "I asked you when this happened, and I would have an answer."

Piers turned and stretched a hand out, feeling for the wall. Then he leaned his arm against it, his head turned away from her, his wrath apparently spent. He was still naked, and Aisley tried to ignore the bulging muscles of his back, his taut buttocks, his long legs. A golden god he was, his body still a marvel to her....

"Months ago!" he spat out.

"How?" Aisley asked.

"In battle," he answered. "I wasn't wearing a helm, only a coif, so that my eyes were unprotected when one of the cursed Welshmen took me down on the ground. He nicked my face and then sought to finish me, but Alan caught him from behind. His axe still fell—into a rock next to my head. I was showered in blood and sparks, as if afire, and..." Piers's words trailed off. "I remember naught else but the pain."

Aisley's heart constricted, spreading life through her again. She longed to walk to him, to wrap her arms around that massive back—to hug him to her and make him whole again. But she stood still, unwilling to enrage him again and unable to bear it should he flail her further with his sharp tongue. "I know a little of healing. Maybe I can help," she said.

Piers pushed away from the wall, snorting loudly. "Don't you think I've tried?" he shouted. "I've had every sorcerer, quack and woman pretender brought here, but nothing can be done!"

Aisley stood firm as he stepped toward her, one great fist raised in the air as if to smite her. "I know nothing of these others, but I do have a fair knowledge of healing. Let me try, at least," she urged.

"Why?" Piers asked, his tone mocking. "Because you wish to have a real man to husband? A knight who can protect your holdings, not a blind fool, hanging on to something that can be wrested from him in an instant?"

"You are not helpless," Aisley replied. "You have men, and Alan to lead them—"

Piers cut her off with a snort. "A fine show, but 'twill do us little good if the truth gets out! This cloak of sorcery will only protect us for so long," he explained roughly. "'Tis only a matter of time before someone questions the legend and tries to oust me, or challenges my right to the property *you* brought to me."

"But surely, the king—" Aisley protested.

Piers laughed bitterly. "Think you Edward needs a blind vassal to protect his interests? To fight his wars and guard his borders? I think not! He knows of my uselessness, and he has let me be, but he cannot protect me. Sooner or later, the myth will crumble and we will be overrun. And then what of you?"

"Then we will do what we must," Aisley said evenly.

Piers laughed again, a cruel sound. "What think you now of your fine choice, my lady?" he asked, his voice taunting her. "Do you not regret it?"

"No!" she shouted back at him. "I regret nothing, and you cannot make me for all your hateful words!" She broke off into a sob, and before she knew what he was about, he was there, pulling her to his hard chest. She slid her arms around him and pressed her cheek against his skin. In truth, she regretted nothing but his harsh speech, which lost some of its chill in the warmth of his embrace.

He did not mean it; Aisley knew that as surely as she could hear the steady beating of his heart. Piers did not wish her dead, nor did he want her to renounce her choice of husband. He had spoken from vulnerability and from a pain so vast that she could not even begin to comprehend it. Here was a great warrior used to living out-of-doors, a strong, clever leader of men who was reduced to hiding himself away—first in Dunmurrow and then, after she'd come, exiled in the great chamber, sightless and alone.

It was a heartrending image, but struck suddenly by the utter absurdity of her previous suspicions, Aisley giggled. Although she felt his body stiffen, she could not help the tremulous bubble of laughter that escaped her. "And I thought you were a creature of the devil, bound to the darkness by some pact for your soul," she muttered, shaking her head against his chest.

"All the horrible stories about you that Edith told me...I swore not to credit them, but what else could I believe? I tell you this now, Piers Montmorency, I would much rather be in love with a blind man than some evil demon!" she said.

Piers tensed, and his head jerked up. "What say you?" he asked.

"I thank God you are not the man that you have painted yourself," Aisley whispered. "For whether you intended it or not, I—I was afraid that you might be."

His hands found her face, and he lifted it, running his fingers over her features as if consuming her with his very touch. His own face held an intensity she had never seen in anyone before, and Aisley was again struck by the strength of his emotions, which soared and dove to depths beyond those of other men. He was still holding himself back, Aisley could tell, but even so, the force of what she sensed inside him, barely restrained, made her tremble. "And?" he asked hoarsely.

"And I love you," Aisley said simply. She shivered in his arms with the release of her fears, with the acquisition of new ones and with the knowledge that come what may, she loved. And though 'twas bittersweet, Aisley would rather have known that love than to have lived a long, empty life without it.

She thought he might kiss her then, but he only hugged her to him, so tightly that she could barely breathe. "Aisley..." he whispered, the word seemingly torn from his throat. She could hear his heart hammering in his chest, as if he held all of his great passion inside him and soon, very soon, it might burst its bounds. For a moment, she thought he might say more, shattering his control, but he only embraced her silently.

Finally, she drew back and lifted her head. "Come, sit by the fire and let me have a look, at least," she said. Taking his hand, Aisley led her husband to the hearth, where she righted the settle and bade him sit. Then she touched a hand to his rough cheek and gazed into his beautiful blue eyes.

They were such a bright color, so alive, that it was difficult to believe they were useless. "Do they hurt you?" she asked, her heart breaking at the thought. Piers merely grunted, which told her that he was in far more pain than he would ever admit. Aisley swallowed hard. "From your tale, I suspect that shards of rock or metal were buried in your eyes," she said, though she could see nothing there now. "You washed them out after it happened?"

"Yes, for all the good that it did," he said.

Aisley pressed her lips together. Usually such things came out, but perhaps the slivers had scarred his eyes in some way, so that Piers would never see. She frowned, refusing to accept that his condition might be permanent. "I learned much from an ancient herbalist in our village before she died," Aisley said evenly, while her mind raced over possible solutions.

Her patient snorted. "I have drunk enough noxious mixtures to kill me!" he answered. "And the last one nearly did. I writhed for days with stomach cramps, and that was that. I sought no more *healing*," he said dryly.

"But you spoke with a doctor?" Aisley asked.

Piers grunted. "I saw many a so-called physician," he said, "though I gave them not my true name. The last was a traveling surgeon who wanted to remove one eye that I might regain my vision in the other!''

Aisley gasped in horror and stroked his cheek possessively while she tried to think of something, anything, that might help him. "There's a Lady's well near Woolpit in Suffolk for diseases of the eye," she said.

"No! I believe not in such foolishness," Piers grumbled.

Aisley sighed. "Then I shall make a draught for you that will ease the pain."

"I have eaten my last toad's liver, thank you!" Piers said.

"I shall make a draught," Aisley repeated. "And you will drink it, for I am your wife, and I fear not the Red Knight's wrath." Dropping her hand from his cheek, she was suddenly aware that her husband was sitting naked before her, his big, golden body shining in the firelight.

Her heart pounding at the sight, Aisley lifted a finger and trailed it slowly down his hard chest. "You are beautiful, Piers," she said softly. She heard his quick breath, and feared that he might fling her to the floor in a frenzy. Not that she would mind. But at long last she could see her husband, and she wished to explore every inch of him—at her leisure.

"Hold still now that I might complete my...ministrations," she said brokenly. She leaned toward him, resting a hand on each of his wide shoulders, and pressed kisses to his cheek, his jaw and his strong neck. Her mouth moved down his smooth skin to his broad chest, where she ran her tongue round one of his nipples, then drew it into her mouth.

His great body seemed to leap to life, and he grunted fiercely, but Aisley laid a hand upon his thigh to still him. Power, barely restrained, throbbed in his muscles, and she felt a heady rush of warmth sweep through her. This was her husband in all his manly glory: gentle lover, fierce warrior and vulnerable man. Aisley traced with her tongue each scar that marked him, ran her hands over his thick arms and legs, and pressed him back onto the settle when he would have surged from it.

"Let me, Piers," she whispered. "Let me see all of you, finally.... You are so very beautiful." He growled low, and his knuckles tightened as he gripped the edge of his seat. With her heart racing, Aisley knelt between his legs and kissed his inner thigh. His maleness was huge and hard in the light, and she hovered over it, listening to his harsh breathing, before putting her mouth on him.

For a moment, Piers's whole frame went rigid, then she felt his big hands in her hair, clutching the locks, pulling her head toward him, and he growled low in his throat, a sound that made her wet between the legs and caused her to bend more thoroughly to her task. Her fingers dug into the muscles of his thigh, and he pushed forward, bucking against her, grunting and groaning, until his great body shuddered again and again and a shout of pleasure was torn from his throat.

"How did you manage to hide such beauty from the world?" Aisley asked as she made lazy circles with her fingers across the wide planes of her husband's chest.

Piers snorted beside her. He crossed his arms behind his head and rested against them, while Aisley admired the muscles that corded them. The light from the fire danced upon the golden body lying in her bed, and Aisley sighed contentedly.

"I hate to disillusion you, Wife," Piers said in the particularly dry tone of his, "but women have rarely gushed about my beauty before."

It was Aisley's turn to snort. "Ha! I do not believe it, Piers Montmorency! Why, a woman would have to be..."

"Blind?" Piers supplied.

"Sorry," Aisley muttered, burying her face in his side. "But 'tis true! A woman would have to be sightless or half-dead not to swoon at your feet," she said.

Piers laughed, the deep, rumbling sound sending shivers of delight through her, and Aisley thought he was so wonderful that she might burst with joy for the love of him. "The only women to ever swoon at my feet were the ones who heard I was marching on their lands," he noted wryly.

"But surely, at court..." Aisley could not finish her words as she envisioned Piers surrounded by ladies batting their eyelashes and giggling and thrusting their bosoms at him.

"I've rarely been to court, Aisley," he said. "I have spent most of my life in the field, and once I acquired my bizarre reputation, I was not the man most women wished to meet."

Aisley sensed there was something he was not telling her. "I still don't believe you. You have probably had ladies vying for your attentions since birth," she protested.

Piers's generous mouth curved up at the corners. "Not quite. When I was a young man in Normandy, I had my share of conquests, but when I joined with Edward, someone called me his pretty vassal. Perhaps I tried too hard to live that down in battle and swung opinion to the other direction with my fierceness."

Aisley smiled. "So you were glad when the king dubbed you the Red Knight?" she asked.

"'Tis better than being called the Pretty Vassal," Piers replied with disgust.

Aisley laughed against his chest. "But really, Piers, how is it that you came not to be wed sooner?"

His smile was bitterly self-mocking. "I was too busy making war."

"Making a name for yourself as a blood-thirsty devil," Aisley teased.

"That, too," Piers agreed. "I had no time for maidens while I sought to better my lot, and later, my fearsome reputation did little to draw them to me—with one notable exception," he said, stretching out an arm to rest a hand in her hair.

"I am happy that your beauty is the best-kept secret in the kingdom, for I wish to share you with no one," Aisley noted. "I find, now that I am married, that I am very possessive of what is mine."

"Didn't I say something like that myself?" Piers asked with a grin, and Aisley was dazzled by the sight of his strong, white teeth.

"I believe you did . . . on the night you first came to my chamber," she whispered.

"Good. I'm pleased we agree on something," Piers said. His easy expression changed then, and Aisley recognized the intensity that came over his features as he brought down his other arm. "Shall I remind you that you are mine, my wife?" he asked, his hands roaming over her body in slow, exquisite strokes.

"Please . . ." Aisley whispered, and she pulled his head down to meet her kiss.

"Good morning, Husband," Aisley breathed as she stepped away from the window. She had opened the shutters, and now she pulled the hangings away from the bed, so that the pale light of Christmas morn shone through the narrow opening onto the sleeping form of the Red Knight.

Aisley drank in his features like one whose throat was parched. His figure had been a dark mystery to her for so long that she knew she could never see enough of him, would never tire of looking upon him.

Thick, golden hair fell in waves about a face that was sculpted like a god's—a god of war, Aisley thought, for the scar that ran across his temple, coupled with a smaller one at his mouth, proclaimed his profession to the world. And yet, those imperfections were nothing when met with the stark glory of his rough-hewn features: the strong jaw, the narrow nose and the firm lips, curved in repose. Piers Montmorency was the most beautiful man she had ever seen.

"You opened the shutters," he said.

Aisley started at the words, for she had thought him still slumbering. But Piers was a knight first and foremost, she remembered, and knights were not trained to sleep soundly while at the mercy of others. "How did you know?" she asked.

"I can feel the draft. Were you admiring me again, Wife?" he asked in that dry tone of his. He opened his eyes, and she was startled anew by the intensity of their color, the rich blue of a robin's egg.

"Yes," Aisley answered wholeheartedly. "I vow you are the handsomest man I have ever seen." She sighed with pleasure just to see his face, to see his generous lips curved in amusement. "Oh, Piers, you have a wonderful smile!" she said. She was prevented by elaborating further by a strong arm that pulled her down against his hard chest and his mouth, warm and coaxing, upon her own.

Aisley felt his magic, his man magic, work into her soul, hot and blissful, but she could not succumb this time. She pulled away, resting a hand on one of his massive shoulders. "I must hurry or I will miss morning Mass," she said. She wriggled out of her husband's arms and off the bed.

"Mass? How? With what priest?" Piers asked, a bit annoyed to have his pleasure postponed.

"That is why I must not be late!" Aisley said, rushing around the room. "I am he!"

"You have taken up the cloth now?" Piers asked wryly. He sat up in bed, revealing his gleaming chest to Aisley's hurried gaze.

She paused at the sight. "Oh, Piers, you are so beautiful! Would that I could stay and love you again in the daylight, but I must be gone," she said, her voice heavy with disappointment.

"Tell me this tale of your new vocation first," Piers ordered. "Need I fear your imminent promotion to bishop?"

Aisley laughed as she put on her gown. "No. Although I have requested a chaplain for Dunmurrow to administer to its people and the villagers, it is much too soon to expect a response." She paused as she buttoned her sleeves. "You don't mind, do you, Piers?" she threw over her shoulder.

His response was somewhere between a groan and a laugh. "Would it matter if I did?" he asked.

Aisley bit her lip. "If they send one, you won't frighten him away, will you? Or annoy him into getting you excommunicated?" She eyed her husband warily across the room, but he was grinning at her. Crossing his strong arms behind his neck, he shook his head.

"Thank you, Piers!" Aisley said as she donned her slippers. Then she rushed over to the bed. "In the meantime, we have no one to say Christmas Mass, so I will lead a few prayers in the chapel before the feast."

"Ah," Piers grunted, still grinning. "'Tis good that you are not taking on the robes permanently, for I would not care for the vow of celibacy attendant upon such duties."

"Stop such talk," Aisley admonished, though she giggled. Fully dressed, she hopped onto the bed beside the glorious warrior that she had married. "You are misnamed, my lord," she said softly as she reached out a finger to trace the hard expanse of his chest. "In truth, 'tis a golden knight you are."

He grabbed her wrist so swiftly that she knew his reactions had not been slowed a bit by his blindness. "Cease and desist, my lady, unless you care to remove the clothes you just donned so diligently," he warned.

Aisley sighed. "You are right. I must go, not only to chapel, but to check upon the preparations for the feast. We will throw open the doors to the villagers and are prepared to feed them all! There is no boar's head, of course, but we have oxen aplenty, and venison and hare and fish—an abundance of dishes to whet your appetite, my lord," Aisley said proudly.

"Aisley," Piers cautioned. "I cannot attend your feast. You know that."

She paused just a moment in regret, although she knew that he could not. They were both aware that if his blindness were discovered, it would not be long before some greedy foe tried to take his lands. "I know," she agreed. "I shall join you later, but I would beg a boon for myself this Christmas day, Piers."

"And what is that?" he asked, his thick brows lowering suspiciously.

"Come outside with me," Aisley urged. She put a finger to his lips to halt his reply while she sought to convince him. "'Twould be only us two. You could wear a helm, and we could ride out just a little way," she pleaded. "I—I want you to come with me to look for the white stag."

"The white stag?" Piers asked, perplexed.

"Yes," Aisley said with a nod. "If you see a white stag on Christmas Day, 'tis an omen of good luck to come."

Piers snorted. "I have never heard of such a talisman."

"Perhaps it is a Celtic tale, for Edith told me of it when I was little, and each year I have gone out to try to spy him."

Although he could not see, Aisley knew that her husband sensed more than was visible to the eye, and he proved it. He lifted a hand to run his fingers through her hair. "Are you telling me that my efficient, organized chatelaine—my lady of the accounts—is a romantic at heart?"

"No!" Aisley scoffed, suddenly embarrassed. "I just . . . 'tis simply a tradition, is all," she mumbled, flustered.

Piers laughed, the deep, rich sound making her tingle all the way to her toes. "'Tis no crime, Aisley, to have a woman's heart," he said. She opened her mouth to argue, but he slid a heavy palm to where her heart throbbed in her chest, as if to prove its existence, and her body's swift, pleasurable reaction kept her from speech. "But as to your request ... is there naught else I might give you for Christmas?'' he said, his fingers grazing her breast.

Aisley drew in a breath. ''Yes, Piers,'' she said softly. ''But there is nothing I want more than to go outside with you in the day.''

He dropped his hand and frowned. '''Tis too dangerous.''

''Then have Cecil come along and remain at a discreet distance,'' Aisley suggested.

Piers snorted, but she would not give up. ''Please, Piers?'' she asked. She took one of his hands and covered it with both of her own.

He scowled, a truly disquieting look that transformed his handsome features into a forbidding visage, and Aisley could see from whence some of his fearsome reputation had sprung. She did not draw back, however, but squeezed his fingers tightly.

''Later, when your guests are deep in their cups,'' he answered shortly.

''Oh, thank you, Piers. You won't regret it. We shall have a lovely time, and perhaps this year we shall see him!''

''Who?'' Piers growled.

''The white stag!'' Aisley said. Then she dropped a quick kiss upon his lips and rose from the bed. ''I must go! Shall I lay out some clothes for you?'' she asked.

''No,'' Piers said, a hard edge still in his voice. ''Just send Cecil in to me. And, God's wounds, close the shutters!''

Chapter Thirteen

They rode silently at first, for Aisley wanted Piers simply to enjoy being out-of-doors. And there was much to enjoy. It was a mild day, the air bracing and clean, and winter birds could be heard, trilling their songs from the barren trees. Glad to be free of the castle's gloom, Aisley sighed contentedly. How could Piers not feel more alive in this glorious world? Though it was she who had begged the boon, Aisley thought the outing a fitting gift to her husband.

After a time, she began to describe the countryside to him, including little things that normally she would hardly notice: the sparkle when the sun caught a puddle, the shine of wet bark, the shapes of branches, stark against the sky, the burrowing of a mouse under a log.

She wanted to take Piers to the waterfall that Alan had showed her, but they were not far into the woods when he reined in his horse. "We are in the forest," he said accusingly.

"Yes," Aisley answered, wary of his tone. "I wish to show you something."

"Show me?" His voice was heavy with sarcasm.

"I wanted to take you to a special place, a beautiful spot in your demesne," Aisley explained.

"Aisley," Piers began, his voice thick with emotion. "You forget . . . not the woods," he said. *For I cannot pro-*

tect you. He did not speak the last aloud, for he could not force himself, could not sound out words he had never thought to say.

The bastard son of an earl, Piers had learned early how to take care of himself, how to fight for his own, and he had proved himself. He had proved himself again and again, until finally he had earned Dunmurrow.

It was not the most prosperous of lands, but Piers would have been well satisfied with it had it not been for the great irony—the irony that when what he'd fought for was finally within his grasp, he no longer had the wherewithal to keep it. Oh, he had Alan, and his men, quartered away from him, rarely seeing their former lord, in readiness still. But without him could they really defend his own?

The question chafed him constantly, but not as personally, never as fiercely as now, when the reality of his situation was reduced from defending rich ground and villagers and an old keep to protecting one single, perfect woman— one dainty being more precious to him then all else. And to know that he could not do it filled him with self-loathing.

"There is a pool...." Aisley said. The hesitancy, the hurt in her voice should have cooled his rage, but it did not. Did she not realize the dangers that lay among the trees? Although Cecil followed behind with a guard of six, the threat of brigands and wild beasts increased his own sense of deficiency until he could taste the bitterness on his tongue.

"Aye, I know it," he said.

"You know the pond with the waterfall?" Aisley's voice was as lilting as a harp or the song of a bird, and her excitement was plain. "You have been there?" she asked.

"Aye, I have seen it," Piers answered shortly.

"I thought you had never viewed your lands," she countered.

Piers grunted. "I came the moment I could get away, to see my newfound treasure," he said, more sharply than he intended. His lands had since lost their luster, for, as he had mused so often before, he would give up all just to have his sight restored. But it wasn't Aisley's fault, and he tried, with difficulty, to soften his words. This was, after all, the Christmas boon she had begged. "'Twas a lovely spot when I saw it in summer, the leaves lush and green and crowded around the pool. I washed there, and the water was clear and clean," he added.

"I knew it would be a wonderful bathing place!" Aisley said. "Come. 'Tis not far."

Against his better judgment, Piers acceded to her wishes, letting his great destrier pick its way along beside his wife's palfrey as they traveled deeper into the woods.

"We are here," Aisley finally said, and they halted. Piers could hear the stream rushing over rocks to fill the pool and the attendant sounds of water and barren trees creaking in the cold air. He could picture it, but he did not want to. He sat still and silent, refusing to share his wife's enjoyment and eager to be gone.

"Piers!" Aisley's voice, low and full of wonder, dragged him from his sullen mood. "I see him!"

"Who?" he asked in alarm.

"The white stag!" Aisley breathed.

Piers snorted. Did she think him a toddling infant to be entertained by her fancies?

"No, Piers," she whispered. "Do not scoff. He is there, at the edge of the trees, all white, a great buck with gigantic antlers. He is staring right at us...."

Piers would have rolled his eyes if the action didn't pain him so. What was this odd turn his wife had taken? Clever and accomplished, Aisley was happiest assuming the myriad duties of a busy household, not playing at childish games like some of the beetle-headed court women—unless she thought *he* was beetle-headed enough to believe her! Perhaps she suspected the loss of his sight had affected his intelligence. "Enough," Piers growled, and then he heard it— a movement in the brush.

He strained to listen as Aisley gasped. "Go to the left, Piers! 'Tis running directly to us!" she warned.

It? What? Before Piers's unseeing eyes flashed images of the wild boars that were known to provide good holiday hunting. Sweet Mother of God... As he urged his mount to the left, his hand went to his sword, but uncertain of Aisley's position or what she would do, he dared not unsheathe it.

The sound of hooves thundering past him assailed his ears, and then Aisley's horse snorting in fear and kicking the earth. And all the while Piers clutched the hilt of his blade, adrift in a horrible dream, blind and helpless. Then his very worst nightmare came to life. Aisley screamed, and a loud splash erupted as her mount fled. When the noises died away, what remained was even more frightening. The wood was utterly silent.

"Aisley?" Piers breathed her name into the stillness, but he was met with no reply. Either she had been swiftly and quietly abducted by a lone horseman, or she was in the pool, unable to answer him. His pain at the thought was physical, and he threw back his head, letting loose a roar of anguish that rent the air more loudly than any of his battle cries. Piers knew his guard would come, but how soon? How long could Aisley survive?

Without hesitation, he slid from his destrier, threw off his helm and his cloak and waded through the dead grasses at the waters edge. He knew the pool and tried to form a picture of it in his mind, but the brain that had functioned coolly through innumerable battles was fogged by dread. He bellowed again, in both fear and frustration, and cursed his own uselessness. Then something—a gurgle of movement in the water—caught his attention, and with the hope that it was Aisley and not some winter fowl, he dove in.

It was icy cold. Piers was up in a moment, gasping for breath, but he forced his lungs to take in more and went under again, swimming toward the noise that drew him. He surfaced again, blowing out air loudly, and then listened. Nothing. In that brief heartbeat, Piers said prayers more deeply felt and humble than all those he had sent up since his blindness.

The supplication seemed to dull the piercing edge of his panic, and he told himself that the pond was not large, that he had time, that he would succeed. The other thought, the insidious, hideous, black notion of life without Aisley, tapped at his consciousness, but he could not face it. Taking a long, slow breath, Piers sank to the bottom and began walking, his arms outstretched, feeling in the cold, black wet void for something other than the plants that fought with him, impeding his progress.

He surfaced only long enough to gulp in air and returned to his search, moving as fast as he could along the uneven bottom, his hands constantly groping through the depths. If only he could be certain that he kept in the right direction, without veering, without retracing steps already taken, exploring the same area over and over....

He pushed aside a mass of water weed and stumbled on, then stopped and turned back. Was it his imagination or had his fingers brushed against something smooth that might be a cold limb? Wildly, he flailed at the vegetation until he found it, and then he was touching the sweet curve of Aisley's slender calf. Dizzy from lack of air and giddy with thanks, Piers gathered his wife's body to him and shot above the water.

Gulping in great, healing breaths, he swam with strong, sure strokes to the pool's edge. There he lifted her in his arms and waded out, stumbling among the dried reeds that choked the area. Swearing softly, Piers clutched her tighter and straightened, treading as carefully as he could until he felt solid ground beneath his feet once more.

The cold assailed him, but he ignored it, for his wife lay like a lifeless thing in his arms. What if all his prayers and efforts had been for naught but to drag her body home?

"No!" Piers screamed the word into the blackness of his existence. He would not have her death and, as if the force of his will could revive her, he set his wife upon her feet. Leaning her over one arm for support, he pounded her back, desperately trying to force out the liquid she may have swallowed. "Aisley, Aisley, love, my love, please..." he whispered, panic surging through his veins. "Aisley... breathe!"

When Piers heard her begin to choke and spit and cough, he felt as weak as a newborn babe, and when he heard her speak, he could have wept with joy.

"Piers," she gasped, leaning against his chest. After a long, painful minute laboring to catch her breath, she was finally able to speak again. "What happened? I'm freezing!" He swayed on his feet, so overcome with emotion that he wanted to sink to his knees, and he clutched her hard against him, sending up his thanks like a litany to the heavens.

"My lord!" At the sound of Cecil's voice, Piers's head shot up. Although it seemed as if an eternity had passed since Aisley had disappeared with a splash, he knew that in reality very little time had passed. His men had come as quickly as they could, and Piers could fault them not. In truth, they had never been more welcome.

"Cecil! Give me your cloak for my lady," Piers directed. He heard his servant giving orders to the members of the guard, sending them back a distance, then felt the heavy fur-lined mantle in his hand. "She will go up before me," Piers said brusquely. "She is never riding that damn palfrey again."

"It was the stag!" Aisley protested through chattering teeth. "That wretched white stag came right at me, as if it meant me harm! I swear to our Holy Mother, Piers, I will never, *never* believe one of Edith's ridiculous stories again."

Piers smiled at her raging, glad that he held an angry woman instead of the cold, limp doll he had grasped in the pond. Alive and breathing fire was his lady, praise be to God.

"A talisman! An omen of good to come!" Aisley railed. "What rot!" She stepped away from him, muttering as she moved toward the destrier.

His arms empty, Piers stood alone for a moment, his body racked by trembling. Whether it was from the cold or simply his reaction to the near disaster, he did not know. Rubbing his arms to try to warm himself, he realized that, against all logic, he had saved his wife from drowning, a feat that amazed even himself.

Dripping wet and chilled to the bone, he blinked, suddenly puzzled, for amid all the discomfort attendant upon the rescue, he noticed something was different. It came to him slowly, like a secret born on the wind, too unbelievable to be easily discerned and too wonderful to be ignored.

For the first time in months, his eyes did not pain him.

"A white stag...what rot!" Aisley grumbled again, and, with a slow shake of his head, Piers walked toward her voice.

"Perhaps," he whispered to himself in wonder. "And then, perhaps not."

Aisley huddled by the fire in the great chamber while Cecil brought water to fill the wooden tub sitting nearby and Piers unceremoniously stripped off his wet clothes. When the tub was full and steaming, Piers dismissed his servant. "You may go, Cecil. My wife will attend me in the bath," he said.

If he could see her now, wet, shivering and bedraggled as a drowned rat, he would probably think twice about his order, Aisley thought ruefully. She glanced up at him and was startled by the sight of her husband in all his glory. The fire lit the small area before her, encompassing the wooden bath and Piers, and Aisley admired the man she had but recently seen.

As conscious as he was of his blindness, Piers certainly had no modesty for the rest of himself, for he stood, a great work of strong, hard muscle and sinew put together in the most manly of forms, boldly resting his hands on the side of the tub. The blaze cast a red glow upon his glorious frame, and Aisley drew in her breath. Here and now, he truly did look the Red Knight, large and powerful and deadly.

"Come, Aisley, into the water," he said. "Need you assistance with your wet clothes?"

"No," she said, rising, for she could hardly imagine summoning Edith to the red one's lair. She fumbled with her wet gown and heard a splash as Piers entered the water. Soon all her clothes lay in a heap by the hearth and she stood totally naked with Piers but a handbreadth away. Aisley felt hot and cold and bashful suddenly, for they had been intimate many times, but usually in the darkness....

There was something erotic about the red, glowing light, glistening off the wet expanse of her husband's chest, his wide shoulders, his gleaming hair.... "Do you want me to bathe you?" she asked, her voice suddenly hoarse.

Piers grinned. "I do, but get in before you freeze to death, Aisley."

"You want me to get in there...with you?" she asked.

"I do," he affirmed. "Are you suddenly shy, my wife?" he asked wryly. "Is this the same woman who only yesterday forced me to be still while she plied me with her hands and mouth?" He reached out to her, his grin wide and sensual.

Aisley could not deny him. She felt his warm fingers close over her own and stepped into the tub. Seating herself across from him, she sank down until the water lapped at her shoulders. Though large, the wooden bath was not big enough for them both to stretch out, so Piers had raised his knees, and Aisley was acutely conscious of her legs, also bent, brushing against his. She felt dizzy.

"Shall I bathe you first?" he asked. The firelight glittered upon his eyes, and for a moment she could swear that he saw her. She remembered them from this morning, bright and intensely blue. Aisley could not voice an answer, but it mattered not, for he moved toward her, lathering the soap in his grip. Then he took her ankle and lifted one dainty foot, and oh, dear heaven, he washed her with warm, wet hands.

Aisley watched him, finding it suddenly freeing that he could not see her. She noted his every movement, saw him close his eyes in pleasure as he touched her, and she felt the spiraling heat of his caress burning her within as his fingers slid along her legs and then her arms. When his palms, slick with soap, moved over her breasts, she moaned aloud. "Piers, Piers . . ." she whispered.

He leaned closer, and for the first time, Aisley actually saw him put his mouth to her breasts, sleek and glistening. For the first time, she saw the dark gold of his hair resting against her skin as he suckled, and she moaned softly at the sight, squirming in the water, longing already for surcease. He sucked harder, and she lifted her hips, relieved when he touched the throbbing juncture of her thighs.

Piers stroked her beneath the water as his tongue raked her breasts, his massive shoulders filling her vision, and Aisley could do naught but whimper as she thrust herself up to meet him. When his fingers entered her, she cried out her pleasure, and he let her, shuddering at the sound, a shudder that matched her own release.

Putting her arms around him, Aisley pressed her face against his wet neck, astonished at the power he had over her, a power she knew now that was not of evil or sorcery, but of love. "Now let me . . . bathe you, husband," she said, and Piers grunted his assent, sitting back in the tub.

Aisley could see his face was taut with need, but she took her time, reveling in her task. She marveled at the feel of his solid body beneath her soapy fingers, his muscles gleaming and smooth, his legs hard and covered with golden hair, and there, between them ... Aisley dropped her hand, closing it tightly around him in the water, and heard him growl in pleasure. The sound urged her on, and she saw him lean back his head and close his eyes.

She thrilled to watch his features, a pleasure so long denied her, but the intensity there was daunting. Aisley panted, wondering again if his passion, fully loosed, would overwhelm her.... Then suddenly his eyes flew open and he took her by the hips, lifted her over him and lowered her down upon his shaft, hot and eager. Water splashed onto the floor as he moved her, guiding her to a rhythm that trilled in her blood. Aisley felt the hard muscles of his legs behind her as he raised his knees. "Good...so good, Aisley," he whispered, his hands roaming over the slick surface of her skin, caressing her breasts and squeezing her nipples.

With something akin to reverence, Aisley watched his face, his eyes closed, his rough-hewn features alive with pleasure. "Kiss me, Aisley," he demanded, and she met his mouth with hers. His lips were bruising, his tongue thrusting inside her mouth even as he thrust himself inside her. Around them, water surged over the side while the slippery friction between their bodies spiraled into an unbearable summit.

Finally, Aisley tore her lips away to shout his name. Then she came, her shudders nearly painful in their intensity, while Piers's hands grasped her hips in a crushing grip. He pulled her down hard, sheathing himself to the root, and emptied his seed inside her as he growled his pleasure, a fierce cry of triumph that echoed into the darkness.

Aisley was weak and gasping when they finally left the cooled water for their bed, and she curled up against her husband, utterly serene for the first time since she had entered Dunmurrow Castle. I love you, Piers, she repeated to herself, and she smiled. Who would have thought that her choice of husband would ever prove to be so right?

She had never dreamed of falling in love with the Red Knight, and she certainly had never imagined the delights to be found in his bed—and bath. Aisley blushed at the memory of Piers's lovemaking. Although she certainly could not fault him before, tonight he had been positively exuberant, perhaps because they both realized how very precious life was, she mused. Having come so close to drowning, Aisley appreciated her existence more fully, and she could think of no better way to celebrate it than by loving her husband. "Thank you for saving me," she whispered.

Piers grunted. "You are worth saving," he said as he squeezed her buttocks.

Aisley rested her head upon his chest, content with his gruff words. Although he didn't deign to say so, Aisley knew that the Red Knight, so disgusted when forced to wed her, had obviously mellowed in his feelings. Why else would a blind man throw himself into a pond in the dead of winter? The very thought of the danger she had put him in made Aisley shiver. "You could have drowned or frozen to death," she said.

"I believe the swim did me good," Piers said. Something in his tone made her lift her head to look at him. His lips were curved softly.

"How?" Aisley asked, puzzled. She had expected him to scold her for dragging them into the woods. Piers had been proven right about the dangers of going outside, and yet, he did not appear angry. He seemed, oddly enough, quite pleased.

"For the first time since the battle, I feel no pain," he answered. "My eyes do not hurt me." He said it softly, as if in awe himself, and Aisley gasped in surprise. Something had soothed him....

"Why? What was it, do you think? The cold? The water?" Aisley sat up and looked at her husband closely, as if his face might reveal a clue. But the bed, as usual, was enshrouded in darkness, and his features told her nothing.

"Perhaps the temperature deadened the ache for a while," she said.

"So I thought, but every inch of me was heated up in that bath," Piers noted dryly, "and I still feel nothing."

Aisley smiled. So that was why tonight was different. . . . For once, Piers had not been struggling with the pain that had heretofore been constant. "But if not the cold . . ." Aisley mused aloud. "It must be the water! Do you often wash them out?" she asked tensely.

"I did after it first happened, but the various solutions did no good," Piers said. "The pain continued."

"But that was so long ago," Aisley protested. "If you did get shards of rock in your eyes, some might have been buried so deep that they took months to work themselves out. The water probably loosened them further, and now they might be gone! Perhaps your sight will return!" Her voice rose in anticipation.

She felt Piers's great body tremble beside her, but he tightened his arm around her, pulling her back down to him. "Hush," he ordered roughly. "I believe not in miracles."

"No?" Aisley asked, her excitement refusing to be quelled. "You believed not in the white stag, and look what happened! He appeared and did no ill, but good, by tossing me into the pond!"

Piers grunted. "You are far too superstitious, Wife," he said.

Maybe, Aisley thought, but she remembered the way the beast had looked at her, eyes wise with intent, and she smiled. There were some things worth believing in, and at Christmas, she knew, all things were possible.

It happened gradually.

It was but a few days before Epiphany when Piers noticed that something was different. Every morning, Aisley opened the shutters of the great chamber, whether he willed it or no, and she was not deterred by finding them shut when she returned from her tasks.

Since she carried on quite foolishly about his looks and could usually be coaxed back to bed with just a few glances at his body, Piers did not deny her. As soon as she left, however, he bade Cecil to once again plunge the room into shadow. He had a morbid fear of someone stumbling upon him and learning his secret, betraying him to his enemies and tearing down the haven he had made here at Dunmurrow. The darkness protected him.

Today was the same as any other, except that when he heard the creak of the shutters and felt the draft of cool air from the window, Piers became aware of something else: light. He lay where he was, unmoving, stupefied by the odd sensation, the strange lifting of the blackness that had besieged him for months.

"Piers, I must hasten!" Aisley said, commanding his attention. "I am setting up the weaving room today. Perhaps we shall all soon have some new clothes to keep us warm."

Piers grunted. "I prefer you without a stitch upon your smooth skin," he said. Aisley laughed, a light, musical sound that usually made his heart lurch, but this morning he was concentrating too much on the blessed light. What had caused it?

"Ah, if only I could linger," Aisley whispered, and he felt her fingers trailing along his chest.

He grunted again. "Tease me not, wench," he warned, and swatted her on her backside. She giggled, but he could hear her moving about the chamber, dressing for the day.

"Tonight, then, husband," she promised, leaning over him, and he was enveloped in her scent, musky and inviting.

"Mayhap at dinner," he said and stole a warm kiss before she pulled away. "See that you do not miss it."

"Shall I send Cecil in?" she asked from the other side of the room.

"No," Piers answered. "I shall call him when I want him." He heard the door close behind her, and for once he was glad of her departure. Although he usually missed her with alarming intensity after she left, this morning he wanted her gone, for he was not yet ready to share his discovery.

He did not even summon Cecil, but remained where he was, frozen in his place, for he suspected that the light was only a fleeting thing, a new facet of his illness destined to taunt him. Would the room dim again when he closed his eyes? Piers was conscious of his heart picking up its pace as if he were going into battle, and, truly, he was more fearful now than he had been in any skirmish.

Yet he knew he must act, so slowly and firmly, he shut his eyes. Then he counted to ten silently and opened them again, only to find that it was not his imagination. The world that had been black for so long was now lighter.

Piers turned toward the window, and the brightness that met him made his eyes water. It was passing strange, this change, and why? With a shudder, he leaned back against the pillows and shut his eyes again, this time against a surfeit of emotion—against hope.

Piers said nothing to his wife. And he still said nothing when, after more days passed, he could see shadows, forms in the grayness. He ordered Cecil to light candles in the great chamber, but if Aisley thought it odd, she did not say so. Presumably, she thought he was doing it for her, and Piers did not tell her otherwise.

He heard her footsteps and lifted his head, searching out the sound, and there she was: his wife. She was standing before the fire. Piers found it difficult to maintain his composure as he watched her, actually saw the outline of her slim figure, standing in front of the light, for the first time in his life. He made a sound deep in his throat. It was beyond his control.

Aisley mistook it, thought it a noise of need, for he heard her voice, her beautiful voice, teasing him. "Do you not wish to wait for our supper, Piers?" she asked.

"No," he answered huskily, his thoughts turning easily to her soft warmth. "I wish to take you now, down among the rushes," he said. He pictured her riding him there, before the fire, with the light illuminating her body, and he grew hard. He heard her sharp breath and smiled.

"But Cecil—" she protested.

"Cecil be damned—the both of them!" Piers said, grinning. Then he was on his feet, moving toward her, and she was trembling when he took her in his arms, his hands moving to her small breasts, his mouth taking hers as they fell upon the floor before the hearth.

Chapter Fourteen

Aisley was in the hall when the messenger from Belvry arrived.

"'Tis a young man named Benedict, my lady," the guard told her.

"Let him in!" she said, delighted at the prospect of news from her former home. She had known Benedict for many years and had watched him rise in the household to become assistant to her steward.

"Edith, see to some ale and food for our guest," Aisley said. She glanced about the hall, but found nothing amiss. Although not as lovely as Belvry, it was warm and comfortable and no longer gloomy, making her content to receive the young man.

She strode across the tiles to greet him, holding out her hands warmly. "Benedict," she said, "how wonderful it is to see you again.". He took her outstretched hands, but his own were cold, and the look on his face made her wary. Was something wrong at home?

"You look well, my lady," he exclaimed, and Aisley smiled. Perhaps it was not something at Belvry that was responsible for Benedict's odd expression, but Dunmurrow itself. In the blissful days since Christmas, she had forgotten the black rumor that surrounded the Red Knight and his keep.

"How kind of you to say so," she said. "I am very well. Please, be seated. You must rest after your journey."

Benedict seemed to relax once a cup of ale and a trencher of stew were put before him, or perhaps it was the presence of Edith, clucking over him in her usual manner before turning to scold Willie for something, that put the young man at ease.

Or mayhap it was only that he was hungry, for he attacked the food with gusto, while Aisley told him of her improvements to Dunmurrow and asked after the friends she had left behind at Belvry. It was only when he pushed aside the vessels, cleaned of every crumb, that his features again turned grim, and Aisley knew it wasn't Dunmurrow, but Belvry that was bothering him. Something was wrong, something that her steward, Matthew Brown, did not trust to a letter.

"What is it, Benedict?" she asked evenly. "Why have you come?"

"My lady," he said sadly. "I am afraid I have ill news for you. Lord Hexham has grown restive in your absence. He disputes our borders, harasses the villeins and freeholders and has taken the manor at Isenglade as his own."

Aisley gasped. "How dare he?"

Benedict shook his head. "He is lawless, my lady, and each day he grows bolder. Matthew expects that someday, perhaps as soon as the weather breaks, he will attack Belvry itself." His pale blue eyes lifted to hers helplessly, while Aisley stared at him in horror. Then he cleared his throat uncomfortably.

"There is more?" Aisley asked, her voice tight.

The young man looked down at his hands, resting before him on the table. "Hexham claims that your marriage was not a true one, that your father promised you to him—"

She broke in before he could finish. "That cursed liar!"

"Yes, my lady," Benedict agreed with an unhappy nod. "He says you are his by right and so, therefore, is Belvry."

Aisley's ire rose swiftly, and she clenched her fists at her sides in frustration. "That bastard! Edward himself arranged my marriage! How dare Hexham dispute it? We must get word to the king...." Her words trailed off as she saw an odd flicker in Benedict's blue eyes. She hesitated then, for she knew what the man was thinking as surely as if he had spoken. Why should she pester Edward, when she was married to the most fearsome knight in the land?

Aisley felt her shoulders slump in defeat, for she knew her blind husband could not help her. Then who could? She could send a message to the king, but when would it find him, and what, truly, did he care for Belvry? There was no love lost between Edward and herself, and she certainly had not endeared herself to him with her choice of husband.

Although Hexham held no special place in Edward's favor, neither did she, and Hexham could promise a strong arm to his liege, while she...what had she to offer? Nothing. And Piers? His fighting days were over, and his lands were not rich enough to buy the royal favor. How much would his past triumphs weigh in the balance? Aisley felt her throat thicken with despair, and she swallowed hard.

It was unthinkable that Hexham, her arrogant, unscrupulous neighbor, could take Belvry. It was unthinkable, but very likely. Aisley stood up. No matter how hopeless it appeared, she was not ready to give way.

"Come, Benedict. I would that you tell all to my husband, Baron Montmorency," she said. The relief the young man obviously felt was palatable, and Aisley could have laughed. Expect not the fierce Red Knight to aid you, she thought dismally, but she felt no bitterness. She loved her husband and would stand by him, even though it meant the loss of everything she had formerly held dear.

Benedict was cowed by the midnight ambience of the great chamber, Aisley could tell. She tried to remember when the eerie red glow of the room had daunted her, when Piers, seated among the shadows and flanked by his great dogs, had seemed threatening, but all she saw was a chamber full of warmth and enough love to chase away any degree of darkness.

"My lord," Aisley said. "This is Benedict of Belvry, assistant to my steward. He brings us news that I would have you hear."

"Sit," Piers said, and Aisley motioned the young man toward the settle. Then she stepped into the gloom, ignored by the huge dogs, to stand behind her husband. She rested her hands on his massive shoulders, and he raised one of his arms to cover her fingers with his own, a comforting gesture that made her want to weep.

"Speak, Benedict," Piers said. He listened silently as the young man repeated, in a nervous tone, what he had told Aisley.

"And what does this Hexham say of me, Benedict?" Piers asked.

There was dead silence. "Go ahead, Benedict," Aisley urged. "You may speak freely here."

She wondered what new slander Hexham brought against the Red Knight, for the young man appeared to dread answering. Finally, he nodded, as if accepting his fate. "Hexham says the Red Knight must be dead and that Aisley hides here behind a shadow, but will not escape him."

Aisley felt anger surge through her husband, and for a moment she feared that he might burst to his feet in one of his rampaging rages. But he remained seated, though tense beneath her fingers.

"Now isn't that interesting?" he asked. When Benedict, who appeared to be quaking in his boots, made no reply, Piers spoke again. "Does our enemy mean to attack Belvry or Dunmurrow?" he asked.

Aisley saw Benedict's blank look and felt dismayed herself before understanding dawned. "I see your point, my lord," she said then. "Perhaps the cowardly viper hopes to draw you out and then take Dunmurrow in your absence. Such a scheme would suit him," she added.

"Which do you think the man wants more, Belvry or Aisley?" Piers asked.

While Aisley watched, Benedict seemed to weigh the question. His eyes flicked to her, though she must be only a dark figure to him in the shadows, and he finally spoke, with more confidence now. "Hexham wants my lady, make no mistake, but he has always coveted Belvry, lands more prosperous than his own, with more hands to till the soil. He has already taken one manor. If you want my opinion, I would guess that he will not stop until he has taken it all."

Aisley walked out into the bailey with Benedict to say her farewells. The young man appeared much heartened, having received instructions from Piers for her steward and staff concerning Hexham's threats. It was hard not to have faith in the Red Knight, Aisley realized, but when Benedict rode away, her encouraging smile faded and she stayed outside, staring into the distance, unwilling to return to her husband.

If she wept over the loss of her home, it would only frustrate Piers, who was frustrated enough without this new threat to his manhood. Truly, Aisley did not want to return to the great chamber at all, for she recalled the last time Piers had thought himself less than a man, and she shuddered at the memory of the night he had smote the quintain.

Dusk finally sent her inside, and calling herself a coward, she went to face Piers's rage. She was surprised to find candles lit in the room, and Cecil serving supper, as usual.

"I have sent for Alan," Piers said when she entered. "I would consult my vassal, but I think I shall have to divide my forces. Perhaps if Alan takes most of the men to Belvry, a show of strength will send Hexham to ground."

Aisley drew in a sharp breath of surprise, her eyes flying to her husband. He was seated at the table, his huge, powerful body seeming too big for it, looking as clever and fierce as his legend would have him. His brow was furrowed in thought, and he appeared absolutely serious. "You mean to challenge Hexham?" she asked.

"No, but I do not plan to let him take Belvry, either," Piers said. His brows lowered, and he cocked his head to the side as if considering her. "Did you think I would do nothing?" he asked.

"No! Of course not," Aisley lied, flustered. God knew she had no wish to rile him. "But have you enough men?"

"Since Benedict could provide little information on Hexham's forces, I cannot answer that as yet," Piers said. "I certainly do not have as many as I would like," he admitted, "but Dunmurrow was never under any threat, so there was no need for more."

Aisley felt guilt seep into her pores and pound through her blood. Although Piers did not accuse her of anything, she knew that she was to blame. If not for her, his home would not be in jeopardy. If not for her, he would be left here, undisturbed . . . . Aisley turned away and walked to the fire. "Perhaps we should just let him have it, Piers," she said softly.

"What?" The word was invested with astonishment, as if Piers thought he had not heard her right.

Aisley cleared her throat. "Perhaps we should just let Hexham have Belvry," she repeated. She turned then to face him and saw the dismay and fury on his features. "Belvry means nothing to me now," she explained, though that was not entirely true. "My life is here at Dunmurrow with you."

She waited, her body tense, for his response, and relaxed when she saw the anger leave his face. "Aisley...my wife," he said, calling her to him hoarsely. She went, and he drew her down upon his lap, his muscular arms closing tightly around her. The strength that she had shown all day threatened to vanish there, and Aisley longed to do nothing more than to weep into his chest, in the comfort of his embrace, for her old home, for her guilt and for the joyful, peaceful pattern of their lives that now was shattered.

"If I do nothing, 'twill be worse," Piers whispered against her hair. "But if I show him that we will not be bullied, perhaps he will slink back into his hole."

Aisley smiled crookedly at his words, for already he understood Hexham very well. "Fear not, Aisley. Just because they are not quartered here does not mean I have no men. They follow Alan now," he noted, a tinge of bitterness in his voice. "And Alan travels where I send him. He will go forth, taking the legend of the Red Knight with him, and perhaps 'twill be enough to discourage our enemies."

Alan arrived a few days later with all the men who had been garrisoned throughout Piers's demesne, and when Aisley looked out to see them, camped beyond the walls and crowded in the bailey, she felt heartened for the first time since the news of Hexham's treachery had reached her. Surely such numbers would be enough to change his mind, she thought, for Aisley knew that despite his boasting, her neighbor was essentially a coward.

Piers and his vassal spent the afternoon closeted together, presumably planning their strategy, while Aisley made sure that all the extra bodies were fed. By the time Cecil came to fetch her for supper, she had lost all track of time, and the meal was already set out when she entered the great chamber.

"Good evening, my lord," Aisley said, noting with approval the warm glow of candlelight. 'Twas such a relief to see one's food! And there was Piers's vassal, looking travel-stained and weary beside her husband. "Alan, how nice to see you again," she said.

"My lady," Alan said. Stepping toward her, he took both her hands in his and shook his head. "It hardly seems possible, but you have grown more beautiful in my absence."

"Thank you," Aisley said with a smile, but she promptly removed her fingers from his grasp. "And you have grown more eloquent!"

Alan laughed, while Aisley, mindful of Piers's excessive jealousy, quickly moved to her husband's side. He slid an arm around her, pulling her even closer in an obviously possessive gesture.

Alan did not look a bit surprised or heartbroken by Piers's behavior. He simply grinned wider. "I assume that you two have worked things out to your mutual satisfaction. Is everything out in the open now?" he queried, seating himself at the table.

"What?" Piers asked, a bit testily.

"Your marriage," Alan answered. "'Twas plain enough to everyone that 'twas a love match. What was all that nonsense before? I fairly laughed when the two of you claimed to be strangers and that the wedding was arranged by Edward. Why all the secrecy surrounding the union?" he asked. When Piers and Aisley both looked at him blankly, Alan shook his head. "Someday, when I pull the full tale from you, 'twill have something to do with this noxious Hexham, no doubt," he said, breaking off a big chunk of bread.

Holding it up, Alan shook it at the both of them. "You could not fool me," he scolded with a chuckle, "for I knew that no woman in her right mind would choose someone with Montmorency's reputation, unless she knew him well."

Aisley stared at Alan, dumbfounded for a moment, then buried her face in Piers's side, giggling uncontrollably, while the sound of his booming laughter filled the room.

The next day, Aisley was laying out stores for the Red Knight's army when Edith rushed up to her, her round face pale. Accustomed as she was now to seeing her servant happy, Aisley was taken aback at the distress so clearly etched on her face.

"What is it, Edith?" she asked.

"Oh, my lady, 'tis Willie," she said, clasping her hands together. "He's been called back to join Alan's forces."

"Oh," Aisley said hollowly. "He is a soldier—"

Edith did not let her finish. "But he's no longer a young man, my lady!" she protested.

"'Tis the life he chose," Aisley said, dismissing Edith's arguments. Then she paused to imagine how she would feel if it were Piers leading the men instead of Alan.

Aisley knew she would be proud, yet she developed a sickening sensation in the pit of her stomach at the thought of her husband going off to battle, maybe never to return. She shot Edith a glance. "Perhaps we can persuade Alan to let Willie remain a member of the guard here," she suggested, for she knew that Piers planned to split his forces, leaving some men to protect Dunmurrow.

"No, my lady," Edith said, wringing her hands. "He won't do it. The stubborn fool wants to go off to fight!"

At a loss for words, Aisley looked at her servant helplessly. What would she do if it were Piers who was determined to leave? She drew in a long breath. "Maybe if you told Willie how you felt, how worried you are, and asked him to stay here with you, begged him to—"

Edith cut in, her face flushed. "I've never begged a man for anything, my lady, and I don't intend to start now," she said haughtily. Then she stormed off, muttering under her breath.

Apparently she had a change of heart, however, for later that day Edith appeared before her mistress again. This time she was smiling smugly, while Willie, hanging back beside her, fingered his belt nervously. "We wish to be married, my lady," Edith announced.

"Edith! How wonderful!" Aisley said with a smile, but it faded as soon as she realized there was no priest to perform the ceremony. "But how?" she asked.

It was decided, after taking the case to Piers himself, that Edith would go with the soldiers back to Belvry, where the chaplain there could officiate. On the journey, Edith would be escorted not only by her own guard, but by scores of others, so she would be well protected.

The possibility that they might meet up with Hexham's army on the way did little to dampen Edith's spirits, for she was too eager to be wed. Aisley grinned, amazed at the woman who had wept in fear over the Red Knight, but now marched off to battle without a qualm. With a sigh, she sent her servant to pack.

Aisley did not see Edith again until the woman came to attend her before supper. "Shall I dress your hair for you, my lady?" Edith asked. She appeared a little constrained, and Aisley knew she had come to say her goodbyes, since Alan was to leave with his men on the morrow.

"No, thank you, Edith," she said, for she knew that Piers liked her hair down and loose. "But you may brush it for me." Edith smiled, as if glad for a task to keep her hands busy, and she picked up the brush, drawing it gently through Aisley's long locks.

"I want to thank you, my lady, for making all the arrangements for me to go to Belvry," Edith said.

"You're welcome, Edith. I am glad to help you, and if you and Willie wish to stay at Belvry, I'm sure Matthew can find something for you both to do there," Aisley said.

"Oh, no, my lady," Edith protested, her hand abruptly halting in its strokes. "I would never abandon you here." For a moment she seemed to be as horrified as she used to be by the specter of Dunmurrow.

Aisley laughed. "I assure you I shall manage just fine. We are acquiring more servants every day. I'm sure I can find someone to attend me," she noted.

Edith seemed a bit miffed. "Well, we shall be back, and what's more, I shall bring some of our own people with me," she replied.

Aisley turned to meet Edith's gaze. "Only if they are willing to move, Edith. I want no one to be unhappy here," she said.

Edith had the grace to look guilty and then nodded. Taking up the brush again, she said, "My lady, I—I'm afraid I gave you some wrong information, though 'twas no fault of my own." The odd tone of her voice made Aisley glance around to see the servant blushing scarlet. What now? she wondered.

"When you..." Edith paused, took a deep breath and began again. "On your wedding night, my lady, I told you some things," she said, "that I have since found not always to be true."

"Oh? What was that?" Aisley asked, trying not to smile.

"The marriage act, my lady. I told you 'twas brief and painful, when 'tis not necessarily either one," Edith said firmly. "Actually, it can be quite...pleasant and...lengthy."

Aisley had to clench her teeth to keep from laughing. When she finally determined herself able to speak, she said, "'Tis all right, Edith, for I discovered that for myself."

"Did you, my lady?" Edith asked, no little wonder in her voice. She stopped her task and held the brush poised in the air, a startled look on her face. "You mean that the Red Knight..."

"I mean," Aisley said, unable to contain the wicked grin that spread across her features, "that the Red Knight's reputation for all else pales in comparison to his skills...in bed."

When Piers awoke, darkness met him, and for a moment he was back in the black hell he had lived in for so many months. Then memory returned, and he knew that it was only the bed hangings that cloaked his world and that his

sight was growing stronger. He refused to say it was returning even in his own mind, for he knew himself unable to face
the prospect of hopes dashed.

Piers expected nothing more each morning than he had
received the day before, only that the utter darkness not return; even with Aisley at his side, he doubted if he could
bear facing that hell again.

Aisley. She stirred beside him, and he lifted a long lock of
hair in his hands, letting it fall between his fingers. Her hair
was so smooth, so fine. Like silver, they said it was. Piers
tried to imagine it, white-blond, sparkling in the sun. Although he could see colors now, the shade of his wife's hair
eluded him, and when he tried to picture her, as he did so
often, her image refused to take shape.

"Hmm. Good morning, Husband," she said softly, and
he smiled. How the woman could come awake so easily,
while his own head seemed fogged, was beyond him. With
a light kiss to his forehead, she climbed over him, making
him hard when a silky thigh slid across him.

"Come back here, wench," he growled, but already the
bed hangings were opening. He closed his eyes in sweet
pleasure, in no hurry to leave the warmth of his bed. How
he enjoyed waking up with her, sharing this time together
until the responsibilities of the day intruded, until he must
face his long isolation in frustration, while she went about
her duties. Piers heard the creak of the shutters and his
wife's gentle sigh.

"'Tis a beautiful day, Piers!" she said. Her voice, as
musical as a waterfall, beckoned him, and he opened his
eyes to turn toward her. For a moment, he thought his very
heart would halt in his chest, for it thundered and then
stilled when he looked toward the window, and he stared,
uncomprehending, at the vision before him.

'Twas his wife. Not a shadow or an indistinct glow of
color, but Aisley—the first sight to meet his eyes in so very
long. And he could not believe what he saw.

Piers knew she was lovely. He had heard others marvel about her charms, but he was still struck speechless. None of his dreams of her had ever come close. Aisley was so piercingly beautiful that she took his breath away.

She was looking out the narrow slit, the early light shining on her face, illuminating features dainty and fine and bright with life. Hair, so pale that it seemed white, yet so lustrous that it seemed to reflect the morn, fell in a long straight mass to her waist.

She was naked. In his astonishment, Piers had barely noticed that, but now he did, marveling at her luminous skin and her breasts, small but jutting upward, their tiny nipples hard in the cool air. Her waist was slim, her legs slender and shapely, and his groin immediately ached painfully. But he ignored it. As much as he desired her, Piers was loath to break the spell that held him, for fear she would disappear into a blur of color, never to be seen clearly again.

His attention returned to her face, her quiet beauty breaking his heart as she gazed out the window. For a long moment, he stayed thus, hardly breathing as he watched her, drinking in the image of his wife. With almost painful clarity, Piers knew he would remember this moment for the rest of his days.

Aisley, Aisley, Aisley, he wanted to shout. And suddenly, it was as if what he felt for her coalesced and grew until he could hardly contain it. All that he had held back, forced down and hidden away because of his blindness now threatened to explode and burst from his body. It was like a dam breaking, the blocked water surging through its barrier, and Piers shuddered with the effort to restrain it.

Perhaps he made some sound, for she turned her face toward him, and he could see her eyes, bright and clear as newly wrought silver, and her lips. Those lips . . . the softest pink and dainty, like the rest of her, yet capable of setting him afire with their touch. "Piers?" she asked, her delicate brows drawing together. "What is it?"

He couldn't speak. He made a noise, and she was at his side in a moment, leaning over him in the bed. She looked at him intently, worry clouding her features, but he could do naught but stare at her, unable to tear his eyes from the silvery depths of hers, so intelligent, so loving. God, her entire heart was there for him to see. To see . . .

"Piers!" She was sobbing, then weeping. He had never known her to cry, yet tears coursed down her cheeks unheeded as she dug her fingers into his arms. She knew, he realized, and yet still he could not respond. "Piers!" She tried to shake him, and her feeble efforts against his heavy body wrung a smile from him.

"Hush. 'Tis no cause for weeping, but rather rejoicing, Wife," he said huskily. He was almost afraid to touch her, afraid to unleash the boundless emotions inside himself.

All his life, he had struggled to keep them in check, and he had managed well enough until his blindness. Then he had lost his tenuous control, raging like a rampaging beast at his plight. Yet Aisley had replaced his fury, filling him with feelings he had never dreamed of having, and they were so strong that he could no longer contain them. . . .

Piers lifted a hand to her soft cheek, so lovely, so silky. "Aisley. . ." he groaned. "Aisley, Aisley. . ." And then something burst inside of him like a white-hot explosion, and he cried out her name. He rolled her under him and found her mouth with a fury that could not be denied. His hands moved over her pale skin roughly, possessively, as he pushed his tongue into her mouth. She did not demur, but met him eagerly, and he growled with the strength of his unleashed passion.

He cupped her breasts, lifting them to his mouth, and sucked hard and endlessly, unable to stop. He could hear her low panting and knew he was not being gentle, but could not help himself. He spread her legs wide to receive him. "Aisley, Aisley," he groaned in apology as he lifted his head, but she arched up to meet him, taking his thrust as he sheathed himself to the root. He clutched her buttocks, trying to get closer, deeper, and he made a compulsive sound when she wrapped her legs around him, aiding him, seeking the same.

Piers looked down at her then, her silver hair fanned across the pillow, her dainty face flushed, her eyes closed, her lips parted to draw in shallow breaths. "Aisley..." he growled, and he took her mouth in a bruising kiss, trying to release all that was in him. Then he was moving mindlessly, harder, faster, only vaguely aware that his wife was biting his shoulders or that her nails were cutting into his skin.

The heady surge of her convulsions as she clenched him tightly and shouted out his name made Piers dig his fingers into her flesh, drawing her up to him for one final thrust that left his body wracked with shudders. "Aisley..." he roared.

When he could think again, Piers rolled to his side, taking her with him, running his hands gently over her back, trying to soothe the bruises he knew he had made. While the thundering of his heart slowed, he kissed her forehead tenderly, and she lifted her eyes to him, beautiful silver eyes swimming with love and tears of joy.

"I always feared that your passion, if unleashed, would overwhelm me," she whispered.

Piers froze, his hands tangled in the length of her hair, his gaze locked to hers. "And?" he asked, finding his voice only with effort.

"And, like all my other fears about you, 'twas for naught," Aisley said, smiling tremulously. "When did your sight return?"

"It happened gradually," he said, his fingers threading through her tresses.

"Why didn't you tell me?" she asked.

"I did not want to raise your hopes—or mine," he answered honestly. "I was afraid that it would not last, that any day I would be plunged back into the darkness."

"What? The Red Knight afraid?" Aisley asked, a smile wavering upon her lovely face. "I don't believe it."

Believe it, Piers thought to himself, but aloud he said nothing. In truth, he did not think himself capable of more speech. He looked into her silver eyes, awash with her tears, and with a groan, he pulled her face into his chest, unable to look upon her any longer. If he did, he feared that he would squall like an infant himself.

Chapter Fifteen

"**P**iers! Come," Aisley said suddenly. "Get up!" She climbed out of bed, took hold of his arm with both hands and tried futilely to drag him from his position. It was like attempting to budge a giant oak, firmly rooted. "You cannot deny me now," she warned, undeterred.

When Piers looked at her skeptically, she said, "Don't you understand? We can leave this room—together! We're free, Piers!" Releasing his arm so that she might dress, Aisley nearly tripped over the dogs, who, sensing her excitement, nosed about her legs. Pushing them aside with a couple of distracted pats, she donned her gown quickly, for she was in a hurry to prove to the people of Dunmurrow that their lord was no demon, but the handsomest man in the land.

Aisley threw open the lid of her husband's chest, looking for something suitable for the occasion, and found a bloodred surcoat. It was beautiful, she thought, and with Piers's coloring, it would make him a sight to behold. She held it up, deciding it was the perfect garment for the Red Knight's return to the world.

"Wear this," she said. "I want to show you off." She sat back on her heels. "Oh, if only Edith were here! She was always filling me with tales about you, till I suspected you had two heads and cloven feet! I wish she could see you now."

Piers's response was a snort, but he rose from the bed, and when he stood before her in all of his finery, Aisley nearly swooned. He looked resplendent in the crimson over a soft yellow tunic, with a heavy gold belt that echoed the color of his hair. In awe, Aisley lifted a hand to touch the burnished locks. "You have such beautiful hair," she whispered.

He laughed and lifted a long lock of her own off her breast. "'Tis yours that is beautiful, my wife. Though 'twas described to me many times, 'tis a shade beyond imagining. 'Tis glad I am to see it," he said huskily. He rubbed the strands against his lips, his eyes never leaving Aisley's, and she felt a surge of warmth spread through her that made her knees weak.

The Red Knight was a sorcerer, in truth, she decided, for what a spell he weaved with his voice, and now, his eyes. She drew in a breath and smiled. "Come, before your mind turns to other things," she teased.

Aisley felt as though she did not release that same breath until they left the great chamber and walked down the dark, spiral stair to the hall below.

If she had hoped to make a dazzling impression upon the first person they met, she was disappointed, for it was Cecil who saw them initially, and his usual serious expression remained unaltered. "'Tis good to see you, my lord," he said, without a hint of surprise at the sight, and then went on his way.

The sudden appearance of the baron got more of a reaction from Glenna, who walked in next from the kitchen, carrying a tray of cups. "Glenna, my lord is joining us for dinner today," Aisley said happily. The cook then took one look at the Red Knight and dropped the platter to the floor.

"Oh, let me help you," Aisley said, rushing to the woman's side. As they righted the vessels, Aisley cast a surreptitious glance at her husband, and unable to contain her enthusiasm, she lowered her voice for Glenna's ears only. "Well, what think you? Is he not handsome?"

Glenna turned wide brown eyes that held a dazed look toward Aisley, then back at Piers. "Well, uh, my lady, he—he looks a bit fierce," Glenna mumbled.

"Fierce?" Aisley sat back on her heels to gaze anew at her husband. He was huge, of course, taller than any man she had ever known, and his muscles were evident under the taut line of his clothes. He stood with his hands on his hips, surveying the changes in his hall, his generous mouth pressed into a firm line and his brows furrowed a bit in concentration. The scar that ran from his eye was apparent. But fierce? Piers was far too handsome to look the least bit menacing. Intent in her admiration, Aisley released a sigh of pure contentment before she noticed Glenna staring at her in wonder.

It was obvious to the servant that Montmorency's new bride was blinded by love, and it did not take long for the news to make its way throughout the castle and down to the village. The ferocious Red Knight was out and about, tamed by his beautiful wife, who, in turn, sighed dreamily at his harsh visage.

With the return of Piers's sight, Aisley's world took on a perfect glow, like an exquisite gem sparkling each day with new facets. He indulged her, going riding and hawking with her, eating in the great hall, visiting the village and acceding to her every whim, although, in truth, he seemed to enjoy the outings as much as she.

In the evenings they played chess or tables in the great chamber, its shadows banished by the soft glow of candles, while the dogs rested at their feet. And they made love. Her fear of strong feelings overcome, Aisley embraced the emotion that poured out of Piers like a tide. She had been right, of course. When unleashed, the force of his passion was overpowering, but she met it, responding in kind, though she had never dreamed that possible.

Weeks passed full of idyllic days, and gradually the weather broke, heralding the coming spring. Piers began working with his men again in the bailey and outside the walls, training them and honing their skills. Although Aisley sometimes watched in admiration as the Red Knight handled a heavy sword, his huge body deadly and graceful, his muscles hard and bulging, she more often felt trepidation at the scene.

For there was one drawback to the miracle that had occurred. A sighted Piers would be able to fight, and Aisley could not bear the thought of letting him go to battle. Hexham was the sole bit of darkness in the unclouded joy of their hours.

So far, Piers had been content to remain at Dunmurrow, for all was quiet at Belvry. Alan and his men were comfortably ensconced there and had seen naught of the treacherous baron, while Edith and Willie remained there, too, happily married. It appeared, for the time being at least, that Piers had been right. A show of might had sent Hexham scurrying back to the warmth of his own hearth. But like a viper in its nest, was he poised to strike, perhaps with the spring?

Aisley was assailed by doubts and by the horrible feeling that the days and nights she shared with the Red Knight were numbered.

She was in the buttery, sorting herbs and preparing a tonic for one of the servants, when Kendrick told her the news. A group of soldiers had arrived from her old home, and their leader was meeting with the baron right now. Kendrick was excited, as only young men can be about knights and the movements of fighting men, but Aisley's heart sank.

It was as if the moment she'd dreaded had arrived, and she stayed where she was, slowly finishing her work, putting her materials away and dusting off her hands carefully before heading to the great chamber to hear a report that could only be bad.

When Aisley entered the room, she noticed, as usual, the changes that had been wrought since she had first stood here, daunted by the Red Knight. Although the room still had a glow to it, for the walls did, indeed, have a red tint to them, today there were no shadows to cloak the lord of Dunmurrow. The shutters were open, letting in a fair amount of light, which fell across the table where Piers was seated with a soldier.

As soon as he noticed her presence, Piers nodded to the man in dismissal, and the fellow rose to leave. Although her feet felt leaden, Aisley walked to where her husband sat, and when she heard the creak of the door closing behind the visitor, she lifted her gaze to his face. It was grim, as she'd expected, and she drew in a sharp breath.

"Hexham has issued me a direct challenge," he said. "I cannot refuse."

She raised her chin and nodded in acceptance. "When will you leave?" she asked, surprised by the steadiness of her voice.

"As soon as possible. A day or two, no less," Piers answered. Aisley could see the regret in his face, and she tore her gaze away, walking toward the window, her eyes shut tightly against the ache of parting. So accustomed was she to finding her way through the darkened chamber that even without looking, she found the arrow slit. Then she opened her eyes to view the lands of Dunmurrow, fresh with the first signs of spring.

Aisley heard his steps and knew he halted behind her, for his great body radiated heat to her back. "Do you remember when I visited the village healer?" she asked.

"Yes." Piers's reply was gruff, and he made no move to touch her.

"'Twas to break the spell you had put upon me," Aisley said softly. "But 'twas a spell that no simple potion could break," she noted. "The old woman knew that, of course, but wished to teach me a lesson, I think."

"Aisley..." His voice was low and broken.

"And she did," Aisley continued. "I decided, then, to accept my feelings for you, and they grew until now I glory in them. But at this moment, 'tis easy to remember why I asked for the potion—to spare myself this pain."

His arms encircled her, pulling her back against his massive chest. "Aisley..." he whispered into her hair. "I'm sorry, Aisley. I feel it, too. Think you that I want to leave you now, when I finally have all that I could ever desire?"

She did not answer, and he went on, "When I lost my sight, I prayed, I wept and I raged to get it back, but after you came...my thoughts were only toward keeping you."

Aisley couldn't help herself; she had to say it. "Then don't go," she whispered.

She heard his sigh and felt it too, a great heaving of his chest against her. "Even if it were not for the sake of your lands or for the sake of my honor, what of the future? If I do not stand up for what is mine now, will we spend the rest of our lives fighting off greedy neighbors? I would like to make this a safe home for our children," Piers said softly.

Aisley smiled bitterly. She knew he was right, but that knowledge did not make the ache any easier to bear. She loved, and now she must pay the price. "All right, but I would have you home soon—and safe."

"What?" Piers asked, sounding affronted. "Have you no faith in the Red Knight?"

Aisley was up before the dawn to bid him goodbye. Though spring was showing its green buds, the morning was still damp and chill, and she clutched her cloak tightly around her as she left the keep.

Piers was seated atop his great destrier, the men who had come from Belvry surrounding him, along with a contingent from Dunmurrow, for he had no wish to be cut down before reaching his destination.

Aisley thought he had never looked more powerful, nor more deadly, dressed in his costume of war, his mail glinting in the dim light and his helm tucked under one arm. He looked up, surprised to see her dashing across the bailey.

"Aisley, love," he said roughly when she reached him. "I didn't expect you."

"You cannot slink away from my bed without me knowing it," Aisley teased, a too-bright smile upon her face. Piers's own generous lips curved up in a grin that struck her heart painfully. "But here, I have something for you," she said.

Her throat thick with unshed tears, Aisley held up what she had crafted during the hours he had spent training and preparing for this day. With a flick of his strong wrist, Piers unfurled it. It was a bloodred banner with a white stag stitched upon it.

"I did not think you had a device of your own, so I put the de Laci emblem on the crimson background," she said softly.

"'Tis beautiful," Piers said gruffly. "Thank you." He called for his squire, who rolled it up and stowed it with his things. Then he looked at her intensely, as if the passion he hid inside his warrior's frame was just a moment away from escaping.

"Aisley..." He opened his mouth to say something, but did not. Instead, he leaned over and lifted her up for a quick, brief kiss that left her breathless. By the time her feet found the ground again, Piers was riding away, into the darkness before the dawn.

Aisley bent over her bench in the buttery, mixing a tisane to ease the pain of one of the villagers, who had a bad leg.

When she had finished, she straightened up and put aside her medicines, her thoughts turning to her own distress. If only there were something she could take to dull the ache inside her, which had not diminished in the weeks since Piers had left.

But she knew that neither she nor the Widow Nebbs had a curative for what ailed her. She missed him. Although she was even busier now, with the planting to supervise, gardens to be laid out and a myriad other duties, Aisley felt his absence like a lesion. Her days were full, but a part of her was empty.

"My lady?" Aisley was drawn from her melancholy thoughts by the appearance of one of the castle's new residents, a girl who worked in the weaving room.

"Yes?" Aisley answered with an encouraging nod, for Clovis was still rather shy.

"I was in the village today to see the Widow Nebbs," Clovis said, eyeing Aisley's own medicines apologetically.

Aisley smiled, for she knew that old habits died hard, and she certainly did not take offense because the girl had sought treatment elsewhere. "Yes?"

"She gave me something for you, my lady," Clovis said, rummaging in her pockets.

"Oh?" Aisley had not been back to see the widow, the memory of the potion that had sickened her still fresh in her mind. Although Aisley felt guilty for neglecting the old woman, she did not feel guilty enough to return to the strange, dark hut where the widow made her home.

"Yes, my lady," Clovis said, handing over a small packet. Aisley stared at it a moment, then quickly put it down on the bench. She told herself she was not superstitious, only that there was something about the Widow Nebbs that made her nervous.

"She said you are to take that to help the babe sit well in your belly," Clovis said matter-of-factly. Startled, Aisley looked at the girl blankly. Babe? What babe? Before she could even begin to examine that statement, Clovis screwed up her face as if trying to repeat something from memory. "I am to tell you, too, my lady, to fear not...because..." She paused, as if the rest of the message had her stumped, then forged on ahead valiantly, "because the magic of the—the...deer goes with you."

Aisley simply stared, at a loss for words to respond to such an outrageous comment. Clovis did not appear to expect a response, however, for she nodded happily, her mission completed, and left the buttery.

Aisley gaped after her. Drawing in a shaky breath, she realized she ought to laugh. And she would have, but the hairs on the back of her neck were standing on end and that was not conducive to amusement. A magic deer? Before, she had thought the widow a strange, but wise old woman. Now she wondered if the lady had not gone mad. She reached for the packet, intending to throw it away, for were she dying, she would probably not accept anything from Widow Nebbs. The woman's last brew had made her far too ill.

A babe, and a potion to seat it. Aisley managed a crooked grin at the thought. Then her fingers froze, a hairbreadth away from their goal, as she tried to recall the last time she'd had her monthly flow. Her mind flew over the past weeks, during which she had tried to keep herself as busy as humanly possible, and earlier, when she had been so upset over Piers's departure.

'Twas possible. 'Twas entirely possible, Aisley thought wildly. No, she decided, shaking her head. 'Twas probable. 'Twas more than likely that she *was* carrying Piers's child and had been too busy and worried to notice! But how had the widow...?

Aisley abruptly jerked her hand away from the herbs and retreated from the bench with a wary frown. Backing out of the room, she ran into Cecil and nearly jumped out of her skin. The impassive servant eyed her dispassionately, as if people were always wandering around backwards, and Aisley did not explain herself.

"Cecil," she squeaked. "I left a packet on the bench in there. Would you please dispose of it for me?"

"Certainly, my lady," he answered without question.

"Thank you, Cecil. You're very good," she added gratefully. Then she headed toward the great chamber to think, to plan and to dream about her son or daughter, the emptiness inside her suddenly filling up again.

Aisley spared no further thoughts for the discarded potion, for she suspected it was only an excuse to bring the babe to her attention. She often wondered, however, about the rest of the widow's message, and if the redoubtable Clovis had garbled it somehow. What had the old woman really meant to tell her? Aisley was curious, but not curious enough to visit the widow and find out for herself.

Aisley was in the hall when they told her of a visitor at the gates. "'Tis a man named Benedict from Belvry," the soldier said.

"Send him in!" she cried, her heart twisting in her chest. She didn't wonder why Benedict had come instead of her husband's man; she wondered only if he brought word of Piers.

Aisley called for ale and food and then walked toward the hearth to warm her hands, suddenly ice cold though she felt no draft. If anything had happened to her husband... Piers! Piers! His name thrummed in her blood, but she tried not to think, not to guess, not to anticipate.

She lifted her head when Benedict came in, cloaked and hooded and much taller than she remembered him. He did not speak, but stood to one side while a servant brought a treacher and a cup and returned to the kitchens, leaving her alone in the hall with Benedict—only it wasn't Benedict.

Aisley remained utterly still, uncertain if she should call the guards or scream for help. Although the man made no threatening moves, she knew something was very wrong. Who was he? Why was he masquerading as Benedict? Aisley knew instinctively that he was her enemy, yet what did he hope to gain, one man alone in the hall of Dunmurrow, with guards outside the keep and a small garrison in the bailey?

Whoever he was, he obviously felt no fear, for he had watched her quietly and now, as if receiving his cue from her, he stepped forward majestically and threw back his hood in a dramatic gesture.

Aisley stared at the familiar face and gasped, unbelieving. "Hexham!" she whispered. "Are you mad? What are you doing here?"

"I've come to rescue the fair maid, of course," he said in that arrogant way of his. Hexham was as dark as Piers was fair, his skin almost sallow in color, his hair black as a raven's wing. He was thought handsome by some, but by none so much as himself. He held a hand toward her. "Come, Aisley. I will take you from this dunghill and back to Belvry."

Aisley edged away from his outstretched arm. "What are you saying?" she asked in astonishment.

"I'm saying that I have come to deliver you from life in this crumbling excuse for a keep and return you to the luxury that you are accustomed to, that is your *due*," he said. Hexham held himself very straight, his chest puffed out proudly, his dark eyes flashing, and she realized abruptly that he did, indeed, see himself in the role of her savior.

Aisley blinked at him, for she recognized now that he had planned it all very carefully. The challenge that had drawn the Red Knight away from Dunmurrow and left forces here at a minimum had been issued only so that Hexham could seize her. Even then the gutless bastard had not dared to try to breach the defenses, but had sneaked inside under disguise.

Aisley could not forestall the look of contempt that appeared on her face. It was just like Hexham to slither around like a snake. Where Piers would ride boldly up to the door and demand entry, Hexham would ever use deceit and treachery to meet his ends. Although he stood alone before her, she knew he must have men waiting outside the keep, for he was not brave enough to come by himself, even to aid what he thought was a willing maid.

And willing he thought her, that was obvious. Hexham spread his arms, expecting her to dash into them, grateful that he had sent her husband from her side and stolen into her home to take her away.

Aisley nearly laughed aloud.

Although there'd been a time when Dunmurrow was uncomfortable and her husband had made her uneasy, she had never thought to leave. Despite much prodding from Edith to flee, she would never have gone, for that was the coward's way. And here, before her in all his glory, was one great coward.

"Come, Aisley," he said, his hands motioning her forward.

If she had thought his motives pure, that he came only to help her, Aisley could have forgiven him his fool's errand. But Hexham, she knew, did naught that didn't profit himself. "Why?" she asked baldly.

She saw a flicker of anger cross his features, but he soon replaced it with an ingratiating smile. "We will have time to talk on the journey. Let us go now before we are discovered."

Aisley shook her head. "Why, Hexham? What did you plan to gain by coming here?"

"I want only to free you from this place. Now come!" he urged. He stepped toward her, no longer able to hide his irritation at her delay.

"No," Aisley said calmly. "I am going nowhere, Hexham. This is my home."

The baron's face grew taut with anger. "This is a tiny pile of rocks!" he snarled. "Your home is at Belvry, beside me!"

"What could you possibly have to do with Belvry?" Aisley asked coldly. "It belongs to my husband."

"Husband! I see no husband," Hexham scoffed. "Your father promised you to me! He wished to ensure that his lands were protected, and what better way than to join them with my own?"

Aisley gasped at his lies. "My father promised you nothing. He thought you a useless braggart and wanted naught to do with you! He would rise up from his grave rather than see you in his stead."

"Enough!" Hexham said, no longer smiling. His lip was curled in disgust, as if Aisley exuded some noxious odor. "I shall have your precious Belvry soon enough."

"You will never have Belvry!" Aisley snapped.

He stepped toward her menacingly. "I will! Once I have you with me, none will gainsay me!"

"If you so much as touch me, Hexham, my husband will kill you," Aisley countered. She spoke with such deadly assurance that the baron hesitated.

Then he barked out a laugh. "Ha! You have no husband! Let the Red Knight come forth and show himself!" he said mockingly, lifting an arm to take in the hall with a sweeping gesture.

Aisley smiled grimly. "He cannot, for even now he sends your pitiful army to rout!"

Hexham looked at her sharply, but Aisley only returned his gaze. "You lie!" he protested, as if trying to convince himself. "No one has seen Montmorency! He is either dead or a feeble old man who rode out at my summons, only to be cut down by my soldiers! If you are truly wed, which I doubt," Hexham added with a sneer, "we will have this marriage dissolved when we reach Belvry."

"Nay, Hexham," Aisley returned softly. Deliberately, she lowered a hand to her belly. "For even now I carry his babe." She saw the flash of surprise in his dark eyes, followed by disgust and uncertainty. "Montmorency lives," she asserted, seeing her opening. "And he is no weakling, but the Red Knight—a great warrior possessed of strengths beyond your imaginings."

A flicker of fear passed over Hexham's face, and Aisley pressed her advantage. How much had he heard of Montmorency's reputation? How much would he believe? "He has stayed here for a time, honing his skills, gaining more knowledge and power than you have ever dreamed," she said. "Why should he leave, for who would deign to challenge him? Only a fool such as you, Hexham, would anger the Red Knight, whose wrath is as red as blood—your blood, which he will spill!"

"Shut up, bitch!" Hexham ordered. He raised a hand to strike her, but the dogs, lying forgotten under the tables, growled low in their throats, halting his motion, and Aisley stepped back, out of his reach. He dropped his arm, but it was trembling with the force of his anger.

At first, Aisley had thought only to be rid of him, to convince him that he was no savior of hers and send him from her sight. But his violence and his words made her change her mind. She remembered his duplicity, his challenge to her husband, who even now might be battling for his life, while the man who had called him out was sneaking into his home to steal his wife, and she knew she could not let him go unpunished.

The baron tried again. Aisley watched him garner control of himself and put on his gracious mask and his most cajoling voice. "If this knight is as fearsome as you claim, then I give you a chance to escape him. Come with me, to Belvry," he coaxed. "I care not about the babe."

Although the man waved his hand in a studied gesture of carelessness, Aisley knew it was a lie he spoke. He was appalled by the babe, and should she go with him, he would never let her keep it. The thought made her blood rush through her veins and pound in her ears, filling her with rage and contempt and loathing such as she had never known. "We can still have the marriage dissolved. We belong together, Aisley, you know that," Hexham said, his tone gentle.

She laughed. "I have always detested you, Hexham, and I cannot think you so blind as to not realize it. But even if I did not, I would not want you. I belong with Montmorency. The Red Knight is my lord," she said calmly. "He is more than I could ever desire."

"You are bewitched!" Hexham snapped. "That you would lie with this devil and spawn a child by him is insanity! Come, and I shall break you of his spell soon enough." He reached for her again, but Aisley was quicker.

"Castor! Pollux! To me!" Aisley said softly, and before Hexham could take another step, the dogs, large and intimidating, stationed themselves on each side of her. Hexham backed away, cursing. "As for you, my gallant rescuer," Aisley added, her voice laden with sarcasm, "I will have you trussed up in the dungeon to await my husband's leisure."

Aisley saw shock travel across Hexham's face. Obviously, he had never expected her to refuse him, let alone take him prisoner. The desperation that flashed in his eyes should have warned her, but Aisley felt bold and brave with the dogs at her side. She was not afraid of the treacherous knave before her.

"Need you more ale, my lady?" So intent was Aisley upon her foe that she had not noticed Glenna's approach, but the servant now stood much too near to Hexham, holding out a vessel and nodding toward the table where the meal for Benedict sat untouched.

"No," Aisley said. She opened her mouth to say more, but before she could utter a warning, Hexham grabbed the servant. The pitcher fell to the floor, ale spilling across the tiles, while the man held a dagger to Glenna's throat.

"Call off the dogs, my lady," he hissed at Aisley. "And come with me, or I shall slit this wench's throat."

Aisley drew in a sharp breath. She had no doubt that Hexham would do it. He was ruthless, and she had backed him into a corner—foolishly, she now knew. She thought of Moira, running in to find her mother bleeding to death on the floor, and she swallowed hard. "All right. I will go with you."

"Send the dogs into the kitchens," Hexham snapped.

"Castor! Pollux! Out!" Aisley ordered, pointing toward the arch that led out of the hall. The dogs whimpered and growled, but went, and she stepped toward the baron, amazed at how quickly he had gained the upper hand. Too late, she realized that she had underestimated him, thinking him only a weak fool, and now she would pay the price for her miscalculation. "Let the servant go," she said.

With one quick movement, Hexham thrust Glenna away from him and grabbed Aisley by the arm, drawing her close and putting the knife to her own throat. "Do nothing or I shall kill your mistress, woman," he said, glaring at Glenna. The servant had fallen to the floor and cowered near the table, her gown wet with ale, her dark eyes wide.

"You will never get through the gate alive, Hexham," Aisley warned.

"Oh, yes, I will," Hexham promised. He pushed her toward the door. Lifting a hand, he removed his cloak in a swirl and passed it over her hair around her shoulders, so that none could see the weapon that threatened her. "You will make it easy for me," he said. "You will tell the guards that we are going into the village, and you had better make it convincing, or you will die."

Aisley clenched her fists in frustration. Would he really kill her? Hexham had always coveted her. She could remember even when she was young how the neighbor had looked toward her with a lecherous eye—and that while his wife still lived, locked away in his keep.

Yes, Hexham wanted her and all that she stood for as chatelaine of Belvry. But he was desperate now, and she could not imagine him surrendering gracefully. His dark face was hard and cold, with a look of a man pushed to the edge, and she shivered. If it were only herself clutched in his grip, she would struggle, scream for a guard or run from him, but it was not just her. Aisley put a hand protectively to her belly and thought of Piers's babe, and she knew she could not endanger it.

As she had suspected, a small group of Hexham's men surrounded them as soon as they left the keep, and Aisley was sickened when she saw that they wore the colors of Belvry, the masquerading devils! At the stables, Hexham took a fresh mount, and Aisley her palfrey. She thought to ride from his side, shouting to her husband's men, but as if reading her mind, Hexham kept a tight grip on her reins, grinning evilly.

Aisley hoped that the drawbridge would stop him, but it had been lowered to increase traffic between Dunmurrow and the village and was raised only at night or if danger approached. No one had known that this small band, ostensibly friends from her former home, could pose such a threat to her.

Although soldiers milled about the bailey and along the walls, none gave the two more than a cursory glance, and Aisley realized with growing horror that they did not recognize her under the heavy cloak. She rode onto the drawbridge without anyone lifting a hand to stop her or raising a voice in question. Powerless, she watched each moment carry her farther away from Dunmurrow and heard each fall of her mount's hooves ringing in her ears like a death knoll.

They were nearly across when a guard standing outside the walls finally noticed her under the voluminous cape. "My lady," he called out, approaching them. Although they came to a halt as he bade them, Aisley saw Hexham's hand tighten on her reins.

"My lady would show us the village," Hexham said smoothly.

The soldier, a massive fellow with bristling gray hair, eyed her companion speculatively, then looked hard at Aisley. "I cannot let you go without an escort of my own men, my lady," he said. "'Twas my lord's orders."

Aisley silently thanked the man, who was obviously well trained, for his refusal. Surely, he must sense something was wrong, but could he act quickly enough to save her? Opening her eyes wide, she sent him a message full of fear and danger, and hoped that her hood did not obscure her features.

It all happened in an instant. As the guard put his hand to the hilt of his sword, Hexham leaned toward Aisley and snatched her into his arms. Dragging her in front of him, he drew his sword across her throat. "Out of my way!" he shouted. Then he spurred the horse to motion, and the guard was forced to stand aside or be cut down by the beast and those of Hexham's followers.

The world flew by as Hexham gave the steed its head, and Aisley could hear shouts rising up behind them. She suspected that a party was forming to pursue them, but what could the Dunmurrow guards do, short of aiming an arrow very carefully. Any attempt to cut down Hexham would kill her, too. If the men-at-arms were fast, they might surround Hexham's group, but she would still be before him, his blade against her throat.

Aisley's heart sank as she realized that she could not count upon help coming from the castle. She was on her own, with only her wits to save her.

Chapter Sixteen

Aisley's wits were of little help. Although Hexham had lowered his sword, she could only cling to the horse as it raced across the open land leading to the forest, for she had no desire to fall and be trampled.

Hexham slowed the animal but little when they entered the woods, and Aisley watched, dismayed, as some of the men took different paths to foil pursuit. She realized that the baron had planned every detail, and yet, despite all, he feared the soldiers from Dunmurrow, for he rode like a madman.

Aisley held little hope of rescue from that quarter, but she could not seem to devise a plan of her own. Her body rebelled at the horrible closeness of Hexham, and she was sure his steed would stumble amid the roots and brush on the forest floor. Her usually nimble thoughts seemed scattered as the party raced onward, eating up the ground beneath them.

Closing her eyes, Aisley let time drift by unheeded, until finally a vision of her husband came into her mind, bringing some sense of order. She thought of Piers, of his might and his love for her, and the calm that had been eluding her settled over her— as if, by some miracle, he had sent her some of his strength.

With her head clearer, Aisley realized she could do naught for now, at least until they stopped, and then…perhaps she could escape. Hexham was ruthless, but he was not as smart as she. Even as she tried to reassure herself, however, Aisley wondered how superior intellect could prevail over bodily power and force of arms.

Hexham finally slowed, then stopped to listen, his blade moving across her again, and Aisley held her breath. To her dismay, she heard the rustle of leaves and the faraway songs of birds, but not one sound of following riders. The men beside them laughed confidently, and kicking the horses to speed, they crashed through the trees into open country—straight into a group of heavily armed soldiers.

Aisley gasped in surprise, her initial fright giving way to hope as, for one brief moment, she thought they were from Dunmurrow. It soon became obvious, however, that the men who gathered around them were not from Piers's castle nor her own Belvry. They were Hexham's men, stationed here to wait for him. It was easy enough to determine because the cowardly Hexham did not balk, but continued laughing, flush with the thrill of his victory.

While Aisley swallowed that bitter discovery, Hexham dropped her to the ground and slid down behind her. Gripping her tightly by the arm, he snapped something under his breath to the closest man, and the fellow handed Hexham a short length of cord, which the baron used to bind her wrists behind her back.

"What's this, my lord?" asked one of the other men. "I thought you were rescuing the lady."

"The lady needed a bit of persuading," Hexham answered tersely. "She's been bewitched by that devil Montmorency."

At mention of her husband's name, Aisley heard the familiar rumble of rumor rise around her, and she turned a steady gaze upon the men who talked of him.

"The Red Knight! Is that his wife?" one soldier asked.

"I've heard of him," another said, crossing himself. "They say he's akin to the devil himself."

"Bah!" Hexham showed his disdain by spitting on the ground at her feet. "He is naught but a shadow, unseen for God knows how long. He is either dead or so old that he cannot lift a sword."

Aisley turned solemnly back to Hexham. "He is young and strong and powerful beyond your imagining," she said evenly. "Already he has learned of your foul deed and hunts you down."

"He knows nothing!" Hexham shouted. He lifted a hand to strike her, and then dropped it, laughing. "I shall ride you so hard and so long that you will forget him soon enough," he said. Several of the men chuckled at Hexham's promise, but Aisley noticed others who glanced at her uneasily, and it was to those that she spoke.

Drawing herself up straight and eyeing Hexham calmly, she said slowly, "Mark me, Hexham, the Red Knight will come, and he will eat your heart for supper."

Montmorency's legend seemed to burst to life then, becoming a presence in the group. Aisley heard more muttering and saw men step back, away from her. She smiled confidently.

"Be quiet," Hexham snorted at her, "or I shall beat you senseless." He turned to his men. "Stop your chattering. And put the bitch on a horse. We ride home."

Alfred Morling lifted his helm and looked out over the empty fields, his practiced eye searching for signs of Hexham. He rubbed his neck roughly, as if he could already feel his head parting from his shoulders. He knew that unless he found the baron, that would surely happen, for he had been responsible for the protection of Dunmurrow.

Montmorency had left him to guard it, had specifically charged him to protect the lady of the keep, and Alfred had failed. Someone had ridden straight into their midst and stolen her from her own hall, right under their very noses. And according to one of the servants, 'twas that bastard Hexham, the very same who had issued a direct challenge to Montmorency himself.

Alfred shook his head. Only the most cowardly of men would draw a knight out on the field and then sneak behind his back to steal his wife. 'Twas unthinkable, and yet it had happened. He rubbed his neck again, knowing that if he did not retrieve Lady Montmorency soon he would be a dead man. Yet night was falling, and they had lost the trail in the forest.

"Clyde!" he shouted. A young warrior rode up at his command, and Alfred wearily gave him the duty he knew all of them feared. "Ride ahead of us, straight toward Belvry, and find Baron Montmorency. Tell him that Hexham has taken his wife."

"Yes, sir," the young man said, his face paling. All who knew the Red Knight's temper shied from the task, but it had to be done. The baron had a right to know. "I will tell him," Clyde said. He turned his steed and was gone.

Aisley shifted on the hard ground. For days they had ridden like demons, as if the very hounds of hell were at their heels—or before them, she thought with a grim smile. Although Hexham professed to have no fear of her husband, still he set a brutal speed, and Aisley suspected he was becoming anxious about Montmorency. For her part, she goaded the baron daily, calmly telling him that the Red Knight would come for her. And though he scoffed, she could see that her confidence burned like a nettle under his skin.

Aisley was glad of the pace, for each night, Hexham was too tired to do aught but chew his food and fall asleep. Sometimes she caught him staring at her and fear pricked at her, for she knew that sooner or later he meant to have her.

That she was another man's wife and carrying another man's child meant nothing to him.

She sensed that he left her alone only because he was weary, and though it would come to rape in the end, Hexham's enormous pride would not let him force her in front of his men. He saw himself as too lordly, too handsome and too gracious to take her here on the ground, so Aisley considered herself safe, for now, unless she pushed him too hard or baited him too long.

When they reached their destination, however, Hexham would no longer feel any constraints, Aisley knew. She frowned anxiously, resting a slim hand on her slender stomach, and hoped that the Red Knight would come before then.

That was all she could do, for a chance to escape had not presented itself and looked unlikely until they arrived at Hexham's home. Her hands still bound, she rode during the day, and at night she slept surrounded by the baron and his men.

Aisley lifted her lashes to take an assessing glance at the group. Although all were asleep, two guards remained awake, one scouting the perimeter of the camp and one close by, watching her. It was always the same, and try as she might, she could form no plan to elude them. . . . Aisley felt exhaustion overwhelm her, and the heavy fog of sleep drew a cloak over her busy thoughts.

She dozed with the image of the guard in her mind, only to waken at the touch of a hand on her arm. Alert instantly, she opened her eyes to find the very same guard bending over her. "Come," he whispered roughly. "I'll help you get away."

Aisley raised up on one elbow, her heart sending a rush of blood through her that made her nearly faint. Get away?

"Hurry!" he said hoarsely, his fingers digging into her arm. Aisley looked at his face, but it was hidden by darkness. Struggling to her knees, she gazed up at him again, to see hi grin, evil and gap-toothed, in the moonlight. Abruptly, as if she were having a vision, Aisley pictured herself leaving with the man, only to be raped and cast aside, her bruised body thrown under some bushes. She shivered.

He pulled her to her feet, and Aisley fought against him, determined now to call out to her other captors. But before she could utter a sound, the nearby trees suddenly burst to life. Her companion stiffened and pushed her back to the ground, then drew his sword. Aisley, the breath knocked from her, fought for air, while she heard men in the camp stir and something crash from the cover of the woods.

Oaths. Several of the men were cursing. Then there was a brief frenzy of activity, followed by someone's laughter. Aisley turned onto her side to view what was happening, but whatever it was, it was apparently over. Most of the men were up now, standing about. Some were holding weapons, others putting theirs away, so they obviously felt no threat.

"Curse you, Rhys, for the clod that you are," Hexham said. "That stag would have made good eating."

The man who had try to compel her into leaving with him backed away, muttering to himself. Another man ran a hand through his hair and shook his head in the darkness. "Can't shoot a white stag, my lord," he said. "'Tis bad luck."

"You stupid curs!" Hexham hissed. "You are as ignorant as blind beggars and twice as slow! Rhys will keep double watch, and you—" Hexham said, pointing at the man who had spoken "—you may join him! Between you perhaps you may have the sense of one man!"

"'Twas a white stag?" Aisley asked in the silence that followed.

"So what if it was?" Hexham said angrily. "Its meat would taste as good as any other."

"'Twas not for eating," she said solemnly. "'Twas a sign from the Red Knight. He comes."

For a moment, Aisley thought she had pushed Hexham too far, and that even his thin veneer of civilized behavior would be broken. But he only glared at her, while the men looked on in various shades of disbelief and horror.

"Somebody shut the bitch up," Hexham said softly. When no one responded, he moved himself. "Here, give me that rag," he snapped to one of the men. Leaning over, he shoved a rancid cloth in her mouth and tied it. "Now we will all be spared your pretty tales," he whispered close to her. With a smug look, he patted her cheek. "Be good, Aisley, and soon you will be sucking on something more pleasant."

Piers lifted his helm and mopped his brow. After waiting for days for some sign of Hexham's army, they had gone out in search of it, only to send it easily to rout. Too easily. Surmising that the retreat might actually be a trap, Piers had let the enemy skulk back to their own lands, and they had, retiring quietly. But Hexham had yet to show his face.

Since the baron had issued the challenge, Piers suspected some treachery. Aisley had warned him that her old neighbor would not fight fairly on a field of honor. In truth, she had not wanted him to come, and that memory added to his frustration. He felt an odd tingling sensation in the back of his head, as if something was, indeed, very wrong.

The arrival of one of the soldiers he had left at Dunmurrow did little to improve his mood, and he glanced immediately at Alan. Perhaps the challenge had been nothing more than a lure to draw him away from his demesne. If that bastard Hexham had attacked Dunmurrow while Aisley was there...

"What is it?" he snapped at the young rider. Piers spared no thought to the man's condition, haggard and hungry and tired, as if he had ridden for days without rest. Neither did he spend a moment on formalities. He could not, for he could barely maintain control of himself.

"My lord," Clyde said, his pale gaze meeting Montmorency's. "My lord, Hexham has taken your wife."

The roar that erupted sent a chill through the Red Knight's own men, while any lingering enemy soldiers cowered and ran for cover. Piers lifted his sword high as if to smite Clyde where he sat astride his horse, but Alan nudged his steed closer.

"Where did he take her? Is he asking a ransom?" Alan asked. His was the voice of reason, a calming influence on Montmorency's rage, and the Red Knight's arm dropped as he listened.

Clyde's hand trembled on his reins, for he knew how close he had been to death, and he silently thanked his lord's vassal. Yet, when he looked at the Red Knight, he felt as though the blade had, indeed, pierced his heart, the anguish on the great warrior's face was so painful to see.

Montmorency loved his wife. It was a revelation to Clyde, a simple soldier who knew naught of such things, and he tore his gaze away from the Red Knight, as if he had intruded on the baron's privacy. He managed to shake his head. "We don't know. He rode in this direction, so we assumed he was taking her to Belvry. A servant woman said 'twas Hexham, but he asked no ransom from us."

"Perhaps he now draws us into a trap," Alan said.

"Now?" Piers said, his voice rough with anger. "He has already trapped me neatly, the whoreson!"

Aisley nearly fell from her mount, weariness draining the life from her. If she could only sleep! Regardless of her chafed wrists, and her dry, swollen mouth, still stuffed with cloth, she would sleep forever, if she could.... The baby sapped her energy, and the gruelling pace was too much. Aisley drifted, nodding, and wondered when Hexham would let them stop for the night.

A jolt forced her to open her eyes, and she looked around her, trying to stay awake. Nightfall was coming and would bring a halt, she hoped. Then she drew in a sharp breath as she recognized the stream that ran along this stretch of road. They were nearing Belvry.

Aisley felt despair wash over her, for she was too tired to grapple with the questions that rose in her mind. What would Hexham do now? Was he going to his own castle or to Belvry, or to one of the outlying manors? Was he in possession of her home? Where was Piers? Hexham obviously anticipated no threat, because he rode with little regard for caution.

They were nearly a dozen strong and fully armed, enough to contend with any brigands. But what of Piers? His name returned to her, over and over. Did Hexham not know of the Red Knight's army, or was he simply too foolhardy to be wary? Aisley was heartened by the hope that they might be riding directly into a trap. In that case, she knew she must stay alert enough to avoid the ensuing battle, for she had no wish to be killed along with Hexham and his men.

Aisley's hopes were fed by the appearance of a lone rider in their path. It was dusk, and the nearby trees would make a perfect hiding place for others. Aisley eyed the woods anxiously, but Hexham apparently was not concerned, for he drew up before the man himself. "Move aside or be cut down," the baron snapped.

The rider did not stir. "Know you that you are on de Laci land?" he asked. Aisley peered at the stranger in the deepening gloom, her initial excitement shadowed by fear. Dressed as a knight and wearing a helm, the rider could well be one of Piers's men, but why then hadn't he called the land Montmorency's?

"This is *my* land, fool, and you had best be off, or I shall have your head!" Hexham warned. His men crowded around him, and Aisley felt sorry for the single rider, who would surely meet the baron's wrath with his death.

Aisley eased her steed away from what looked to be a cold-blooded murder, but as she did, shouts rang out, and horses poured out of the woods. Although she could not tell how many, she knew there were enough to overwhelm Hexham's small band. Weary as she was, she managed to move away, not wanting to be caught among the warriors when the blood lust was upon them and no one could see clearly in the twilight.

If Aisley's first thoughts were for her own safety, her next were to escape. She had no idea who these new men were, and she had no intention of giving herself up to their uncertain care. She tried to break free from the group, but one of the massive destriers moved in front of her, cutting off her route and making her horse balk. With difficulty, she managed to turn the beast around, but the battle raged thickly behind her. Was there no way out?

Aisley shook her head, as if to clear her mind, and then, spying the stream, she sent the animal into the water. She knew the course here was shallow enough, although fast moving, and she rode away from the melee as quickly as she could. Her heart beat faster with every length of her horse's stride, and freedom called to her. It waited for her ahead, if she could only escape the notice of those fighting behind her.

Just as she began to think she was safe, Aisley heard the splash of hoofbeats at her back. "Hold!" a man cried, and she slowed, not daring to risk her baby or her life for her liberty. Drawing a deep breath, she turned to face her adversary, and she knew immediately that Hexham had not won the day.

His upset brought even more confusion to her. She was glad to be rid of the baron, and yet she had no notion who these men were who had attacked him. With one look at the cruel face staring back at her, Aisley knew that she might have landed in far worse trouble than Hexham's company had brought her.

"'Tis a woman!" the man shouted over his shoulder to his fellows, and Aisley prayed these were Piers's men, who would do naught to her but guard her carefully until she was safe at her husband's side again. Should she make her name known, or would brigands use that knowledge to hold her for ransom?

"Bring her here!" another shouted. Aisley tried to get a look at the one who spoke, since he was obviously the leader, but she could see only his back. She rode forward, intent upon judging what manner of man he was before giving her name. Then she wondered if any of Hexham's men remained alive to gainsay her if she did not tell the truth.

Aisley tried to summon her wits as she approached the leader. In the gathering darkness, she saw that he was taller than Hexham And more muscular, but could tell little else. Then he turned and grew still, staring at her as if he had seen a ghost. "Holy God!" he said.

While Aisley sought for an appropriate response to that odd greeting, he shouted at his man, "Get the gag out of her mouth!" His voice sounded oddly strained, making her wonder if she had heard it before. She had no time to search her memory, however, for she soon felt the cloth being removed and licked her dry lips gratefully.

"Aisley! Don't you know me?" the man asked. Then he lifted the helm from his head, releasing a crown of dark hair, and Aisley gasped. She took one look at the familiar face and slipped slowly from her mount in a dead faint.

She would have hit the ground if it were not for the quick hands of the cruel-looking man beside her. Unfortunately, Aisley was unaware of his kind deed, and when she woke up to find herself sprawled across his lap, she shrieked. She was not comforted when he smiled, as if he were quite accustomed to holding screaming women.

"Aisley! 'Tis Nicholas, your brother," someone said sharply. Tearing her gaze away from the scar on the face above her, Aisley glanced over at the leader—as if her eyes could ever convince her that she was seeing a dead man. She closed them again and moaned.

"Are you all right?" Nicholas asked impatiently, and Aisley suspected he was more irritated than concerned. It had been a long time, but she recognized the general tone of the males in her family. "What were you doing with that bastard Hexham? What did he mean, saying that these were his lands?"

Realizing that the specter had no intention of leaving her be, Aisley finally opened her eyes again and looked at him. Even in the lowering gloom, she could tell it was her brother. Nicholas had all the height that Aisley lacked, height inherited from their father, and he had the thick brown hair of their sire, too.

No one would have suspected them of being siblings, and yet she knew their features were enough alike that close scrutiny might reveal their relationship. Nicholas was uncommonly comely for a man, a trait that he despised, and he had been forever brawling with his brothers over his pretty looks. Were they gone now or just hardened by experience? In the twilight, he appeared to have aged far more than would be expected in the five years since Aisley had seen him last. "You're dead," she said.

If Aisley expected him to be surprised at her pronouncement, he was not. "I know. 'Tis a long story, Sister, and the night grows dark. Tell me, where does Hexham go?"

"Go? To hell, I hope," she answered wearily.

"Aisley!" At his urgent command, she finally sat up, elbowing the man who held her on his lap.

"Hexham is gone?" she asked.

"Yes," Nicholas answered bitterly. "The viper has fled, as usual, but he will not escape. Where does he go?"

"I don't know," Aisley said. "He never told me. I assumed we were going to his castle, but he acted as if he owned Belvry now."

"Does he?" her brother asked in a voice she did not recognize, a voice so filled with hatred that it made her draw back.

"Again, I do not know," she answered. "He snatched me from Dunmurrow after drawing out my husband with a challenge."

"Your husband?" Nicholas's eyes narrowed, and Aisley was somehow irked by his surprise. "You have wed?" he asked.

"Yes," she answered. "My husband is Baron Montmorency, the Red Knight. Have you heard of him?"

Nicholas shook his head. "No, but I have been away," he said roughly, "too long."

"So that is why you said de Laci land," Aisley whispered as the truth finally dawned on her. With her father's son alive, this fight was no longer Piers's. Not only that but... Aisley gaped in amazement, realizing that she need never have wed at all.

The thought of all that could have been avoided by her brother's presence made Aisley weak, yet she knew a physical pain when she considered a life without Piers. She was glad then that Nicholas had disappeared, whatever his reasons, for she did not regret her marriage. She regretted only that Piers was in danger for the sake of her brother's lands. "You are rightful heir to Belvry," she said.

"Yes," Nicholas replied. "Though I've no doubt Hexham would dispute it." He paused. "Will your husband?"

"Piers?" Aisley nearly laughed. "No, he has his own lands. He never wanted Belvry. 'Tis yours, brother, but first we must find my husband." She slid from the grasp of the man who held her, feeling her tiredness slip away, her body invigorated by the hope that her brother might see her reunited with Piers. "Have you a horse for me?" Aisley asked.

Nicholas nodded. "Get my sister a mount," he said. "For now we shall let our snake crawl away to his hole, but we will soon run him to ground." Turning to Aisley, he said, "We ride for the manor at Chiswill. The rest of my men are there."

"You have more?" Aisley asked in a stunned voice, as someone helped her onto a great, black steed.

"Yes," Nicholas said. "I have men of my own and mercenaries."

"Then you knew there would be trouble when you returned?" she went on, tightening the reins.

"Yes," Nicholas said curtly. As usual, his answers were short and emotionless, and Aisley could see that his brief interest in her had waned, since she could provide him with no further information.

She sighed as she watched him flick a cool glance of dismissal her way, and she could not help comparing her brother to her husband, who could be described as anything but cold. Both men were strikingly handsome, but there the similarities ended.

Aisley was loath to quit her bed at Chiswill Manor, a warm and welcoming reminder of her former life as the daughter of Clarence de Laci. Yet she knew that Nicholas would demand to leave early, and she wanted a bath after her days on the road. How odd it was to think of her brother alive and well in the hall below!

Although they were not close, Aisley still felt a sister's pleasure at his homecoming, and she felt immeasurably lighter to be relieved of the burden of Belvry. She had never thought to part willingly with her old home, and yet she knew she could do so now without a qualm. Its beauty and its luxuries no longer held allure when compared with the more powerful attraction of her husband.

After her time spent as Hexham's prisoner, trussed up and frightened, a simple bath was a luxury, and the peace and safety of Chiswill, a small, insignificant holding, became precious. As a measure of her new mood, Aisley nearly wept with joy to find that some of her old gowns were still stored in the wardrobe, never having been removed during her last visit in the halcyon days of summer before her marriage.

Slipping a hand to her stomach, she was awed by how much happier she was now, despite all the difficulties she had faced. Yes, she had been content then, enjoying the season and busy with Belvry, but she had been lonely. She admitted that she had crowded her days with work to avoid an emptiness inside her—an emptiness now filled by her husband.

Drawing in a deep breath, she said a prayer for Piers. Would that she would find him alive and well, and could tell him about the child he did not know he had conceived.

Something had forced Hexham's hand, Piers thought as he led his men to greet the approaching army. Was it Aisley's kidnapping? Although he knew he had to consider the possibility, he could not bear to think of her in the possession of another. He turned his mind instead toward war, for, whatever the reason, Hexham was finally acting. Piers had been right before not to walk into the baron's trap, because Hexham had more men lying in wait, soldiers whom he now sent out boldly.

They were a match for Piers's force, and he regretted leaving a contingent at Dunmurrow, for it had done little enough there. It had failed even to protect his wife, he noted grimly. The irony of this fight was not lost upon him—that he should risk his men and his life over a meaningless castle, while the woman he cherished more than all else had been stolen from him.

Pride, Piers thought with a shake of his head. Pride and honor were often a man's downfall, as well as his reason for living. For once in his life, he regretted riding to war.

As he assessed the enemy, Piers also regretted the blindness that had kept him out of the fray for so long, depleting his forces. Still, Alan had rallied those who remained, and now they must prove their mettle, as must he. It was time for the Red Knight to live up to his name. With fierce calculation, Piers put aside thoughts of all else and turned his attention to killing.

Chapter Seventeen

Although Piers knew his men were fighting valiantly, Hexham was calling on fresh reserves, loosing an endless supply of mercenaries, who attacked on every flank. Pulling back to assess his position, Piers lifted his helm and wiped his brow, the sweat pouring into his eyes under the heavy mail coif. When he saw Alan approaching with a grim look on his face, he knew his vassal did not bear good news.

"Hexham's man said he is willing to discuss terms," Alan said as he reined in.

"Terms?" Piers scoffed, as he usually did at such words. "Why do you even delay me with such news? You know I never talk when I can fight."

Alan looked uncomfortable, and a flush stole over his features as he held Piers's gaze. "I thought perhaps . . . the baron might say something of your lady," he explained.

Piers felt his insides tighten at the mention of his wife, by necessity forgotten in the heat of battle. "Has he asked a ransom?" Piers asked, his voice thick.

"No," Alan answered, "but Hexham's man did not say much. Perhaps he plans to offer your lady in return for Belvry."

Piers grunted. One woman for the whole of a huge, profitable demesne? 'Twas an unheard of exchange, and he scowled as a lifetime of soldiering, of honor and pride conflicted with what was truly important: his wife. "Let us hear him out, then," Piers said roughly.

They eyed each other dubiously when they entered Hexham's tent, however. The baron was seated on a great chair with a rug under his feet, like some Eastern infidel or rich Italian merchant. Although he was dressed in the finest costume of war, it was plain from the shiny glint of his mail that Hexham had not been part of the fighting. Piers could only stare scornfully at a man who did not lead his own into battle.

"So this is the fearsome Red Knight?" Hexham asked. The baron lifted his brows in a decidedly mocking expression, and Piers caught Alan's warning glance. Was Hexham provoking him deliberately? He was not sure, but the greeting made him determined to keep his head, despite his precarious temper.

"Yes, my lord," said the man who had brought them. He slipped out, and they were left alone before the baron and his men-at-arms. Although a contingent of his own waited outside, Piers began to feel uneasy. Hexham was a slippery villan who had already proved his treachery. Had he planned some mischief instead of talk?

Hexham regarded them at length. Then, leaning his elbows on the arms of his chair, he put the tips of his fingers together and placed them under his chin. "It must be obvious to you now, Red Knight, that you are sorely outnumbered. Why don't you surrender gracefully, and I shall let you and the rest of your men live." He waved a hand magnanimously. "There has been enough bloodshed today."

Piers did not answer, but stared at the arrogant ass who preened before them. This "discussion" was useless. Surely the man had not stopped the fighting for this? And what of Aisley?

Apparently unnerved by Piers's stoic glare, the baron snapped at them, "Well? Answer me!"

Piers lifted his hand to the hilt of his sword. "What of my wife, Hexham?" he asked, his fingers tightening upon the weapon. "Where is she?"

Hexham appeared surprised at the question, and for a moment Piers wondered if the man really had captured Aisley. He quickly recovered his poise, however, and smiled evilly. "Your wife? Oh, you mean Aisley de Laci."

"Aisley Montmorency," Piers correctly, his lips tightening into a hard line. "What have you done with her?"

"Why, nothing of course, except tie her to my bed and take my ease with her," Hexham said lightly. He dropped his elaborate pose to flick at a fly on his arm. "I'm afraid I rode her a little too hard, and she lost that babe she was carrying, but no matter. I will plant other seeds in that white belly of hers."

Piers's roar of rage shook the tent. His sword flew out of its sheath with such speed and such deadly aim that Hexham had to scramble out of its path to avoid being pinioned to his chair. Still, the blade sliced down his arm, drawing blood, and he screamed.

The men-at-arms behind him rushed forward, but Piers cut them down like stalks of grain, murderously intent upon his objective—Hexham, who was fleeing from the tent without any thought of defending himself. And all the while Piers's bellow of wrath rent the air like some pagan death cry.

Aisley felt her impatience grow as they approached Belvry, and she urged her horse out of line, sending it closer to her brother's great destrier. They had been on the road since dawn—Aisley, Nicholas, the men who had fought against Hexham's band and an even larger number who had been waiting at Chiswell—holding to a steady pace to reach Belvry before evening.

She looked back at the ranks behind her. They were an impressive sight, for each man appeared battle hardened and dangerous. Sometimes Aisley caught a glimpse of browned skin and dark, mysterious eyes, and she wondered where Nicholas had gathered his force. They moved silently, obeying him without words in a manner that seemed strange and foreign, and Aisley shivered, glad they followed her brother and not Hexham.

"Aisley!" She turned to hear her brother's voice, low and clipped. "Get back until we see what awaits us," he ordered.

Aisley opened her mouth to protest. The crest of the hill lay ahead, and beyond it Belvry and perhaps Piers. She had come so far, and did not want to tag along behind. And though the faint sounds of men drifted up to them, she would swear it wasn't the noise of battle. Before Aisley could respond, however, the stillness was broken by a ferocious roar, as if some wild beast were on a rampage.

"Piers." His name escaped her lips in a hushed whisper.

"What the hell was that?" Nicholas asked.

Piers. "It was Piers," Aisley said, more firmly. "He has lost his temper."

"That is a man?" Nicholas asked, his eyes narrowing in disbelief. "That is your *husband?*"

"Yes!" Urging her mount forward to the crest of the hill, Aisley looked down upon the fields before Belvry, only to find them filled with soldiers, and from the midst of them arose Piers's unmistakable bellow. "I know it is!" she said, turning to her brother. "Oh, Nicholas, he may be in trouble."

"Get to the back then, Aisley." Turning toward his men, he said, "Make sure she has a guard around her at all times. The rest of you, be prepared to attack at my signal. But remember—" Nicholas paused, his handsome face twisting coldly "—remember that Hexham is mine."

When Piers finally broke out of the tent, he was sweating and bloody enough to merit his name. Hexham was nowhere to be seen, but he, Alan and the small contingent from Dunmurrow were being overwhelmed by a very large part of the baron's army. Whether Hexham had hoped to trap them there amid the enemy, Piers did not know, but because he had lost his temper, they were now well and truly caught.

They made a rush for their horses and managed to mount in the melee caused by their rush from the tent, but when Piers scanned the area for an escape route, he saw none. They were an island in a sea of Hexham's soldiers, with too great a distance between them and their own to possibly reach safety. Fighting for his life, Piers tried to cut a swath toward the high ground, but when he glanced up, suddenly he saw more men, mounted knights and mercenaries, cresting the hill and marching straight toward them.

We are lost. For the first time in all his battles, the words entered Piers's mind, and he thought how ironic it was that only a few months ago he would have willingly gone to his death proudly, while now...now, by God's wounds, he wanted to live!

"What the devil?" shouted Alan from beside him.

Piers followed his vassal's gaze to the hilltop and stared in puzzlement as one of the approaching knights unfurled a black banner. Alan groaned when the sign of a leaping white stag was revealed. "I've seen it in Belvry. 'Tis the sign of the castle," he said, despair creeping onto his face.

"No," Piers protested. He shook his head slowly and then, turning swiftly, reached back and grasped his own flag, given to him by his wife and forgotten. He tossed it to Alan, who let the wind take the bloodred material that, unbound, sported an identical leaping stag. It rose above their small group, snapping in the wind like a vivid warning to all who would threaten them, as Alan eyed him questioningly.

"'Tis the device of the de Lacis," Piers shouted, grinning.

It was over quickly then. Hexham's forces retreated under the new onslaught, their leader nowhere to be found. Piers drew up in front of Belvry's walls and ordered th drawbridge lowered, so that the wounded might receive attention. Although he led a force into the bailey, he did not intend to linger, for he vowed to pursue Hexham and finish the job he had begun in the baron's tent.

"The Red Knight! The Red Knight!" Inside the walls, the residents of Belvry cheered his arrival, and Piers realized that he was, indeed, covered in blood, none of it his own. As Edward once said, he seemed to attract it. With a sigh, he slid from his horse, and would have called for a fresh tunic, but did not want to do so when time might be of the essence. He had underestimated Hexham before; he would not do it again. The bastard could not be allowed to escape, and, more importantly, he could not be allowed to take Aisley with him.

With a warrior's discipline, Piers forced from his mind images that would interfere with his task, especially visions of Aisley tied to the baron's bed. Right now he needed to gather those men best fitted to the task before him and seek the viper in its nest.

Alan approached, and Piers nodded toward the black banner, still visible out on the slopes before the castle walls. "Who heads our saviors?" he asked.

The vassal shook his head. "The men are a tight-lipped lot. They say only that they serve de Laci."

"What de Laci?" Piers asked. The only de Laci he knew had no men and was probably trussed up for Hexham's pleasure. *A babe,* the baron had said. Was it true? Had Aisley carried his child, only to lose it to Hexham's brutality? Removing his helm, Piers wiped the sweat from his eyes and told himself not to let himself feel anything, or he might be overwhelmed right where he stood.

"Montmorency?" A new voice spoke behind them, and he looked up to see a strange knight astride a prime piece of horseflesh.

"Yes. I am Montmorency," Piers said, stepping closer. The warrior dropped from his black stead and approached. He was tall, nearly as tall as Piers, although not as broad,

and he moved with a natural grace that hinted at noble
lineage. As he walked, he doffed his helm, revealing a head
of thick, dark hair.

His face, although finely drawn and handsome, held a
cold, hardened look that Piers had seen on many a soldier.
Perhaps that was what made him seem familiar, Piers
thought. Then their eyes met, and Piers felt an eerie sense
of surprise. He recognized those eyes, such a peculiar shade
of gray as to be almost silver....

"I am Nicholas de Laci," the man said.

"But you're..."

"Dead," Nicholas finished for him. "I know. 'Tis a long
story, better shared when we are at our ease in the hall. Suf
fice to say that I am grateful to you for guarding my hold
ings so well in my absence. My sister speaks highly o
you—"

Piers couldn't help reaching out to grab de Laci's arm
perhaps too forcefully. "Aisley! She is here?" He recog
nized the desperation in his voice, but he was beyond car
ing.

"Yes," Nicholas said. He nodded his head toward a trai
of men behind him. "She is—"

Piers didn't wait for Aisley's brother to finish. He did no
pause to discuss the battles that lay behind them or ahead o
them, nor to share his plans for Hexham, nor to settle th
affairs of Belvry. Tossing his pride and his honor aside as h
did his mail gloves, he ran to his wife.

She was already dismounting when he saw her, and the
she ran toward him in turn. They met upon the green gras
before the walls of Belvry. Without regard to dirt, sweat o
the blood that soaked him, his wife threw herself into hi
arms, against the hard mail that covered his chest, and h
lifted off her feet, pressing hot kisses to her eyelids and he
face.

Piers realized she was weeping, but she was laughing, too
so glad was she to see him, and he ignored the tears to kis
her soundly on the mouth. It was only when he finally le

her slide to the ground that he heard the cheers of the men around him. Although he flushed at the sound, he could not tear his attention away from his wife. "You are...all right?" he asked hoarsely.

"Yes," Aisley said, her smile radiant, her gray eyes, so like her brother's, glowing like molten silver.

"Hexham did not harm you?"

"No," Aisley answered. "Hexham was too afraid of pursuit from Dunmurrow to dally with me. He kept up a grueling pace until we reached Belvry lands, and then Nicholas overtook us."

Piers saw truth in her gaze. He trusted her, and yet he had to hear the words. "He touched you not?"

"No," Aisley whispered, her eyes never leaving his own. "Hexham never even raised a hand to me, though I made certain he was sorely tempted many times."

Piers felt relief wash over him in waves. Hexham had lied; the bastard had not tied her to the bed. There had been no rape and no miscarriage. With a shudder, Piers drew her into his embrace. Thank you, God, he silently prayed to the heavens. If no miscarriage, was there even a babe?

"You met my brother?" Aisley asked, drawing him out of his thoughts.

"Yes," Piers answered. He lifted his head and realized that now was not the time for any further intimacies. With reluctance, he released her, though he kept one arm draped around her slim shoulders, and started walking back toward where Nicholas waited.

"He was worried that there might be a dispute over Belvry," Aisley said, "but I told him that you did not want it."

Piers paused to look down at her, his brows lowering. "You gave him one of the largest and most profitable holdings in the region without even a word to me?" he asked dryly.

Aisley laughed, unperturbed by his scowl. "Was I wrong? I distinctly remember on several occasions you growling that you wanted none of my wealth, and most ferociously,'' she added.

Piers groaned. ''And so I have fought for what is now my brother's?'' Aisley's trilling giggle was her only response, and he felt his heart constrict with the force of his love for her. By God, if he could, he would be carrying her in his arms right now, and to the devil with Hexham. He would take her up to his chamber and show her just how much he had missed her....

Unfortunately, those pleasant musings were interrupted by Aisley's brother, who was striding toward them, his squire leading his horse behind. ''Baron Montmorency,'' Nicholas said when they met. ''My apologies for a hasty departure, but I cannot allow Hexham to escape.''

''Of course not,'' Piers said. ''I will get some men and come with you.'' He ignored the touch of Aisley's fingers on his arm, as if to stay him.

''That is not necessary,'' Nicholas said. ''You have done more than enough for me, and let me assure you that Aisley will receive a generous marriage portion.''

Piers lifted a hand as if to dismiss his words, but the younger man's face grew even harder. ''I insist, my lord,'' Nicholas said. ''I am grateful to you, but I will be indebted to no man.''

Aisley tightened her grip upon Piers's arm, warning him not to lose his temper, but she need not have been concerned. Piers had known men like Nicholas before. ''Naturally, I shall be happy to receive a settlement from you. I have lost men here, of course, and they must be replaced. As for Hexham...'' Piers paused. ''He challenged me directly. He drew me out so that he could sneak behind my back and steal my wife from my own keep. I intend to see him dead.''

''Baron,'' Nicholas said. He hesitated, and shifted his weight as if impatient to leave. Was he in such a hurry to go after Hexham, or was he simply uncomfortable with words? Aisley's resurrected brother was an interesting puzzle that would bear further scrutiny, Piers decided. "Please, do not take this as an insult," Nicholas said, "but Aisley is fine. She is safe and unharmed, while I... What lies between Hexham and me goes much deeper."

Piers wondered what could go deeper than kidnapping a man's wife, but he held his tongue. Nicholas stood very still, his gray eyes as cold as stone, while he awaited a reply. It took about one minute for Piers to decide to hell with honor and pride, and one more to decide just what he was going to do while his new brother-in-law was slaughtering his enemy for him. "All right. He is yours," he said.

Nicholas nodded his thanks, yet his gaze remained serious, his face rigid. Then he mounted his magnificent steed and, without a backward glance, he was off, calling to his men in an unusually soft, low voice. They rode after Hexham like hounds scenting a kill, but Piers did not share their eagerness. He was weary of fighting and death, of the acrid smell of blood and the sour taste battle left in one's mouth. Honor and pride had their place, to be sure, but he would rather find his ease between the thighs of his beautiful wife.

As if sensing his thoughts, Aisley tugged at his arm. "Come," she urged. "Have you seen my Belvry?" Piers looked down at her, noticing that her lovely blue gown was smeared with blood and filth.

"A bath is called for first, my wife," he said huskily.

She beamed. "Thank you, Piers," she whispered, leaning into him.

"For what?" he asked, truly bewildered.

"For not going with Nicholas," she answered. "I know you wanted to go, but I couldn't bear it, not when I just found you again and—"

Piers put a finger to her lips. "Believe me, Aisley," he said huskily. "'Twas no great sacrifice on my part."

"Your breasts seem larger, heavier," Piers said, stroking the object of his interest. "Have you been rubbing them with special oils?" he teased.

Aisley made a face. "Of course not!" she said, outraged. She had never even done such a thing in her youth, having never had the slightest interest in her form. She knew why her breasts were fuller, and she had a sudden suspicion that Piers did, too.

"Good!" he answered. "For I liked them just as they were, small and perfectly shaped to my mouth," he said, nipping her flesh.

"Piers..." Aisley's thoughts were scattered by the feel of his tongue laving her nipple. How could he arouse her so easily? She had thought herself totally exhausted and sated after the heated passion of their reunion, and yet... His mouth moved down to lick her navel.

"Have you something to tell me, Wife?" he asked.

His words sent Aisley's languid mood fleeing, and she sat straight up, bumping his head with her quick movement. "You know!" she accused.

"Know what?" Piers asked innocently as he spread her legs.

"About the baby!" Aisley retorted, annoyed that he had spoiled her surprise.

"What baby?" he asked.

She cuffed his blond head, which had dipped to one of her thighs. "Our baby!"

"We're having a baby?" he asked, his familiar dry tones teasing her even as the moist pressure of his lips made her bones melt.

"Yes!" Aisley said in exasperation as she fell back against the pillows.

"'Tis good news," Piers commented from between her legs. "Shall I send him a kiss?" Aisley's breath eased out of her in one long moan as he lifted her in his hands and touched her with his tongue.

Aisley was starving. She silently consumed all the food in her trencher and was snatching bits from Piers's while he eyed her indulgently. "Just how many babes are in there?"

he asked, pointedly eyeing the robe that was knotted across her flat stomach.

Aisley laughed and finally sat back in one of the beautifully carved wooden chairs that graced her parents's chamber. Piers's chamber. Nicholas's chamber, she amended.

"What think you of my brother?" she asked.

Piers gazed at her fondly. "I think you were right. He is not the tickling type," he said dryly. "You are lucky, though, because I am," he added, a wicked grin on his face. Aisley shrieked and raced across the room, but she was not fast enough, and soon Piers tossed her upon the bed, landing beside her with such force that she thought the massive oak platform would rend in two.

"Stop. Stop, or I shall loose my supper!" she warned. Her husband stilled, suspended over her, his huge hand resting on her waist, his eyes, the warmest and sweetest of blues, bright with laughter.

"'Tis the first time a woman has ever told me that!" he protested. Aisley laughed softly, her hand lifting up to caress his cheek. How could he possibly be so dear to her?

"Piers," she said softly. "You were right. Nicholas is not the tickling type, nor the hugging type, nor the loving type, and I fear he looks even harder now than he did when he left five years ago." The thought made her sad for him.

Piers sighed, leaning back against the pillows. "Battle often breaks a man or else molds him into something other than he might wish to be."

"Do you think he might warm up to us after a while?" Aisley asked. She remembered her brother's hooded gaze traveling over her like a stranger's as she rode beside him. He had never asked if she was happy, if her husband was a good man....

"I don't know," Piers answered softly.

She sighed, and he entwined her fingers in his, bringing them to his lips for a gentle kiss as they both lay on their backs, staring up at the timbered ceiling. "You know, it is strange, Piers, but Nicholas was always so very handsome.

He was thought a great prize by the ladies and had a reputation for being honorable and gentle and fair," Aisley said.

"I am sure he still is," Piers said.

Aisley drew in a breath. "But when I look into his eyes, it is as if he is cold inside," she whispered. She shivered, and Piers drew her close. Nicholas, heir to Belvry and comely besides, was just the sort of knight women were eager to marry, while Piers was not. For most of his life a landless knight, he had never possessed the fortune to attract a lady, and his reputation was enough to scare the most stout-hearted damsel. Still, Piers was by far the greater prize, Aisley mused. "He is frightening, Piers, more frightening than the Red Knight ever was."

"Even at my most grim?" Piers teased, nudging her.

"Even at your most grim," she retorted, smiling. The thought made her remember her own contributions to his legend. "I told Hexham you would eat his heart for supper," she noted.

"Oh, thank you," Piers said, groaning. "I can see why he didn't find you particularly seductive. I can just picture you yammering like some old village crone about my black powers."

"But you do have powers," Aisley crooned softly, her hand roaming freely over his body.

"You aren't going to toss up your food, are you?" Piers asked dubiously.

"I promise," she said.

"Well, then, I suppose I will just have to bewitch you, my wife." And he did.

Nicholas returned a few days later, his mood even chillier than when he'd left. He strode into the great hall as if he owned it—which he did, Piers reminded himself—tossed his helm onto a chair, shook out his long hair and snapped, "Hexham escaped."

Piers lifted his eyebrows, not so much at the words, but at the tone the younger man used. Was Nicholas accusing him of something? "I am sorry to hear that," he said evenly.

The silver eyes dropped from his own, as if he recognized his mistake, and Piers relaxed. The boy was angry and was lashing out at everyone. Watching his wife protectively, Piers hoped that would not include Aisley.

She was already on her feet, ordering food and drink for her brother, but if she expected any sort of greeting from him, she was not going to get it. Piers felt a stab of annoyance. No wonder Aisley had at first seemed so contained, so unemotional, if this was an example of the familial affection with which she was raised.

"I will find him," Nicholas promised, his voice hard. He sat down, and Piers was reminded of Aisley's movements—graceful yet very controlled. De Laci held himself as a soldier, and Piers had a feeling that the man's guard was rarely let down. For a moment, Piers felt sorry for Nicholas and whatever had made him into the man he had become.

"Don't worry, Montmorency, I shall track Hexham down. He is too stupid to evade me for long, and when I find him, I will kill him," Nicholas said.

"Call me Piers. And I am hardly worried. If you want my advice," he continued, knowing the young man didn't, "I would tell you to forget about the baron. Find yourself a lovely wife, get yourself some heirs and enjoy your fruitful demesne and the peace you have won for it."

Nicholas shot him a look of amused disdain. He thinks I'm a doddering old fool, Piers thought with some surprise. He regarded himself thoroughly, noting that he had regained the weight lost during his blindness and had, by necessity, forced his body back into rigorous shape. He was still the Red Knight, even though he did not share this pup's lust for blood, and he suspected he could best his new brother in any contest of arms. Piers sent Nicholas a warning glance to put him in his place.

Nicholas got the message and looked away. When he turned back, his fine lips were drawn together in a grimace. "I cannot let Hexham go," he said. He hesitated, as if loath to say more, then continued, "I went to the Holy Land to fight the infidel, little knowing that a viper among my peers would be far more dangerous than the pagan hordes," he said coldly.

"I was wounded, but not mortally, and I waited for one of the men to find me. 'Twas Hexham." Nicholas breathed the name like a curse. "Instead of helping me, he dragged me under some brush and left me there to bleed to death."

Piers saw Aisley draw in a sharp breath, and he reached out a hand to cover hers, while Nicholas went on, "I would have died but for a peasant woman who heard my cries. She nursed me with her own hands in her tiny hovel. Unsure of what Hexham planned, I took another name. When I regained my strength, I sought him out, but he was gone. 'Twas then I knew that he coveted Belvry," Nicholas said.

"Father was no fool, so I saw no need to come rushing home," he explained. "I made my own fortune and gathered men to me against the day I might need them. 'Twas not till recently that I heard of my father's death. Then I knew the time had come for me to rise from the dead."

"Does Hexham know you are alive?" Piers asked.

Nicholas shook his head. "I don't think so. My men were sworn to silence. I'm sure the sight of the de Laci banner surprised him, but unless he was fighting near me, he would not know."

Piers snorted. "'Tis doubtful he was fighting at all. I nicked him in his tent, and he took off, crying like a babe. He probably ran then, long before we could turn our attention to pursuit."

Nicholas frowned. "Perhaps, but I will find his trail, and eventually he will meet his end by my sword."

Watching the young man's countenance, Piers felt suddenly weary. "Do not let your life be ruled by revenge, Nicholas," he advised, but the look he received warned him to mind his own business. Piers felt Aisley's hand tremble and knew she was worried about his temper, but Nicholas did not anger him. He pitied his new brother. He had seen men like Nicholas before—men whose lives were fueled by hate until it ate them up. And what would happen when he finally killed Hexham? Piers suspected there would be nothing left inside Nicholas de Laci.

"He might have gone to court, to plead his case before Edward," Aisley suggested.

"Perhaps," Nicholas acknowledged. "In any event, I leave tomorrow to pick up his trail from here." Piers saw the quick flash of disappointment come and go on Aisley's face, and now he *was* angry with the thoughtless young man before him.

"I wanted to explain the situation to you before I left. And I will, of course, see to my sister's marriage portion," Nicholas added carelessly. Oh, you noticed her, did you, Piers thought, annoyed. To look at the two, one would never even know they were related. The only thing they had in common was they way they acted, each cool and unreachable.

"Aisley, could you excuse us for a moment?" Piers asked with what he hoped was a gentle smile. "I would like to discuss your marriage portion with Nicholas."

Aisley nodded and left the room, grace in her step, pride in her bearing, and he wanted to wrap her up in his love. He also wanted to punch Nicholas de Laci in the face.

Piers rose and walked toward where his new brother was seated. Accustomed to using his size to intimidate, he simply stood over the young man and looked down into those cold gray eyes. "I don't give a blessed damn about your money," he growled.

When Nicholas made to rise, Piers sent him a look that told him to sit down. "I, too, fought in the Holy Land," he said. "And I campaigned with Edward in Wales for years. Not being heir to a profitable demesne, I earned my small holding by the blood of my sword. And I have been through a trial in the past year that would make your brush with death seem like a summer frolic.'' Piers's voice was hoarse with pain, despite his effort to control it. "So know you that you are not the only man whose life has been other than he would wish.''

His hand moved to the hilt of his weapon. "I counted myself fortunate to be able to fight here—to preserve your holdings and my wife's memories of her home. I just want one thing from you in return.'' The gray eyes flicked up to his as Nicholas watched him stoically. "I want you to treat your sister as if she exists.''

Nicholas's brows lifted in surprise.

"I don't care if you curse my name to hell or disappear to the ends of the earth once we leave Belvry, but while we are here, I want you to treat your sister as if she is a living, breathing relation whom you respect—for keeping this castle running in your absence, if nothing else,'' Piers said.

Without waiting for a reply, he turned on his heel and left the hall to find his wife. He decided it was a good thing Aisley had embellished upon his reputation, because any more scenes like this would surely destroy the myth of the fearsome Red Knight.

Chapter Eighteen

At supper, Piers congratulated himself, for it seemed his little talk with his brother had done wonders. Nicholas spent the meal conversing quietly with his sister, while Piers looked on fondly. Perhaps the young man wasn't so bad. Perhaps he had just let his revenge get in the way of more important things, and all he needed was a little reminder of life's priorities.

The evening passed quickly and pleasantly, and though it grew late, Piers was loath to quit the hall. It was filled with people who loved his wife, from villagers celebrating their safety to women who had served as her attendants for years. Seeing so many eyes on Belvry's chatelaine, Piers begged her to sing, and the throng immediately hushed.

Apparently all were familiar with her talents. Piers smiled when he saw an old servant lean back and close his eyes as Aisley's voice rang out, clear and lovely, but he himself could not bear to shut his against the beauty that was before him. He had spent too many evenings listening blindly to the angelic sounds, and now he greedily watched her every movement. His gaze caressed the long silver hair he insisted she wear loose and followed the supple lines of her body, which seemed far too dainty to be nurturing his babe.

When she finished, Aisley was inundated with praise. Her women moved around her, their faces wreathed in smiles, while she flushed at the attention. Even Nicholas told her how much he enjoyed it. "I had forgotten how beautifully you sing," he said, and Piers felt the man spoke honestly.

It was late, and despite their enjoyment of the evening, Aisley appeared tired, so Piers called her to his side and told the rest of those assembled good-night.

"Aisley," Nicholas said softly. "I would bid you good-bye, for I leave early tomorrow."

Aisley nodded, her face impassive. "I wish you well, Nicholas," she said.

"And I, you," her brother answered. "You may stay as long as you wish, though I know not when I will return. Oh, and Aisley..." Nicholas paused, and gray eyes met gray across the tiles. "Thank you for taking such good care of our home."

Aisley smiled sweetly. "You are welcome," she said. Then she turned and shot Piers a look that told him as certainly as words that she knew he was responsible for her brother's speech.

Piers glanced away and said nothing until they reached the great chamber, but if he thought his wife would forget the incident, he was mistaken. As soon as the door was closed, she elbowed him in the stomach and started giggling. "What was that for?" he asked, unhurt by the gentle prodding.

"You are a sham, Red Knight!" she said, doubling over with laughter. "What a fearsome beast! What spell did you lay upon my brother to make him part with that bit of praise he gave me?"

Piers tried to look innocent, but that only made her laugh louder. "If you only knew how unusual his behavior was, you would not try to deny it. I swear Nicholas has never complimented me in my lifetime—unless it was for not getting killed when I once took a horse far too large for me." Aisley fell back upon the big bed, her laughter turning into gentle sighs of contentment.

"I have half a mind to let word of this get out, you know," she warned. "The legend of the Red Knight would surely be tarnished by the news. I suppose you don't even realize how the servants avoid you, how everyone in Belvry hangs back because of your fearsome reputation?''

Piers had not noticed it, but he gave it no regard, simply stripping off his surcoat and folding it neatly. "I don't know why you are complaining," he commented. "I thought you relished the legend of the Red Knight. You're the one who put it about that I eat people's livers—"

"Hearts," Aisley amended, giggling again.

Piers smiled. He put the tunic down on one of the many elaborately carved chests and thought how truly sumptuous the room was. Belvry was vastly different from Dunmurrow. Built far more recently, with comfort in mind, it was more spacious and warmer and filled with chambers and furniture and tapestries. No wonder Aisley had scorned his home, dark and cramped and cold.

With a sigh, he walked to the window and gazed up at the stars. For a brief moment, he wished he could give all the riches in the world to his wife, but he put such thoughts aside as a waste of energy. He knew he was lucky to be able to present her with a whole man, and he was thankful for it.

Down in the bailey, soldiers moving in the night caught his eye. Nicholas left on the morrow. How long would Aisley wish to stay at her old home? Piers could not blame her if she wanted to summer here, or even stay to birth the babe in familiar surroundings. But he felt the pull of his own castle, his own holdings. Were men more possessive than women about such things? Dunmurrow was not much, but it was his, and he had fought long and hard to win it.

"You are nothing but a great, gentle wonder, and I love you," his wife remarked sleepily from the bed.

Piers ignored her teasing, his mind on more serious matters. "Do you wish to have the child here, Aisley?" he asked, steeling himself for her answer.

"No," she replied. Piers looked over at her then. She was stretched out in the glow of the many candles, her silver hair glittering around her like a translucent veil, her gown riding up to reveal beautiful, slim legs, and at that moment, if she had said she wanted to have the child in the Holy Land, Piers didn't think he could have denied her.

Lucky for him, her request was not so outlandish. She said simply, "I want the baby to be born at his own home, Dunmurrow."

Compared to the frantic pace that had taken her to Belvry, the journey home was a long and leisurely one. Aisley knew that with a baby on the way, she would not want to travel later, so they stopped at the outlying villages on Montmorency lands, talking with the residents and gathering to them any who wished to live at Dunmurrow.

They were greeted with varying degrees of fear, suspicion and welcome, for these people knew their lord only by black and menacing rumor. Aisley could see that many women, and men, too, were surprised to find that the golden-haired, handsome man beside her was the Red Knight. Though he might still appear fierce to them, it was better by far to see a man in the flesh than to hear only of his dark legend.

Aisley knew that her presence eased the Red Knight's way, for when people saw how much he cared for his wife— something she subtly, but easily maneuvered him into demonstrating—they often changed their attitude toward him. She was glad of her role, because she was proud of him beyond measure, and she wanted acceptance for him, for her and for the baby she carried home.

Word of them traveled ahead, and by the time they reached Dunney, Aisley knew the villagers would be looking for them. She wondered how they would be received, for of all the places they visited, Dunney was the only one where the Red Knight had shown himself before going off to fight. 'Twas also the place where he was most feared.

Aisley did not have to wait long to discover the mood of the town, for they had barely passed the first of the huts that were scattered along the narrow road when the cheering started. She shot a surprised glance at Piers, who had the oddest look on his face. "Red Knight! Red Knight!" rose the chants, and as their party rode further, villagers lined the way on either side, sending up shouts of welcome for the returning lord and lady of Dunmurrow.

Aisley felt a stinging behind her eyes to see them all—men, women, old and young. Some she knew, many she did not, but it seemed as if everyone had come out to greet them. In the center of the village they halted, and a hush fell over the crowd, the only sound being the smart snap of their banner, bloodred and white, held by Piers's squire. All eyes turned in expectation to the Red Knight, who sat staring at his people, looking much too fierce, Aisley thought. She wet her lips, prepared to fill the breach, but then he spoke.

"Thank you for your fine welcome," Piers boomed out in his warrior's voice. Although his words were kind, he still appeared great and powerful and a bit forbidding, his huge body astride his massive destrier, his golden hair ruffled in the breeze. He surveyed them all. They looked back—intimidated, Aisley realized. Then, suddenly, he broke the mood with a wide grin. "'Tis good to be home!"

The cheers were deafening, and their horses began moving forward again, Piers firmly in control of his audience, his spell cast upon an entire village, Aisley thought with a smile. She tried to see everyone and wave to those she knew, but she was hampered by the tears that threatened to spill out joyfully at Piers's acceptance. She could not help seeking out one particular hut near the edge of town, and, as she'd expected, there was the Widow Nebbs seated outside her door, waving a spoon gleefully and cackling, for all the world, like a delighted witch.

For the most part, it was a good journey, especially at its end, but Aisley was glad to be home. She looked forward to spending the summer comfortably at Dunmurrow in their own soft bed in the great chamber.

Although it was normally her busiest time, she found herself seated more than once in one of the two new chairs

Piers had insisted upon having built. She gazed out over the hall with a proprietary air, enjoying the breeze that floated in through the high windows while she sewed a tiny gown for the infant.

With a smile, Aisley realized that in the weeks since their return, Piers had slowly and quietly assumed many of her duties or had passed them on to Cecil or Edith or Willie, who now found himself a permanent resident of the castle, doing whatever no one else had the time to do. Willie's soldiering days, Aisley suspected, had been over the moment Edith married him, but he seemed content, as did all who resided here. Dunmurrow was peaceful and quiet, and Aisley was happy beyond her imaginings.

She glanced up from her work one day to see Glenna walking across the room, and was about to consult with the cook about supper when she noticed a priest enter the hall. Surprised, Aisley put aside her sewing and rose to greet him. Although she had requested a new chaplain, so far she had received no response from the bishop, the delay owing, she suspected, to the Red Knight's rather unsavory reputation. Perhaps this fellow had a message for her or had come to claim the position himself, she thought hopefully.

"Good day to you," Aisley said, walking toward the visitor. She halted a few steps later when she saw Glenna throw her a horrified look and scurry from the room. Did the cook not want a man of the cloth at Dunmurrow?

"And you," the priest said roughly. Aisley had no more time to question Glenna's behavior, for suddenly the man rushed forward, dragging her to him and putting a short sword to her throat.

"Hexham!" Aisley gasped. "Are you mad?"

"Perhaps," he hissed. "If so, 'tis because your cursed brother has made me so. He has hounded me like a dog, Aisley, like a cur, until I cannot escape. London, the countryside—no matter where I go, he follows me. He tracks me even where I leave no trail. He is led off the scent by no one." Hexham paused, trembling with emotion. "He is...inhuman."

Aisley heard the raw desperation in his voice, the unusually high pitch that bespoke a man driven beyond his limits to the very edge of sanity. And with that realization came a fear of him that she had never harbored before, for a man who has nothing to lose rushes headlong toward any escape.

She licked her lips nervously. "However did you manage to get in here?" she asked, speaking slowly and deliberately in an effort to calm him.

He smiled then, a remnant of his old self responding to her implied flattery. "I heard in the village that you had sent for a priest. 'Twas easy enough then to bribe my way in."

"You came alone?" Even knowing the present state of his mind, Aisley was impressed by his daring.

"I had no choice," he spat. "I have no one left to aid me! Your brother has seen to that. His men have chased mine down, killing them or driving them away until no amount of money can buy their allegiance."

He turned to her, and when Aisley saw his dark features, gaunt and haunted, she knew he was not a man newly brave, but a man frightened beyond endurance. Pressing the blade tightly to her throat, he flinched and began moving back across the hall, pulling her with him.

"But 'twill do you no good to take me," Aisley protested. "Belvry is lost to you now."

"Yes, Belvry is lost!" he snapped. "Devil take the foul place! I want only to reach a safe haven, and you will make sure I do. With you in my hands, your brother will not touch me."

"You would hide behind a woman's skirts, Hexham?" Piers's voice boomed out across the hall, and Aisley felt weak with relief. He stood by the door, a fearful Glenna behind him, and Aisley knew the cook must have recognized Hexham and run to fetch her husband.

Hexham did not appear to realize his danger, for he snarled scornfully. "We meet again, so-called Red Knight. But you have given lie to your own legend, for you have proved yourself devoid of all the skills and powers attributed to you. If Aisley's cursed brother had not come to your aid, you would be dead, destroyed by my army!"

Aisley shivered, waiting for Piers's violent temper to erupt, but he remained calm and watchful, his mouth twisted into a grin. "Ah, but you did not think it an accident that he arrived so precipitously, did you?" Piers asked smoothly. "'Twas solely for your benefit, Hexham, that I called him back from the dead."

By great effort of will, Aisley choked back a gasp. She eyed her husband with new respect. He was good, very good.... She had never known him to use his own legend, but standing there in a bloodred surcoat, huge and forbidding, his eyes hooded, his lips tightened in a fierce smile, he looked as if he just might have powers normal men did not.

Hexham was not unaffected, for Aisley could feel him tense behind her, his muscles taut. He was afraid, but he would not show it. He laughed again, but the sound seemed forced. "A fairy tale," he scoffed. "Feed it to the villagers, who might be kept in line by such nonsense. Now, move aside, or I will slit her throat." He gripped Aisley harder and edged toward the door with the strength of a man close to madness.

"Let her go now, Hexham, and I will let you live," Piers said evenly.

Hexham spat on the floor. "Do your worst, Red Knight. Call up your demons and have them smite me!" he taunted.

"All right," Piers said grimly. Then he gave a quick whistle, and suddenly two gigantic black shapes bounded out of the shadows under the chairs. The dogs, unseen and unheard before, leapt for Hexham's throat, taking him down before he could lift a finger. Released from his hold, Aisley fell to her knees, rubbing her neck in amazement while Hexham lay upon the tiles, writhing and screaming under the dogs' attack.

A word from their master called off the animals, preventing them from tearing Hexham to pieces, but still he did not rise. The point of Piers's sword kept him down. "I've a mind to kill you now and be done with it," the Red Knight said in a deadly voice. "But I have no wish to anger my brother. Unfortunately for me, Nicholas has claimed you for himself."

"No!" Hexham shrieked. He scrambled for his fallen blade, but Piers was quicker, and Hexham fell back, pierced through the heart.

Aisley turned away in horror. She heard Piers replace his weapon and give orders to the gathering servants. Then she felt his arms around her, lifting her from the floor to hold her against his chest. She buried her head in the warmth of his neck, drawing in shaky breaths.

"I believe, my wife, that your troubles with neighbors are over," he said softly.

"Nicholas will be angry," Aisley noted, mentioning the first thing that popped into her mind.

"Yes. Your brother will be very... frustrated," Piers agreed, carrying her toward the dark staircase to their room.

Behind them, Aisley heard the muttering of the servants and then Glenna's high voice. "But how did the dogs get there?" she asked. "I didn't see them when I left."

Aisley thought back herself, and she could not remember the beasts being present, either. Surely neither Castor nor Pollux had been under her chair while she was sewing. Very slowly, Aisley lifted her head to look at her husband, but he only crooked a brow at her and grinned.

"They were there," he said. "You must not have noticed them."

Maybe, Aisley thought to herself, and then again, maybe not. Perhaps there was a grain of truth embedded in the legend of the Red Knight.

* * *

Nicholas arrived the next day, presumably having followed Hexham's trail to Dunmurrow. His face was hard and his manner cold when Aisley greeted him in the great hall, and she wondered if he had already heard of the baron's death.

She saw to it that he had some ale, but she felt constrained in his presence and knew a measure of relief when Piers joined them. She and her brother had never been close, but since his return, Nicholas was like a stranger to her, and never more so than now.

"'Tis good to see you again, Nicholas," Piers said. He sat down in one of the chairs and eyed his new brother impassively.

"I have tracked Hexham here," Nicholas said curtly. "Have you seen him?"

"Yes," Piers said. He heaved a sigh and leaned forward. "He came through the gates but yesterday with a group from the village. He was dressed as a priest and again tried to take Aisley hostage."

Aisley saw Nicholas's eyebrows lift slightly, and she knew he was questioning the lax security that would allow Hexham to sneak into Dunmurrow not once, but twice. Piers's own brows drew downward, as he noted the insult, and Aisley silently hoped that he would not lose his temper. He did not, but he was obviously annoyed. He sat back in his chair and gazed stonily at Nicholas. "I was forced to kill him," he said bluntly.

Nicholas turned as pale and still as death, and Aisley drew in a quick breath in dismay. He looked, she thought, like a man who had spent his life on a quest, only to have it snatched from under him at the last moment. Perhaps he had. He appeared so lost that Aisley wanted to go to him, but she knew he would not appreciate her comfort.

"He was mine," Nicholas finally said, flashing Piers an accusing glare.

"He was in my hall, threatening my wife," the Red Knight replied.

Aisley watched the two uneasily and wet her lips. "Hexham led you a merry chase?" she asked, trying to lighten the mood, thick with tension, that had settled over the hall.

"Yes," her brother answered, without even glancing her way. "He did go to Edward to plead his case, but the king took no part in his cause and chastised him for harassing his neighbors." He lifted his head to look at Piers with new respect. "Apparently, you are quite high in the king's favor."

Piers accepted the admiration with a swift shrug. "I served Edward for many years," he said simply.

"Piers did not intend to kill Hexham," Aisley broke in. "He told Hexham that he would save him for you, but our neighbor apparently feared you above all else, and risked death rather than face you."

Nicholas fingered his weapon absently. "Yes, I have no doubt that is true." He frowned. "My apologies, Piers, for reacting so harshly to the news. You did what you had to. You must understand, 'tis a bitter draught to swallow, knowing that I will never be revenged."

"'Tis over now, Nicholas," Piers said. "'Tis time to get on with your life."

The knight appeared dazed, as if he could not comprehend Piers's directive, and Aisley wondered what kind of life her brother had led for the past five years. "Belvry is yours, Nicholas," she said softly. "Although Matthew is a good steward, he still must take direction from you." She had hoped that the mention of Nicholas's home, his heritage, would move him, but he still seemed more dead than alive.

"Yes, you are right, of course," he said dully. "I should be going now."

"No!" Aisley protested. "I did not mean to send you off. You must stay with us for a while, at least."

"Yes," Piers said. "You have been on the road for weeks. I will have Cecil show you a room so that you may rest, and I will see to your men."

Like one in a dream, Nicholas rose and let the servant lead him to the steps.

"What will become of him?" Aisley asked quietly, staring after her brother.

"He needs a wife," Piers replied. Moving to stand behind her, he rested his great hands on her shoulders. "Perhaps Edward can be persuaded to arrange something. I have a feeling that, like his sister, he will wed only when forced to do so."

Aisley smiled at his teasing, but shook her head. "I don't know, Piers," she said. "Though he is my brother, I would pity the poor woman who became his bride."

"Nonsense," Piers said, sliding his arms around her. "Perhaps right now some female is scheming how to get him for her own."

"I did not scheme to get you!" Aisley said, bristling at his insinuation. She turned her head to glare up at Piers, but he was laughing at her outrage, and the sound always tugged at her heart. He pulled her back against his chest and rested his chin upon her head.

"Then I thank God that your schemes have a tendency to go awry," he said.

"I resent that," Aisley whispered with a smile as her hands closed over his thick arms. "My decision to choose the Red Knight did not go awry, but aright."

Epilogue

"Good morning, Wife," Piers said as he opened the shutters. The bright light of Christmas Day shone through the narrow window to bathe Aisley in a soft glow.

Returning to stand by the edge of the bed, Piers marveled at her beauty. Ever since the moment he had first discerned her form, when she had become something other to him than shadows, he had not tired of gazing upon her. Her hair was spread upon the pillow, a mass of blond threads so light as to be nearly white, and so rich they seemed to sparkle upon the cloth.

She looked like an angel fallen down from heaven, and Piers felt a pressure behind his eyes that had nothing to do with his former blindness. As she discerned his attention, Aisley's lashes fluttered open, and he was met with true silver, glittering brightly in the light.

"Were you admiring me, Husband?" she teased.

"Yes," Piers admitted wholeheartedly. "I vow you are the most beautiful woman to grace this earth."

"Your eloquence is inspiring, but unconvincing," Aisley said, chuckling softly at she patted her misshapen form. "So begone with you. You must hurry, so you do not miss morning Mass—again." Her brows lowered accusingly.

"Yes, we should be going," he said with a sigh. "I hope the new priest does not talk overlong."

"Piers!" Aisley admonished.

"'Tis only that I so look forward to this feast of yours," he said, grinning. "Now that you have your boar's head, 'twill be nearly perfect, will it not? The lord and lady of the castle presiding over all in a hall rich with tapestries and cupboards and filled with food and drink aplenty for the villagers—and the now-numerous folk of the keep."

"Piers," Aisley began. She licked her lips in what he knew was a nervous gesture.

"What?" he asked suspiciously.

"I'm afraid I will not be able to attend this feast."

"Why?" Piers asked, his voice growing louder than he intended in his dismay. The celebration was to be his wife's crowning glory in a year of achievements.

Once his sight had returned, Piers had been astounded to view the improvements to Dunmurrow, and he had insisted that she continue to make the keep more habitable. Aisley had succeeded beyond his expectations, creating a warm, luxurious and efficient home out of Dunmurrow. The harvest had been good, assuring a winter without want, and now they were to stand together and publicly welcome the people of his demesne. She deserved to be at his side, and, selfishly, that's where he wanted her.

"Don't blame me, Piers," Aisley said, putting a delicate hand to her swollen belly. She smiled ruefully. "'Tis the fault of this son of yours. He demands to be born today."

"What?" Piers laid a hand on her stomach. He had been proud at first, proud and thrilled to learn she was carrying his child, but now that the time had come, he felt panic gripping him. It was the same panic he had felt a year ago when his wife had gone into the pond, and a blind knight was all that stood between her and death.

"You will be all right," he growled, expressing his concern in the only way he knew how.

"Yes," Aisley agreed. She patted his hand, comforting *him*, sweet wife that she was. "All will be well, you will see. When the feast is done, you will have a lusty son—or daughter—to greet you."

Piers looked down into those silver eyes, and he felt something snap inside. "Aisley," he said hoarsely. "There is something I have never told you...."

"What is this? If you are going to say that you have another wife, 'tis too late for that," she teased. "Or is it that you truly are a sorcerer and have bewitched me these many months?"

Piers shook his head, emotion overwhelming him. "'Tis not as dire as all that," he said. He tried to speak lightly, but he could not. "I should have told you a long time ago, but when I could not see, I did not want to bind you further to one so useless."

"Piers," she said, reaching out to him.

"Then, when my sight returned, I was ... I wanted to be sure that it would stay with me," he said gruffly. He looked down into eyes that pierced his heart. "Aisley, my wife, my own," he whispered, "I love you."

Aisley smiled. "Is that all? My fierce Red Knight, I have known that for a long time now," she said, "but 'tis good to hear you say it."

Piers took her delicate face in his hands and kissed her gently, surprised to find that his eyes were filling with liquid. He was truly healed now, in all respects.

Aisley caressed his cheek. "Since you are in such a good mood, my husband, I would ask a boon of you this Christmas Day," she said.

"If it is to go chasing after that white stag, you may as well wish for something else, for I shall not," Piers warned.

"No," Aisley said with a laugh. "'Tis that you preside over the feast today in a festive manner and make all that do not know you aware of your goodness."

"'Tis impossible, Wife, for you are the only one to see such goodness," Piers growled.

"No," Aisley protested. "'Tis not true. Even Edith likes you now. So go! Send her to me, and then you must attend to the people at the most wonderful Christmas celebration ever."

Piers did, though his heart was not in it. He sat through Mass, but his prayers were with his wife. He presided over the table, talked with his knights, presented bounty to his tenants and the villagers in a more-than-generous display, but his thoughts were in the great chamber.

All knew that their lady was big with child, so none questioned her absence, as they might have even a few months ago. Then they would have whispered that the Red Knight had done his worst to her. And perhaps he had, Piers thought bitterly. He knew how women could die in childbirth....

Mindful of her request, he did not end the feast early, but let it continue into the evening hours, only leaving when the household was bedding down for the night in the great hall. He made sure a garrison was sober enough to watch the walls and took it upon himself to walk along the battlements.

From the top of the keep, he looked out into the darkness, his now-keen eyes scanning the surrounding countryside for anything out of the ordinary. A few torches dotted the road to the village, lighting the way of some straggling revelers, and down in the bailey, men held to their posts. Otherwise all was still.

Piers looked around one last time, his gaze caught by a flash of white at the edge of the forest. He stared intently, trying to make it out, his heart pounding a little faster. With Hexham's death, he had thought himself free of enemies, but anything was possible....

He made a low noise in his throat, unable to believe what his eyes were showing him. Perhaps 'twas only a trick of the moonlight, but for a moment, he thought he saw a great, pale deer—the white stag. Piers shook his head to clear it, but the beast was still there, looking up at him with wisdom and intent, as if sending him some message. Then it tossed its enormous antlers and disappeared into the trees. Piers shivered. 'Twas only a bit of snow blowing in the wind, he decided, and yet...

He hurried down to the great chamber as if fire licked at his heels and thrust open the door just as his child launched itself into the world and the arms of the midwife. Aisley was lying back upon the pillows, gasping for breath, her face pale but lovely, and Piers strode to her side.

"'Tis a girl, Aisley, a daughter!" Edith, hovering near the midwife, said excitedly.

"A daughter, Piers," Aisley whispered.

"You are all right?" he asked hoarsely.

"Yes," she said with a smile.

The midwife placed the small bundle into Aisley's arms, and Piers marveled at the precious life they had made together. He had a daughter! And he could see her—every one of her tiny fingers. Had it been little more than a year ago that he had been buried here in the darkness, blind and bitter? And then, by some miracle, Aisley had burst into his life to set it all aright—more than aright.

"Thank you for my daughter," he said gruffly as he looked down at his wife. "And Aisley..."

"Hmm," she murmured contentedly.

"I know not whether God or man or magic had a hand in our union, but thank you. Thank you for choosing the Red Knight."

* * * * *

Harlequin® Historical

First there was **DESTINY'S PROMISE**...
A woman tries to escape from her past on a remote Georgia
plantation, only to lose her heart to her employer's son.

And now **WINDS OF DESTINY**...
A determined young widow finds love with a half-breed
Cherokee planter—though society and fate conspire to pull
them apart.

Follow your heart deep into the Cherokee lands of Georgia
in this exciting new series from Harlequin Historical author
Laurel Pace.

1994 MISTLETOE MARRIAGES
HISTORICAL CHRISTMAS STORIES

With a twinkle of lights and a flurry of snowflakes, Harlequin Historicals presents *Mistletoe Marriages*, a collection of four of the most magical stories by your favorite historical authors. The perfect way to celebrate the season!

Brimming with romance and good cheer, these heartwarming stories will be available in November wherever Harlequin books are sold.

RENDEZVOUS by Elaine Barbieri
THE WOLF AND THE LAMB by Kathleen Eagle
CHRISTMAS IN THE VALLEY by Margaret Moore
KEEPING CHRISTMAS by Patricia Gardner Evans

Add a touch of romance to your holiday with *Mistletoe Marriages* Christmas Stories!

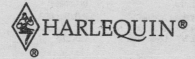

Maura Seger's BELLE HAVEN

A colony in New England. A farming village divided by war. A retreat for New York's elite.

Four books. Four generations. Four indomitable females....

You've met Belle Haven founder Amelia Daniels in
THE TAMING OF AMELIA, Harlequin Historical #159
(February 1993).

And the revolutionary Deanna Marlowe in
THE SEDUCTION OF DEANNA, Harlequin Historical #183
(August 1993).

Now, in November, watch Julia Nash turn New York society upside down in THE TEMPTING OF JULIA.

And in early 1995, Belle Haven comes of age in a contemporary for Silhouette Intimate Moments.

Available wherever Harlequin books are sold.

"HOORAY FOR HOLLYWOOD" SWEEPSTAKES

HERE'S HOW THE SWEEPSTAKES WORKS

OFFICIAL RULES — NO PURCHASE NECESSARY

To enter, complete an Official Entry Form or hand print on a 3" x 5" card the words "HOORAY FOR HOLLYWOOD", your name and address and mail your entry in the pre-addressed envelope (if provided) or to: "Hooray for Hollywood" Sweepstakes, P.O. Box 9076, Buffalo, NY 14269-9076 or "Hooray for Hollywood" Sweepstakes, P.O. Box 637, Fort Erie, Ontario L2A 5X3. Entries must be sent via First Class Mail and be received no later than 12/31/94. No liability is assumed for lost, late or misdirected mail.

Winners will be selected in random drawings to be conducted no later than January 31, 1995 from all eligible entries received.

Grand Prize: A 7-day/6-night trip for 2 to Los Angeles, CA including round trip air transportation from commercial airport nearest winner's residence, accommodations at the Regent Beverly Wilshire Hotel, free rental car, and $1,000 spending money. (Approximate prize value which will vary dependent upon winner's residence: $5,400.00 U.S.); 500 Second Prizes: A pair of "Hollywood Star" sunglasses (prize value: $9.95 U.S. each). Winner selection is under the supervision of D.L. Blair, Inc., an independent judging organization, whose decisions are final. Grand Prize travelers must sign and return a release of liability prior to traveling. Trip must be taken by 2/1/96 and is subject to airline schedules and accommodations availability.

Sweepstakes offer is open to residents of the U.S. (except Puerto Rico) and Canada who are 18 years of age or older, except employees and immediate family members of Harlequin Enterprises, Ltd., its affiliates, subsidiaries, and all agencies, entities or persons connected with the use, marketing or conduct of this sweepstakes. All federal, state, provincial, municipal and local laws apply. Offer void wherever prohibited by law. Taxes and/or duties are the sole responsibility of the winners. Any litigation within the province of Quebec respecting the conduct and awarding of prizes may be submitted to the Regie des loteries et courses du Quebec. All prizes will be awarded; winners will be notified by mail. No substitution of prizes are permitted. Odds of winning are dependent upon the number of eligible entries received.

Potential grand prize winner must sign and return an Affidavit of Eligibility within 30 days of notification. In the event of non-compliance within this time period, prize may be awarded to an alternate winner. Prize notification returned as undeliverable may result in the awarding of prize to an alternate winner. By acceptance of their prize, winners consent to use of their names, photographs, or likenesses for purpose of advertising, trade and promotion on behalf of Harlequin Enterprises, Ltd., without further compensation unless prohibited by law. A Canadian winner must correctly answer an arithmetical skill-testing question in order to be awarded the prize.

For a list of winners (available after 2/28/95), send a separate stamped, self-addressed envelope to: Hooray for Hollywood Sweepstakes 3252 Winners, P.O. Box 4200, Blair, NE 68009.

CBSRLS

OFFICIAL ENTRY COUPON

"Hooray for Hollywood"
SWEEPSTAKES!

Yes, I'd love to win the Grand Prize — a vacation in Hollywood —
or one of 500 pairs of "sunglasses of the stars"! Please enter me
in the sweepstakes!

This entry must be received by December 31, 1994.
Winners will be notified by January 31, 1995.

Name _____

Address _____ Apt. _____

City _____

State/Prov. _____ Zip/Postal Code _____

Daytime phone number _____
                              (area code)

Account # _____

Return entries with invoice in envelope provided. Each book
in this shipment has two entry coupons — and the more
coupons you enter, the better your chances of winning!

                                                    DIRCBS

OFFICIAL ENTRY COUPON

"Hooray for Hollywood"
SWEEPSTAKES!

Yes, I'd love to win the Grand Prize — a vacation in Hollywood —
or one of 500 pairs of "sunglasses of the stars"! Please enter me
in the sweepstakes!

This entry must be received by December 31, 1994.
Winners will be notified by January 31, 1995.

Name _____

Address _____ Apt. _____

City _____

State/Prov. _____ Zip/Postal Code _____

Daytime phone number _____
                              (area code)

Account # _____

Return entries with invoice in envelope provided. Each book
in this shipment has two entry coupons — and the more
coupons you enter, the better your chances of winning!

                                                    DIRCBS